FLINT AND SILVER

Pirates of the Caribbean meets *Flashman* in this rip-roaring prequel to *Treasure Island!*

Having just killed six pirates, John Silver's career in the merchant navy looks set to end, until the pirate captain makes him an offer he can't refuse. On the other side of the world, Joseph Flint is planning a bloody mutiny. When these two gentlemen meet they forge a deadly and unstoppable partnership, amassing a vast fortune, but the arrival of beautiful runaway slave Selina triggers sexual jealousy that turns the best of friends into sworn enemies! So the legend of Treasure Island begins, and all the questions are answered ... including the big one – why did they bury the treasure?

FLINT AND SILVER

For my beloved wife
Most precious
Most special
Most dear

FLINT AND SILVER

by

John Drake

Magna Large Print Books
Long Preston, North Yorkshire,
BD23 4ND, England.

British Library Cataloguing in Publication Data.

Drake, John
Flint and silver.

A catalogue record of this book is
available from the British Library

ISBN 978-0-7505-3055-2

First published in Great Britain by HarperCollins*Publishers* 2008

Cover illustration by arrangement with HarperCollins Publishers

Published in Large Print 2009 by arrangement with
HarperCollins Publishers

Magna Large Print is an imprint of Library Magna Books Ltd.

Printed and bound in Great Britain by
T.J. (International) Ltd., Cornwall, PL28 8RW

Acknowledgements

I thank my agent, Antony Topping, and my editors Julia Wisdom and Anne O'Brien for their thorough professionalism and sound advice. They have made this a better book than otherwise it would have been.

John Drake,
September 2007

Chapter 1

15th March 1745
Off Madagascar

Ria de Ponteverde carried guns; most merchantmen did: carriage guns, with powder and shot, rammers and sponges, trucks and tackles. They differed from ships of the various royal navies only in the relatively small degree of their armament, as compared with the exclusive concentration upon artillery that marked out the man-o'-war.

And it wasn't just a broadside battery on the main deck. It was swivels on the gunwale, and small arms in the lockers down below: muskets and pistols, pikes and cutlasses, and all the gear that went with them – cartridges, flints, powder horns and small-grained pistol powder. All this was a fearful expense and a burden upon trade, for there was not one farthing's profit to be made by honest seamen in hauling defensive arms and ammunition across the seven seas.

Unfortunately there were others on the seas who were not honest seamen, and whose business it was to become very rich, very quickly by selling cargoes without the bother of paying for them. Hence the need for guns, because sometimes – indeed often – these gentlemen could be seen off by force. Sometimes, but not always. And now, six miles off the Bahia de Bombetoka, a general slaughter was about to begin.

The Portuguese brig *Ria de Ponteverde* and the buccaneer *Victory* were locked yardarm to yardarm in a stinking cloud of powder smoke that barely shifted in the hot, tropical air. The brig was beaten. She was broken, bloodied, smashed and splintered; her helm was shot away, her sails in shreds and *Victory*'s boarders were pouring over her sides.

A tall yellow-haired Englishman stood with his Portuguese mates by *Ria de Ponteverde*'s mainmast among the shattered spars and dismounted guns, the silent dead and the howling wounded, as the boarders came through the smoke cheering and hacking and killing. Firearms boomed and jumped on either side. Right next to the Englishman, his captain, José Carmo Costa, took the flash and thunder of a blunderbuss at close range, blowing large parts of his heart, lungs and breastbone clear out through the back of his shirt.

Then it was cold steel, hand to hand, and no quarter asked or given.

The Englishman swung a cutlass with all his might. He was a big man: muscular, quick and agile with long limbs and not a scrap of fat on his body. The blow came down like the wrath of God and caught his first man – fair, square and smack – on top of the head.

The heavy blade clove to the teeth, slicing bone, brains, meat and gristle. Number one dropped twitching and shivering, and the blade jerked free with a disgusting *schlik*. Then a dozen men, jammed in ferocious fight, rolled into the Englishman and a bedlam of noise beat at his ears.

Arms, blades and bludgeons worked busily all around and instinctively he kicked and elbowed with enormous strength, clearing a fighting space around him, and – seizing the instant chance – ran the point of his weapon into the middle of his second man, who yelped and twisted and tried to pull free. But the pirate stumbled and went over face down, and the Englishman stamped a heel snapping and crunching into the base of his victim's spine while he leaned mightily on his sword arm, driving the blade through the wriggling body and into the planks of the deck, even as the dense press of combat knocked him clear, still gripping the slimy hilt.

He cut down number three with two strokes: the first shearing fingers, the second splitting a face. Four and five took just a single cut each, one to left and one to right; a tall black with rings in his ears, and a squint-eyed barrel-chested fellow armed with a boarding pike.

Six was the hardest. He was a small man with a straw hat, striped breeches, quick feet and a straight-bladed sword honed to a wicked point, which he used to the exclusion of the edge. This man was a swordsman, which the Englishman was not – he had now to learn or to die.

Sweat flew as he wrenched his cutlass to and fro, trying with sheer speed and force to overcome skill. Ssssk! The cutlass blade sliced a larynx without killing. Jab! Jab! Jab! The rapier missed twice then sank an inch into the Englishman's side, before he beat it clear with a clash and a scrape of steel. Jab! Into his hip. Chunk! And the tip of the swordsman's elbow was off like the top of a breakfast egg. Jab! Into the Englishman's cheek. Swish! Through the straw hat, slicing away hair and a patch of scalp. Then a blur of light and the Englishman cut hard into the right side of the other's neck, sinking the blade through flesh, fat and marrow to within an inch of the left-hand side, almost but not quite taking the head clean off.

He gasped and shuddered as his man went down. He'd fought before, but only with his fists. It'd been just fights over girls or drink, or because a man had given offence. For that he'd drawn blood and cracked heads. He'd grown up in a hard school. But he'd never before fought with weapons and the serious intent to kill. In fact he'd never killed a man ... except that now he had. He'd just killed six of them.

Now he looked around and saw that he was the last man standing of *Ria de Ponteverde*'s crew. The others were either dead or dying, or having their throats cut before his eyes by the buccaneers. The fight was over and the enemy ringed him, raising their weapons warily. There were no guns left loaded or they'd have shot him for sure. They'd won the fight, but they'd taken the measure of this fair-haired killer who stood head and shoulders taller than any of them, and they were being careful.

He spun on his heel, chest heaving and breath coming in deep gasps that left the taste of blood at the back of his throat. He screwed the sweat out of his eyes with his left hand, and took a firmer grasp of the cutlass hilt. The edge was nicked like a saw, but it would still cut. They edged in closer all around him: angry faces, pike heads, swords, dirks and hatchets.

'Bastard!' said a voice. 'You done for my mate.'

'Skin him!' said another.

'Boil him!'

'Woodle him!'

'Burn him!'

'Come on then!' he roared. 'Come one, come all!' His voice was high and cracked. It was near a shriek. He was in an uncanny state of mind: wound up tight with the blood of battle, heart thundering, nerves at hair-trigger. He was outnumbered beyond hope, but still highly dangerous, and none of those around him sought the honour of being next to fight him.

'Aaah!' he cried, and stamped forward a pace.

''Ware the bugger!' they shouted, and *'Cuidado!'* and *'En garde!'* They fell back, only to close in behind him. He slashed at a pikestaff thrust by a big-nosed fellow with lank black hair. He clashed blades with a hanger wielded by a bare-chested mulatto with a face scarred in a dozen fights. He spun round to catch a red-haired Irishman trying to spit him on the sly. Red-hair darted back, howling from a shoulder slashed to the bone, and lucky it wasn't his skull.

'Henri!' cried a man in the front rank, yelling back over his shoulder and holding up an empty musket, *'Apporte moi de la poudre et balle!'* There was a swirl in the crowd and a cartridge was thrust into the Frenchman's hand.

'Aye!' they roared. 'Drop the sod, Jean-Paul!'

'Je déchargerai la tête du con!' he muttered, and bit his cartridge, priming the pan and snapping down the steel. He grounded the butt, stuffed the

rest of the cartridge into the muzzle and drew out the ramrod to firm home the charge down the long barrel. The Englishman leapt forward, trying to cut down the musketeer before he could reload. But they'd thought of that. They were already clustered protectively around Jean-Paul, with pikes presented to keep him safe.

There was a rattling clatter of steel against ash, and the Englishman was driven back bleeding from a stab to his shin, and another to his arm. Frustrated, hopeless and fearful, he watched Jean-Paul finish his loading, cock the musket and slowly take aim.

He saw the round, black muzzle come up and fix on him. He saw Jean-Paul's eye glinting over the breech, alongside of the lock. He leapt to the right. The musket followed. He leapt to the left. It followed again. And behind Jean-Paul, others were busy loading. It was no good. Muskets were not renowned for accuracy, but Jean-Paul's was no more than ten feet from the Englishman's chest.

'Fuck you, you bastard!' he spat. Jean-Paul bowed extravagantly.

'Merci, monsieur,' he said. *'Et va te faire foutre!'*

'Go to it, then!' said the Englishman. 'And a curse on the pack of you!' He threw down his cutlass, spread out his arms and closed his eyes. At least it would be quick. Not like what they'd threatened.

John Paul took up the slack on the trigger. He squeezed harder. The lock snapped. It sparked brightly. The gun roared. Three drachms of King George's best powder exploded, driving the heavy musket ball violently out of the barrel ... to soar in a majestic parabola, higher than a cathedral steeple, and then to curve down into the sea, where it fizzed viciously for a few feet until its power was spent, and then proceeded gently on its way down to the sea bed, where the fishes nosed it for a while and then ignored it.

'Belay there!' cried a loud voice, with all the confidence of command. Nathan England, duly elected captain of the buccaneers, had just knocked the barrel of Jean-Paul's musket skyward.

'I say we keep him!' he said, pointing his sword at Jean-Paul's target. 'You there!' he said. 'You can open your eyes... *Ouvrez les yeux...! Entiendez...? Capisce?*' England's crew were the dregs of half a dozen seafaring nations and he was used to making himself understood in whatever tongue suited.

The Englishman blinked. He stupidly ran his hands over his body to feel for a wound.

'Portugês?' said England. *'Français? Español?'*

'English, damn you!'

'Huh!' said England. 'Rather *bless* me, you ungrateful bugger, for I've a mind to let you live. I'm several men adrift, courtesy of yourself, and I don't see why you shouldn't make up some of the loss.'

'I'm no bloody pirate!' said the Englishman.

'Neither am I,' said England. 'Nor my men, neither. We're gentlemen of fortune! Brethren of the coast!'

'Horseshit!' the Englishman sneered. 'Same bird, different name.'

Hmm, thought England, taking the measure of the big man with his broad, square face – pale for a seaman – and his stubborn jaw and angry eyes.

'Now see here, my bucko,' said England, 'I've neither time nor inclination to educate you. The fact is, I saw you fight Little Sam, who was the best among us. And you killed him.'

'And why not?' said the Englishman, not realising he was being praised. 'Didn't you take our bloody ship and kill my mates?' he pointed at the body of Captain Carmo Costa, still smouldering from the charge that had killed him. 'That's my captain there, and him not a bad bastard neither.'

England frowned. He was not a patient man. He stuck his thumbs in his belt and drummed his fingers on the tight leather. 'Now, here's the long and short of it,' said he. 'We must come to a swift agreement, you and I, my lad. I like the way you fight, and I have the fancy to admit you into our company. So you can either sign articles and join us...' Glancing over his shoulder at Jean-Paul with his smoking musket, England commanded, *'Recharges, enfant!'* Then he nodded at the Englishman and concluded with a smile: '...Or you'll be shot where you stand.' As far as England was concerned, the matter was resolved.

Quickly, another cartridge was found for Jean-Paul, and he grinned merrily as he plied his ramrod. Meanwhile Captain England drummed his fingers on his belt.

'So, what's it to be?' he said. 'For as soon as *mon ami* has loaded, he may open fire, and that's the truth.'

'Damn you all!' said the Englishman, and Jean-Paul cocked and aimed.

'Je tire, mon capitaine?'

'Last chance, my cocker,' said England, as Jean-

Paul began to squeeze the trigger.

'Avast!' said the Englishman, and made the only choice that any decent man could make in the circumstances. A precious saint might have said no, and the Lord Jesus Christ certainly would have, but who wants one of them for a shipmate, anyway?

With all matters of recruitment concluded, England's men set briskly to work aboard the two ships, mending and splicing above, plugging and hammering below. These things they did with practised skill, and did them well, since the lives of all aboard might depend on the work. They also buried the dead with due respect, and they cleaned and scoured the decks after their fashion. As for the wounded, they were attended by the drunken butcher that served England for a surgeon. He was of the 'boiling pitch' school when it came to staunching bleeding, and the crew were more afraid of him than of the hangman. But he was what they'd got.

Victory and *Ria de Ponteverde* sailed in company within hours of the battle, and that evening the yellow-haired Englishman was welcomed into England's crew as a fellow gentleman of fortune. The ceremony was half farce and half deadly earnest, with all hands mustered round the mainmast and the rum flowing freely. England presided in his best clothes, a plumed hat, and seated on a massive carved armchair brought up from his cabin.

The proceedings owed much to the horse-play of crossing the equator, with a ludicrous bathing and soaping, and the postulant stripped naked and blindfolded. Finally, England hammered on the deck with the narwhal tusk he carried as a staff of office.

'Now, brothers,' he cried, 'we stand ready to admit this child as a free companion. So pull the blindfold off him, Mr Mate, and put a sharpened sword into his hand.' This was done and the Englishman stood blinking and puzzled and looking about him. The mob of armed men were swaying in silence on the heaving decks, bracing themselves with such ease that they weren't even aware of doing it.

'So,' said England, 'if any brother knows of any just impediment why this child should not be admitted, then let him speak now or for ever hold his peace!'

This parody of the wedding ceremony served the entirely practical purpose of ensuring that any man who'd lost a friend to *the child* must challenge him at once or accept him as a shipmate in good faith. With six dead to his credit, this was an interesting moment for the crew, and there was much hopeful shuffling and muttering and looking to those who had lost their messmates. One or two of the bereaved found it expedient to consider their boots at this moment, while others brazened it out with fixed smiles and knowing winks. But much to the disappointment of those free of obligations, nobody wanted to fight.

'So be it!' cried England when he thought sufficient time had passed. 'And now, brother-that-you-have-become, I asks you to sign articles as all others have done before you.'

At this, England's first mate stepped forward

and laid down a big book upon a barrel that was set before England as a table. Pen and ink and a sand-caster were ready to hand. The book was black-bound in leather and had once been the master's journal aboard an honest merchantman. But the long-dead navigator's written pages had been cut out and a series of numbered items entered in a large, bold hand on the first remaining page.

'Are you a scholar, brother?' said England. 'Or will you have me read these articles to you, before you make your mark?'

'I know my letters,' said the Englishman.

'Well enough to read?'

'Aye!'

'Oh?' said England, for, saving the mates and the gunner, not one other man in his crew could do the like. 'Then read, brother, and read boldly for all to hear!' The Englishman picked up the book and held it close to a lantern to catch the light.

'These articles ...'

'Louder!' cried England. 'So those aloft can hear.' He pointed to the tops where the lookouts were stationed.

'These articles,' roared the new brother, 'I do enter into freely and volunteerly and thus do I solemnly swear. Article one: that I shall obey the commands of my captain in all matters of seafaring and warfare, upon pain of the law of Moses, viz: forty lashes – barring one – upon the bare back...'

And so it went on. There were twenty-three articles in England's book, mainly self-evident statements of the need for discipline on board any ship that ever went to sea in all of mankind's history. There was much other good sense too, on such matters as forbidding the dangerous business of smoking below decks, and the filthy business of pissing in the ballast, which lazy sailormen will do who can't be bothered to go to the heads on a dark night. Anyone caught doing *that* was obliged to drink a pint of the same liquid, piping hot, donated by his messmates. Also, there were ferocious punishments for taking private shares of the loot before its formal division. In all these matters, the articles were similar to those in use by numerous other freebooters and buccaneers currently doing business in the Indian Ocean and Caribbean.

But England's articles had some extras. He punished rape by castration, torture by hanging, and sodomy by dropping the offenders over the side, bound together, with roundshot tied to their feet. These eccentricities the crew took in good part (even the astounding prohibition of rape) because England was a fine and lucky seaman with a nose for smelling out gold.

So the new brother worked his way through the list till he came to the end, where followed four clear signatures, one obviously that of the draughtsman of the articles, plus a few painfully worked names such as children might attempt, then several hundred crosses, marks and scrawled drawings: some of fish, or birds, or animals, some of hanged men, some skulls-and-crossbones, and one splendid likeness of a face, the size of a penny piece, as finely drawn as the work of any London caricaturist, which was the mark of an illiterate man who nonetheless had this remarkable gift. Each mark had a name beside it in the draughtsman's hand. Many (including the likeness) were neatly ruled out in red ink, with a date beneath it. These were the dead.

The Englishman sighed. He took up the pen, dipped it into the ink, and paused. In fact he was only half an Englishman, for his seafaring Portuguese father had married an English girl and settled in Bristol. The son had taken his father's size and strength, his mother's yellow hair, and at thirteen had run away to sea to escape his father's belt. His name, as given to him by his father, had been João De Silva: a foreign-sounding name to some and therefore tainted, but not to him. Unlike the vast body of land-rooted, home-fast Englishmen, he had no disdain of things foreign, because seafaring men are an international breed taught by hard reality to know that all races have their strengths and weaknesses, and the only thing that matters is how your shipmate behaves when the sea turns nasty – and certainly not the land of his birth. But for all that he was still an Englishman in his loyalties, and so he signed with a flourish as...

John Silver

Chapter 2

4th January 1749
Aboard HMS Elizabeth
The Caribbean

Captain Springer controlled his anger with effort. 'Lieutenant Flint,' he said, 'I swear that if I hear that tale once more, I shall put you in irons.'

'Will you, though?' said Flint. 'Then I pray that you may be cursed as I was. Four years under Anson, suffering scurvy, shipwreck and sores, only to see thirty-two wagons full of gold unloaded at London, and not a penny piece was my share!'

Springer glanced around the quarterdeck. The mids and the seamen were muttering and looking sly. Mr Bones, the master's mate, was staring attentively at Flint as if waiting for some word of command. Springer ground his teeth, Bones was Flint's man through and through, while next to him, Dawson, the sergeant of marines – who was loyal to Springer – was glaring his contempt at this public squabbling.

'Mr Flint,' said Springer, 'a word.'

Springer walked up the sloping deck to the weather side and waited for Flint to join him while the crew looked on in wary fascination. Springer was pure tarpaulin: lumpish, heavy and elderly with a fat lower lip, watery eyes and a bristling white stubble that no razor ever conquered, while Flint was smooth as a cat, with an olive, Mediterranean skin. He moved like an athlete and had a beautiful, brilliant smile. He was slim-built and only of average height, but men always thought of him as tall.

Together, these two opposites stood locked in argument in their long blue coats with the brass buttons.

These uniform coats were badges of rank which few officers were wearing as yet, for they were an innovation introduced only the previous year. But *Elizabeth*'s officers all had them, thanks to Lieutenant Flint, who, wanting a smart ship, had spent his own money to get them – including one for Springer, who'd never have bothered if left to himself.

But if the coats were uniform, nothing else was: not the shirts, nor breeches, nor shoes, nor the big straw hats the two men wore against the sun. Nonetheless, the coats served their purpose of marking out the wearers as officers of His Majesty King George II. In fact, since *Elizabeth* was sailing with a reduced, peace-time, crew, they were the only two commissioned officers on board, and it was sheer madness for them to be seen in open dispute before their men.

'Mr Flint,' said Springer, 'look about you. If we continue in this manner, there'll be no discipline worthy of the name in this ship. So, listen to me: I am resolved to proceed to São Bartolomeo according to my orders–'

'And leave a fortune in prize money to pass by?' said Flint. 'We named this ship *Elizabeth* when we took her, but she was *Isabella la Católica* before that, and she's Spanish from keel to main-truck. We could use that to come alongside of any Spanish ship–'

'But we ain't at war with the Dons!' said Springer. 'Can you not appreciate that, you bugger? Not since last year!'

'Bah!' said Flint. 'There's no war, but there's no peace neither. Not out here. It's dog eat dog: us and the Dons and the French! And I know ports where a prize'll be bought for cash money and never a question asked.'

'No...' groaned Springer, and he wavered. He distinctly wavered, and Flint spotted it instantly and changed tack. He was very charming when he chose, and now he spoke sweet and friendly.

'See here, Captain, sir,' he said, 'there's a way to square the matter between us, I do declare. Indeed, I take my oath on it, for I'd not see a brother officer suffer in such a matter.'

The words meant nothing, but they were so fairly spoken that Springer relaxed. The scowl left his face and he gave Flint his entire attention.

Ah-ha! thought Flint, and rejoiced, for it was his guess that deep within Captain Springer there was greed that was just itching to be squared with duty, if only the means could be found.

'The fact is, sir...' said Flint.

'Aye?' said Springer.

'...I lost my share of the greatest treasure ever taken because of that bastard Anson, and I'd not see you lose your own best chance–'

But Springer snarled like a wolf as Flint struck a wildly false note by harping back upon the great wrong that had scarred his life.

Flint had sailed with Anson on his famous circumnavigation of 1740–44, when the Manila galleon was taken: the most fabulous prize in British naval history. But before that, Flint's ship *Spider* had foundered going round the Horn, and Anson had taken her people into his own ship, *Centurion*, where *Spider*'s officers had nothing to do and were rated 'supernumeraries'. As Flint told the story, this meant that they fell into legal limbo and got no share of the loot: a monstrous injustice, but one that a man got sick of hearing about.

'Mr Flint,' roared Springer at the top of his voice, 'you will attend to your duties this instant, or I'll not be answerable.'

Barely in control of himself, Springer turned away and yelled at Sergeant Dawson, 'Turn out your men, damn your blasted eyes! Bayonets and ball cartridge!'

Dawson yelled and hollered and a company of marines doubled up and formed on the quarterdeck with steel gleaming at the tips of their musket barrels.

'Mr Bones!' cried Springer. 'Muster all hands!'

'Aye-aye, sir!' said Mr Bones, and after a deal of cursing, kicks and blows, and a rushing of bare feet, Springer's eight-score seamen poured up from below, and down from the rigging, to fill the waist. There they stood, squinting up at the quarterdeck in the sun, on the hot deck, in the mottled shade of the towering canvas high above their heads.

So, with his officers and marines behind him, Captain Springer reminded his crew of their duty under his orders from Commodore Sir John

Phillips, which orders were to occupy, fortify and hold the island of São Bartolomeo. He reminded them of the strategic importance attached to the island by Sir John. He further reminded them of the dreadful penalties provided for disobedience under the Articles of War.

The crew stared sideways at one another, for they knew all this already. They also knew all about Flint's 'secret' plans for privateering. They knew because Lieutenant Flint had made it his business that they should know, and thereby they knew that Springer's speech was not for themselves but for himself and Lieutenant Flint. Springer no longer trusted either, and was parading the power of the King's Law to deliver the two of them from temptation. And for a while, the stratagem worked.

So His Majesty's ship *Elizabeth* sailed steadily southward from the Caribbean, heading for a certain latitude and longitude that Commodore Phillips had got from the last survivor of a Portuguese barque wrecked on the coast of Jamaica. *Elizabeth* was a big ship, of near eight hundred tons, mounting twenty brass guns. She was old fashioned, with a lateen sail on the mizzen, a spritsail under the bow, and steered with a whipstaff. But she was well found and comfortable and, with so few men aboard, and fair weather and no war actively in progress, *Elizabeth* should have been a happy ship. But she was not.

As far as the foremast hands were concerned, *Elizabeth* was becoming a hell-ship. This was thanks to Mr Flint, who, having failed to bend Captain Springer to his will, was taking out his spite on those beneath him. As first officer, he had unbounded opportunity for this, together with a natural aptitude for the work.

Naturally he flogged the last man down off the yards at sail drill. Naturally he flogged the last man up with his hammock in the morning. Any vicious brute would think of that. But it took Joe Flint to punish a mess by making them serve their grog to another mess and stand by while it was drunk. And it took Flint to set the larboard watch tarring the decks for the starboard watch to clean – and vice versa.

His repertoire was endless and creative. A man who prized his three-foot pigtail was made to cut an inch off it, for the crime of *sulking*. Flint contrived to detect a repetition of this crime each day until the pigtail was entirely gone. Likewise, a man caught sleeping on watch was made to throw his savings overboard, and another who doted on a particularly fine parrot was obliged to give it up to Flint, though in this case a quirk of Flint's character drove him to take the bird – for its own good, he said – in order to save it from the filthy words the lower deck were teaching it.

This he believed to be a cruelty, which he despised. For, whatever his attitude towards men, Flint could stand no cruelty to animals, and undoubtedly the bird flourished under his care as never before. Soon, he and it were friends, and he went about with it riding on his shoulder, which was a great wonder to the crew.

But mostly Flint's tricks were cruel, and a particular favourite of his was to offer escape from flogging to any man who would play 'Flint's game' instead.

'Mr Merry!' said Flint, the first time this offer was made. 'I see you've been spitting tobacco juice upon my clean decks. There's two dozen awaiting you for that. Is not that so, Mr Bones?'

'Aye-aye, Mr Flint!' said Billy Bones, who followed Flint like a shadow. 'Shall I order the gratings rigged, sir?'

George Merry stood trembling in fear of the cat, while his mates bent to their work and looked down, for it was unwise to catch Mr Flint's eye when he was in a flogging mood.

'No,' said Flint. 'Here's Mr Merry that would escape a striped back, if he could, and I'm resolved to give him that chance.'

Billy Bones stared in amazement, and George Merry's face lit up with hope.

'Will you play "Flint's game" instead, Mr Merry?' said Flint, tickling the green feathers of his parrot.

'Aye-aye, sir!' grinned Merry.

'Good,' said Flint. 'Fetch a small cask and a belaying pin, Mr Bones, and put it down here.'

Flint had George Merry sit to one side of the cask, cross-legged, while he sat on the other, and the heavy oak pin was placed on the cask between them.

'Gather round, you good fellows,' cried Flint at the furtive men watching from afar, and soon a crowd surrounded the cask. 'Now then, Merry,' said Flint, smiling, 'here's the game: I shall put my hands in my pockets, while you shall put your hands on the rim of the cask.'

Merry did as he was told and an expectant

silence fell.

'Now,' said Flint, 'choose your moment, Merry, and pick up the pin. If you pick it up, you go free.' Merry leered confidently at his messmates. 'But,' said Flint, 'if you fail, the game continues until you choose to take two dozen as originally promised.'

Merry considered this. He looked at Flint. He looked at the belaying pin, only inches from his fingers. He stuck his tongue out of the side of his mouth to help himself think ... and reached for the pin.

Crunch! The pin beat down on Merry's fingertips, drawing blood from a broken fingernail. Flint had moved faster than thought. A roar of laughter came from the onlookers, Merry howled in pain, and the parrot on Flint's shoulder screeched and struggled and flapped its wings in disapproval of the proceedings. It stamped and cursed and nipped Flint's ear.

'Ouch!' said Flint. 'What's the matter with you?' And he shook the bird off to fly free and nestle in the maintop, chattering and muttering to itself. Meanwhile Flint smiled and replaced the pin and stuck his hands in his pockets.

'Play on, George Merry,' he said, 'or take the alternative.'

Merry instantly snatched at the pin ... and *thud!* It smashed blood out of his thumb, to more laughter from all sides. And so it went on, until Merry could stand it no more and begged for a flogging, which Flint graciously allowed.

As for the parrot, in time it came back to Flint, since no man beneath him dared feed it, and Captain Springer – drunk or sober – did not care to. It even seemed to be begging his forgiveness, for it began preening him, taking a lock of Flint's long, black hair and gently pulling its formidable hooked bill down the length of the strand.

Ever afterwards it took flight whenever men were flogged or abused. Eventually it developed a frightening prescience of Flint's moods, for it had grown to know him very well, such that even before Flint grinned and gave the word, it flew off because it could not abide the cruelty. The bird was innocent, but the foremast hands saw things differently. They hated the parrot. They called it Cap'n Flint, and on those fell occasions when it flew from its master's shoulder, and no man knew what might follow, they groaned and whispered:

'Watch out, mates ... the bird's in the maintop!'

And yet there was still worse to come from Flint and all hands soon had warning of it.

The formalities of the service had to be observed before George Merry could be flogged, since only the captain could order it, and Merry was clapped in irons awaiting his captain's judgement – which was indeed a formality but took time. Thus Merry had to wait for his punishment, which took place during the forenoon watch of the day after he'd played Flint's game, when all hands were mustered to witness the defaulter lashed to a grating to receive his promised two dozen. Being already in severe pain from the battering he'd had from Flint, George Merry took his flogging with much groaning and weeping, which disturbed an already unhappy crew far more than a usual flogging when a brave man clenched the leather between his teeth and refused to cry out.

Once Merry was taken down, and the decks hosed clean, eight bells were struck for the turn of the watch, when the navigating officers took their noon-day observations; for which ceremony Mr Flint demanded an absolutely silent ship. After that, the hands were sent below for their dinner, the best time of the day, with full platters and the happy communion of messes clustered at their hanging tables on the gun-deck, where pork, pease, pickles and biscuit were shovelled down throats with a generous lubrication of grog.

It was a noisy, happy time, except for George Merry and his messmates. George himself sat painfully upright, bound in the vinegar and brown paper that the surgeon declared was the best thing for a flogged back. With his broken fingers, he could eat and drink only because his messmates fed him and held his mug to his lips.

'Ah, George Merry!' said a voice from the next-door mess, 'I sees you be in poor straights.'

'That I be, Mr Gunn,' said Merry, nodding politely towards Ben Gunn and his messmates, who were quartermasters, rated able to steer the ship. They were the elite of the lower deck and aboard *Elizabeth* they were always addressed with the honorific 'Mister'.

'So,' Ben Gunn declared, 'you thinks you be in pain?'

'Aye, Mr Gunn,' said Merry, and bit his lip.

'And you thinks you be hard done by?'

'That I does!'

'Then listen,' said Ben Gunn and beckoned his messmates and George Merry's to lean closer. Ben Gunn was a serious and sober man, if a little strange. He was much respected for his skill, but was distant – even odd – in his manner, as if his mind steered a different course than that of other men.

'You've heard Flint tell of the Manila galleon,' he said, 'and how he was done out of his share for being supernumerary?'

'Aye!' they said, and could not help but look over their shoulders in fear of Flint.

'Then heark'ee, my lads, for he don't tell the whole tale.'

'No?' they said, barely breathing.

'No, he don't, not the half of it, for I had it in full from a poor soul, long gone, what sailed in *Spider* under Flint.' Now they were transfixed and, sensing the mood, men from other messes were leaning close. 'Supernumerary, he was,' said Ben Gunn, and tapped the table in emphasis, 'for Anson diddled him, and he didn't even diddle him fair! He done it – which is to say, he *said* he done it – 'cos of what Flint had done aboard of *Spider.*'

Now the whole gun-deck was listening. They were listening, but Ben Gunn was gone off in his own thoughts.

'What was it, Mr Gunn?' someone prompted. Ben Gunn started.

'Why, it were the *Incident,*' he said, and lapsed into silence again.

'What Incident?' said a voice. 'What'd he do, Mr Gunn?'

Ben Gunn sighed. 'He meant it for a good thing,' he said, 'for he were a fine officer in them days, and he meant no harm. But it got twisted into a cruel thing...' He looked around, fixing men's eyes in emphasis. 'It got twisted ... and not entirely by his own fault, mark you! And it became such that, by comparison, we be living like lords aboard this ship today, and happy that we ain't in *Spider*.'

'Tell on, Ben Gunn!' said his messmates, looking at one another, for even they'd not heard this before.

'It were known as the *Incident*, for that's how Anson named it when he used it as an excuse to do Flint out of his share.' He looked round again. 'Flint were betrayed, shipmates. Anson betrayed him, and Flint were *turned by* that betrayal, for he worshipped Anson.'

'So what happened, Ben Gun?'

Ben Gunn struggled within himself, searching in his limited store of words for the things he would have to say. These were not things that decent sailormen talked about. The task was dreadful hard for Ben Gunn, and the whole deck waited in silence for him to speak.

Chapter 3

21st May 1745
Aboard Victory
The Indian Ocean

John Silver and Captain Nathan England walked the quarterdeck side by side, with every other man deferring and keeping clear of their private conversation. The weather was hot and good. The ship sailed easily, the guns were secured, and most of the men idling.

'Articles, John! Articles is what makes us what we are.'

'Which is pirates,' said Silver.

'No!' said England. 'If I'm a pirate, then Drake was a pirate, and Hawkins and Raleigh too, and all the rest of 'em that did what I do. And didn't they come home to knighthoods and estates?'

'But the law – King George's law – will hang us if they catch us.'

'Which they won't.'

'But they *would*.'

'God bless your soul, John! And wouldn't Queen Bess've hanged Drake, if she'd caught him at the wrong time? She'd've done it to please the King of Spain! She did what she had to, and so do I.'

'But …' said Silver.

'JOHN!' yelled England, loud enough to shake the t'gallant masts, and all hands turned to look. England's face reddened with anger. 'Avast, you swabs!' he cried. 'Look to your duties!' And every man turned away and found something to be busy with. They did as they were told, without resentment and of their own free will.

'There!' said England. 'D'you see that? Was that *pirates*, or free companions?' He waved a hand at the crew. 'That's real discipline, John. The discipline of free men. That's *articles*.'

'Bah!' said Silver.

'God damn you, you ignorant bugger!' said England, biting down on his temper. Then, 'Ah!' he said, as an idea struck him. 'Come along o' me, John Silver, and I'll show you something, by God I will!'

England stamped off, slid down a companion-way, and led the way below decks to the great cabin, right at the stern of the ship. Unlike some, England used his cabin not for display but as a place of work, where he could bring together his officers when he needed to make plans. There was a big table and some chairs, and a profusion of cupboards and drawers and pigeonholes for the storage of charts and other papers.

'Secure that hatchway!' said England, pointing at the door. 'Not that I don't trust the hands, but some things are best kept out of temptation's way.' Then he fumbled for a key, unlocked a cupboard and pointed to the big, black ledger that lay inside.

'Book of Articles!' he said with reverence. 'The very same in which you signed your name. And here beside it is the flag beneath which we buries the dead.' He laid a hand on the black cloth. 'And then there's this!' He took out a snuff box. It was nothing special. It wasn't gilt or enamelled. Not the sort of thing that would have graced a gentleman's waistcoat. It was a large, plain box, neatly carpentered from some hard, black, African wood.

'Now you just look at this, my boy, and you tell me if that was the work of bloody pirates!' He held out the box. Silver took it.

'Well?' said Silver.

'Well, open the bugger!' said England. Silver fumbled for the catch, and sprung the box open. He looked inside and saw nothing ... just two round pieces of paper, each about an inch across, each faintly dirtied with charcoal that had long since rubbed off.

'Aye!' said England, seeing Silver's expression. 'Not much to look at now, are they? But each one of them got rid of a captain. By one of 'em Davies was removed by Latour, and by the other Latour was removed by myself.' Silver took out one of the papers. He turned it over. The single word *Deposed* was written on the fresh side. The same word was on the other paper.

'What are these?' said Silver.

'The black spot, my son,' said England. 'This is the means whereby the lower deck gets rid of a captain it doesn't like.'

'The black spot?' Silver said, grinning. 'Sounds like boys at play!'

'Huh!' said England. 'You just hope you never see one handed to you! For it's a summons from the crew to stand before them and be judged. No man may harm one who gives him the black spot, nor stand in his way as he seeks to deliver it. No man may even lay a hand on one who is found in the act of *making* a black spot. And as for him to whom they deliver it – why, he must stand judgement by vote of the whole crew, be he even the captain himself.'

England reached out and took the papers. He held them up one at a time before Silver's eyes.

'This one was for Captain Danny Davies who had greedy fingers for other men's shares. Him they hanged from the yardarm. And this one was for Captain Frenchy Latour, that brought bad luck upon us one time too many! Him we stripped bollock-naked and heaved over the side to see if he could swim to Jamaica from ten miles offshore.'

'Aye,' said Silver, 'but what does it mean?'

'It means, my son, that we sail under the rule of law on board of this ship. We sail under the rule of law every inch and ounce as much as if we were on board of a ship of King George of England, or King Louis of France, or King Philip of Spain! Their laws is all different, ain't they? And ours is too, but it is *law!* It is articles! And that's why we ain't pirates!'

He spoke with such passion and such obvious sincerity that Silver nodded. He'd now heard these same arguments repeated so many times that he was losing the will to fight them; and in any case, nobody likes to think the worst of himself, so even the cleverest man will accept a weak case if it suits his self-esteem to do so.

'Now then,' said England, 'no more o' this, for it ain't why I sent for you.' He stared at Silver thoughtfully. 'You're a good man, John Silver, and the crew like you. You know what they call you?'

Silver grinned. 'Aye!' he said.

'Well?' said England. 'Out with it!'

'Long John,' said Silver.

'Aye! Long John Silver, 'cos you're the tallest man among us, and one o' the best. You're a seaman to the bone, and there's not a man here that would dare to fight you. You're a man that others will follow.' Silver shrugged, England laughed. 'It's true,' said England. 'So here's the case, Long John Silver. I have it in mind to make an officer of you on board of this ship. You have the natural gift of command, and more than that you know your letters and your numbers, which is as rare among seamen as balls on a eunuch! I shall rate you as third mate and start your education this very day.' He clapped Silver on the shoulder. 'What say you, Long John?'

'Thank you, Cap'n,' said Silver, beaming with pleasure and raising a hand to his hat in salute.

'Good!' said England. 'So what do you know already? Can you steer a course?'

'Aye!' said Silver, confidently.

'Then show me,' said England. 'We'll go this instant to the ship's wheel!' He smiled and led the way.

'Cap'n!' said the first mate, who was standing by the helmsman.

'Cap'n!' said the helmsman.

'Let Mr Silver take a turn,' said England. 'The course is north by northwest, Mr Silver, and keep her as close to the wind as she'll bear.'

The helmsman waited till Silver had taken a firm hold on the other side of the big wheel with its out-jutting handles, and when Silver nodded, he stood back and left the ship to Silver's hand, with England and the first mate looking on.

It was easy. Silver had done this a hundred times before on other ships. He was a fine steersman, keeping careful watch on the sails, and holding the ship true to her course with minimal pressure on the wheel. The task is harder than it seems and few men could have done it better. England grinned. The mate grinned, and word ran round the ship that Long John was at the helm.

'Would you change the set of her sails, Mr Silver?' asked England, nudging the mate.

'I'd shake a reef out of the fore topsail, Cap'n,'

said Silver. 'She'll bear it, and she'll steer all the easier.' And when this was done, and *Victory* did indeed answer the helm more sweetly, there was an actual cheer from the crew, now eagerly looking on.

'Well enough,' said England. 'Stand down, Mr Silver, and we'll look at the transit board, and you shall tell me its purpose aboard ship and how it is kept.' Again, Silver smiled. He waited till the helmsman had control of the wheel, then stepped forward to the binnacle housing the compass, and picked up a wooden board hanging on a hook. It had a series of holes drilled in it, radiating out from the centre in the form of a compass rose. There were a number of pegs to go in the holes, each peg attached to the board by a thin line.

'Well, Cap'n,' said Silver, 'every quarter-hour by the sand-glass, the log is hove at the stern to find the speed of her through the water.'

'Aye,' said England. 'Let's say the log's been heaved, and her speed is five knots...'

'So,' said Silver, 'that's five knots for a quarter-hour, north by northwest.' And he set a peg in the board accordingly, and looked at England. 'For that is the purpose of the board, Cap'n: to keep a reckoning of her course and speed, every quarter-hour, throughout the watch.'

'Splendid!' said England. 'And what happens at the end of the watch?'

'Why,' said Silver, 'the officer of the watch–' he instinctively touched his hat to the mate – 'he takes the board and marks out how she's run – her course and speed – during the watch.' He paused for he was now entering unknown waters.

'He marks it out on the chart, Cap'n...' Silver blinked. 'Which is all I knows o' the matter.' His smile faded a little.

'We'll come to that!' said England confidently. 'But first, here's the end of the forenoon watch about to be struck...'

Clang-clang! Clang-clang! Clang-clang! Clang-clang! The bell sounded from its little temple at the break of the fo'c'sle.

'Eight bells! Change the watch!' yelled the boatswain, and there was a rumble of bare feet on the boards as the hands of the starboard watch ran to relieve the larboard watch, who were now standing down. They doubled to it like men-o'-warsmen because Captain England would have it no other way. At the same time England's servant came up from below with a big triangular wooden case. He opened it and presented it to England.

'Cap'n,' he said respectfully, and England took out a complex ebony instrument with brass scales, a miniature telescope, and lenses, filters and other mysterious appendages besides.

'This is a quadrant, Long John,' said England. 'For this first time, I shall instruct you in its use, but afterwards, the second mate shall be your teacher.'

He nodded at the second mate, who touched his hat respectfully before taking his own quadrant out of its case and standing beside the first mate, who already had his quadrant ready.

''Tis noon,' said England. 'The ship's day begins at noon, each day, and at that time we...' England paused. 'Long John?' he said. 'What is it?'

Silver was looking at the quadrant. It unsettled

him. It worried him. He'd seen officers using quadrants and the like ever since he first went to sea. But he'd never before been asked to use one, and he stared in morbid dread at the unfathomable complexity of the thing. Some men are disturbed by heights, some by spiders or snakes. Some cannot bear to be enclosed in a small space. Long John was weighed down by the thought of having to swallow such an appalling meal of abstract thinking, which was so different from the simple, physical seamanship that he'd learned by hard labour.

'No matter, Cap'n,' he said. 'Show me the workings of her.' Long John was no coward. So he took the quadrant when England offered it, and he paid his best attention to the explanations, so carefully given, and he did his best to ask questions.

But it was no good. The worry turned to fear: fear of being exposed as an incompetent before England and the crew. Later, in England's cabin, when the captain tried to explain latitude and longitude and how a ship might find its way across the empty oceans, it was even worse. Long John tried to the very utmost of his ability, but the bearings and degrees and minutes had no meaning to him. Instead, his head felt thick and hot, a band of pain clamped round his brow, and his eyes watered like a blubbering child's. Finally, as England waved a pair of elegant brass dividers with blue-steel needle-points, trying to explain dead reckoning, Long John Silver swayed and stumbled with nausea, and had to be helped into a chair by a dumbfounded Nathan England.

'What is it, John?' he said. 'Have you got the

ague? Is it some damned fever? What is it, shipmate?'

'Can't do it, Cap'n,' said Silver. 'Show me any other task. Let me dive for gold on the sea bed. Let me lead boarders into a three-decker's broadside. Anything.'

'What d'you mean, lad?' said England, more concerned than he'd realised. England had no son. He had no family at all. He'd taken powerfully to John Silver and it had become England's hope and pleasure to see the younger man advanced in his profession.

'Can't do it, Cap'n,' Silver repeated. 'Not with charts an' all. Please don't ask me.'

'Nonsense!' said England. 'Everyone thinks they can't do it at first. We shall persevere.'

And so they did. Neither man was one to give up easily. They persevered for weeks. Sometimes Long John even thought he was getting a grasp on the thing. But the best he ever achieved was like the performance of a clumsy musician who sounds one plodding note after another, to the dismay of those around him, and to his own despair, recognising his failure.

'How can it be, John?' said England at last. 'I've seen you calculate the value of a ship's cargo down to the penny – and that done in your head without pencil and paper. How can you manage that, yet not master this piece of glass and wood?' He held up a quadrant.

'Cargoes is things I can touch,' said Silver. 'But that bloody thing...' he stared hopelessly at the instrument '...that's black magic!'

England sighed. 'It's no good, is it, shipmate?'

'No,' said Long John. 'And happy will I be to try this no more!'

'So be it,' said England. 'I shall rate you as an officer, nonetheless: whether it be coxswain, master-at-arms or something of my own invention, for I still say that men follow where you lead. But the fact of it is, John Silver, that only a gentleman and a navigator may command a ship, and I fear you will never be one.'

Chapter 4

4th January 1749
Aboard HMS Elizabeth
The Caribbean

Flint crept silently down a companionway, drawn by the unnatural silence on the dinnertime gundeck, which should have been rattling and echoing with noise. The silence could only mean some punishable insubordination and it was his delight to catch them at it. He was enjoying the anticipation of a hunter who takes his prey unawares, especially when at last he stepped through a hatchway and caught sight of the whole crew gaping at Ben Gunn, their stupid mouths hanging open, still speckled with food and dripping with grog.

This was the delicious moment. The moment just before the trap was sprung, when a word from him would jump the swabs out of their skins. Prolonging the pleasure, he nuzzled his parrot and held his hand over its beak to keep silence. Flint wondered what the solemn and miserable Ben Gunn might have to say that could so captivate them.

Had he been only a little more patient he would have found out; and then he too would have been captivated. He would have been captivated, bound in chains and sunk beyond soundings in the limitless depth of interest in what Benn Gunn was about to reveal ... but he couldn't contain himself. The anticipation of the moment was too exquisite.

'What's this?' he boomed. 'Is there disaffection among the hands? Is there wickedness in the wind?'

A hundred men leapt in terror as the fear of hell took their hearts with an icy claw, for they'd spun round to see Flint, smooth and shining, neat and suave, with his parrot on his shoulder. He gazed upon the sea of terror and shook with laughter, tickled beyond bearing by their comical faces. His parrot flapped and cackled, he snapped his fingers and stamped his foot in glee. Then he walked up and down between the mess tables, making jokes and clapping men on the shoulder in merriment. The coin of Flint's character had spun and come up bright, and now he worked black magic with his charm and his wit, and there wasn't a man present who could help but like him, and smile in admiration of him.

Afterwards, though, nobody could ever persuade Ben Gunn to finish his story, and the mystery of an unspeakable past hung about Flint and made them fear him more than ever.

And all the while Springer watched in dull,

uncomprehending hatred. He was sixty-two years old. He'd been at sea fifty years. He'd learned his trade in King Billy's time, when precious gentlemen despised the service, and he knew no other way than a rough way. He'd kicked arses and knocked men down all his life, and he believed flogging was the only way to keep idle seamen to their duties. What's more, *Elizabeth* under Flint's hand was the tightest ship Springer had ever known. And yet ... there was something about the way Lieutenant Flint went about his duties that upset Springer, and it nagged at him that he couldn't make out what it was.

The sorry truth was that Springer had not the wit to distinguish the ruthless, straight discipline that he practised himself – and which seamen respected – from the sadism inflicted upon them by Flint. So Springer avoided Flint and spent many hours in his cabin, reading and re-reading Commodore Phillips's orders and studying the rough map that Phillips had got from the hands of the dying Portugee. Phillips's eyes had blazed over the island, thinking it would be another Jamaica: a sugar island to coin money. Springer hoped Phillips was right, and he hoped he might get his hands on a little of the money.

Then he'd roar for his servant to bring a bottle, and he'd damn the lure of Flint's plan, which he knew might bring a quick return, whereas any benefit from the island was far distant and entirely dependent on the goodwill of the commodore, whose arse was as tight as a Scotchman's purse.

In fact, Springer need not have worried about Phillips's greed, because the commodore would soon be incapable of enjoying that deadly sin. In a matter of weeks, a violent storm would run Phillips's squadron on to a reef off Morant Point, Jamaica, with the loss of over a thousand men. This catastrophe would leave all knowledge of the island of São Bartolomeo exclusively in Springer's command, to the degree that even the name São Bartolomeo would never be heard again.

What Springer should have worried about was the temper of his crew under Flint, whose reign over the lower deck was unpredictable in the extreme. On the positive side, Flint had some excellent qualities. He knew the name of every man on board, and all their characters and peculiarities. He was a superb seaman and navigator, and his exacting standards were evident in the gleaming brass and snow-white decks. Above all, men leapt to his orders like lightning.

Many of the crew, led by Billy Bones, would have followed Flint into the cannon's mouth. Billy Bones was a big, plain, simple man with a dog's need for a master. He had enough education to find his latitude and plot his course. He had enough – plenty enough and more – of muscles to knock down any man he didn't like. Beyond that, he had the wit to recognise Flint's talents, and to envy the swaggering style and bearing of the man – a style and bearing which shone so brightly compared with his own, with his leathery face, his knotted hands and his tarred pigtail.

But Billy Bones saw no further and no deeper, and certainly acknowledged no fault in Flint. This was partly because he didn't want to: he'd found his idol and that was that. But there was more. There was fear. There was a great fear that Billy Bones bowed down to and which made his idol all the greater.

With Flint, everything hinged on fear. At a deep and instinctive level, all men look at each other on first meeting to assess who'd prevail in a fight, but no man had ever looked into Flint's eyes without blinking, for there was something about Flint that was manic and unholy, something best left unchallenged. Something that resonated with the horrors hinted at by Ben Gunn.

In some officers, this could have been a strength: an instant source of discipline. But in Flint's case it was an iron lid screwed down on a boiling pot. As his cruelties grew steadily worse and resentment festered among the men, Captain Springer, who could not bear what Flint was doing, stayed mostly below decks, thereby removing the restraint his presence would have had on Flint's behaviour. It was a situation that could not last. The lid must eventually blow off the pot.

But Phillips's mysterious island came first. Having run up the Trades to get wind of the island, according to the rough chart, *Elizabeth* ran south-southwest and made a commendable landfall. Springer and Flint (and even Billy Bones, with deep-furrowed brow and tongue stuck out of the corner of his mouth) had completed a most effective piece of navigation.

The hail of 'Land ho!' from the masthead brought a surge of excitement, and the hands ran to the fo'c'sle and into the foremast shrouds to see. Even Springer came up on deck, bringing his chart. Flint raised his hat and smiled. All hands cheered, and for a moment everyone was happy.

'The anchorage is to the northeast, Mr Flint,' said Springer, offering Flint his first sight of the dead Portugee's map.

Flint studied the crude sketch and sneered.

'Pah!' he said. 'Damn near useless. No soundings, no bearings. We shall have to go in like an old maid in a dark bedroom.'

'Not at all, Mr Flint,' said Springer. He'd become protective of the old chart and, besides, he hated Flint. 'This is a good, safe anchorage, and we have no need to fear.'

'Hmm,' said Flint, spotting the bleary-eyed look on Springer's face and wondering how much drink he'd got down him. 'We'd be as well to sway out the launch, though, and sound ahead as we go, don't you think, Captain?'

'Aye-aye, sir!' said Billy Bones, at Flint's elbow, and he turned to give the order. Springer's face filled with indignation.

'Belay that!' he cried. 'Mr Bones, keep your bloody trap shut, you insolent sod! I'm master here and I shall con this ship safe to her anchorage, and there won't be no need for bloody boats!'

Flint blinked in amazement and Billy Bones's jaw dropped.

'But–' said Bones.

'Shut your mouth, you mutinous bastard, and attend to getting the guns run out!' said Springer, and turned to his bulldog. 'Sergeant Dawson,' he cried, 'muster your men! I'll have an armed landing party ready against any eventualities.' Springer turned to Flint and Bones: 'Against *all* eventualities!'

Some hours later, the big ship worked round the northernmost tip of the island, keeping well out to sea, for vast rollers thundered ashore at every point, throwing up clouds of spray off huge rocks where hundreds of black beasts, glistening like monstrous slugs, cavorted and displayed themselves in the waters. Those who'd seen the like before named them for their mates as 'sea lions'.

A line of great hills, one a small mountain, rose up from the island, and trees of every kind covered the land. Huge pines towered above the rest, and sea-birds swooped and rose over all. There was some muttering that this was too small an island to be another Jamaica, but for all that the spirits of the crew lifted as it rose from the sea and revealed its secrets.

'There!' said Springer. 'See the anchorage, Mr Flint? Good enough for a first-rate, say I!'

Flint looked through his glass and nodded.

'Room enough, Captain,' he said. 'But I'd still like to know what depth of water was under my keel as I went in.' Having already heard Springer's views on the matter, Flint paused and chose his words with utmost care, before adding, 'Could we not send the launch ahead, sir, sounding as she goes, just to be sure?'

'Nonsense!' said Springer, so poisoned with hatred for Flint that he would deny his own half-century of experience in order to prove the man wrong. He was damned if he would pay attention to anything Flint said. Not if the sod fell on his knees and begged.

'Strike the courses and reef the topsails,' said Springer loudly. 'And I'll slide her in as pretty as poke up a tart's arse!'

He glared at all around him defying any of them to say otherwise, and men sniffed and muttered and went about their business, while Flint shook his head and turned away. Springer was captain and Springer had his way.

The eastern side of the island was more sheltered and less battered by the waves. The anchorage was about three cable-lengths across at the mouth, which opened between low cliffs like a softer, southern version of the fjords of Norway. Inside, it widened somewhat and ran for a couple of miles to a sandy, white-and-yellow shore, with thick undergrowth and green-top trees bent over the beach. Behind that, the land rose fast and sharp to high ground on all sides. It was indeed a fine anchorage, fit for a squadron of the line.

In a ship steered by a whipstaff, the helmsman – Ben Gunn on this occasion – wielded the big, vertical lever from beneath the quarterdeck, and looked out through a scuttle, giving him a view of the sails and the sky. He had a compass to steer a course by, but could see nothing else. Consequently, when coming into an anchorage, he relied entirely on the orders of his officers. Thus Springer stood by the scuttle and Ben Gunn awaited his commands.

Meanwhile, the marines remained ready to defend the ship, the gun crews stood by their pieces; the boatswain's crew assembled at the cathead to cast off the ring-stopper and let go the anchor; the few idlers aboard got themselves where the best view was to be had, and all hands enjoyed the thrill of expectation that comes from exploring a new land. There might be gold, silver, tigers, unicorns, drink, savages ... women!

The island stretched out its arms and folded them in, and waited dark and mysterious. The waters were calm, the wind was fair, the ship glided deeper and deeper into the anchorage. She came in bold and confident at a cracking pace, so that Captain Springer might show Lieutenant Flint how to come to anchor like a seaman, and not a lubberly fop... And just at the very second Springer was drawing breath to give the order to drop anchor, eight hundred tons of timber, spars, rigging, iron, brass, biscuit, salt-pork, gunpowder, canvas and men came to a full and shocking stop as the *Elizabeth* ran judderingly aground.

Two men fell out of the rigging into water too shallow to cover their knees. The fore topmast snapped and came down in ruin. Flint stamped his foot in disgust, the boatswain swore, everyone else looked at his mates and sneered, and Captain Daniel Springer knew himself to be a bloody fool.

Chapter 5

1st June 1752
Savannah, Georgia

The news of Flint's arrival ran through Savannah in minutes, and every soul – man or beast – that was not physically chained down, ran to the riverside to see Flint's ships work slowly up river, through muddy waters that ran some forty feet below. Soon the best part of a thousand people lined the banks, shouting, calling, waving and pointing out the sights to one another. There were redcoats, slaves, children, merchants, dogs, whores, seamen and even a few Indians, all shoving and jostling for a place. Flint's men were renowned as big spenders and their arrival would benefit the whole community.

Down on the river, Captain Flint himself strutted his quarterdeck in a fine new suit of clothes, and his first mate Billy Bones bawled and roared and drove the crew to their duties as the three ships came to anchor, flying British colours out of respect to His Majesty King George II. *Walrus*, Flint's own ship, was the biggest of them, followed by the brigantine *Chapel Yvonne* out of Le Havre, and the scow *Erna van Rijp* out of Amsterdam. Both the latter showed signs of damage to their masts and rigging: damage temporarily repaired for a short voyage.

Up on the river bank, Mr Charles Neal, a stocky, respectably dressed man, sweated in the oppressive heat, and shoved as close to the edge as he dared, to catch Flint's eye. At once, Flint swept off his hat and bowed low.

'Ah,' said Neal, and raised his own hat. He sucked his teeth and hissed in irritation at the damage to the brigantine's mainmast. He could see that he would have to replace it before the vessel undertook a proper voyage. He shook his head and wondered if the likes of Flint ever considered the consequences (that is to say, the *cost)* of damaging so expensive an item as the mainmast of a ship. He supposed not.

'Boy!' he said, summoning the slave who followed him about with a big parasol to keep off the sun. 'Best speed now! Run back to the liquor shop. Tell Selena to get out all the best. Every table and chair in the house, and all the girls washed and cleaned. Tell her I'll be along later with Captain Flint.'

Neal thought of Selena. She would do the job. She was his best girl. For that matter, she was his best *man* – he laughed at his little joke. She was the only one he could trust. The best of all his people, and she'd been with him only thirteen months, and even she didn't know how much he now relied on her. It was his good fortune that she had come to Savannah. But then, where else could she have gone? This squalid colonial outpost on the banks of the Savannah River was the only place where she could hide.

The town was no place for a man like Charley Neal, who'd been destined for the Inns of Court (or at least their Dublin equivalent) until his temper and fists intervened. Savannah sweltered and stank. It festered with diseases. Its houses were hovels of rough-hewn timber shared by men, hogs, horses and slaves, all living in a constant shadow of danger from the Indians in the surrounding forests.

Mother of God, thought Neal, *it's worse than a bog-house shit-hole!*

But then he shrugged and reflected that here, at least, he did not need to watch his back as he would have done in Ireland. Here, almost everyone was welcome: English, Irish, Scots, Swiss and Germans – even dissenters and Jews – and all were left alone, and none pursued for little sins in past lands. Little sins like the mashing and smashing of a holy Jesuit Father who'd tried to take an unholy interest in one of his pupils.

Only Spaniards were banned outright from Savannah since their king had his own ideas about who owned Georgia and who did not. Spaniards were banned and Catholics very unwelcome, so Cormac O'Neil had trimmed his name slightly, and risked his soul considerably, by affecting the protestant religion. And now, Charley Neal consoled himself that Charles was not the most protestant of English royal Christian names, and hoped that God might forgive him in the end.

More to the point, Savannah was teeming with growth. It was close enough to the Caribbean sugar islands to trade with them – and there were other opportunities too. Very profitable ones, since it was acknowledged that, in Savannah, King George's law ran only on Sundays. And in the absence of law, business worked excellently on trust. Thus Neal's dealings with the likes of Captain Flint were conducted on that basis. Flint trusted Neal to receive the ships he brought in and to turn them into cash, while Neal trusted Flint to cut his throat if ever he attempted deceit.

Half an hour later, a roaring crowd of townsfolk arrived at Neal's liquor shop, following at a respectful distance behind Flint, who was arm-in-arm with Charley Neal himself. The liquor shop was a long, dark timber shed with seating for hundreds on low stools arranged around long tables, with fresh sand and sawdust on the earth floor. There were storerooms attached for the drink, and a cook-house to provide food. At one end stood a row of jugs and barrels from which the drink was served. Here stood Selena in front of a row of girls, mostly black, waiting like gunners at their pieces before battle was joined. Neal looked at Selena as he entered and nodded in approval.

Their eyes met and she nodded solemnly, and without smiling, the little madam, as if he didn't know all about her.

In fact, he did know all about her. She was a runaway. Worse, she'd committed murder. Selena had turned up on his doorstep with a sack made of bedlinen, crammed with gold and silver items she'd stolen from her master's 'special house'. She had money too, doubtless taken off his dead body when she'd finished shoving a knife in him, or shooting him, or bidding farewell to him by whatever means a slender girl finds to do away with a fourteen stone man. And then she'd got as far as Savannah!

Neal shook his head in wonder. How did a sixteen-year-old manage that? She'd run in the night, with no plan and nowhere to go in all this wild land with its scalping, cannibalistic savages. No doubt she'd bribed and paid her way, either with money or that other currency that God gave women for the temptation of men. That would have been easy enough. She was uncommonly shapely and her face was pretty as a doll's.

'Ah well!' he said. He was over sixty and not greatly troubled by these things any longer. His passions focused on his strongbox. So he'd taken her into his household, claimed an honest quantity of her money, and made her his own legal property, safely secured with all necessary papers and her life's history washed clean of all stain.

And now she was amassing her own small pile of gold, running the liquor shop – and running it well. As Charley Neal had anticipated, everything was ready to receive his guests. A host of horn tankards stood deployed like a regiment on parade. Corks were drawn and barrels tapped. The cook was blowing up the ashes of her fire while her helpers sliced the pork and slit the fish, and the shutters of the long windows were thrown open for the air, with shades of sailcloth braced outside to keep off the sun. In one corner, the house band of musicians were already playing. There were two fiddlers, three pipers, a horn-blower and a mulatto drummer, groaning, twanging and battering away at a pace to set the pulses racing.

Thus entered Flint and Neal, followed by Billy Bones in the company of Mrs Polly Porter, owner of the biggest breasts in Savannah, who never laid down for less than gentlemen or those in possession of a Spanish Dollar. Then came Flint's officers, his men, and all the lesser folk, until the house was filled to the very limit of its capacity to receive them.

It was instant bedlam. Selena and her girls were run off their feet, dealing with the wants of the mob and keeping eager hands out from under their skirts. Food and drink poured down throats, cash poured into the strongbox. Songs were called for, and roared out to shake the walls. Those who felt capable got up and danced. Men piddled in corners, fights flared and died, hogs scavenged scraps, and here and there a copulation beneath a table caused the pots to shudder above, while folk peered below the planks and urged the amorous couple to go to it.

Selena herself served Neal and Flint.

'Selena!' said Neal, taking his rum punch.

'Mr Neal!' she said, and 'Sir!' to Flint, who was handsome, with a most beautiful smile and gorgeous clothes. He was by far the finest man she'd ever seen.

'My dear,' said Flint, looking her over.

Ah ha! thought Charley Neal, spotting advantage. 'Be nice to the captain,' he mouthed at Selena. But Selena had other work to do, so this duty passed for the moment.

Meanwhile Selena cast an eye over Flint and his crew – and was fascinated by what she saw. She was surprised at how young they were. Aside from some of the officers, they seemed mostly in their early twenties. They were tanned like old leather, and dressed in their best shore-going rig: white ducks, buckled shoes, coloured shirts and stockings, and silk handkerchiefs bound round the skull. They were tattooed and pierced with gold earrings, and each man bore enough arms to start a small war.

But what marked them out from common seamen even more than the pistols and blades was the fact that every man had the authentic look of trouble about him. Savannah was no place for weaklings, but even by Savannah standards, Flint's 'Chickens' stood out as hard cases. Fortunately, today they were in the best of spirits.

When, after some hours, they managed to drink themselves unconscious and things became quiet again, Flint and Neal withdrew to Neal's house to discuss business, leaving Selena and her crew to clear up the mess. She was in the storeroom, sorting out full bottles from empties, when a sound made her turn around. Selena jumped when she saw the man. This wasn't one of the drunken swine from the main room, risen on his hind legs to search for more drink; he was stone-cold sober and his clothes were fresh. She'd not seen him before. And yet she already knew him. Or at least she'd heard of him. Flint and his men were the talk of Savannah, and she'd heard plenty about them from Charley Neal, whose business it was to know what went on among his dangerous clients. These men could have one leader one day, and another on the next. Neal had to be ready for such changes and did his best to keep up with the various plots and rivalries.

So Selena already knew quite a lot – by reputation – about the man who'd just come in. He was very tall, with yellow hair, long limbs and large hands. His face was wide and his eyes large and intelligent. He was remarkably neat and clean, and everything in his manner and bearing told her that here was a man quite out of the ordinary. He looked down into her eyes and smiled.

'John Silver at your service, ma'am!' he announced, and bowed like a courtier, sweeping off his hat.

'Long John!' she said. 'You're the one they call "Long John".'

He smiled again, as if pleased with her.

'The very same, ma'am,' said he. 'An' a smart little thing you are an' all, to spy me out so quick. Smart as paint, you are, I saw it the instant I clapped eyes on you.' He cocked his head on one side in surprise. 'And gifted with the speech of a lady, too! Now I wonder how that might be?'

Selena shrugged off this potentially dangerous question and threw back one of her own.

'Long John Silver,' she said, 'the one that Captain Flint is afraid of?'

'What?' said Silver, surprised. 'And where should a pretty little thing like yourself hear such wicked lies?'

'From the trash in there,' she said, glancing towards the big room with its stupefied inhabitants. 'They say you were great friends once, but he's afraid of you now.'

'Ah, well, there we have it,' he said, nodding wisely as if perceiving some happy explanation of what had seemed like bad news. ''Tis clear that some of the poor lads...' he ticked off names on his fingers: 'George Merry, Mad Pew, Black Dog and some others...' He frowned and shook his head like a parson reflecting on favourite pupils who can never *quite* get the catechism right. 'And even Mr Billy Bones himself... 'Tis plain that some o' my shipmates just cannot keep a hitch on their jawing tackle, once the first bottle has gone down.'

But then his smile came back and he reached out a long arm and patted Selena's bare shoulder in avuncular fashion.

'So there y'are, my dear. Weren't no cause to believe none o' them. Not at all.'

Selena frowned in her turn and shook off his

hand. She didn't follow the logic of his argument, nor really what he was talking about.

'But whilst we're on this tack,' said he, genuinely curious, 'just what were those lubbers a-saying about old Long John? And why in heaven's name should Joe Flint be afeared o' me?'

'Because you want to take the ship from him,' she said, repeating what she'd heard from a score of drunken lips.

'Shiver me timbers!' said Long John, staggering back with every convincing show of horror and amazement. 'Me heart fair bleeds to hear of such wickedness from so sweet a child as yourself.' He grinned and shook his head. As far as Long John Silver was concerned, there was no captain other than Flint, whatever might be the gossip on the lower deck, and whatever Flint's little weaknesses.

But then Silver moved a pace closer and ran his hand lightly down her cheek. She twitched away as she realised that he only wanted what all the others wanted. She tried to slip by him, but he was too quick and kept between her and the door.

'I can prove my loyalty to the dear captain,' he said, manoeuvring her into a corner, 'for if I had wanted the ship, then ... why, I'd have took her!' He seized Selena's wrists and pulled her close. 'For I'm a man as takes what he wants, my dear.'

'But you can't!' she said, once more quoting from the drunken gossip of Flint's men. 'Because you can't set a course, not with charts and quadrants and dividers.'

Silver's face worked horribly as Selena's words stuck a red-hot iron right into his most tender, most shameful, and most agonising weakness.

'Can't I?' he snapped.

'No!' said she. 'You can't, because it's gentleman's work, which Captain Flint can do because he is a gentleman!'

'Flint?' he choked. 'Flint ... is ... a ... *gentleman?*'

'Yes,' she said. But he did not reply. The spasm of laughter was so uncontrollable that he could barely breathe, let alone speak.

Chapter 6

30th January 1749
Aboard HMS Elizabeth
The island

With the entire crew looking at him in judgement, and the ship fast aground in proof of his guilt, Captain Springer reddened and seethed and trembled.

Springer was not a clever man nor a gifted one, nor even one with any particular aptitude for his career. He'd only gone to sea in the first place because his seafaring father had sent him, and he'd learned his seamanship through hard work and hard knocks.

He had managed, through a certain dogged bravery, to win promotion in action. He was well aware that he was lucky to have risen as far as he had, and that his skills were few: he knew how to stand the enemy's fire and how to keep the lower deck to its duties; he knew how to run down his latitude to a destination ... and that was it. He hadn't the cleverness of Flint, and nowhere near his skill as a navigator, and now he felt himself the victim of some plot of Flint's. Well, he was having none of it. It weren't his fault, so it had to be someone else's.

'You bloody lubbers!' he roared at everyone in general. 'You whore-son, bastard, nincompoop parcel of landsmen...'

He raved and swore, ignoring the cries of the men who'd been thrown overboard by the impact of the ship's running aground. It was lucky for them they were in such shallow water or they'd have surely drowned. He damned and blasphemed and blasted and cursed, and comprehensively lost the respect of his people in a rage of temper that every one of them knew ought rightfully be directed at himself.

'Sergeant Dawson,' he screamed, at last and inevitably, 'rouse me out that sod of a helmsman and I'll see the backbone of him at the gratings before five minutes is out. And all the lookouts too, and all the shit-heads that went overside ... and ... and...'

He cast about in anger and every man wisely dropped his eyes, though one was too slow, *'And that sod there!'* he cried. 'Him as dares to look his lawful captain in the eye in that insolent manner!'

This was a desperately bad course to steer.

For one thing, Springer was ignoring the accustomed usages of ship's discipline that required the boatswain and his mates to administer discipline. To employ the marines was an affront to every seaman aboard, as well as being a naked display of direct rule by musket and bayonet. Even worse was Springer's singling out Ben Gunn the helmsman – a man so respected by the entire ship's company that it would be deemed a severe insult to the lower deck to flog him, unless his dereliction of duty was severe and was obvious to all hands, whereas in this case it was *physically impossible* for Ben Gunn, in his station at the whipstaff, even to have seen what hazards the ship might be running on to.

What Springer was doing was bad and despicably stupid.

But one after another the five men were stripped, triced up and given two dozen – including Ben Gunn, despite growls of anger from the crew, to which Springer responded by ordering his marines to level their muskets at the hands. This was utter madness, and even the marines were groaning as the cat fell, stroke after stroke, on Ben Gunn's skinny back. When he was taken down, the poor creature was no longer the same man, for his pride was broken and his mind was wounded far worse than his body.

To say, therefore, that *Elizabeth* was an unhappy ship would be a very masterpiece of understatement. The mood of the ship's people was even worse than it had been under Flint; then, at least there had been moments of laughter. Everything that later happened on the island stemmed directly from Captain Springer's staggering failure of leadership. An explosion was now inevitable. But for a few weeks the disease festered under the skin and no eruptions were visible. This was thanks to the urgent need for action to get the ship afloat again.

First, Springer tried to warp her off. In theory this was a simple task which involved passing a hawser ashore to be made fast to a strongpoint such as a mighty tree. The hawser would then be bent to the capstan and all hands would heave the capstan bars around to haul the ship off the sandbank.

In practise, the effort failed. Despite the disciplined effort of teams of men passing the line ashore in the launch, sweltering their way along the shoreline to find a suitable tree, and despite the combined strength of every man aboard, pushing their hearts out on the capstan bars, *Elizabeth* never budged. Springer had brought her in at the flood of the high tide, such that there'd never be another inch of water to be had under her keel to lift her off. In fact, each time the tide went out, she appeared to settle in deeper. So each high tide, Springer tried another trick, each more desperate that the last, each seeking to give the capstan a better chance to pull the ship clear.

'Give a broadside, double-shotted, to shake her off, Mr Flint!' cried Springer. 'That'll break the suction.' So the island echoed to the boom of *Elizabeth*'s guns. But the ship never moved. 'I'll lighten her, Mr Flint,' said Springer. 'Strike all topmasts! All boats out of the ship, and all spare sails and spars.' That failed too. 'Guns and carriages ashore, Mr Flint,' said Springer wearily on the fourth day. 'And all stores out of the hold. Everything that ain't scarfed and bolted into the hull.' But, despite the enormous labour, *Elizabeth* – now more hulk than ship – simply wedged herself deeper into the sand.

As the boatswain's pipe delivered the final call of ''Vast hauling' and a hundred sweat-drenched men collapsed at the capstan, Springer chewed his knuckles in despair. Around him his officers were glaring at him in open contempt and the men were seething with hatred for Springer, and with fear at the prospect of being unable to get off the island. The crew were exhausted. The ship was gutted. Ashore lay a vast pile of ship's stores: arms and artillery, food and drink, clothing and tools, all under a miniature town of spar-and-canvas tents above the tide-line. And in the midst of it all Captain Springer was helpless, hopeless, guilty and angry. For the first time in his career, he did not know what to do.

And so, Lieutenant Flint, who'd watched incredulous as his captain dug himself into the pit, saw that his moment had come. Thanks to Springer's disgraceful behaviour certain wicked temptations had been laid before Lieutenant Flint, which even *he* fought off at first, but when they came knocking at his door, grinning and winking, day after day after day. Well, finally he gave up the fight and embraced them.

'May I speak, sir?' said he, all humble and respectful.

'Damn your eyes, you evil sod,' said Springer, 'this is all your doing.'

'Aye-aye, sir,' said Flint, ignoring the words, which in truth had no meaning anyway. Springer wasn't even looking at him.

'I have a suggestion, sir,' said Flint.

'Bollocks!' said Springer.

'Aye-aye, sir,' said Flint. 'But we can make Portsmouth yet, sir, and do our duty to the Commodore.'

'What?' said Springer, beginning to take notice. 'Can't you see it's hopeless, you prick-louse?' Springer gestured at the ship. 'She'll never come free. Can't you see that, you slimy sod?'

'Indeed, sir,' said Flint, 'the ship is lost. But we can build another from her timbers. We have all the tools and the necessary skills. We could easily build a vessel capable of reaching Jamaica, let alone the Spanish Americas.'

Springer gaped at Flint, consumed with relief ... and then with envy and hatred. Why hadn't he thought of that? It was bloody obvious once it was pointed out.

'I further suggest, sir,' said Flint, 'that you might consider bringing the men together at once to announce your decision, and that you might further consider the issue of double grog to all hands in respect of their exceptional labours.'

Billy Bones, standing as ever in Flint's shadow, grinned to himself. He'd make sure everyone knew whose idea it was to get them back home.

'You back-stabbing bastard!' said Springer bitterly, and he glared at Flint. 'It's all you, you sod. It's a plot!'

'Indeed not, sir,' said Flint, and permitted himself the hint of a sneer, for although there had been no plot before, there was one a-hatching now.

But Springer had no option other than to make the best of it. He had all hands piped to the quarterdeck rail, then he made his speech and ordered double grog. They cheered him for that, knowing there was a way home tomorrow and a roaring debauch tonight. Double grog meant a full pint of strong Navy rum per man, and even sailors got drunk on that.

For the next two days, Springer's crew were the happiest tars in the service, since on the first day they were mainly unconscious and on the second they were recovering in a warm bliss of recollection. On the third day, Flint, Billy Bones and the boatswain's crew set them to work with the aid of rope ends knotted tight and soaked in salt water to give a good whack. The crew had had their fun, and now it was time to put the captain's (that is to say, Lieutenant Flint's) plan into operation.

The carpenter and his mates set about erecting a small shipyard ashore and hacking planks and timbers out of the ship herself. Another team, under the gunner and his mates, erected sheer-legs, block and tackle, and with the steady labour of twenty chanting seamen, dragged cannon bodily up to the cliff-tops at the mouth of the inlet, and established batteries to command the sea approaches.

At the same time, half the marines under one of the midshipmen began exploring the island to determine whether any danger lay at their backs. The other half, under Sergeant Dawson, deployed on the outskirts of the shore-works, in open order with ball cartridge loaded, to give warning of any attack.

Meanwhile, the cook and his mates served up victuals, the cooper filled the ship's butts with fresh water, the surgeon drew splinters and sewed up cuts, the sailmaker cut up *Elizabeth*'s sails and re-sewed them according to the new pattern designed by Lieutenant Flint, and the boatswain's crew steadily stripped the rigging and fittings out of the ship, and set up a store tent ashore. And just to keep them busy, those men not already employed were sent out in a boat, rigged for sail, with another midshipman in command, to take bearings around the entire island, and to take soundings besides. This would enable a proper map to be made.

The true master of all these works was, of course, Lieutenant Flint, who excelled himself in the efficiency with which he flogged the men to it, and in the ingenious punishments devised for those who incurred his displeasure.

'Three days without water for you, my chicken,' for a boatswain's mate who'd smashed his toes with a dropped roundshot, which Flint interpreted as malingering.

'The one to lash the other, by turns,' he pronounced on two seamen who'd dropped a compass out of a boat in twenty fathoms. 'And to continue until one or the other drops,' he smiled. 'So lay on, my hearties, for whichever beats the hardest will take less back.'

And so it went on:

'Gagging with a marlin spike, while lashed to a spar in the sun.'

'No grog until within soundings of England.'

'No sleep for two nights.'

'Ducking to the count of fifty.'

'To play Flint's game, or take two dozen.'

The result of all this was, firstly, that – in the absence of a maintop – Cap'n Flint the parrot spent a lot of time perched among the trees; and secondly that *Elizabeth*'s crew were prevented from being mended and made sound by the busy works that Flint himself had set in motion. Under any hand other than Flint's, the men would have recognised the good sense of what needed to be done. They would have rejoiced in the escape from marooning, and they would have given of their best.

Alas, Flint could not deny himself these vicious pleasures. As for Captain Springer, he was worse puzzled than he'd been when at sea with Flint. He still couldn't put a finger on what was wrong with his first lieutenant, and was furthermore weighed down by the guilt of running his ship aground and not knowing how to get her off. So he took to skulking in his tent and emptying bottle after bottle to take away the despair. He left everything to Flint, unless Flint positively forced him to play a part.

One day, three weeks after they'd come ashore, Flint came to his tent with just such an intrusion.

It was hot, terribly hot. Springer's tent, rigged under the shade of trees along the shoreline, kept out the sun, but not the still pressure of heat. As usual, all work had ceased for the middle hours of the day when the sun blazed fiercest. A cable's length away, where the new vessel was growing, the steady thud, thud, thud of the carpenter's adze had come to a halt, along with the battering of mallets driving in trenails, and the groaning of saws shaping the timbers afresh. All hands were asleep, save those unfortunates on watch. Clad in an open-neck shirt, wide ducks, bare legs, with the sweat glistening on his heavy face, Springer snored in his hammock.

Two figures came scrunching across the shimmering white sand and into the dark of Springer's tent. Flint and Billy Bones were coming to call. Flint with his eternal parrot on his shoulder, and Billy Bones in his wake.

'Cap'n, sir?' said Flint, rapping his knuckles on the spar that acted as a tent post.

'Uh? What?' said Springer, starting out of his doze. Flint nudged Billy Bones and nodded his head quickly towards the empty bottles under Springer's hammock. Bones leered back. They'd become very familiar, these two.

'Sorry to disturb you, Captain, sir,' said Flint, advancing into the tent with a paper rolled up in his hand.

'Damn you, you bloody sod,' said Springer with reddened eyes. 'Whassit now, you rat-piss streak of piddle?' He reached for a pistol that he kept by him and cuddled its heavy brass butt.

Flint saw the movement and smirked. Springer's face swelled and his teeth ground together. He hated Flint beyond reason, and the more so because he didn't know why. But his fingers twitched and lay still. He was a law-abiding man, incapable of putting a pistol ball through another officer in cold blood. Anyway, he was half asleep, half drunk, and having trouble keeping awake.

'Here's the chart, sir,' said Flint, displaying the finished map of the island. 'You'll see I've taken the liberty of naming the prominent features: Spy-glass Hill, Mizzenmast Hill, North Inlet, and so on.' He pointed with his finger: 'And here, sir, you can see that there is a better harbour than this, to the south.' He nudged Billy Bones again, craftily so Springer could not see. 'But, of course, we never got the chance to try it.'

'Damn you, you whore's whelp ... you walking abortion ... you...' Springer mumbled on and Flint spoke over his incoherent curses.

'I'm glad you approve of the chart, sir,' he said sarcastically. 'For it was drawn entirely by myself.'

He rolled up the chart and produced another paper showing the lines of the little sloop that the carpenter's men were building. 'But that is not why I am here, sir, disturbing your rest.' He made a show of presenting the plans to Springer. 'Here's our little *Betsy*, sir. She'll be sixty tons, two masts, sweet as a nut, and able to bear six guns.' He flicked a glance at Billy Bones, then continued: 'Six guns and maybe forty men. Fifty at the uttermost, sir. We cannot build her bigger.'

'Damn you...' murmured Springer and fell completely asleep.

'So most of the people must stay on the island, sir...' said Flint, making a pantomime of deference to the unconscious Springer, '...while *Betsy* sails to bring rescue to those who remain.'

It was the plain truth and Flint had known it from the moment he and the carpenter had designed the new vessel. There was only so much that make-and-mend initiative could achieve, and some of *Elizabeth*'s timbers were rotten besides. The carpenter had been sworn to silence under pain of death at Flint's own hand, should the secret leak out, plus the promise of being one of those to be embarked in the new ship.

But it would eventually become obvious to even the stupidest among the crew that there would not be room for all of them aboard *Elizabeth*'s child. Any decent officer would therefore have summoned his men, given them the truth at once, and trusted to their good nature as seamen to understand that there simply was no other way forward. And any decent crew would have understood. But Lieutenant Joseph Flint had fallen so deeply into temptation that he was now driven by quite another logic than that which applied to decent officers who led decent crews.

'Thank you, sir,' said Flint, as Springer – lost in sleep – snorted and gargled like a hog. 'Bah!' said Flint. 'Will you just look at the swab?' He plucked out the pistol from under Springer's hand and turned to Billy Bones. 'Give me your chaw, Billy,' he said.

'What?' said Bones, his brow furrowed in puzzlement.

'What, *sir!*' said Flint. 'Just spit out your chaw, at the double now.' Flint held out his hand.

'Me chaw?' said Bones, tested beyond comprehension. 'Into your hand, sir?'

'Spit!' said Flint. 'Now!'

'Aye-aye, sir!' said Bones. He'd seen the look in Flint's eye and dared not disobey. So he leaned forward and spat out a plastic gob of black-brown tobacco, sticky and slimy with saliva. It splattered into the palm of Flint's hand. Flint smiled without the least sign of disgust. He squeezed and moulded the tobacco to his liking, then he filled half the barrel of Springer's pistol with sand, and rammed the sticky plug of tobacco down on top of it as a wad. Finally he deftly replaced the pistol without waking Springer.

'There,' he said quietly as he wiped his hands on Billy Bones's shirt. 'Just in case he ever gets the courage, eh, Mr Bones?'

'Aye-aye, sir,' said Billy Bones.

Then they walked out again into the fierce heat and the high, blazing sun.

'We'll set them building the blockhouse tomorrow, Billy-my-chicken,' said Flint, 'and you can let the word out among the people that Captain Springer is going to abandon them.'

Billy Bones licked his lips. He blinked and trembled. He muttered and groaned. He summoned every grain of his courage ... and he ventured to dispute the matter.

'Bugger of a risk, this mutiny, begging your pardon, *Cap'n*,' said Bones, instinctively adding that last word – the supreme honorific of his vocabulary – in the hope that it might protect him. It was an arm raised in anticipation of a blow.

'Billy-boy, Billy-boy,' said Flint in a peculiar soft voice, without ever giving Bones so much as a glance, reaching instead to pet the green bird that clamped its claws in his shoulder and chuckled and nuzzled his ear. 'Don't ever question my orders again. Not so long as you wish to live. Do you hear me?'

Billy Bones was armed equally as well as Flint with pistols and cutlass. He was the bigger man, being taller and broader in the chest. He was a man in the prime of his strength and was used to keeping discipline over the scum of the lower deck. But he gulped and swallowed in terror, he bowed his head, he shook in fright. Then he took refuge in the seafaring man's universal safe response to the words of his betters.

'Aye-aye, sir!'

Chapter 7

1st June 1752
Savannah, Georgia

As Long John laughed, he took care to keep an eye on the girl. He laughed till his belly ached at what she'd said. He laughed wildly over the thought that – of all the warped and twisted fiends that came in nightmares – Flint might be a *gentleman*. It was the solemn way she'd said it. It was the innocence of it, God love her, with her plump little arse and her big eyes and her bouncing tits. So even with the tears blinding his eyes, Long John kept a close watch on her, and on the room itself, Charley Neal's liquor store.

The door was the only way out. The walls were heavily built, with one high window covered by an iron grille to make sure that the liquor did not wander off during the night. Still laughing, Long John kicked the door shut behind him, and leaned himself against it to make entirely sure she'd not escape.

He took these unconscious precautions because *Walrus* had been months at sea and not a sight of anything female had Long John taken in all that time, and when coming ashore to Chancy Neal's house Long John was as used to making up for lost time as any other seafaring man.

Finally, Long John drew forth a handkerchief and wiped his eyes. He took a deep breath, sighed happily and smiled at Selena, who all the while had kept an even closer watch on him than he had upon her. She was watching and waiting. She knew precisely what was in the man's mind, and she knew that all the other girls were at that very moment laid on their backs with drunken sailors snoring contentedly between their legs, breeches blown to the four winds and hairy buttocks displayed to the world. She knew too, that each girl would be clutching a fistful of gold, which (after Neal's percentage) they would keep for their own selves.

'Now then, my girl,' said Silver, 'what might your name be? For I've taken the most powerful fancy to you, and no mistake!'

The words were true in a constricted sort of way. Long John looked at Selena in the dim light of the hot storeroom and he liked what he saw. The cheap cotton gown was her sole garment and it was thin. It covered her nakedness for decency's sake, but all the pleasures beneath jutted and curved most appealingly.

'My name is Selena,' she said. 'And I'm no whore.' She had made her decision and set down the rules. All she had to do now was enforce them.

'Indeed you ain't,' said Long John. He smiled and produced a large gold coin. He held it up and turned it so it gleamed and shone.

'It's no use,' she said.

'Oh?' said Silver, and looked at her afresh. 'Aye,' he said thoughtfully, and nodded. 'You ain't like some o' them dog-faced drabs neither, nor ain't you neither. You're quality, my girl. That you are!' He produced another coin. She sneered. He produced a third. There was now more money on offer than Selena could earn in years by any other means.

'I told you, John Silver, it's no use. I've never been a whore, and I'm never going to be one.'

'Oh?' he said, with a sneer of his own. 'Don't tell me there's been a virgin found in Savannah, for there ain't never been one yet!'

She blinked, considering her own precise status in that regard, following attentions pressed upon her by a certain Mr Fitzroy Delacroix, who had once been her owner. Long John grinned, mistaking the signs.

'Well, there you are then, my little bird,' he said. 'What was good for them, is good for me. And I ain't no Jew nor Scotchman when it comes to paying the reckoning.' He flourished his three gold pieces. He set them on a nearby barrel. He thought the matter settled. 'This'll do nicely,' he said, looking round the room. 'Private like, and quiet as a church.'

He threw off his hat and pulled his shirt over his head. He was a fine-muscled man: strong in the arms, flat in the belly, with a dominating physical presence. Selena crushed the impulse to run because there was nowhere to go. Instead, she stood her ground.

'I said, I am not a whore!' she cried, with all the force in her body, but she was seized by two powerful hands and hoist up off her feet, her eyes level with his.

'Well then, madam,' said Long John, glancing at the gold pieces, 'just what *is* the price, then?' He grinned. 'And don't I get a little something for what I already laid down?'

He tried to kiss her lips, but she turned her face away. He ran his tongue all over and around the silky black column of her throat. She stayed rigidly still. He gave up. He set her down. He was puzzled and annoyed.

'Beach and burn me, girl!' said Silver. 'Just how much d'you expect? You're a rare fine shaped 'un, I'll grant you that, but this ain't Paris nor London, and you ain't King George's mistress!'

'I told you. I'm not a whore!'

'Oh yes you are!'

'Oh no I'm not!'

'No?'

'No!'

'You bitch!'

'You bastard!'

'Whore!'

'I AM NOT A WHORE!'

In his anger and balked desire, Silver swung back his hand. But when it came to it, he couldn't bring himself to strike the small, helpless figure. So he sighed and growled and cursed. And then, eventually, and very late in the day, it occurred to him that it just might be a good idea to pay some attention to what she'd been saying.

'Are you *really* not a whore?' he said.

'Are you deaf!'

'But all Charley's girls are.'

'EXCEPT ME!'

'Oh ... well ... I...'

He fumbled for words. He was a stranger to the art of apologising and no words came. Instead a heavy guilt fell upon him: the guilt that sits on a man who knows he's behaved very badly. Beyond that, as he looked at Selena, a tiny barb had been driven into Long John Silver, and it smarted. For a long time he didn't even recognise what was happening, because he'd not had such feelings for years.

He picked up his clothes and his money and left, slamming the door thunderously behind him. And later, when he encountered Polly Porter, who'd gone out for a breath of air while Billy Bones was asleep, and she – ever open for business – welcomed him with open arms, he couldn't bring himself to do it. There was no joy in a sweating copulation with a fat tart when his mind was full of the small, lovely, black figure staring back at him with fierce determination.

When Long John was gone, Selena was seized with a terrible shaking. She'd kept herself bold and calm while danger threatened and, now that it was gone, her legs shook and her teeth chattered, and there were tears too. There was a great quantity of these. She was very young and entirely alone and the world was a very hard place.

Chapter 8

20th February 1749
The island

Billy Bones trod heavily across the sand, making his way towards the marine sentry on guard at the latrine trench.

It was night but there was a bright moon and the marine recognised Mr Bones easily by the hulking shoulders and the blue officer's coat with its rows of shiny buttons. Also there was a heavy 'Pfff! Pfff! Pfff!' of exhaled breath in time with the laboured footfalls, which was unique to Mr Bones. It was his unconscious and wordless protest at the need to struggle over soft sand in a hot climate.

The wretched marine drew himself to attention and reviewed all those little sins of omission and commission in the doing of his duties of which private soldiers can be found guilty by any superior officer who has a mind to do so.

It was bad enough being stuck out here by a stinking bog-pit to make sure that the bastard matelots shovelled sand over their shit when they'd shat, but it weren't fair – not at all –for Mr bastard Billy Bones to come out to check that all was to rights. It was usually one of the mids, and they were all right. A quick 'All's well?' and off the little bastards went, holding their bastard noses. Then a shudder of ice ran down the marine's backbone.

'Mygawdamighty!' he said as he realised what a fool he was, being afeared of Mr Bones, for if the bastard officers were walking the guard posts themselves and not sending of the mids ... then the next one might be... Oh my eyes and soul ... the next one might be *Flint!*

'Stand easy there!' said Billy Bones. 'All's well?'

'Aye-aye-suh!' said the marine, looking rigidly to his front.

'Huh!' said Billy Bones. He looked all around into the dark, as if a horde of wild savages was creeping inwards with sharpened spears. It was all for show, of course, as everyone now knew the island was uninhabited.

'Keep a sharp look out,' said Billy Bones.

'Aye-aye-suh!' said the marine. But Billy Bones lingered, cleared his throat, spat, and condescended to conversation.

'Damned hot,' he said.

'Aye-aye-suh!'

'Shouldn't wonder if we don't have fever on the lower deck before the week's out.'

'Aye-aye-suh!'

And so they continued for some little time until one Emmanuel Pew came out to relieve himself in the trench. Pew was known to his mates as Mad Pew for his speaking of the Welsh language, and for being not quite right in the head.

'Ah,' said Billy Bones, and he waited until Pew had finished grunting and heaving, and had hauled up his breeches and buckled his belt. Then he turned and affected to take note.

'You there!' said he. 'Damn your blasted eyes! Shovel away there with a will, like the blasted surgeon says, or I'll flay the living skin off your blasted back!'

Pew jumped in terror and filled in half the trench in the excess of his desire to please Mr Bones.

'Now, back to camp at the double,' said Billy Bones. 'And I'll walk beside you so you don't drown yourself falling into the blasted ocean.'

The marine went limp with relief as the big figure rolled away, puffing and cursing beside the thin, nervous, dark-eyed matelot who'd become the target of his attentions.

'Serve the bugger right!' thought the marine. 'Bleeding mad bastard that one is an' all, that bastard Pew.'

But the aforesaid Mad Pew was the objective of Mr Bones's walk out to the latrine trench. As ever, Billy Bones marvelled at the acuteness of Flint's observation, and his penetrating knowledge of the characters of the men.

Flint knew that Pew went to shit well after lights out, because at that time there was nobody there, and he wouldn't be jostled and hurried. Some men are like that, and Flint's knowledge of Pew's habits enabled Billy Bones to get him alone for a few minutes' conversation in the dark, with no possibility of being overheard. It thereby enabled Billy Bones to put certain proposals to Pew, and to ask certain questions of him, without risk of a hanging for the pair of them. And of course – did Mr Bones but know it – the fact that Lieutenant Flint was no part of the conversation meant that there was absolutely no risk to Flint himself. Indeed, Flint would have been the first to denounce Billy Bones as a traitorous mutineer, should the need arise.

So Billy Bones sounded out Pew and explained that Captain Springer was going to abandon him to his fate, but that there was a way out which was very much to Pew's advantage. Pew nearly dropped in his tracks with amazement once or twice, to hear such things from Billy Bones. But he saw reason.

Over the next few weeks, Billy Bones had similar conversations with a number of others, all carefully chosen by Flint, and always in circumstances where Flint was saved harmless from any consequences, and always where nobody could see or hear what passed between Billy Bones and the other. Each man chosen was a skilled seamen, and together they formed the nucleus of a crew: Benn Gunn the helmsman, Israel Hands the gunner's mate, Peter Black (better known as *Black Dog)* the carpenter, and Darby M'Graw the master-at-arms. These, together with Mad Pew the sailmaker, were the principal figures in Flint's plan, but there were others too: foremast hands to haul on lines and work a ship.

Thus all this dangerous, careful work was planned by Flint, while all the actual risks were taken by Billy Bones. In this secret division of labour, Joe Flint wasn't quite the perfect judge of men that he thought he was, for Flint believed it was no end of a joke that Billy Bones should stand between himself and danger, and what a fool Bones would think himself should he ever find out. But the truth of the matter was different. So great was Billy Bones's devotion to Flint that he'd gladly have volunteered for the duty, if ever it had occurred to Flint to be honest with him. But such a thing would never have occurred to Joe Flint.

All the while, up at the North Inlet, close alongside the hull of the dead *Elizabeth*, the building of her daughter *Betsy* came forward in promising style. The carpenter's crew laid her keel, raised up her ribs and planked her hull. They set her beam ends in place and fashioned old spars into new masts, and fitted her out with pumps and capstans, gratings and ladders, and all the complex gear that must be crammed into a sea-going vessel.

As these vital works proceeded, Mr Flint kept himself mightily busy – and clear away from Billy Bones – in building an impressive fortification at the other end of the island. For this major work he took nearly half the able-bodied men, with a month's supply of food, and all the tools the carpenter could spare. They tramped across the island, and Flint took some more detailed observations of its geography as they went. Finally he chose a site on a thickly wooded hill, with a spring of clear water welling up near the summit.

'You will fell all the trees within musket-shot of this point,' he told the two midshipmen he'd brought with him as his subordinates.

He reached up and scratched the poll of his green parrot. This had become a habit of his when wrapped in thought. The midshipmen looked at one another and at the size of the pines on the hill, and they were glad that they wouldn't personally be doing the physical labour.

'You will trim and shape the trunks, and they

will be used to build a blockhouse according to this plan,' said Flint. He produced a rolled-up paper and looked around the hot, thick, pine-smelling forest with its buzzing insects and soaring trunks. There was not a rock or a bush or a bank of earth; only columns of living wood and the sandy soil beneath. There was nothing to rest the paper on.

'You there – Billingsgate!' he called to a seaman standing a respectful distance away, burdened with a heavy bundle of canvas for making tents. 'At the double now! Here, Fido! Here, Prince! Good dog!' He smiled his shining smile and the seaman dropped his bundle and sped forward. 'Down, Rover!' said Flint, forcing Billingsgate on to all fours. 'And don't you move, not on fear of a striped shirt.'

The man's back formed a sufficient table to spread Flint's plan. Like everything Flint did, it was beautifully done. It showed a loop-holed blockhouse of heavy timbers, with an encircling palisade of split logs. The mids leaned forward and examined the design. The more intelligent – or perhaps not – of them, Mr Hastings, frowned and spoke up.

'Please, sir,' said he, 'don't this plan more readily suit a defence against armed men already ashore? So wouldn't we be better strengthening the seaward batteries up at ... ugh!'

He shut up as the elbow of his less – or perhaps more – intelligent comrade, Mr Midshipman Povey, caught him hard in the ribs. He looked up to see the deadly smile splitting Flint's face, for Mr Hastings had spoken the unchallengeable truth.

Flint's blockhouse was a nonsense. Any threat could only come from the sea and was best countered by batteries covering the few places on the island where ships, or ships' boats, could make a landing. But from Flint's point of view, the blockhouse was a most wise and sensible thing to build, since it kept himself so visibly away from Mr Bones's politics at the other end of the island.

'Mr Boatswain!' he cried, and acting-boatswain Tom Morgan came doubling through the tree trunks. 'Get yourself a cane, Mr Morgan, and stripe this insolent child a couple of dozen across the fat of his arse.' The colour drained from Mr Hastings's face and he swallowed hard. Flint turned his face to the other mid. 'And then deliver two dozen unto this one, for he's as insolent as the other.' Flint smiled and tickled his parrot. 'I'll not have nasty young gentlemen answering back to their betters.'

Two weeks later the blockhouse was built and ready for occupation. Where only virgin forest had stood, there was now a great clearing with a massive log-house in the centre, surrounded by the stumps of the trees that had been sacrificed for its construction. As a fortification, it was thoroughly well made, commanding a clear field of fire in all directions, while the six-foot palisade was well placed to break up an assault, but too insubstantial to enable an enemy to take shelter there.

Had there been any real need for such a building, it would have served to perfection, and Flint even attended to minor details such as the fact that there was no natural basin around the spring from which water might be drawn. He had a large ship's cauldron brought up, and the bottom knocked out of it, so it could be sunk in the ground at the spring-head to provide an artificial tank that constantly filled and brimmed with fresh water.

With the blockhouse built, Flint left a guard of four marines to occupy it, and marched his command back to the North Inlet, the *Elizabeth*, the *Betsy*, and Captain Springer. The long, straggling column, heavy-laden as it was (by Flint's own design), laboured heavily to complete the journey and suffered various casualties. One man broke his leg, one got lost, four developed severe blisters from the straps of their packs and fourteen presented themselves to the surgeon with rashes from poisonous jungle plants.

Flint dealt promptly with all these accidents. He had the gratings rigged and awarded a dozen each to the rash-sufferers for carelessness, two dozen to the lost soul for stupidity, three dozen to the blister brigade for incompetence in lashing their kit, and four dozen to the broken leg (so soon as he could stand on it) for wilfully rendering himself unfit for duty.

With these punishments and others, there was now hardly one man of the three hundred foremast hands and petty officers that once had been *Elizabeth*'s people who had not felt either the lash or some more spiteful punishment. The mood of the crew was sullen and resentful, and only one push was needed to drive them to the great leap that Flint had planned: some of them ... enough of them ... sufficient for Flint's purpose.

By now, too, *Betsy* looked like a ship rather than

a collection of timbers. Her lower masts were stepped, and her standing rigging in place. The carpenter and his mates had even contrived to serve her hull with pitch and paint, to offset the worm. All she needed was men turning the capstan and she'd warp herself sweetly down the greased slide-way already laid out before her, and she'd swim in the waters of the North Inlet.

Flint saw that things had reached the moment of truth, and he held a conference that very night, safely away from the camp and out in the dark forest, with Billy Bones and some others including Israel Hands and Black Dog, who were the most intelligent, and others who were the least stupid of the chosen ones. Flint explained what each of them had to do, and made each man repeat it until it was clear they'd understood. Hands and Black Dog learned fast enough, but for the rest Flint had to keep his temper entirely under control. For once, he had to be patient and encouraging as these morons stumbled and mumbled and struggled towards learning their parts.

He could not afford any noise or dispute at this stage, for now he, Joseph Flint, was personally involved, and the danger to himself was acute.

Chapter 9

3rd April 1751
The Delacroix Plantation, South Carolina

Selena fought all the way, but her mother was twice her weight and three times her strength. The woman just put her head down and took the blows she received from her daughter and never gave back one – which amazing behaviour frightened Selena more than anything. Instead, her mother got sullen and angry and tried to persuade.

'What you do, girl?' she cried as she pulled Selena along. 'You think you not like all women? You think you better? You ... you ... you ...'

But her words failed. She'd never learned English very well and she switched to the liquid speech of her homeland, which the youngsters like Selena barely understood – for it earned the toe of the overseer's boot to be heard 'talking African'.

But this time Selena's mother didn't just speak it: she bellowed it. And since it was dusk, and the day's work was done, the people came to the doors of their shacks as Selena was dragged by. They came to see what all the fuss was about. When they saw, they understood and they laughed or pitied according to their individual character. Mostly the men looked at Selena and licked their lips and thought their own thoughts, but the women screeched and laughed and slapped their sides in happy chorus.

'It's your time, girl!' they cried. 'Now you just like all the rest!' And they nodded to one another in righteous enjoyment at the fall of one who had put on such airs.

'Where's Miss Jeanie?' they mocked. 'You want me to call her from Paris?'

And the children hopped and capered along behind, laughing and mimicking, even though they didn't understand. But they would, given a few years; especially the girls.

Yard by yard, Selena was hauled away from the neat line of shacks and out towards the big house. The crickets sang, the moon came out, the stars shone, and soon the children scampered back home with final jeers, for they were getting too near the big house, and knew better than to make trouble there.

The big house was ablaze with light and music. The master and mistress were entertaining. White-folk visitors were come from far away beyond the plantation, where no slave was allowed to go. There were carriages drawn up outside the big house, but that was at the front, which was forbidden to Selena and her mother. Instead, Selena was dragged the last few hundred yards to where Sam the overseer lived in his smart, plank-built house with the veranda and the whitewashed walls. Sam's house stood way out from the shacks where the common folk lived, and close enough to the big house to be ready for the master's call.

Sam was a greatly privileged creature. He wore shoes and a white man's hat, and was even trusted with a gun, and now he sat with this badge of office across his knees as he rocked on his own porch.

Selena's mother dragged her up the steps and brought her before Sam. He was a big, hard young man, chosen for his ability to knock down any other slave with his fists. But he smiled and shook his head in admiration of Selena.

'My oh my!' he said. 'Ain't you just ripe and ready.' He slid his hand into Selena's cotton dress and reached for one of the hard breasts that were bouncing so appealingly as she struggled.

'No!' barked Selena's mother, and caught Sam's arm a blow with her fist. 'She not for boy like you!'

Sam snarled and raised his musket butt to smash the woman flat. He was top dog and didn't take no crap from nobody.

'Hold you hand, nigger-boy!' cried the woman. 'My Selena, she be Master's girl – *yes?* Master do what she say – *yes?* Selena say, "Flog Sam black ass" – *Master flog Sam black ass!*'

Sam froze. It was true. It could happen. So long as the master's fancy lasted, he'd give a girl most everything she wanted ... especially if it was so little a thing as flogging an uppity slave. Sam had seen too many floggings to suffer one on his own sweet hide. He doused his anger and lowered his gun.

He said nothing, but got up and led the way to the 'special house' down in the hollow by the river, among the trees and out of sight of the big house, where it had been placed by a thoughtful husband to spare the blushes of his wife. What the mistress did not have positively thrust before her eyes, she could contrive not to know. Indeed, as far as the mistress was concerned, what went on in the house in the hollow served the invaluable purpose of focusing her husband's attentions where they would do the most good and the least harm.

Sam had the keys to the special house. He unlocked the door and lit the candles inside. He looked sidelong at the two women to see their wonder at the fine things on display, things no field slave ever saw: the curtains, carpets and furniture, the silks, satins and linen, the wines and food, the big bed, the great mirrors and the gold-framed paintings of naked white women, luscious and plump. Tonight there was also a big bathtub, with water, soap and towels, and a selection of brightly coloured dresses.

'Now you get that girl ready, you hear?' said Sam, for the benefit of his dignity. 'You get her clean and dressed up right pretty, or it gonna be *your* black ass gets flogged!' With that, he straightened his shoulders and marched off, master of the field.

Selena's mother sighed.

'Get you clothes off, girl.'

'No!'

'Get you clothes off. How me clean you, if you not take off clothes?'

'Take me home. I wasn't bred for this!'

'No! You stay here. You stay!'

'Why?'

This simple question finally broke the dam of Selena's mother's emotions. The woman burst into loud slobbering tears and called Selena a wicked girl who'd see her ma and pa sold away and all her brothers and sisters too.

'Sold away!' cried Selena's mother, voicing the dread fear of the plantation slave. 'Sold down-river. Me never see you. Me never see me man. Me never see me childrens. Never never never. That what you want? You *creature!*'

'No!' screamed Selena, and stamped her foot, 'But why should it be me?'

''Cos Master want you. That why he let you live in the big house! That why you get fancy clothes and fancy words. You got them 'cos he want you for *fancy piece!*'

'No! Miss Eugenie – Jeanie – she loved me!'

'Huh! She love you when you small. You was her nigger doll. And now she gone to Paris for schooling and left you behind when she could've taken you with!'

'No!'

'No? So why you back in fields? Why you sleep in Mumma's house and not Miss Jeanie's room?'

'It's all your fault! You told me to smile at the master in the first place!'

Selena's mother bit her lip and the strength drained out of her indignation.

'Well,' she said, searching for words. She searched hard and came up with a powerful word: a white man's word. 'I told you to smile 'cos it *proper,*' she said, and nodded in satisfaction.

'Huh!' sneered Selena. "Proper", you say? I say you just want all the things I can get you while I'm the master's girl!'

If a woman with skin the colour of black velvet could have blushed, then Selena's mother would have done it. Since this was impossible, she took her daughter by the hair, stripped her naked, lifted her bodily into the bathtub, and doused and soaped and scrubbed the slippery body as if she'd have the skin off it. Then she laid on with the towels, bound up the girl's hair to look nice, and crammed, jammed and rammed her into the first dress that came to hand.

'Now hear me, Selena,' she said, with a face as grim as a bulldog's. 'Me don't want no more. You always stamping and cussing. You always having you way. Me always let you. Me let you, 'cos you fine and you pretty.'

She stood back, hands on hips and leaned forward so her nose was an inch from Selena's.

'Now you pay me back, girl,' she said. 'You bump you ass for Master. You bump real good. You think on me. You think on you father. You think on you brothers and sisters.' In a final burst of anger, her voice screeched in fury, hitting a pitch previously unsurpassed. 'If you not do, then no place for you in me house. Not food, not fire, not water. Nothing! NOTHING! You hear me?'

There was silence as the two looked at one another, balked in anger. Then, seeing the faintest flicker of a downcast eye from Selena, and seeing that the girl made no move to run, the mother said, 'Huh!' loudly. Then she cleaned up the bath things, made everything neat and tidy, hauled the bath outside and emptied it, and marched off back to her own place, and her husband, and the rest of her eight surviving children.

She was a good woman. She was doing her best, under iniquitous rules, for all those who depended upon her. She was the exact moral equal of a noble commander who wins glory by sacrificing a regiment to save an army. She wept all the way home, nonetheless.

Left alone, Selena first did some weeping of her own. Then she threw some things about and broke glass and china. Then she looked at herself in a mirror, admired the incredible gown, and then she sat down on the big bed to think. Ideas sped and tumbled through her head with the wild energy of a sharp and penetrating brain. But she saw no way out, other than the one her mother had specified.

Thus she came to a decision. First she brought herself to face and accept her betrayal by Miss Eugenie. She cleared that monstrously difficult fence with valiant courage and with maturity beyond her years. She did it all by herself and with none to advise her. Next, she accepted her duty to her mother, to her father and to her family. Finally she lay back on the bed, spread her gown to best advantage, and waited for the master. But the master did not come, and eventually, being unused to staying awake at the end of a hard day's work, Selena closed her eyes and went to sleep.

She was awakened by a fumbling at the front of her gown and a man's drink-loaded breath wheezing in her face. A fat belly pressed down upon her with the buckles of his clothes scratching. Hands squeezed her breasts and a foul mouth pressed on hers, licking and sucking.

At forty-six years of age, the master, Mr Fitzroy Delacroix, had long since established his etiquette where slave-girls were concerned. He liked them young, he liked them slim, he liked them full-breasted and he liked them virgins. The delight of slave-girls, to his way of thinking, was that you could do *what* you damn well liked to them, *when* you damn well liked, and not have to waste hours bringing them to the boil like you did with decent white women. As for whores, slaves beat them every time because you didn't have to pay and you couldn't get poxed.

Added to these usual benefits was the particular one that Selena had been his own daughter's playmate, raised alongside her, and equipped with the speech and manners of a white girl to the degree that – for some time now – Delacroix had been just itching to get his hands on her. Thus it was very much the case that his daughter's desire for a wider education and her hopes of fluency in the French language were far from Delacroix's only reasons for sending Miss Eugenie to Europe.

Not sharing Delacroix's point of view, Selena struggled furiously and got a ringing box round the ears in reply. Delacroix laughed and threw her skirts over her head. Holding her down by the wrists, he buried his nose into the soft recess between her thighs and gorged like a hog at a trough. Enjoying himself hugely, he rolled to one side to unbutton himself and haul out his shaft. But, freed from his weight, Selena leapt up and darted to the door ... which was locked.

Delacroix positively roared with laugher, and staggered after her with his drawers round his ankles and his paunch wobbling over his upstanding lust. He grabbed at Selena, but he was full of drink and she ducked under his arms, snatched up a silver candlestick and swung it at his head. He just managed to raise his arms in defence and the blow thumped painfully into his left elbow. He fell back, stumbled and sat down heavily on the floor, legs stretched out in front of him.

'Ow!' he said, rubbing his elbow in surprise. 'Well, I'm damned!' And he doubtless was, for those were his last words on earth.

With a huge quantity of food and drink in his stomach, and sick from the pain of the blow, Delacroix suddenly vomited heavily, gulped and choked ... and inhaled a good lungful of half-digested beef and claret. He then throttled and kicked for a minute or two, before expiring purple-faced and pop-eyed at Selena's feet, with his tongue lolling out of his open mouth.

Philosophers would argue that Delacroix was entirely responsible for his own death – and a shameful death too – from gluttony and attempted rape, but Selena knew that the world would see things differently. A slave found with her dead master was just meat on the hoof. They'd not ask her what had happened. They'd simply hang her.

Fear and panic surged out of the dark corners of the room. There was no refuge on the plantation. They'd hang any slave who tried to help her, and her mother's house was the first place they'd look – even supposing for one minute that her mother would take her in. But beyond the plantation was the great, wide world: the outside world that Selena had never even seen, let alone visited. And now she had to get out into that world and make her way, and not get caught. And all she had to guide her was her own native wit.

Chapter 10

24th March 1749
The island

On the morning after his secret conference, when Flint had taken his irreversible step and now stood at risk of betrayal by too many men for him to face down, he went to Captain Springer.

The man was sunk beyond belief in drunkenness. As far as Flint could judge, Springer was a worse hulk than *Elizabeth*. He was decayed and rotting in his tent. Flint sighed. By the look of Springer, this would delay vital preparations by a week or more; or at least by however long it took to get Springer off the rum and looking like some passably good imitation of an officer. But since Springer was unconscious, Flint went and found Springer's servant and put Billy Bones to work, kicking the servant's unfortunate arse around the camp for sufficient time to drive home the message that the captain was to receive no more strong drink, no matter what threats or entreaties he might offer.

In the event, Flint was lucky. Springer came from a tough old breed, and his liver was so powerfully exercised by its life's work that it had him sobered up that very evening.

Then, after a day spent in blinding headaches and purgative vomits, Springer was fit to walk, talk and to be washed and shaved and put into a clean shirt by the morning of the day after. Flint duly presented himself at the captain's tent, and – as his deputy and representative during the captain's *indisposition* – he gave Springer an account of all the island's news that was masterly in the very small proportion of untruth that was added in order to deceive Springer completely, and to set him off on the false trail that Flint had planned.

When Flint was done, and was standing humbly before his captain with his hat in his hands, Springer glared at him with bloodshot yellowed eyes and with hatred that could have been cut into blocks and sold by the pound as rat poison. But Springer knew his duty (or so he thought), and he never hesitated.

'Muster the men, you bloody lubber!' he growled. 'This is your fault, as I've always said, and I'll see you broke for it as soon as we rejoin the squadron!'

'Aye-aye, Captain,' murmured Flint, with downcast eyes. And after suffering a sufficient quantity of oaths and curses from Springer, Flint withdrew, found Billy Bones, and gave his final instructions.

Half an hour later, every soul on the island, excepting the four marines still guarding the useless blockhouse, were mustered on the beach under the hot sun, before the tented encampment and the almost-completed *Betsy*, while stuck on her sandbank a cable's length off, the empty corpse of the *Elizabeth* was a constant reminder of past failures, and a spectator to what happened next.

Springer got up on a chest, the better to speak to the men. He sweated heavily in his uniform coat and cocked hat, and his shirt and stock. But these were the indispensable icons of his rank, especially given the shockingly ugly mood of the men. Springer had never seen the like before, and he stuck out his chin and clenched his fists in anger. He wasn't the man to tolerate skulking and scowling from the lower deck, as they would bloody soon learn!

Around him, in their blue navy coats, stood Lieutenant Flint, Acting-Master Bones, and five midshipmen. The surgeon and the purser stood to one side of them, with a group of senior warrant officers including the boatswain, the gunner and the carpenter. Further off still was the comforting block of twenty-nine marines, drawn up with bayonets fixed, under Sergeant Dawson and two corporals.

Facing Captain Springer, divided into starboard and larboard watches, stood well nearly two hundred lesser folk and foremast hands of the manifold varieties of their kind: topmen, coopers, waisters, cooks, afterguard, boys and so on. Springer ground his teeth at the muttering and scowling that came from them, and the insolence on their stupid faces.

'Avast there!' he bellowed. 'Silence on the lower deck!'

They looked at him and waited, still defiant but listening to what he might have to say. When it came, it wasn't very much, and it wasn't very clever. Springer was no maker of speeches: he simply stamped and spouted and told them to do their duty and God help them as didn't! Since the men had already been flogged and punished beyond all reason, this was the last thing they wanted to hear. But Springer didn't know that, for Flint hadn't told him, and finally, the captain got round to the subject of leaving the island.

'Our new ship lies a-waiting and ready to bear away for Jamaica!' he cried, pointing to the *Betsy*. 'She's well found and ship-shape and will bear fifty men...' At this there came a deep, animal growl from the belly of the crowd. 'Silence!' yelled Springer, but all he got was a chorus from the play so lovingly crafted by Mr Flint, who nearly choked with laughter as his actors delivered their lines.

'What about the Dons?' cried one.

'What if they come back?' cried another.

'AYYYYYE!' the crowd roared.

'What?' yelled Springer. '*What* bloody Dons?'

'Them as was seen from Spy-glass Hill!'

'Them as was looking for a landing!'

'They'll murder every man jack of them as gets left behind!'

Now other voices joined in, genuinely frightened of a mass slaughter at the hands of the Spaniards. Frogs and Dutchman was one thing; even the Portuguese; but they'd get no precious mercy out of the Dagoes!

'Mr Flint?' said Springer, looking down at his subordinate. 'What the poxy damnation are the sods blathering about?'

'I cannot imagine, sir,' said Flint with a sneer. 'Why don't you ask the men?' In that instant, seeing the look in the other's eyes, Springer came as close as he ever did to understanding Flint and to guessing what was actually underway.

'You whoreson bastard!' he said, and he cast

about, this way and that, wondering what to do next. He was the very picture of indecision, and to the angry mob in front of him, he looked exactly like a man who'd been found out.

'See!' cried Israel Hands. 'The bugger knew it all along. He's leaving us to the bloody Dons!'

'No!' cried Springer. 'No! No! No! The ship'll take a good fifty, maybe more, and I'll come back for...'

'And who's to say who goes and who stays?' cried George Merry, in wild terror. Swept on by the furious emotions around him, Merry – who in any case was not one of the brightest – was now so deep into the role given him by Flint, that he actually believed it.

'ARRRRRGH!' roared the crew.

'Sergeant Dawson!' screamed Springer, as the mob rolled forward. But Dawson was already giving his orders.

'Make ready!' he barked, and twenty-nine muskets snapped into the left hands of their bearers, enabling the right hands to cock the locks. A howl of fright went up at this show of deadly force.

'Bastards!' cried Israel Hands and, reaching the climax of his own part, he produced a hidden pistol: a little one, small enough to hide under his few clothes. He took a breath. He ran forward, and while the marine's muskets were still pointing harmlessly upwards he let fly with his pistol.

'Ahhhh!' screeched a marine, and dropped his musket as the ball took him in the face and smashed his jaw. It was the first blood. The wretch continued to bawl and groan, but his mates straightened up, as they'd been taught, and faced front.

'Present!' cried Dawson, and the muskets swept down to bear on the mob.

CRACK! Another shot came out of the mob: Black Dog this time, with the second of Flint's own pair of pocket pistols. The ball flew nowhere. The cries of the mob became general, and a hail of two-pounder, swivel-gun shot (distributed earlier by Billy Bones) was thrown by muscular arms to arch up, and drop viciously down on the redcoats. One marine went down stunned. More shot flew and the mob charged.

'Fire!' cried Springer.

'Fire!' yelled Dawson.

BA-BANG-BANG-BOOM! Twenty-seven muskets blazed together at such close range that powder-flash singed the hair of the maddened seamen at the front of the mob, while Captain Springer hauled out his own pistol and discharged it at Israel Hands, who was running at him with a drawn knife.

Instantly, fifteen men went down, struck by musket balls, and Springer fell backwards off the chest with the thumb and two fingers blown off his pistol hand, and one eye put out by flying fragments of the burst barrel. Being half-blinded, he did not notice that Israel Hands simply ignored him, leapt over his fallen body, and ran off after Flint, Billy Bones, Black Dog, George Merry and about fifty others.

While these favoured ones vanished into the jungle at the edge of the beach, a hideous, murderous fight took place: marines, mids and warrant officers against the remaining seamen. It was bayonets, dirks and swords, against knives and fists. It was entirely hand-to-hand, for the marines had no chance to reload. Consequently the struggle between former shipmates lasted only as long as it took for all parties to exhaust their strength and fall back sickened by what they had done, or rather what they had most cunningly, deliberately and skilfully been *caused* to do, by Lieutenant Joseph Flint.

The final tally was forty-five dead, including most of the marines, Sergeant Dawson, Captain Springer, most of the mids, nearly all the warrant officers and a large number of seamen. Many more were wounded, some grievously. But there was a still worse moral effect of what had been done. This was to place the greater part of those alive entirely beyond the law, and in all probability under delayed sentence of death at the hands of the service they had just betrayed.

The surviving marines were safe. The two surviving midshipmen were safe, as were all the rest who'd fought for their King and his laws. But the rest had shared in a mutiny, and an extremely bloody one at that. They had been a part of the ultimate crime, the crime which the Royal Navy would never, ever forgive – they had slain their captain. They now faced either permanent exile from their native land or being hunted down for a naval court martial, and the short, jerking journey up the yardarm with the aid of a running noose.

Thus the survivors broke naturally into two parties that limped and bled and drew away from one another as far as they could go. The smaller party, perhaps thirty strong, consisted of the mids, the marines and the purser, plus those seamen and petty officers who'd remained loyal. This party had two muskets, a few pistols and a pair of midshipman's dirks between them. The larger party, nearly two hundred strong, carried off the rest of the marines' firelocks and ammunition. Being the stronger, they took command of the camp and immediately broke open the spirit casks and proceeded to get roaring drunk.

In this condition, they were later visited by *Captain* Flint, as he was now known, at the head of the only body of men on the island who were sober, under discipline, and fully armed from the supply of weapons thoughtfully hidden in the woods at Flint's orders. Flint told his followers – Israel Hands, George Merry and the rest – that they were restoring order and conquering mutineers. This was abject nonsense, but it served, and a second slaughter followed, since Flint's real purpose was to eliminate from the surviving seamen as many as possible of those whom he felt unable to trust in the greater purpose which was to come.

When the sun set that night there were less than a hundred men left alive on the island. Flint stood in the dying light and eyed the wreckage and slaughter all around. He stroked his parrot and smiled.

'Well, Billy-boy,' he said to the creature that clung to him even closer than the green bird, 'It seems we are become free men, to go a-privateering after all. Isn't it a shame that Mr Springer never saw reason in the first place, to save me all this trouble?' And Flint laughed and laughed and laughed.

But there had to be a few more risings of that sun before Flint got entirely what he wanted. To begin with, *Betsy* wasn't quite as ready for sea as had been hoped, and vital work remained to be done, and also Flint had to deal with the remaining loyal hands on the island.

Some of them weren't hard to find, since they came limping into the camp at North Inlet in ones and twos, begging for food. The others were hunted down with whooping and halooing and merriment, at least on Flint's part, for he took a lead in all such congenial operations, leaving Billy Bones the task of completing *Betsy*'s fitting out.

'Chop 'em down, lads!' he cried, on the first occasion they took captives. 'Chop 'em down like so much pork!' But in this he was baulked. To his surprise, his men turned nasty as their consciences stirred. After all, as far as they knew, they'd mutinied in face of abandonment and certain death, and then they'd fought the marines when fired upon. But they'd never set out to cut the throats of their own shipmates. What's more, the captives included Mr Hastings and Mr Povey, the last surviving midshipmen: two youngsters who were good officers and popular with the crew.

Flint glowered and cursed, but saw that he could not oppose the men in this matter. He was well aware that not everyone on the lower deck was stupid. Some were capable of working out that Flint had taken command from Captain Springer by force. In that case, what was good for Springer might become good for Flint, should Flint upset the men too much. This gave Flint a nasty fright. It was his first sight of a problem that – for all his cleverness – he had not foreseen, and which would come back to sit upon his shoulder like his parrot. Given his great pride and vanity, it was deeply disturbing.

But the prisoners were spared: all of them.

Finally in late May of 1749 when *Betsy* was warped out into the North Inlet, laden with men and stores and guns, to spread her sails and head north, she towed astern of her a longboat containing the remaining loyal hands. There were twenty-three of them, but the longboat was a good, big one, so they weren't too crowded. They had their own store of food and water too – the crew had insisted on that – and this proved a blessing, since soon after *Betsy* had left the island under the horizon, the towline somehow got slipped during the dead of night.

Flint explained that this had been an unfortunate accident which was all for the best, since it removed those who had unaccountably refused to win wealth and riches by privateering. For their part, with the longboat gone and nobody forced personally to witness what might be the fate of the boat's occupants, the crew allowed themselves to believe Flint's words, and were thereby led down a slippery path towards outright bloody-handed piracy.

In this profession – having at last got what he wanted – Flint proved a passing fair success. Or perhaps he just was lucky. Whichever, he took some good prizes, and beat up and down the Caribbean for many jolly months before fate caught up with him.

Chapter 11

1st June 1752
Savannah, Georgia

In Selena's world there was no time for self-pity. When the shaking stopped, she went back to work.

She picked her way over and around the customers in the liquor shop, and made an effort to clear up the mess that they had made. Some of them were stirring now, and calling for more drink. Selena served them, and prodded the other girls awake to help her.

Later in the evening, after lamp-lighting time, when Flint and Neal came back to the liquor shop, a second round of debauchery was well under way. Flint and Neal were like brothers; satisfied with their business and now looking to take a drop or two in celebration. Flint merrily kicked three or four men out of their chairs and swept their pots and plates off the table to make way for himself and Neal. Roars of approval greeted their arrival, and the musicians woke themselves up and joined in the din.

This time Flint leapt on a table top, threw back his head and led the singing. His men cheered madly when they heard the song, for it was a piece of his own creation, that he sang only when in the best of spirits. Joseph Flint sang beautifully, with a high, carrying voice that was lovely to hear, and once heard never forgotten. He gave each line of the song, with his men roaring out the chorus.

'Fifteen men on the dead man's chest–'

'Yo-ho-ho, and a bottle of rum!'

'Drink and the devil had done for the rest–'

'Yo-ho-ho, and a bottle of rum!'

'With one man of her crew alive–'

'Yo-ho-ho, and a bottle of rum!'

'What put to sea with seventy-five–'

'Yo-ho-ho, and a bottle of rum!'

The song went on, verse after verse, getting steadily grimmer and darker, but with Flint so beaming and charming, acting out the horrors of the story in such splendid good humour that everyone laughed at the wickedness he was proclaiming.

When he finished, he sat down to mighty cheers, and smiled like the sun in his glory. Neal smiled too, though he'd no taste for Flint's kind of music. His mind was still full of delightful calculations concerning the cargoes in the holds of Flint's two prizes. Selena came to their table at once, with rum. Flint raised his glass to her in a polite toast. His sharp eyes swept her up and down. He frowned. He saw the miserable expression on her face and her red eyes.

'What rogue has upset you, my African Venus?' he said. He stood up, and took her chin gently in his fingers, the better to study her. 'I dare swear you've been crying. Just tell me who it was,' he said, in a soft, quiet voice. 'Just tell me his name and I'll have the liver out of him. I'll rip it out, and slice it narrow, and feed it to him in strips.' Charley Neal blinked anxiously. When other men said things like that, they weren't really thinking of opening a man's belly and sticking a hand inside to pull things out. But when Flint made the threat...

'Don't you mind her!' cried Neal, half standing. There were limits to what the colony's trustees would ignore – even for cash payment in gold. 'Leave her, Joe,' he said. 'These black girls are ten a penny!' And he dared actually to reach out and clutch Flint's arm, as if to restrain him.

Flint was not pleased at the gesture. He frowned slightly and turned his eyes first on Neal's hand, and then on Neal himself. The Irishman fell back as if a blow had been struck.

'Sorry, Joe!' he begged. 'Sorry-sorry-sorry!' He raised his hands in placation.

'Thank you, Charley,' said Flint. 'But be assured that this lady is not to be compared with others, and is not to be sold at the price of one tenth of a penny.'

'No!' said Charley. 'No, no, no!' And he shook his head as if to shake it off.

'I am glad that we are agreed,' said Flint, and ignored Charley Neal. Flourishing a silk handkerchief, he made a great play of dabbing it at the corners of Selena's eyes. 'So who was it that offended you, my dear? Only give me a name.'

'It doesn't matter,' said Selena, seeing the imploring look on Neal's face. She could not afford to upset her protector-in-chief. Neal sighed gratefully. Flint shrugged his shoulders and deigned to smile again as he looked at the girl.

'By George!' said Flint. 'Where did you find such a beauty, Neal? Is this what you keep hidden at home?' He laughed and his white teeth shone. He bowed and indicated a chair. 'Will you honour us, ma'am?' Selena hesitated. Neal nodded furiously. As far as he was concerned, Flint could have any girl in the house free of charge, and he could do anything he liked with them.

Flint drew out the chair and ushered Selena to her place as gallant as a nobleman with his lady, and she with her torn and tattered cotton print, and her bare feet.

This drew hoots of laughter from Flint's men, who assumed he was playing some game with the girl, and they extemporised lewd and obscene advice, which they bawled out at the tops of their voices, concerning what he should do next. But they had mistaken their captain's intentions. White showed round Flint's eyes, and Billy Bones – never far from his idol and knowing him better than anyone – silently stood back and took cover.

BANG! BANG! Flint drew and fired a pair of heavy pistols with the speed of thought. Smoke rolled and twinkling red fragments of wadding sprayed about him. He'd aimed left and right at random, not caring where the balls might whiz. He set the smoking pistols carefully back in his belt and produced a second, smaller pair, with which he menaced the room.

'Silence!' he roared, as the women shrieked and men howled.

'Aaah!' moaned a voice. 'Me arm! Me sodding precious arm!'

'Who is hurt?' cried Flint. 'Show yourself!'

'It's me,' said a voice, 'Atty Bolger.' And a man stood up with a ruined arm hanging by a shattered shoulder and the blood in a growing puddle at his feet.

'God bless me!' said Flint. 'Why, it *is* Atty Bolger, I do declare! That's a nasty wound, old shipmate. Does it hurt?'

'Course it hurts, you *cunt!*'

'Uhhhhhhhhhhh!' gasped the room.

'Then shall I help you, Atty? Shall I take away your pain?'

'Aye,' said Bolger, who was not one of the brightest.

CRACK! went Flint's pistol.

'And does it hurt now?' asked Flint, but Atty said not a word. And neither did any other man or woman in the room, where utter silence reigned as Flint held two hundred people by the unaided force of his own terrifying personality.

'That's better,' he said. 'Now ... should any man here have anything else to say about this lady–' he bowed gracefully to Selena '–then let him step up now and say it to Joe Flint ... just here–' he indicated a spot a yard in front of himself. After a due pause and a most remarkable absence of any sound at all, let alone further comment on Selena, Flint smiled his dazzling smile and sat down again. He ignored the rest of the room, and the din slowly returned.

Selena was goggling at Flint with big round eyes. Her ears rang with the detonation of the pistols and her mouth hung open in amazement.

'Pop!' said Flint, flicking a finger under her chin and snapping her mouth shut. He laughed and looked her over once more. Flint had been at sea just as long as John Silver and the others, and like them he had need of a woman. But his needs were more singular. For one thing, Flint was extremely particular where women were concerned. He demanded considerable beauty, and specific circumstances. He had just found the former, and now he set about procuring the latter.

Flint could be very charming when he wanted. He had a store of wit and clever stories, mostly at the expense of others and mostly cruel, but funny nonetheless. He made Selena laugh. He even managed to say something amusing when four men passed carrying the profoundly limp and silent Atty Bolger. In short, Flint exerted himself to please. He was attentive to whatever Selena said. He ordered food and drink for her, and served her himself, anxiously inquiring whether the rum and water was not too strong for her taste.

She was puzzled and flattered. No man, black or white, free or slave, had ever treated her like this. She saw no sign in this fine gentleman's face of the hot passions she stirred in others. And he was clean and didn't smell of sweat and filth like most others did. His teeth were beautiful and his face was handsome, and he was immeasurably the finest-dressed man she had ever seen.

Selena relaxed. She smiled. She laughed.

And all the while Charley Neal thanked the saints that the slaughter seemed to be done for tonight (and all due to *accidental* pistol shots that the authorities would understand) and nobody's liver had been laid out on the floor.

Better still, Charley saw that the topsails of another fine bargain had just hove up over the horizon as, little by little, Flint led the conversation towards Selena herself. Her age, her thoughts, her hopes, her plans: small and piteous as these were, for the blessings of a clean bed, a full stomach and a little kindness. Finally, Flint made his move.

'My dear,' he said, leaning forward with a serious expression on his face, 'if I had a daughter, I'd not let her be bred in such a nest of vice as this–' he waved at everything around them, including Neal (who was already working out the price for what was now, clearly, on its way).

'Forgive the precipitousness of my impetuosity,' said Flint. 'Attribute this to the sincere philanthropy of my intentions.'

Selena chewed hard on these huge and ponderous words, the like of which the plantation and the tavern had not prepared her for.

'What I propose,' said Flint, 'is that I adopt you as my legal ward, my dear, and fetch you aboard my ship to live under my protection.' Selena's eyes widened. Neal's closed in satisfaction. Selena dreamed of freedom. Neal dreamed of profit. 'Will you come, my dear?' said Flint. 'I swear by the Almighty Being who made Heaven and Earth that you shall have nothing to fear.' So powerful was the force of his argument that Billy Bones, watching and listening nearby, nodded in enrapt agreement and mouthed the words, *nothing to fear*.

Selena looked at Flint. She looked at Neal. She looked around the room. She measured Flint against every man she had ever met, and by that sad, debased and impoverished standard, Flint shone like the evening star.

'I will come with you, sir,' she said. And it was settled as far as she was concerned. The squaring of Charley Neal took longer, for he could show impressive papers demonstrating his undoubted ownership of Selena. He also had charge of such money as Selena had hoarded and was honest enough to make clear that it would go with her. It was furthermore very much to Neal's credit that he dared to press Flint for assurances that the money would remain Selena's once she passed into his power.

But eventually all parties left smiling and certain figures in Neal's ledgers were adjusted to his advantage over that of Captain Joseph Flint. When the dealing was done, Flint stood up and offered Selena his hand.

'Mr Bones,' he said, 'lanterns and a boat's crew, if you please. I'm returning to the ship at once.'

A small procession left Neal's house and marched through the warm night to the music of a thousand twittering crickets. Flint led the way with Selena on his arm as they took the short walk to the stairs down to the river. There, *Walrus*'s jolly-boat was launched for an even shorter pull out to the ship herself, and soon Selena was overcome with wonder at the size and mystery of the ship: its crammed and complex machinery of ropes and tackles and bolts and spars, half visible and all the more strange in the night. She wrinkled her nose at the smell of tar and timber, salt and fish, and things faintly rotting in hidden corners.

'Come below, my dear,' said Flint, and the anchor watch and the boat's crew leered and nudged one another. Billy Bones made the ancient gesture of slapping his left palm into his right elbow and jerking the right forearm erect, fist clenched, like a phallus. He did this – but by God Almighty and all His angels – he took care to make sure Flint didn't see him do it.

'You shall have my own cabin,' said Flint, 'and a bath shall be rigged of good fresh water, and clean clothes provided afterwards.' He turned to his men. 'Mr Bones, what slops have we to suit my lady?'

'No women's traps, Cap'n,' said Billy Bones, 'but I'll root out the smallest we've got in shirts and britches.'

'Clean, Billy-my-chicken!' said Flint. 'Let everything be clean.'

Later, Selena was left entirely to herself in Flint's cabin at the stern, below the quarterdeck. It was a fine place, lavishly furnished with tables and chairs, chests and carvings, shining cutlasses and mysterious seafaring instruments. Candles glowed in hanging lanterns and a tub of fresh water, lined with sail-cloth for smoothness, was filled and waiting for her in a space cleared in the middle of the cabin. The result aroused unfortunate memories of a certain 'special house', the only other place Selena had ever seen that had an equal quality of furnishing, and there'd been a bath there too. But here she had privacy, something she'd never known before in all her life, and the thought of it was almost mystical. She locked the door, drew off her single garment, bound up her hair, and slid into the cool water.

Flint was watching her.

He had a sleeping cabin to one side of the main cabin, and his eye was pressed to a fresh-bored hole in the bulkhead. He looked at the lovely round limbs, the high breasts standing out in their youth, the slim waist and the gorgeous female swell of the hips, the beauty of her face, and the girl's natural daintiness. She was a thing of uttermost loveliness and Flint's breath came in gasps. His mouth was wet and drooling and his member rose painfully below his belt.

Flint groaned in shame. It was his curse that he could not penetrate and enter a woman as other men did. The urgent need for virility simply drained the strength from him, and so he turned to stratagems such as this. He thrust his hand into his breeches and worked steadily, as if pumping out the bilge.

Chapter 12

1st February 1750
The Spanish Main

His Catholic Majesty's sloop *El Tigre* came foaming across the enemy's bow and delivered her broadside of double-shotted six pounders one after the other, each gun captain choosing his moment as his own piece bore on the target.

Ten guns boomed and bounded back, gouting thunderclouds of smoke. Ten stabs of flame licked the victim's planking, and twenty iron balls tore through the air. Some missed and fell foaming into the sea, for even at close range it was hard for the gunners to time their moment precisely. But more than half of the Spanish shot crashed, ripped and tore its way from end to end of the island-built *Betsy*. At the stern, surrounded by whirling splinters and dying men, bawling at them to stand and fight, and damning their yellow livers, was Captain Joseph Flint, the celebrated mutineer, who was coming to the conclusion of an eight-month career as a pirate.

His performance in this trade had been erratic. He had indeed taken some Spanish prizes and wallowed in slaughter. He had indeed got some gold under hatches; quite a lot in fact, and thus far, success. But he'd lost half his men in plots, counter-plots and the subduing of mutinies that were entirely caused by Flint himself. With independent command, all his old faults had swollen and grown monstrous large, to the degree that, for all his talents, Flint could never become a leader of men. He could only set one faction against another. If the Spanish navy hadn't very efficiently searched for him and caught him, then his own men would have done for him, soon enough, and he knew it. But that didn't concern Flint at this particular moment.

El Tigre had been battering *Betsy* for the best part of an hour. She was a better ship, better manned, better armed and with a loyal crew. All the Spanish captain was doing now was making sure there'd be no serious opposition when finally he led his boarding party over *Betsy*'s rail. Either that, or he was attempting actually to sink her.

'We must strike, Cap'n!' cried Billy Bones into Flint's ear, over the thunder of the guns. Billy was grey-faced with fright, and crouched almost to the deck, as if that would save him from the hurtling shot.

'Strike?' cried Flint. 'Strike to the Dons?' And he laughed hysterically.

'We're beat, Cap'n,' said Billy Bones, and looked about the deck.

Dead and wounded lay everywhere, all over the shot-ploughed planks. Guns were dismounted and the foremast was working like a loose tooth. Those hands left fit were looking over their shoulders for somewhere to run. That was a bad sign. Next thing they'd be running below, out of reach of shot. Flint waved his sword.

'Death to him that shirks his duty!' he cried, and the men looked at him like the lunatic which he very nearly was. Then they cringed and stared as the foremast went over the side in a great crackling of parting stays and sundering shrouds.

El Tigre's men cheered wildly as she passed completely across *Betsy*'s bow with the wind fair on her larboard quarter. She had totally outmanoeuvred the enemy vessel, which now lay wallowing like a drunken pig. Lieutenant De Cordoba, *El Tigre*'s commanding officer, instantly put down the helm, aiming for the bold stroke of coming round through the wind to bring his un-fired starboard battery to bear. In this he was over-ambitious. Either that or unlucky, for *El Tigre* missed stays and hung in the eye of the wind, with her canvas flapping and roaring and De Cordoba stamping his foot in anger and screaming at his men.

Seeing this glimpse of hope, Flint drove his wavering crew to cut free the foremast and bring the shattered *Betsy* before the wind, under her after sails. Some furious minutes later, *Betsy* gathered way and rolled miserably downwind, discoursing heavily and needing constant helm corrections, and moving away from the Spaniard at a bare walking pace.

She'd covered less than a mile before *El Tigre* was got before the wind and came surging forward with the water foaming under her bow. Fear ran the length and breadth of *Betsy* and the men broke and tried to run away. But Flint cut down the first of them, and the others howled and ran back to their duty ... for a while.

'Tain't no use, Cap'n,' said Billy Bones miserably, 'them buggers is coming and we can't stop 'em.'

'Billy-my-chicken,' said Flint, 'I'll run you through the liver if you say that again, I take my oath on it.'

BOOM! A gun fired and another roundshot flew.

But it wasn't the Spaniard. Heads turned in amazement as a big, fast schooner came plunging down from the north. She was a mile away and closing fast. The lookouts hadn't seen her, for most of them were dead, and the others had eyes only for the immediate enemy.

'By God and the devil!' said Flint. 'See her colours?'

'Stap me!' said Billy Bones. 'The black flag, like our own!'

The schooner flew sable banners from her fore and maintop. Each displayed a grinning skull over crossed swords. She came tearing down, straight for *El Tigre*, which turned away from

Betsy and made ready to receive the newcomer.

The two ships were very evenly matched. They were closely similar in size, in guns, and in the number and skill of their crews. A long engagement followed with much careful long-range shooting as each captain tried to place his ship to some advantage over the other. The result was a great burning of powder, but to little effect, since neither party saw any benefit in closing to a range where hits were certain, for neither would risk a lucky shot that left his own ship dismasted or harmed in her spars, such that the enemy could place their broadside under his stern and hammer him into surrender.

At first, *Betsy* took no further part in the fight, for she'd suffered grievous loss of life, and Flint's methods of rousing flagging spirits were of his own, highly ambiguous and uncertain nature. But eventually he got a spar lashed to the stump of the foremast, and set a sail upon it. Then, with the wreckage heaved over the side, and a few guns manned by crews who were more frightened of Flint and Billy Bones than they were of the Spaniards, *Betsy* made the best of her clumsy way towards the two circling, thundering opponents.

Flint was doing this only because they were now downwind of him, and *Betsy* was incapable of anything other than running before a fair wind. It was his fixed intention to pass through them, or by them, to make his escape, and he'd had guns manned strictly to assist this principal objective. But Lieutenant De Cordoba knew none of this. He only saw a second ship, flying the black flag, coming to join the one that was already his equal.

De Cordoba hung his head, heaved a sigh, and asked God and his king to forgive him. Most of his powder and shot was used up. His guns were so hot that the carriages were smoking. His men were exhausted. They were in no condition to fight two ships, especially if it came to close quarters, since the men of two ships must surely outnumber his one. With utmost reluctance, De Cordoba therefore hauled out of the fight and ran before the wind. From his point of view, it was an un-heroic decision but a wise one.

But to Flint and his men, it was joy. It was relief. It was repeal, redemption and resurrection! They cheered and yelled with delight to see the Spaniard go. And other cheers came across the water from the schooner. This broke the first wave of delight. With *El Tigre* growing smaller with every minute, the schooner swung out her cutter and manned it, and the cutter pulled briskly across to *Betsy*.

When this happened, Flint, and those left standing of his crew lined the shot-broken sides of their ship and wondered if they'd been rescued or simply taken by a different enemy.

They were glad to see the Spaniards go, of course, for the Spaniards would've hanged the lot of them without so much as a trial. But what did the schooner want? Who were her people? They flew the black flag, like *Betsy* did, but what did that matter? It wasn't like one of King George's ships coming to the aid of another. Flint frowned and bit his lip, and considered the oncoming cutter. He'd never go to help another ship; not him! He'd take his Bible oath on it! But there was nothing to do but wait, for even the cutter was faster by far than the half-ruined *Betsy*, and soon it bumped and ground alongside, and men were scrambling aboard by the main chains.

The first of them was a tall man with a mane of fair hair starting out from under his hat. He had long limbs and an active, alert face. He had the air of a man used to authority. He shook his head at the damage done to the ship.

Flint stepped forward and the fair-haired man looked him over.

'English? *Français? Portugés?*' he said.

Chapter 13

10th June 1752
Aboard Walrus
The Savannah River

Billy Bones was the happiest man on board as *Walrus* worked her way downriver and out past Tybee Island. He chucked and smiled, and he kicked the men to their duties in the most good-hearted way, punching their heads cordially and with humour.

'Haul away, you buggers!' he cried to the waisters running with a line to raise the mainsail. 'Pull, you whores' abortions!' he bellowed at the boat's crew labouring to get out a kedge anchor for warping the ship when the wind failed. He laughed and beamed and showed the mettle of his wit by flicking men's ears with the tip of a rope's end and tripping the unwary down hatchways. And all the lower deck nudged and winked, and thanked their lucky stars that Mr Bones was in so jolly a mood.

The cause of all this happiness was that Billy had just spent a week ashore, galloping every tart he could get his leg across, and drinking himself roaring drunk every night. Best of all, he had enjoyed a most delightful, and profitable, prize-fight with a sergeant from the garrison who was reckoned the best exponent of fisticuffs in all the American colonies. A huge crowd had gathered to witness the encounter, which took place at night, by torchlight, on the West Common by the bay.

After only twenty-five rounds of bare-knuckle fighting, the sergeant was showing signs of wear, while Billy Bones was just nicely settling down to work. Taking advantage of the slackening of his opponent's attack, Billy Bones put him down with a cross-buttock, and began industriously to kick him in the kidneys, until he was hauled off by a band of soldiers who broke through the ring to rescue their man.

When the beaters-out had cleared the ring with cudgels, and the fight resumed, the sergeant having been revived with cold water and brought up to scratch, the military man found that his heart wasn't really in it any longer, and Billy Bones polished him off in four or five easy rounds. Later, Billy still had the appetite for three bottles of French wine and a hoggish portion of pork and corn, and he still had the strength to give the redoubtable Mrs Polly Porter one of the most vigorous servicings she'd known in all her professional experience. Indeed, it was the talk of Savannah that Mrs Porter was unable to receive customers for three days afterwards.

Besides all this, Billy Bones was merry because Captain Flint was merry, and that long-nosed, yellow-haired sod, John Silver, was not. Billy had seen the black girl that Flint brought aboard, and had whistled to himself at the look of her and the shape of her. Billy didn't like black girls normally, and would pay over the odds for a white girl, or at the very least a mestiza. But this one, by God, was different. She had a figure like a sand-glass and the prettiest little face, and the most enormous eyes, and the shiniest hair that Billy Bones had ever seen. And all the lower deck thought so too.

Billy turned this over in his mind, since, in the normal way of things, it was bad luck to bring a woman on board – any woman, let alone one like this. But Flint was captain, along with that swab John Silver – even Billy Bones had to admit the truth of the double command – and the crew would take their lead from the captain as long as he brought home the goods. So ... the girl being Flint's property, no man dared oppose her being on board, and it was beyond all imagining that anyone would even *think* of laying a hand on her. Billy Bones alone would see to that, never mind Flint.

So *Walrus* rounded Tybee Island and forged out into the open sea, and the wind came on to blow, and Billy summoned all hands to shorten sail. The thundering rumble of feet on the planks and the yelling of the boatswain's mates brought Flint up on deck, and he smiled his wide smile at Billy

Bones. This simple instant of approval from the man whose slave he was, provided the capping joy for Billy Bones. His simple, brutal heart soared to the heavens and all around him was happiness to the far horizons.

Meanwhile, beneath his feet was the living, straining timber of a fine ship, and above him the topmen leapt to their work among the crackling roaring sails, and above them the gulls wheeled and turned and cried. On deck men were hauling on the braces to trim the mainyard and the well-greased blocks hummed and clacked with the strain. From forrard the salt spray came up like mist from the plunging bow, and the smell of the sea and the freshness and newness of it was all around.

Every seaman knows the thrill of that moment of setting out, with the land falling astern and the whole world opening ahead, and Billy Bones knew it no less than any other. It was the very heart and soul of why men went to sea, and gloried over the miserable landsmen who stayed ashore and never knew such wonders.

Flint came to stand by Billy Bones, alongside the helmsman at the tiller. He studied the set of the sails and then the compass in its binnacle.

'Well enough, Mr Bones,' he proclaimed. 'What course, helmsman?'

'A point north o' southeast, Cap'n.'

'Well enough,' repeated Flint. Billy Bones could see the satisfaction on his captain's face.

He grinned to himself, for he knew exactly what was making Flint so sweet. Billy Bones thought what he'd like to give that little piece of black mischief, if only he could get his hands on her, and never a doubt but that the Cap'n was giving her just the same. Billy Bones imagined the high, jutting breasts and the swell of her black rump from the slender waist, and he cursed hard and silently to himself, and wished mightily that it was himself doing the work and not Flint.

'Ah, John!' said Flint, as the hulking figure of Silver emerged from the quarterdeck hatchway. 'Come and keep me company. I feel the need for honest conversation.'

'Aye-aye, sir!' said Silver with that eternal cheerfulness that turned Billy Bones's stomach. What was wrong with *him?* Why couldn't the Cap'n have *honest conversation* with Billy Bones? Weren't he an honest man?

And so the happy moment was broken, and Billy Bones suffered the bitter jealousy of a child whose best friend has been taken away by another. For Billy Bones loved Flint. He loved him as a son loves his father or a patriot loves his country. He was sunk in awe for Flint's cleverness and his quickness and his terrible ability to strike fear into the hearts of men. And since Billy Bones's admiration of Flint was without end, he didn't mind that Flint treated him like a donkey, because such a man would do that to anyone.

What Billy Bones did mind, was the easy equality with which Flint treated John Silver. As far as Billy Bones could see, there wasn't anything that Silver did that merited this, and Billy Bones sneered. But he turned his head away to do it, and walked to the rail and stared into the sea, that his expression might not be noticed.

'Now where have you been these days past, John?' said Flint.

'Enjoying my shore leave, Cap'n,' said Silver. 'And doing it in those ways that the tradition of our trade requires!'

Flint laughed. 'And myself busy all the while, in action against Neal the Irishman, making the best of our business.'

'And yourself the best man of us to do it,' said Silver. They both laughed and Billy Bones ground his teeth to see the friendship between them, and the obvious pleasure that each took in the other's company. But then there was a stirring and a whispering and a curious murmuring among the hands.

'Bugger ... me ... tight!' said the helmsman, each word forced out between gritted teeth. Billy Bones turned to see the cause of this.

'Jesus fucking Christ!' he said, turning piously to religion in the extremity of his emotion, for he saw that Flint's black girl had come up on deck and was standing, holding on to a rack of belaying pins on the weather side to keep her footing, which she couldn't do without hanging on, what with her being a landsman ... lands*woman*, rather.

She had her hair bound up in a silk handkerchief of deep scarlet, and she was dressed in a shirt and a pair of white duck slops, secured round the waist with a black leather belt. The clothes had belonged to one of the ship's boys: a scrawny, undersized twelve-year-old, and had been given to her on Flint's orders as being nearest to her size. But the result was a tightness around the behind, and bare legs from just above the knees, and a want of buttons around the neck that left more velvet-black skin gleaming in the sunshine than was entirely wise.

She was nervous with the motion of the ship. Billy saw that she'd be casting up her accounts before long, like any green sailor. Then he looked around and saw that there wasn't one man on deck who wasn't staring pop-eyed at her, and those below were being called up by their mates so as not to miss the treat.

For that matter, Billy felt his own desires stiffening, and that was after a glutting, unrestrained debauch ashore that normally left him contented for weeks. Billy Bones entirely revised his opinion of black girls and looked at Flint out of the corner of his eye. By Satan! The captain was a man, and no mistake. He saw the satisfaction on Flint's face at the crew's reaction to his little prize.

'Selena, my dear!' called Flint. 'Come aft!' Billy could see that she didn't know where *aft* was, but Flint beckoned and she half walked, half staggered along the deck to join him. And then Billy Bones saw the most surprising and wonderful thing: Silver was scowling. Silver's beaky nose was out of joint. Someone had shoved a pint of mustard up his arse, and Billy Bones could see who it was. A dull grin broke across his greasy face. He followed everything that happened next with utmost attention.

'Selena,' said Flint, making introductions as if he were on a flagship and she were a duchess, 'may I present my quartermaster and good companion, Mr John Silver.'

Billy Bones saw the fine lips twist and the nose

flare and the hands go to the hips.

'Huh!' she said, and Billy Bones held his breath. Skin, salt, bugger and burn him if this didn't look ripe! The little bitch was facing down Long John Silver like he was a foremast hand caught thieving from his mates; while Silver, by heaven, couldn't meet her eye. Billy actually saw Long John blush and blink and look from Flint to the girl and back again. Billy snorted with glee, and hastily made a show of clearing his throat and going to the rail to spit tobacco juice from the plug he kept eternally working in his mouth. But he came back sharpish to watch the next round of the contest.

'Why, what's this, John?' said Flint.

'We've met,' said the girl.

'Aye,' said Flint, 'in Savannah.'

'Yes,' said the girl, 'in Charley Neal's liquor shop.' She looked at Flint. 'Your friend thought I was something that I am not.'

Billy Bones whistled silently to himself. She was powerful uppity for a nigger-woman. But then he remembered who her protector was.

'If that was the way of it, miss,' said Silver, 'then I'm right sorry, and I take my Bible oath on it.' He turned anxiously to Flint, who was looking on in amusement, 'A word in your private ear, Joe,' he said, but Flint let go a blast of laughter. He slapped his thigh and petted his squawking parrot, and took off his hat and fanned himself. Then he held his sides and started all over again. Once Flint started laughing, it was hard for him to stop.

'Why, John,' he said, between gasps, 'don't tell me we both chased the same hind, and I was the faster?'

'No!' said the girl.

'No!' said Silver.

'No?' said Flint.

'We'd best talk, Joe,' said Silver. 'A woman is the worst luck that's possible to bring aboard a ship.'

Billy saw the fun drain out of Flint in double quick time. Flint's eyes went wide and round and white, which was a dangerous sign.

'Now, would that be *you*, John Silver, questioning *me?*'

'Aye,' said Silver.

'So!' said Flint.

They stared at one another as if no other person was within miles. The moment was intensely painful to each. Their friendship was still at its height. Then Flint shook himself and forced a smile, and tried another laugh – though not a very good one – and clapped Silver on the shoulder.

'John, John, shipmate,' he said, 'let's not you and I quarrel.'

'Never at my choosing,' said Silver, making his own best effort to force things back the way they'd been before.

'Then why ever?' said Flint, and smiled almost naturally.

'But we must talk, Cap'n,' said Silver, glancing at Selena, and Flint's eyes grew round again, but he held his course.

'Aye,' said Flint, 'what can't be cured must be endured, as the doctors say.' And he looked at Billy Bones and Selena. 'My dear,' he said, 'this gentleman is Mr Bones, my first mate.' She looked at him in a way that would have got her the back of Billy Bones's hand under other circumstances.

'And, Mr Bones, this lady is my ward, Selena. I hand her into your personal safe-keeping, Mr Bones, and will inquire of you should any man treat her with less than proper respect.'

'Aye-aye, sir!' said Billy Bones. *Ward* indeed. But if that's what Flint said, then so it should be. 'You can leave the hands to me, Cap'n,' he added.

'Oh, I do, Mr Bones. Indeed I do,' said Flint. 'And now, John, let's settle this matter over a glass of rum, like good companions, eh?'

'With all my heart, Cap'n,' said Silver, and the two of them went below. Billy Bones's spirits fell when he saw that, but he perked up later when a raging and a hollering of voices could be heard coming up from Flint's cabin. Billy guessed the stern windows must be thrown open for the fresh air, since the sound was coming up over the taffrail. He would dearly have liked to get himself and his ears astern to hear what was being said, but he dared not. In any case the little madam was wandering round the deck among the men, and his presence was badly needed beside her.

She was still hanging on to whatever came to hand, bracing herself against the heaving deck which she hadn't yet come to terms with, but she didn't seem one bit afraid, and she wasn't going to be sick after all. She stared at every ordinary item of the schooner's gear as if it was all brand new and she didn't know a jibboom from a jackstay. In due time, the wheels of Billy Bones's mind turned, and he managed to calculate that this was indeed the case, what with plantation slaves not being bred up to the ways of the sea.

The trouble was that Billy knew he must either

follow her round like a nursemaid, or at least take a turn about the ship to warn the hands what would happen to them should they not mind their manners. So he had to abandon the fascinations of eavesdropping just at the very moment when he was learning to relish them.

Round the ship he went, as fast as he could, to give the crew their orders in the hope that he could get back to the stern without delay. But to his surprise he found that the men were not interested in the juicy bit of tail that was parading itself round the deck, because another piece of news had sped round the ship ahead of him. All the crew wanted to hear about was the split between Flint and Silver. And there was a dimension to this that had hitherto escaped Billy Bones's understanding, for he'd been too busy rejoicing at Silver's fall from the post of Flint's chief favourite.

'Which are you for, Mr Bones?' said Mad Pew, way down below where he had a little cabin – dark, close and lantern-lit – for his sailmaking gear. There was no other person present, but Pew looked around as if for hidden listeners in the shadows, and he nipped Billy Bones's arm with hard sinewy fingers in the way he had when talking, which made men's flesh creep. Billy guessed that Pew was frightened, but it was hard to read Mad Pew's expression when he was disturbed in any way, for on those occasions such a twitch jumped in the corner of his eye that it was impossible to notice much else about him.

'Haul off, you bloody lubber!' said Billy Bones, shuddering and shaking off the thin, strong hand. 'What the buggeration d'you mean, "which one"?'

'Flint,' said Pew, 'or Sil-ver?' His Welsh voice made two sounds out of the name.

'Bladderwash!' snarled Billy Bones, 'You fucking mad bastard!' And he read Pew the rule book concerning black girls aboard ship, and went stamping on his way. But the next person he met was Israel Hands, the gunner, coming out of the magazine, and Israel Hands was not mad, nor a fool, nor anything other than a prime seaman.

'Bad business, Billy,' said Hands, with a deadly serious look on his face.

'What is?' said Billy Bones, staunchly managing not to grasp the point.

'Why ... Flint and Silver, shipmate,' said Israel Hands. 'If they steers their separate courses, then some'll go with the one, and some the other.'

'Bollocks!' said Bones. 'Who'd follow any other man than Flint?'

'Aye...' said Hands carefully. 'Who would, an' all?'

'See?' said Billy Bones, believing he'd won the argument.

'Let's hope things don't turn nasty, Mr Bones,' said Israel Hands, 'or none of us'll dare to sling a hammock for fear of a knife from below whiles we sleep.'

Billy Bones thought this over and shook his head.

'No,' he said, 'not aboard the old *Walrus*. Not while we're jolly companions one and all.'

'Aye,' said Israel Hands. 'Whatever you says, Mr Bones.' But he was glad that, as master gunner, he slept in a nice solid wooden bunk.

Chapter 14

30th May 1749
Dawn
Elizabeth's *longboat*
The South Atlantic

'We're all going to die,' said Mr Midshipman Hastings, 'and that's God's truth.' And he curled himself into a ball in the sternsheets of the wallowing longboat.

'Hell and damnation, George,' said Mr Midshipman Povey, kneeling down and putting his hands over his friend's ear so he could whisper without being heard, 'If you don't buck up soon, that's just what we shall do. Now bloody well stand up and do your duty! I can't do it, I'm too small. They won't listen to me.'

'Shan't,' said Hastings, 'it's too much.' He shoved Povey's hands away and looked up at him. 'Just too much! All *that* on that stinking island ... and now this–' He raised his head slightly, peered between the backs of the three marines sat stolidly on the aftermost thwart, as a protective screen from the hands.

Povey followed his gaze. Rough, fearful faces glared back in a mass. The men were growling and moaning. Worse still, some of them were sobbing in despair. Cast loose upon the deep without charts, compass, instruments or any hope of salvation, they were twenty-three lost souls a tiny wooden shell, surrounded by an endless desert of ocean.

If they were lucky and the weather was foul, they might be swamped and drowned. But given fair weather ... it would be a hideous lingering death by thirst: the worst of all ways for a seaman to die. Povey's heart sank.

'Oh, what's the use...' he said.

'What's goin' on!' said one of the hands, reading Povey's expression. He lurched forward, trying to see what the mids were doing, only to be grabbed by a marine and thrown back to his place.

'Fuck you, lobster!' said the seaman, and sneered. 'You ain't got no bloody musket now, have you? Don't you touch me, you bloody lubber!'

'Aye!' growled the rest.

'Where's the rum?' said one.

'AYE!' they cried, and surged forward in a body to seek an answer.

The boat rocked horribly as a fierce struggle took place between seamen and marines. There were no weapons among them – they'd been plucked clean of those – but there was gouging and kicking, and heads slammed hard against the planks.

'George! George!' said Povey. 'For God's sake stand up!'

The longboat was a big one – thirty-six feet long by a dozen broad at the waist. She was ponderous and heavily timbered, but with twenty-one men fighting viciously on board of her, she was rolling gunwale-under and shipping it green.

'George!' said Povey, shaking the other as hard as he could, but Mr Midshipman Hastings sat staring with his mouth hung open, head lolling from side to side with the sickening motion. 'Right then,' said Povey, 'here's the way of it, George Hastings.'

He let go of Hastings and fell back. 'If you won't stand up and do your duty, as the senior of us two, then ... then I'll cut you in town, I'll tell my servants to shut my door to you ... *and I'll never speak to you again!*'

'Oh...' said Hastings, and sat up just as a seaman threw himself clear of the fight and landed belly-down between Hastings and Povey, and got both hands lovingly round the rum cask. His feet were firm caught among the bellowing crowd forrard so he couldn't get up, but from the look on his face, he wasn't ever going to let go.

'Ah!' said Hastings, struck with inspiration. He scrambled to his feet and began kicking the seaman's hands and fingers with all his might.

'Ow! Ow! Little bastard!' yelled the tar.

'Help me!' cried Hastings.

'Aye-aye, sir!' said Povey, and laid in with the toe of his boot.

'Here!' said Hastings, grabbing the cask as the tar finally let go. 'Help me lift it!'

The two mids heaved the heavy cask up and poised it on the rolling, heaving gunwale.

'NO!' wailed the horrified tar. He drew breath and gave out an ear-splitting shout, 'Ahoooooy, shipmates! 'Ware astern! Look what the little sods are a-doin'!'

The instant they clapped eyes on the awful thing the mids were doing, the men gave a collective groan and magically ceased to fight.

'Now then,' screeched Hastings, having been handed his audience without even having to summon it, 'pay attention, you men!' Silence fell. He looked at Povey. He looked at the wobbling cask. 'Can you hold it?'

'Aye-aye, sir.'

'Right!' said Hastings. 'Now listen to me: either I shall have discipline aboard of this ship, or that cask–' the men gaped in round-eyed horror '–goes over the side!' He turned to the other mid: 'Isn't that so, Mr Povey?'

'Indeed, sir!' said Povey, and wriggled the cask.

'Uh!' gasped the hands.

'Now then...' said Hastings, his hands clasped behind his back in the style of an officer. Drawing on all he'd learned in a year and a half afloat, he then *behaved* like an officer and divided the men into starboard and larboard watches, appointed captains of each watch, rated the man with stamped fingers as boatswain (to keep him out of mischief) and rated the eldest of the marines as acting-corporal. He then threatened stopped-grog for all future offenders, reminded them that the longboat was rigged for sail and in all respects seaworthy, and assured all present that he and Mr Povey would now confer to agree a course to the nearest port. Then – putting the larboard watch on duty – he sat down, exhausted.

This cheered the men wonderfully. Gloom vanished. Smiles returned.

'Gaw' bless-you for a young gen'man, sir!' said

a voice.

'Aye!' said the rest.

'Well done, sir!' said Acting-Corporal Bennet.

'By Jove!' said Povey, 'Well said, George!'

'I do hope, so,' said Mr Midshipman Hastings quietly. 'Just as I hope you know how to find the bloody land, because I'm damned if I do.'

Chapter 15

1st February 1750
The Spanish Main

Flint stared at the yellow-haired man, who seemed fluent in a number of languages.

'I am English, sir,' he said. 'My name is Flint, and I am commander of this vessel.' He took off his hat and bowed. He knew himself the weaker party, and so he was polite. To his surprise, the tall man doffed his own hat and bowed in return.

'John Silver, at your service, Captain,' he said. 'John Silver of the good ship *Walrus*, and until this morning under the command of Captain John Mason, God rest his soul!'

'Your captain was killed in the action?' asked Flint – the *action* indeed! He was consciously modelling his bearing on that of this amazing visitor. Flint was in the other's power, so if *he* wanted to play the gentleman instead of the pirate, then *so* would Joseph Flint.

'Aye, sir!' said Silver. 'And him one o' the finest

who ever served under Captain England, the which I had the honour to do myself.'

'Captain England?' said Flint. 'The famous pirate of the East Indies?' That was genuine and not role-playing. Flint had heard of England and the huge prizes that he took.

Silver smiled an odd smile.

'Not *pirate*, sir,' he corrected, 'but a gentleman o' fortune. One of the brethren of the coast, and a true buccaneer in the old style, that was Cap'n England; and Cap'n Mason was one just the same. Why, the instant he saw the Don's colours matched against your own, he sent hands to quarters and made sail to come up with you to take your part. That was England's way, and it was Mason's too.'

Flint clung hard to his reason. He was dumbfounded. He heard the words. He understood the meaning of each one separately. But put the words together, and there was no meaning to be had; not by Joe Flint, at any rate.

'You came to our aid,' he said, in as neutral and careful a voice as he could. His instinct was to be friends with this fellow, and to be just such a creature as he was. This could not be avoided. Not while Silver had the bigger ship, more guns and more men.

'Aye, sir,' said Silver, 'we acted in the old way, as gentlemen o' fortune should.' He smiled and took Flint's hand and looked him in the eye, honestly and without guile. Then he grinned at the parrot nestling against Flint's ear.

'Fine bird that, sir,' he said. 'By repute, they talks as well as a Christian, and they lives for ever mostly.' He reached out and stroked the green plumage, and the bird nuzzled his hand. Flint's eyebrows went up. Most men kept clear of the bird. Most men were afraid of losing a finger, and were justified in their fear.

'Hmm,' said Flint, still in the dark as to Silver's intentions, but beginning to hope that dawn might be approaching. For, as far as Flint could judge, Silver was living out a dream of buccaneering on the Spanish Main, as it had existed forty years ago. Either that or he was plain mad. Flint was inclined to the latter supposition, but decided to wait upon events and to see what the other did, as opposed to what he said.

And again Flint was amazed. Silver and his men bustled about the smashed and battered *Betsy*, going to the aid of the wounded, taking a hand at the pumps, helping to clear away the wreckage, and in every way anxiously seeking to make right and mend. After a while of this, and when everything was done that was urgent, Silver took Flint aside and spoke to him.

'Cap'n Flint,' said he, 'asking your pardon, but it won't do and that's the truth.'

'Won't do?' said Flint. Terror struck him like a knife, and his imagination conjured the horrors of hell. Here it comes, he thought, awaiting a cut throat and a plunge over the side.

'No, sir, it won't,' said Silver. 'Here's you with seventeen whole men, and twenty wounded and your ship leaking and her rigging cut to ruins...' He paused to run a highly critical eye over *Betsy's* timbers and fittings. 'And your ship not one of the best to begin with, begging your pardon.'

'She was built from the ruins of another,' said Flint, stung to the defence of his ship. 'Built on a sea shore under conditions of utmost inconvenience and difficulty.'

'Ah,' said Silver, 'I thought she weren't Bristol-built.' He smiled and continued, 'So let's make the best out of the worst, and fetch away yourself and your people and repair on board of the old *Walrus* and be good companions one and all.'

'Aye,' said Flint, still waiting for a trap to spring, 'but what about the ship?'

'Flotsam an' jetsam, Cap'n,' said Silver. 'One good blow'll see her dismasted and rolling like a barrel. Better you should come on board with us.'

But Flint hesitated, thinking of the loot down below. He thought of it even though he knew it was no longer his. It belonged to the man with the greater strength. Even so, Flint was constitutionally incapable of giving it up willingly.

'But ... ah...' he stumbled for words. Without thinking, he looked towards the hatch in the waist. Silver was far too sharp to miss that.

'I see, Cap'n!' he said, and tapped a finger alongside his nose. 'You've a cargo below decks,' he smiled, 'Well done, sir! But never you mind about that, for we'll hoist it out, and across to the old *Walrus*, and all shall share and share alike: your goods and our goods, and jolly companions one and all.'

'Jolly companions,' said Flint, 'One and all...' And the incredible thought finally occurred to him that Silver actually meant what he said.

'Companions and maybe more,' continued Silver. He tilted his head on one side and studied

Flint. 'You have the look of a gentleman about you, sir,' he said, 'so I take it that you are used to command ... and knows the ways of plotting and setting of a course with a chart and a quadrant and 'rithmatic?'

Again Flint became nervous. Again he had no idea where this line of inquiry might be leading. But Silver continued.

'The thing is, sir,' he said, 'Cap'n Mason was cut in half by a shot, and both the mates killed one way or another. There's still a lad aboard what's learning the ways of it, but there ain't none left as can reliably find his way across an open ocean. We're seamen one and all, who can steer a course. But who's to set one?'

'Ahhhh,' said Flint, and stood six feet taller in the self-same boots. 'My dear fellow,' he declared, 'I dare swear our interests run in harness. Both myself and my first mate, Mr Bones, are proficient in the art of celestial navigation.'

The relief in Silver's face was a delight for Flint to see, and he almost gave up thinking that an elaborate trap was still hiding somewhere.

Within a few hours, *Betsy* was emptied of her treasure chests and the belongings of Flint's men, and everything transferred to *Walrus*. Then the men themselves came across and the dead were honoured. That was the first thing that showed Flint that Silver and his men truly were different, for Silver wouldn't have the dead casually heaved over the side as had been the practise aboard *Betsy*. Instead, everything was done as if under King George's own flag. Silver insisted the sail-maker sewed up each man in his own hammock, with a round-shot at his feet. Then all hands were mustered and made to doff their hats, while two men balanced a plank across the rail and, one after another, the dead were placed on the plank – under *Walrus*'s black flag – and the canvas-shrouded corpses were slid into the deep, with the boatswain and his mates sounding long calls on their pipes.

Flint looked about him. *Walrus* was a ship of another kind in other ways too. She was scrubbed and polished, and there was an easy comradeship among her crew. Later he learned there was no spitting on the decks nor naked lights below. That's how Mason had liked her, and England before. Under Silver's command, *Walrus* was got under way, and at Silver's request, Flint set a course for Savannah, Georgia, where fresh powder and shot was to be had, since *Walrus* had fired away most of her stores just as *El Tigre* had done, and *Betsy's* stores were ruined by the leaks she'd sprung down below.

Once the immediate pressure of work was eased, there followed a great haggling and chattering as Flint's men found themselves berths among Silver's crew and formed themselves into messes. Flint found that he was fascinated with John Silver, or Long John, as he was known. He watched the way Silver went about the ship, nimble and active: skipping down ladders and up into the shrouds with a speed and ease that made light of his bulk. Silver knew all his men and had a joke or a word for each of them. He knew his letters well enough to read and write, and he knew numbers too, and was highly adept at calculating the value to be got out of a prize. But beyond that he was pure lower-deck, with the manners, speech and tar-streaked palms to go with it.

But what impressed Flint most was the respect he was given by every man aboard. They knuckled their brows and leapt to obey, and raced one another to be first to complete the tasks he set them. And all this was done without a blow or a curse, despite the fact that one look at him proclaimed him to be a deadly dangerous man in a fight.

Over the next days and weeks, Flint observed all this and there grew within his damaged soul a positive liking for Silver, which sprang like a bright green shoot out of a dung-hill. If Flint had been an introspective man – which he was not – he would have remarked to himself – which he did not – that everything he liked in Silver was the opposite to everything that was wrong in himself.

Flint never put such thoughts into words. He never perceived them and knew them. But just the same, there was some dim awareness of this underlying truth. And neither was this the limit of Flint's education. A few days after the two crews had mixed, and with gentle weather and all secure and shipshape, Silver mustered the hands – *Betsy*'s men to the fore – and proclaimed that all must now be made regular and articles signed. Flint had not the least idea what this meant. But some of his men did.

'I'll put my mark!' said Israel Hands.

'I'll want to cast an eye, first!' said Billy Bones seriously.

'Cast an eye?' said Flint, struggling with the

incredible fact that Billy Bones had finally managed to do something unexpected.

'Aye,' said Billy Bones. 'Articles, Cap'n. 'Tis the way of things among the brethren of the coast.'

'The what?' said Flint.

'The brethren of the coast, Cap'n,' said Billy Bones, as if to an ill-taught child. Billy Bones had been talking to the half-trained lad who was the nearest equivalent to himself aboard *Walrus*. He'd spoken to others too, and he'd absorbed some of their customs and lore.

'You poltroon!' said Flint in a whisper. 'Brethren of the coast? That was in your grandfather's time, up north, off the...'

'These here is the ship's articles,' cried Silver, producing a book very much like the one he'd signed years ago on England's quarterdeck. 'I'll ask Mr Flint to read it for all those who haven't the schooling.' And he solemnly handed the book to Flint. 'In a bold voice now, sir! So's all can hear.'

Flint opened the book and looked at the handwritten articles. He looked too, at the men crowded all around him: a sea of eyes in sunbrowned, expectant faces, crammed into the narrow space of *Walrus*'s deck. The ship was running sweetly, the wind played in the sheets, lines and shrouds, and the sails rustled up above. Flint shrugged to himself, lifted up his voice and read for all to hear. He stumbled only once, at the place where the name of the captain – Mason – had been struck out in red ink.

'What name shall go here?' asked Flint.

'All in good time,' said Silver. 'Be so good as to hold your course till you come safe into harbour.'

So Flint read on to the end. When he'd finished, he and all those who'd come aboard with him were invited to sign, including the wounded who'd been brought up on deck for the purpose. So they signed: Flint, Billy Bones and a few others inscribing their names, and the rest with crosses or other marks, such that by the end of the ceremony, and much to his surprise, Flint's opinion had been changed. He started out in profound contempt for this nonsense, but ended convinced of its value. Seamen's minds were childlike, and Flint could see the power that the book, and the words, had worked on them. They'd be a better crew for it, and it proved exactly the buttressing of legality – or an approximation of it – that was lost when a crew breaks apart from the King's law as his own crew had done. But there was more to come.

'Now that we're jolly companions all,' said Silver, addressing the whole ship, 'we must elect a captain according to tradition. So will any brother step up and give a name?'

'Long John!' cried a dozen voices, 'Cap'n Silver!'

'No, lads!' cried Silver. 'It can't be. The captain must be a gentleman of the quarterdeck that can guide the ship over the ocean.' Here he looked steadily at Flint, and Flint was as utterly dumbfounded as ever he'd been in all his life.

Is the fool handing over command to me? he thought. *Impossible!* But Long John continued.

'And every man here knows I ain't no navigator!'

'Bugger that!' cried a voice, 'We'll have no cap'n than Long John. Where's the man that could face him? Where's the man that's half the seaman he is?'

‘Aye!’ they roared. They cheered and they cheered for Long John, and waved their swords and muskets to the skies. But Silver shook his head and raised his hands for silence.

‘No! And there’s an end on it, say I. My vote goes for Cap’n Flint – a true gentleman, bred up in King George’s navy, no less. So what say you, lads, to Cap’n Flint?’

They said very little at first, even those who’d come over from *Betsy* – *especially* those who’d come over from *Betsy*, for they knew what to expect from Flint. But Silver talked them round. He was a fine speech-maker, and all by native wit with never a drop of book-learning nor any example set to him by teachers. It was all sincere and from himself.

As for Flint, he watched all this as if from a box in a theatre and with such amazement, and such surprise and such disbelief as could hardly be contained within the body of a single man.

Silver was giving up command – which Flint could not believe. Silver was handing it to Flint on a plate – which Flint could not believe. Silver was doing this, whom Flint could see was possessed of all the natural gifts of leadership. Silver was doing this, whom the men wanted and whom they had called for. It was beyond understanding. Flint’s mind cringed as it was dragged towards an invisible frontier, beyond which men acted for the common good, and not just for themselves.

Every day he spent with Silver, Flint came closer to that mystic line.

Chapter 16

30th May 1749
Night
Elizabeth's *longboat*
The South Atlantic

The two mids sat silent at the dark stern of the longboat, now sweetly heeling under her canvas – gaff and jib-sail – with half the men asleep, the rest dozing. Hastings had the tiller, the sky was bright with stars, the night was cool and comfortable, the seas were easy and the round-bowed long-boat was a good, dry, sea-keeping vessel. Under other circumstances, those aboard of her would have been a merry company, but not now. Hastings and Povey in particular were not merry. They were watching the bright stars as if their lives depended on them, which they did.

'There!' said Povey. 'There's one setting now–' he pointed '–see?'

'Yes,' said Hastings, and gave a touch on the tiller to steer towards it. 'Tell me again,' said Hastings, who'd never paid half as much attention to his lessons as he should have.

'We're steering *west*,' said Povey. 'Sunrise and sunset gives us east and west by day, and the stars set in the west at night, yes?'

'Yes.'

'And better than that, we've got the northern

trades blowing northwest – or close to that – which couldn't be better for a westerly passage.'

'But why are we steering west?' said Hastings.

Povey sighed. "Cos my best guess is that we're somewhere in the latitude of the Windward Islands, and if we're lucky we might make Barbados, which is British, and which lies to the east of 'em.'

Hastings frowned mightily, trying to remember which king owned which islands.

'The Windward Islands...' he said. 'They're French, aren't they?'

'Yes,' said Povey. 'At least, I think so.'

'Not Spanish?'

'No.'

'Good! We'll take our chance with the Frogs, but not the heathen Dagoes.'

The two mids sat silent for a while, then Povey returned to the question which took precedence over all other questions. At least he had the sense to whisper.

'So how long do you think the water will last?'

'They gave us one water-butt. That's about one hundred gallons when it's full.'

'Yes, but how long will it last?'

'And there's twenty-three of us...'

'So how long will it last?'

'I don't know! Can *you* tell me how long till we reach the Windward Islands?'

'Well...' Povey frowned and thought mightily. He looked at the boat's wake, sliding past, 'Well ... we're running at about four or five knots wouldn't you say?'

'Yes.'

'Say a hundred miles a day?'

'Yes.'

'So ... well ... it depends how far we have to go.'

Hastings couldn't bring himself to ask Povey how far that was, because he feared that Povey didn't know. For his part, Povey was immensely relived that he was not asked, because indeed he did not know.

Instinctively, Povey glanced astern. He looked at the dark waters. There was nothing following them, nothing coming after them. There was nothing at all ... except death by thirst.

Chapter 17

16th February 1750
Aboard Walrus
The Atlantic

The partnership of Flint and Silver soon took an enormous prize, and it was entirely due to Flint's skill that *Walrus* was in the right place at the right time, out in the open Atlantic.

He'd explained the way of it to Silver, previously, with a chart spread out over a table in the master's day cabin. *Walrus* was charging along under all plain sail, in a steady blow, and Flint and Silver and one or two others were crammed into the cabin for a council of war. Flint's fingers flicked over the chart table, pointing and stabbing. Precisely, Flint set his fingertip upon the port city of San Felipe, which lay on the eastward side of the island of Nuestro Santissimo Salvador, facing homeward towards Spain.

'Latitude fifteen degrees, three minutes and thirty seconds,' he said. 'Longitude fifty-five degrees almost exactly.' He frowned, 'If we can trust this Dago chart.'

'Looks a good 'un to me, Cap'n,' said Billy Bones, squinting hard at the chart and rubbing his chin. He pointed a thick finger: 'Soundings, bearings an' all. Set out fair an' shipshape.'

Silver frowned and peered at the neat, intricate penmanship, but all he could understand were the tritons and conches that the Spanish cartographer had used to illuminate the margins and name-plate of the map. A thick, heavy headache oppressed him, as always when he tried to get an understanding of these fearful concepts of latitude and longitude.

'It's a rich, fat island with a steady trade with Cadiz,' said Flint. 'And there's a stone fort and a pair of frigates to guard the town.'

'So we can't cruise offshore, for fear of meeting superior force,' said Billy Bones.

'Aye,' said the company, including Long John. That much was obvious.

'Indeed,' said Flint, tracing his finger along the latitude of San Felipe and following it far out into the Atlantic. 'And therefore, we shall cruise along this line, out beyond thc horizon from the port, awaiting a ship coming westward, running her latitude down to make landfall.'

The pain in Long John's head became very great. His eyes watered and the chart swam before him.

'Beach and bone me, if I'll ever understand it!' said Long John, for he made no secret of his limitations in this matter. The others looked at one another and Flint sneered instinctively and thought to stab with sarcasm, but the words came out oddly, for him.

'What's ailing, you John?' said he. 'It is but a trick, this navigation. A trick such as this old bird might learn.' He tickled his parrot, and pulled at her feathers, causing her to squawk. 'Why, this poor creature cusses in five languages, which is more than most men can do.' He looked fiercely at the bird, and shook it.

'Grrrr!' he said

'Mierda! Coño! Tu m'emmerdes!' screeched the bird. Everyone laughed, and Flint – who never cussed at all – shrugged in embarrassment.

'There, there,' he said, calming the parrot. 'Poor creature was taught that by ignorant men. It's a trick, that's all, just like this *mystery* of navigation, which is not a thing to be compared with the gift to put heart into men and lead them forward against the enemy.' Flint smiled. 'That's the mark of a real man and one whom we admire.'

'Aye!' said the rest, for it was not only a handsome compliment but a true statement of Silver's worth. Billy Bones and Israel Hands exchanged a brief glance of amazement, for they'd never before heard Flint say a good word about anyone. Come to that, Flint was puzzled himself. It was the first time he'd ever met a man whom he liked and respected.

As for Silver, he grinned and nodded, and the

pain went out of his headache. He smiled and shook Flint's hand in gratitude – to the further amazement of Mr Bones and Mr Hands – and then reached up to stroke the parrot where it swayed and bobbed on Flint's shoulder.

'Ah, you're a fine 'un an' all, ain't you, shipmate?' he said, and the bird nuzzled his hand and gently nipped it with its great hooked beak – the beak that could crack Brazil nuts to splinters.

'Why, John,' said Flint, 'it appears you have a friend. Are you a rival for its affections?'

'Not I, Joe!' said Silver. 'Not for the bird nor nothing else.'

Wonder was surpassing wonder for Billy Bones and Israel Hands, not least because the parrot was feared by the entire crew, and the last man that had dared to touch it – when they were alone in the maintop and he'd attempted to wring its neck – was Black Dog, who was now missing two fingers off his left hand.

Meanwhile the result of Flint's unique and tremendous act of kindness was that much of Silver's ludicrous guilt over navigation faded away. Never again did he worry quite so much about charts and quadrants and latitude – at least, not while his friendship with Flint lasted, and for that Long John was deeply grateful.

More tangibly, Flint's simple plan – the thousand-times repeated ploy of the pirate or cruising frigate – worked well. On 16th February *Walrus* swooped down upon the three-masted Spanish West Indiaman, *Doña Inez de Villafranca*, giving a broadside of chain-shot into her rigging to tear down spars and sails and paralyse the crew, like the prey of a striking spider.

From the start, Capitan José Martin Ramírez knew that his ship was lost. He'd left Spain escorted by two splendid frigates, heavily armed and manned to guard the cargo under hatches in *Doña Inez*. Having been separated from these ships by foul weather, he'd been chewing his knuckles for a week in fear of precisely what had now come down upon him. But he was no coward and he fired a musket into the packed mass of savages swarming over the wreckage-strewn rail of his ship, and then he used the long barrel to drive his men into line, like a sergeant of grenadiers dressing the line with a halberd. Then he faced the enemy.

'Para Dios, España, et Las Señoras!' he cried – for God, Spain and the ladies! There were six women aboard: wives or betrothed of gentlemen in Santiago. Three of them were virgins, and for any one of the six, he was prepared to give his life, rather than see them despoiled. Unfortunately, not all Capitan Ramírez's men shared this noble sentiment. Some were already wavering, even before the shock of battle.

There came a roar of small arms, and the front rank of the pirates disappeared in smoke, while leaden bullets thumped into the Spanish defenders.

'Fuego!' roared Capitan Ramírez, then, *'Santiago! Santiago!'* the ancient and holy battle cry of the Christian knights who drove the Moors from Spain. There was a thundering volley from his men, then Ramírez was casting aside his musket and charging, sword in hand, to die with honour if need be.

In the event, he spitted one man – straight through the mouth and out the back of his head – killing him instantly; and he left a lifelong scar on Billy Bones's cheek. But then Bones sunk his cutlass deep into Ramírez's shoulder, hard by the side of his neck, and the brave Spaniard went down spouting bright, frothy blood in all directions.

After that there was some screaming and stampeding and some modest butchery before the thoroughly beaten crew were allowed to throw down their arms and beg for quarter. Long John granted it, and to make sure they got it, he went round with a belaying pin, cracking heads among *Walrus*'s people until they left off cutting throats.

Flint watched him in amazement. He'd have skinned and gutted them. He'd have dug their eyes out. He'd have boiled them. He'd have sliced the skin off their pricks. He'd have... He paused and wiped the sweat from his eyes and the slobber from his mouth. Flint knew that Silver's ways made a whole crew and a sound crew, even if he didn't understand why.

'Break open the hatches, lads!' roared Silver. 'Guard the prisoners, and out with the rum and the wine, and the cheese and the pickles!'

Half a dozen of the crew, told off for that purpose, herded the prisoners to the fo'c'sle and the rest roared with delight.

'Three cheers for Long John!' cried a voice.

'Aye!' they roared and cheered lustily.

'Three cheers for the cap'n!' cried Billy Bones lustily.

'Aye!' they cried, and gave Flint his three,

equally loud.

They waved blades in the air and fired off the few firearms left loaded. They embraced their messmates and danced hornpipes. They staggered about, tripping over the clutter of fallen gear and staggering as the vessel rolled heavily under the movement of so many men.

Then they set to with a will, with crowbars and hammers and axes. Off came the hatches and men scrambled to investigate the catch. Down below they broke into the captain's cabin, with its books and carpets and images of saints, and they smashed open everything that was locked or shut. Bales of cloth came up from the hold and were cut into festoons of bright colour. The brandy and wine was found, as were hams and fresh eggs.

Then – best of the best and wonder of wonders – great, iron-bound strong boxes were discovered and smashed open to reveal Spanish silver dollars in countless glittering, clinking, shining profusion. Spanish dollars! The famous *Ocho Reales* that passed in circulation throughout the known world as a sovereign standard of currency.

'Dollars!' yelled the mob.

'Pieces of eight!'

'Pieces of eight! Pieces of eight! Pieces of eight!'

They bawled out the words over and over, and ever after it was a talisman and a watchword among them to say it:

'Pieces of eight! Pieces of eight! Pieces of eight!'

Even the parrot learned the words and every last man was brimming with joy. It was an enormous, fabulous treasure, and they were wild with excitement.

But the biggest roar came when some serious axe-work broke open a sealed cabin on the cable tier, where half-a-dozen terrified Spanish women were hidden. One poor creature, believing all she'd been told about pirates, took her own life on the spot with a little pistol kept for this purpose. She fired straight into the centre of her forehead, spattering blood, brains and bone-fragments upon her companions. The rest, shrieking hysterically, were dragged up on deck to a reception of howling, slavering lust.

But Silver found a still-loaded gun and fired into the air. He knocked men down with the butt, and called upon them all to remember the articles they'd signed.

'No woman that ain't willing!' he bawled. 'You've money enough, now, for every whore in the Indies!'

But all he got was an angry, foul-mouthed, spittle-drenched bellowing from a monster denied its meat. Even Long John's leadership had its limits, and he had now gone beyond them.

'Bugger you, John!' they cried. 'Haul off, you bastard, before we split you!'

BANG! BANG! Flint fired his own pistols into the air, and loaded with furious speed, and sprang forward and stood beside Long John, between the crew and the women.

'Who shall be first?' cried Flint, and levelled into the mob. 'What no-seaman lubber will stand forward and deny our articles?'

Where Flint led, Billy Bones followed, and the three most feared men of *Walrus*'s crew were now standing shoulder to shoulder. Israel Hands hesitated, then crept in beside Long John. And that was the end of the matter.

'Get 'em below and out of sight!' hissed Flint to Billy Bones, who promptly drove the women down the nearest ladder with blows from the flat of his blood-smeared cutlass. It was rough work, but Billy had no Spanish and the women no English. And it was better than repeated violent rape by over one hundred men.

'Now then, lads?' said Silver, turning the subject as hard and fast as he could. 'Who'll lend a hand to get the dollars across to the old *Walrus?*' They growled nastily, still baulked in their lust, and Silver nudged Flint with his elbow, and said in a loud stage-whisper, 'I'd say there's five hundred there for every man of us. What's your tally, Cap'n?'

'At the very least,' said Flint, and stooping forward he snatched a handful of coins from an open chest and flung them at the men. That brought a small cheer and a struggle for the coins, and a merciful shift in the wind of the men's attentions.

'See 'em scrabble, John?' said Flint softly, as the men dived for the chests and fought and bit for the biggest share. They cursed and bellowed and dug. 'Hogs to the trough,' Flint added.

'Aye,' said Silver. 'They lives for the moment, mostly, like all sailormen.' Then he caught Flint's eye and winked. 'Thank'ee, messmate,' he said. 'For a while there, I didn't know who I might count on, but articles is articles.'

'Indeed,' said Flint, shifting uneasily under his gaze.

'Didn't know for sure you was with me,' said

Silver, 'judging from some o' the tales that's told.' Silver looked again at Flint, for some of the details of Flint's past doings were circulating aboard *Walrus* and it was no secret that he'd led a most ghastly and bloody mutiny on his secret island.

'Bah!' said Flint. 'Take no account of tales. I stand by what I sign.'

'Spoken like a man!' said Silver, deciding to judge Flint by his future behaviour – and a thousand leagues from guessing the real truth, which was that Flint's powder was thoroughly damp in this particular respect.

Then Billy Bones came puffing and blowing out through a hatchway. He plunged into the maelstrom of struggling bodies and hauled out two that he thought might be trusted: Tom Allardyce and George Merry. He slammed their heads together to gain their attention, poured fearful threats into their ears, and sent them below with two brace of pistols each, and a powder horn and a bag of bullets. Then he fought through the press to Silver and Flint.

'All secured, Cap'n!' he said to Flint and touched his hat. 'I put the tarts all back in their hole, along with the dead 'un, and them two lubbers to guard 'em.' He jerked his thumb to where Allardyce and Merry had gone below.

'Can you trust them?' said Flint, and Billy Bones smiled – a sight as rarely seen as a polar bear coming ashore at Portsmouth with a penguin lugging his sea-chest.

'Aye, Cap'n!' said Billy Bones. 'They'll be good, for I told 'em what I'd do with 'em if they ain't.'

'Good man,' said Flint. 'And now we'll have

some order on the lower deck. They've had their fun...'

'Avast there!' said Silver. 'What about them?' He pointed to the Spanish seamen huddled on the fo'c'sle.

'Huh!' said Flint, grinning. 'Sssssk–' and he drew a finger across his throat.

'No!' said Silver. 'Maroon 'em, or set 'em adrift in a boat with stores an' a sail. That was England's way. But spare the poor buggers' lives.' He looked hard at Flint. 'For we're gentlemen o' fortune, not common pirates.'

'Oh?' said Flint. 'And what, pray, is the difference?'

'That is,' said Silver.

'Oh?' said Flint.

'Aye,' said Silver.

Flint sighed. He bit his lip. He looked about him, and he reached up and stroked the parrot that, as ever, had settled back on his shoulder once the killing stopped. He paused and thought ... and finally he came into harbour and dropped anchor in the recognition that Silver was wholeheartedly sincere in his determination to live by his precious articles. It was one more reluctant step towards the invisible frontier that might make a better man of Flint.

Nonetheless, Flint was clever enough to realise that, in calling himself a gentleman of fortune, Silver was trying to deny what he had become. So thought Joseph Flint, and he thought this ridiculous. But he liked Silver more than any man he'd ever met ... he who'd never had such a thing as a friend.

'Have it your own way,' he said finally, looking over the ship from stem to stern. 'In any case, this ship's too big for our sort of buyer. They want smaller and more handy craft. For myself, I'd have burned her. But this is what we'll do...'

He paused and fished for words. 'As gentlemen of fortune, and jolly companions all–' Long John quietly nodded '–we'll strip this ship of whatever we want, and then...' he shrugged his shoulders '...why, we'll let them sail away and take their blasted females with them.' He turned and looked to Silver for approval, an incredible act for Joe Flint. 'What say you, Long John?'

'Aye-aye, Cap'n,' said Silver with a smile and with immense relief, for he would think well of Flint, if only he could. 'That'd be the way, Cap'n, and no mistake.'

So *Walrus*'s men cleared *Doña Inez* of everything that glittered or shone, and helped themselves to everything they fancied in the way of drink and victuals. Israel Hands took some extra powder and a splendid nine-pounder for a bow-chaser: a brand-new iron gun from the Spanish Royal Foundry at Barcelona, complete with a supply of shot to go with it. The cooper wanted some water butts, which he thought held water sweeter than those in *Walrus's* ground tier, but he was to be disappointed. The men were already tired hauling Israel's gun aboard and they weren't going to raise sweat for mere water. The cooper complained to Flint, but merely got cursed. Flint had pushed the men as far as he dared today, and in a cause he didn't believe in.

As the sun went down over the Caribbean

islands under the horizon, *Walrus* sailed away and left the Spaniards to mend their wounds, to bend a new suit of sails to the jury-rigged masts, and thank the Blessed Virgin for their lives.

They buried their dead too, including the poor creature who'd blown out her brains in a needless sacrifice to her chastity. Conversely, aboard *Walrus* all was plum duff and merriment, with healths drunk, the fiddler playing, and messes competing to dance under the stars. Flint had found a friend, and thought he'd only temporarily compromised in these absurd matters of how prisoners should be treated. John Silver, too, had found a friend, and thought he'd shown him how to steer a better course from now on.

The friendship, at least, was true. Each man found a vital something in the other that was absent from himself. Together they were stronger than ever they had been apart, and the result was the celebrated career of Captain Joseph Flint – Flint the *pirate*, for the world saw through such dissembling words as *gentleman of fortune*.

The most remarkable thing is that so few people ever knew that Captain Flint the pirate was not one man at all, but a symbiotic partnership between two, and the phenomenal success of Captain Flint lasted only as long as the partnership endured.

Chapter 18

14th June 1749
Elizabeth's *longboat*
The South Atlantic

'That's the last of the rum, sir,' said the boatswain. 'Just enough for one tot. And there ain't a great deal left in the water-butt neither. You'll have to talk to the men, sir.'

Hastings and Povey were clustered secretively round the empty rum cask, with Oliver, the boatswain – he of the kicked fingers – while the three marines, as ever, faced forward on the aftermost thwart, to divide the officers' stern from the men's foremast.

It was very, very hot, and all aboard were tired, thirsty and afraid. Eyes squinted against the glare. Lips were cracked and dry. The skin lay like brown paper on the backs of men's hands, and – worse still – there was almost no wind. They were as near becalmed as made no difference with the sails hanging useless and the rudder unable to bite.

'What will you tell 'em, Hastings?' said Povey.

'Better make it something good, sir,' said Oliver.

Hastings fiddled nervously with a piece of flaked skin on his lower lip, daring himself to peel it off. He blinked and thought, and whispered to Oliver.

'How much water have we left?'

'Dunno, sir,' said Oliver. 'I don't dare fathom it,

sir, for it lays forrard among the hands, and they'll see.'

Hastings sighed. He stood, raised a hand to shade his eyes, and looked at the men. They weren't fierce any more. They sat listless and quiet. They were giving up. That was bad. Once they gave up, they'd start dying. Hastings sighed and sat down and reached for his log. It was a little Bible that his mother had given him in which he kept a record of the long-boat's progress by scribbling in the margins with a bit of old pencil. He studied it briefly.

'Ah!' he said. 'It's Sunday.'

'Is it?' said Povey.

'Probably,' said Hastings. 'I don't know.' He turned to Oliver: 'Mr Boatswain, will you call the hands together for church.'

'Aye-aye, sir!'

'Right, Povey, this is what I'm going to do, so be ready with the rum...'

Aboard ship, 'church' meant all hands dressed in best rig and everything ready for captain's inspection. Under the circumstances, those aboard the longboat did their best. They tidied themselves and the boat, and the two midshipmen put on their uniform coats.

'Off hats!' said Hastings, when finally he stood up before them, 'We will say the Lord's Prayer.' And so they did, the familiar prayer profoundly moving some of the hands, who mumbled the words in thoughts of home and happier days, their faces wrenched with emotion. That done, Hastings asked the Almighty to send them a wind and bring them safe to Georgetown Barbados, or at least the French Antilles, and not to throw them into the pitiless hands of Spain.

'Amen!' said the hands fervently.

'Now then, men,' he said, 'we've had a run of bad luck, which was clearly due to our not giving a name to this ship.'

'Oh?' they said.

'Therefore we shall give her a name, so she can be proud of herself.'

'It's his mother's name,' said Povey, standing, 'which is a damn fine thing, because she's the most tremendous beauty. I know because I've seen her!'

'Ah,' they said, nodding to each other.

'Thank you, Mr Povey, you may sit down,' said Hastings, and turned to the crew. 'We shall name her with a *libation*.'

'What's that?'

'It's a gift of wine – or rather rum.'

Povey handed Hastings a small horn cup which contained the last rum in the boat.

'We shall give this libation to the ship and to the sea, so that it will bless her and bring us luck!'

'AYE!' said the men, touched to the core of their primitive souls. They nodded to one another, in uttermost, fervent approval. It was a sacrifice, and a worthy one.

Hastings turned and poured the rum carefully over the boat's bow.

'I name this ship *Constance*, and may God bless her and all who sail in her!'

And perhaps He did, for they got a good north-easterly wind within an hour of offering Him the rum.

Chapter 19

15th June 1752
Aboard Walrus
The South Atlantic

Selena was coming to terms with a very cruel truth. Deep in thought, and idle as ever aboard *Walrus*, she was on the quarterdeck with Flint and Billy Bones below, while Silver spoke to the helmsman, Tom Allardyce.

When the watch changed, another man took over the helm and Allardyce went below. The new man was not a crony of Silver's and Silver looked around for someone to talk to. He saw Selena and smiled. She'd noticed him looking at her before, and she could see he was trying to make up for what he'd done in Savannah. She was very bored, by then, with nobody for company other than the ship's boys, and they were beginning to snigger and take liberties. As for Flint, he showed less interest in her these days than he did in his parrot. He seemed to have got what he wanted from her, without ever touching her.

And beyond that, like any human creature, she was missing her parents and her brothers and sisters, and she was trying to face up to the fact that she would never see any of them again. Not in this life. Not in this world. Not when plantation slaves could not leave the plantation; and not when a sure and certain hanging awaited her if ever she should return.

As long as she'd lived ashore, even in Savannah, she'd managed not to face the truth, but life at sea had changed everything, so strange and wonderful as it was, and so utterly far from home as it had carried her. Now she was struggling to remember their faces, especially the little ones – the dearest of all – with their young, unformed features that she could no longer picture in her mind.

In the depths of her loneliness, she looked at John Silver's broad shoulders and his intelligent eyes and judged him as if at first meeting. She smiled, offhand and casual, and saw the pleasure in his face; and Providence was kind to her, for she instantly discovered the ancient and fascinating sport that God has made for all the women of the ages in offering enough bait to lure a man forward for closer inspection, while giving not much away. It was a game she'd never have had the chance to play on the Delacroix Plantation. There, she was just cattle to be worked and bred from, while on board *Walrus* she enjoyed all the privileges of a free-born woman, and one with powerful backers.

But the ancient game worked both ways. Silver proved to be charming and amusing company, with a store of tales to tell about strange places and strange things that he'd seen.

'Chinamen, ma'am, with fingernails so long, they bend like the bones in a lady's stays.' She smiled, remembering the wonderful gowns that Miss Eugenie wore, and all their complex underpinnings.

'Monkeys, ma'am? Have I seen monkeys? Why,

baboons is the king o' monkeys. I've seen baboons out of Africa, with jaws like mastiffs, and arses – begging your pardon, ma'am – striped blue and red and all the colours o' the rainbow!'

She laughed to show she wasn't such a fool as to believe this nonsense.

'And great snakes called pythons, in the East Indies, that can swallow a whole hog...' he winked and grew so familiar as to jab her gently in the ribs with a finger '... or a plump little thing like yourself, if he could just clap a hold on you.' She could see that it wasn't just the python that would like to clap a hold on her, given the chance. So she frowned to put him back in his place.

But she carried on talking to Silver. She did it often after that, and found that it infuriated Flint. Perhaps she even did it *because* it infuriated Flint. It was exciting, and she was too young to realise how dangerous it was. Flint reacted by devoting more time to her. He got Mad Pew, the sailmaker, to sew her a dress from ship's stores. Since Pew had never done the like before, and hadn't the least idea how to go about it, the result was not a specially fine dress. But it was a dress, and Flint made her wear it for dinner. Then he had his cook prepare special meals and made his officers turn out to dine with her in their best clothes and on their best behaviour. They were a rough lot aside from Mr Cowdray, who'd once been a surgeon in London, and Mr Smith the third mate, whom the men called 'Parson'.

Selena didn't much care for Parson Smith, because he stared at her breasts with his mouth hanging open whenever he thought nobody was looking, and he had fat, pink little fingers with disgustingly bitten nails. He was clearly ashamed of whatever it was that had driven him from England, and he wouldn't be drawn to talk about it. But Mr Cowdray was much better. He was clever and friendly. He had lived in the great world among ladies and gentlemen. He'd seen the King and Queen and he'd been to the Opera House. In fact, Selena liked him so much, and was so fascinated by his stories about the clothes and hairstyles worn by London ladies, that Flint never asked him to dinner again. And Silver was never asked at all.

From time to time, Selena would be sent deep down below to hide among the coiled mass of the anchor cable. This was when *Walrus* pounced on a ship that the pirates wanted to rob. The hideous noise of the guns, firing over her head, and the stench of powder smoke were so bad that she begged Flint to let her stay on deck at these times. But on this, he was as immovable as a mountain.

'No, my little flower,' he would say, firmly shaking his head. 'It isn't just what would happen should you get in the way of a shot, it's the things you might see.'

And all the while, the poison between Flint and Long John grew worse. There were arguments over everything. They quarrelled over the set of the sails: Silver always wanting less for safety, Flint always wanting more for speed. They quarrelled over swabbing below decks: Silver against, for the damp it caused, Flint in favour for the greater cleanliness. They quarrelled over watering the grog, over setting the watches, over gun-drill, musket-drill, and what to do with prisoners.

Flint always wanted them butchered, Silver always wanted them marooned or set adrift.

But the greatest quarrel was over Flint's wish to bury the wealth that was accumulating below decks, not only from coin and bar silver taken directly from captured ships, but from Charley Neal's payments for jewellery and prizes sailed into Savannah.

Selena felt that this latter argument was different. She didn't begin to understand the bickering and shouting over *ship things,* as she called them – swabbing, gun-drill and the like – for these at least got settled one way or the other, and the arguments stopped. But there was no decision on burying the goods, and the arguments got worse.

Finally one night there was a serious quarrel, even though it wasn't about the burying but a different matter entirely. Long John, Flint, Billy Bones and some of the other officers – every man of the crew who was consulted on important matters – were in Flint's cabin. Selena, of course, was not among them, but she heard the angry shouts right enough. Everyone did, and they listened with giant ears to the noise coming up from below.

'Damned if I'll turn for Savannah!' cried Flint.

'An' damned if you don't!' cried Silver. 'We've beat about and quartered the ocean hereabouts for far too long. Every shipmaster for a hundred leagues knows Flint's about, so it's time for Flint to be gone.'

'Who's cap'n here?' came another voice, that of Billy Bones. He had the loudest voice in the ship and every word came up as clear as if he was standing on the quarterdeck.

'Shut your trap, Billy!' said Silver.

'An' who's to make me?'

'Shut it, Billy,' said Silver. 'I say that one more prize is one too many. The next one might be a man-o'-war out looking for us.'

'Yellow-livered bugger!' came Billy Bones's roar.

At this there was an explosion of anger from below, followed by a rumble and a breaking of furniture, and all the unmistakable sounds of a fight. There was even the bark of a pistol, and the grunts of men giving and taking heavy blows. The eyes and mouths of those on deck grew rounder and rounder as the whole crew came astern, dim figures in the dark, to hear what was going on in Flint's cabin. For the few minutes the fight lasted, there was no proper lookout kept, nor attention to the helm, nor to any other thing that interfered with listening.

Soon the sounds of combat ceased and the crowd dispersed rapidly as Flint and Silver came on deck. They were not on speaking terms and took opposite sides of the deck, glowering into the night and exchanging curt words with a few favoured ones who congregated around them, staring angrily at the other group.

They were followed a while later by Mr Billy Bones: he who'd defeated the foremost pugilist in the Americas. Billy Bones moved unsteadily, hanging on to hand-holds like a drunken man. He violently kicked the backside of the first man he passed, damned his mother as a poxy whore, and told him to haul up a bucket of water. Billy Bones knelt down and plunged his head into this, and washed the blood off his face, and groaned and fingered his bruises. He kept darting nervous glances at Silver and muttering to himself. The crew whistled and drew their conclusions.

But if Silver had won the fight, he lost the argument. *Walrus* did not return to Savannah. Flint had his way. He would not listen to Silver's warnings as he would have done in the past. He would not listen because there now stood between the two men a prickly hedge of mistrust and anger. This was a great pity. It was a very great pity indeed. In fact it is barely possible to put into words how great a pity it was – especially and tragically for Long John Silver – because Silver had been absolutely right and Flint had been wrong.

Chapter 20

21st June 1752
Aboard John Donald Smith
The Caribbean

Mr Eustace Crane, captain and part-owner of the West Indiaman *John Donald Smith* raised his cutlass in a trembling hand and squinted against the fierce sun as he judged the distance. His ship thrashed along with every stitch set and the wind humming in her taut rigging. There wasn't another knot to be got out of her, while the pursuing enemy was coming on like a race horse.

Captain Crane was sick with fear and the blade of his cutlass shook, for he knew about the pirate,

Flint. Indeed, every man, woman and child in the Caribbean knew about Flint. In particular, they knew that any man daring to make a fight of it got sliced like pork. But Crane feared ruin even more, and he feared the pitying contempt of those more fortunate than himself, and he balanced the hideous images of death and mutilation with thoughts of his family in Bristol, turned out of doors by the bailiffs and cast upon the parish as paupers.

And now, Flint's ship was no more than a pistol-shot astern, with the sea boiling under her bows and her wake twining and joining with *John Donald's*. There never had been the least possibility that *John Donald* could outrun Flint's own darling *Walrus*, for the latter – a rake-masted Yankee topsail schooner – was built purely for speed, while the West Indiaman was a fat, cargo-carrying box, with masts and sails added as an afterthought.

And once *Walrus* got alongside, then God help a poor sailorman, for Crane had counted her fourteen guns and he could see at least a hundred armed men crammed on board of her. He stared at them in horror, where they jostled merrily for place as they prepared to board. The speeding schooner was heeled far over, dipping gunnel-under with the weight of bodies crammed along the rail, and white water surged thigh-deep among them. They cussed and swore, and they laughed at the wetting and the sight of Crane and his wobbling cutlass, for not another man Jack was to be seen aboard *John Donald Smith*.

Flint himself leapt into *Walrus*'s main shrouds and called out to his crew: Long John, Billy Bones, Mad Pew, Black Dog, George Merry,

Israel Hands, and all the others. The wretched Crane heard every word.

'Look at them, the sons of bitches!' he cried, pointing to *John Donald*. 'They never dared fire a gun, and now they've run below, shitting their shirt-tails as they burrow in the ballast to hide!' A roar of laughter came from his crew, and they nudged one another and thought their captain no end of a wit.

But Flint had made a nasty mistake. *John Donald*'s decks looked empty only because her people were laid between their guns, behind musket-proof screens of junk and anchor cable that had been raised above her bulwarks. Flint should have spotted that, for it was man-o'-war fashion to build barricadoes. It took time and effort and interfered with the smooth running of a ship. It was not a thing to do without a purpose.

In that instant, down came Captain Crane's arm, and five gun captains jumped up and applied glowing matches to a battery of six-pounders. There followed some long seconds as priming powder smoked and fizzed into life and hot flame darted into the thickness of the iron breeches.

There was surprise and anger among Flint's men. The stupid, like Tom Morgan and George Merry, pointed out what was happening and roared in outrage as if at some piece of broken faith. The clever, like Flint and Long John, dropped smartly on to *Walrus*'s canted deck and grovelled into the planking, trying to squeeze themselves into the seams alongside the caulking.

With a thunderclap bellow, a gout of flame and a vast jet of white smoke, the first gun went off.

Three of its fellows joined in, pizzicato, and the fifth fired three seconds later. The guns were expertly laid: chocked up high at the breech, to play downwards upon the open decks of a ship closing upon her weather beam. Crane had served King George in his youth. He'd fought Frog, Dago and Dutchman, and he knew his business well.

In all five guns the load was 'langridge': shards of iron, old bolts, bent nails, lengths of chain, musket balls – whatever came to hand – and every last scrap of it that could be crammed down the barrels without bursting the guns. Such a broadside was useless at any but the closest range, for it was entirely without accuracy and would scatter and lose its capacity to kill. But Crane was well aware of that, which was why he'd waited until his paint was all but rubbing up against Flint's.

Consequently, well over half a hundredweight of jagged fragments tore into Flint's boarding party, and cut like a thousand lancets. They took off fingers, thumbs, buttocks, faces, knees, elbows and limbs. They threw men down, they opened them up, they blinded, castrated and disembowelled. They ripped out livers and kidneys, lights and pipes, and spewed them hot and slimy on the deck. Thirty men were struck dead on the spot and fifty wounded. The remaining sixty-five whole and untouched men stood wavering in the smoke-reeking slaughterhouse of *Walrus*'s waist, up to their ankles in the wet meat that had recently been their shipmates.

A cheer came from *John Donald Smith* as the smoke cleared and her crew saw the dreadful work done by their fire.

'Muskets, boys!' roared Crane, and showed the way by sheathing his cutlass and seizing a sea-service Brown Bess.

At a range of ten feet, Crane let fly and saw a bloodied figure throw up his arms. Dropping the long gun, Crane hauled out his pistols to empty them at the enemy. Mad with excitement, the *John Donalds* took up their small arms and set to. There were three dozen muskets ready and waiting, plus half a dozen of blunderbusses, and a brace of pistols for every man aboard.

This crackling, battering fire, hard on the heels of the dreadful broadside, knocked the heart out of Flint's men, and all those still able ran below; some beshitting themselves and digging into the pebbles of the ballast, just as their captain had said only a few moments ago.

With the helmsman hauling in his own entrails hand over hand, howling like a broken-backed dog, *Walrus*'s tiller pleased itself where it lay, and the twelve-foot bar slammed and banged to either beam. Finally, with her aftermost sails drawing harder than her foresails, *Walrus* herself decided that she'd bring herself round, bow into the wind, and wallow dead in the eye of it, sails flapping, blocks rattling, and offal, excrement and wounded men slithering across her decks with every roll.

Meanwhile, *John Donald Smith* held her course and ploughed onward at a steady seven knots, a very creditable speed for her which goes to show that Eustace Crane was as good a seaman as he was a gunner – and a desperately poor tradesman. For if Crane hadn't made so many bad guesses, and so many times been deceived, then he'd never have found himself in the position whereby his all and everything was risked in this one voyage. And in that case, he'd never have laid in extra guns and powder, and spent time drilling his crew and making ready for a fight. And in that case he'd have given up the ship to Flint, as so many sensible men had done before him, in order to keep a whole skin and live another day.

Instead, Eustace Crane and the ship of which he was part owner sailed onward and eastward, and in due course dropped anchor in Bristol, and turned a most excellent profit on her voyage.

Afterwards, for the rest of his life, it was Crane's pleasure, whenever he was in congenial company with his back to a good fire and the rum-punch going round, to tell the tale of how he'd driven off that bugger Flint and ruined half his villainous crew. It was the strict truth, and Crane had every right to be proud of it. But even his best friends never really believed him.

Chapter 21

21st June 1752
Aboard Walrus
The Caribbean

Smoke and flame filled the waist as *Walrus* received *John Donald*'s fire. Laid flat on his face, Long John Silver was kicked sideways by a terrific blow as men and wreckage fell all around him. He couldn't see the length of his own arm for the smoke, and for the moment he was deaf from the massive concussion of five cannon less than a dozen yards from his head. But he could still smell: and a hot stench of burned meat and hair filled his nostrils.

He tried to sit up, shoving at the weight pressing him down. The weight – and the smell – was Mad Pew the Welshman, who lay across Long John, mouthing in his mother tongue, and scorched from brow to breast by muzzle-flash. The face was black, the hair was gone, the eyes were white and blank. Mad Pew was now *blind* Pew.

Long John heaved Pew clear and tried to leap to his feet. He couldn't. Something was wrong. Then the smoke cleared and Long John gaped in dismay. His left leg was hideously mangled between hip and knee. The great bone of the thigh gleamed in the depths of the wound, blood sprayed outward, and the remnant of the leg hung by ragged straps of skin and meat.

Flint's face appeared, peering and prying.

'Why, John,' he said, 'they've limbed you!' He grinned wickedly. 'So who's the better man, now, I wonder?' Long John still couldn't hear properly, but he read Flint's lips and he saw that Flint was smooth and unharmed. Not a hair nor fingernail disturbed.

'Bastard!' said Long John, and reached for the long pistol in his belt. But the ship rolled, the mainsail boom swung viciously across the waist, wreckage groaned, and Blind Pew shrieked and fell over Long John's arm.

'Later, John,' promised Flint, as Billy Bones

came up and hauled Flint to his feet.

'Fucking ship's in fucking irons, Cap'n,' said Bones. 'And the fucking crew is run below like a fucking shoal o' fucking washerwomen!'

'Billy-my-chicken!' said Flint. 'Ah, Billy, my Billy! What poets are Pope and Milton compared with thee?'

'Fuck that, Cap'n – beggin'-yer-pardon!' said Bones. 'But look at the fucking state of her. Look at the men–'

'Bah!' said Flint. 'They'll not fight again this day. We'll be lucky to keep them off the rum.' He lurched forward. 'Follow me, Billy-boy, and we'll go below.'

The two vanished down a hatchway, and soon there came the distant sound of pistol shots and clashing steel as Captain Flint and Mr Bones explained to the men that spirits were not to be issued until the ship was put to rights.

Meanwhile, on deck, the wounded threw back their heads and howled to the world for help. The world ignored them, but someone else did not. Selena came up from below and picked her way through the wreckage, eyes bulging at the awful things that slopped and slithered about her feet. She went from man to man, peering into their faces.

'Long John? Long John?' she said.

'Here!' cried a voice from a heap of dead flesh jammed between two guns. 'Selena!'

She darted forward, pulled him clear, and gasped as he screamed in agony.

'Oh my Lord!' said Selena, looking at his wound. 'We've got to get you below. The surgeon's got everything rigged and ready.'

'No,' said Long John. 'Not that!' And he clung to her legs, grey-faced in terror. 'You won't let that blasted sawbones take my leg, now, will you? Not you. Not that.'

'Huh!' she said. 'Never seen you afraid of nothing before.'

But Long John was in terror to the bottom of his soul, and as best he could he cursed, shrieked and fought every inch of the way, while Selena single-handedly dragged and hauled his deadweight down below to the surgeon.

'You'll die, if I don't,' was all she said.

'Ah, Mr Silver,' said Mr Thomas Cowdray in his bloodstained leather apron and rolled-up sleeves. 'I'd thought better of you: *aut vincere, aut mori:* either conquer or die.' He shook his head. 'I see that you have done neither!'

Mr Cowdray had once been an educated gentleman, and still was an excellent surgeon: quick, adept and intelligent, and nothing like the rumsozzlers usually to be found afloat. He'd once practised at St Bartholomew's Hospital in London, and there his brother surgeons had mocked him for his insistence on cleanliness, and on boiling his surgical instruments in a cauldron of water before use. Cowdray had claimed this to be a sovereign remedy against post-operative rotting of wounds, but when it was discovered that he'd learned it from a gypsy sow-gelder, he was laughed out of the hospital. His learned colleagues might have forgiven him the source of his methods, but they could never – *never* – forgive him the superior results that he achieved with them.

His subsequent career – via gin, gambling, and relieving ladies caught pregnant without husbands – had taken Mr Cowdray away from England and to the West Indies, and so by easy stages to privateering, piracy, and finally to his current post as surgeon to Captain Flint.

Cowdray frowned as he saw the extent of Long John's injuries. He looked at the other wounded, made a judgement, and turned to his assistant, a mulatto named Jobo, chosen for strength, who also served as cook's mate.

'Silver next,' said the surgeon, and a wild roar came from Long John, who did his best to climb out of the hold unaided. 'Some of you lay hands on him and bring him here,' said Cowdray.

Selena, Jobo and one or two of the other less-badly wounded, grappled with Long John and got him on to Cowdray's table. They cut off his breeches at Cowdray's command, and Jobo slipped on a tourniquet and twisted till the bleeding stopped.

'You!' said Cowdray to Selena. 'Take the broken leg and hold it out straight,' She hesitated. 'Go on, girl!' barked Cowdray. 'Pick it up! It won't bite!' And he turned to the rest: '*You* – get up behind him on the table and wrap your arms round his chest. *You* – hold his good leg. And, *you* – hold his arms.'

Cowdray reached for a sickle-shaped amputation knife, razor-edged on the inside.

'Rum!' cried Long John. 'Rum, for the love of God.'

'Later,' said Cowdray, and dropped to his knees, facing Long John. He slipped his arm under the injured leg, which Jobo raised to receive him. He bent his elbow back around the limb so the curved knife sat beneath the thigh, tickling the taut skin. He set his teeth and he pulled with all his strength.

Long John howled like a damned soul as the knife cut skin, fat, muscle, tendon, nerve and blood vessel in one almighty slicing cut, right down to the bone. Cowdray leapt up, laid aside the big knife and swiftly ran a lancet around the bone, severing any remaining shreds of tissue.

'Jobo,' he said, 'stump!' And Jobo slid a pair of leather straps into the wound, and hauled on them, squeezing the red flesh towards the hip to expose an inch more of the bone.

Cowdray pounced with a fine-toothed saw and went through the femur in six sharp strokes, leaving Selena holding a severed leg: limp, heavy and dead. The vivid reality of its final separation from the living man caused her to drop the horrid thing and stagger back with her head spinning sickly. She was at – and past – her limits. She hurried away, groping for ladders, in search of fresh air.

Barely noticing her absence, Jobo kicked the dead leg aside and let loose his straps so the flesh swelled forward, burying the cut end of bone so it couldn't stick out of the stump when it healed.

'Slacken off!' said Cowdray, and Jobo let the tightness out of his tourniquet till little jets of blood revealed where the arteries lay. Cowdray caught each one with a long-handled hook, pulled it out and tied it off, leaving long threads trailing after the knots. Then off came the tourniquet and the operation was complete. It had taken less than two minutes, and Silver was still bellowing lustily, while aside from Cowdray and Jobo, every creature present was yellow in the face and sweating heavily.

But Cowdray wasn't quite done. He dressed the wound carefully with lint and linen, and finally added a woollen cap – like a short, fat stocking – to finish the job.

'Next man!' said Cowdray, and Jobo lifted Long John off the table and laid him alongside the others that Mr Cowdray was done with.

'Give him a pull of the rum, Jobo,' said Cowdray, glancing down.

But Long John had to wait, for down the ladders there came a second rush of wounded, bumping and howling and bleeding.

These were not victims of *John Donald*'s artillery but of their own captain and first mate, who'd passed among the surly survivors and reasoned with them after Flint's style until *Walrus*'s crew returned to their duties and the dead and the offal were heaved over the side, and repairs were made, and lines were spliced, and the decks were swabbed till no stains were left. Soon *Walrus* was sailing like a lamb, and all was jump-to-it discipline and jolly fellowship once more, since any man who chose not to be jolly was beaten senseless by Mr Billy Bones.

And all the while, Long John was left to bawl to his heart's content, and nobody paid him the least attention – not with a dozen more doing the same all around him, and a merry little company they made. All it needed was the Devil to join them, scraping his fiddle and beating time with his hoof, and all hands would have known themselves already transported to that very place which was their ultimate destination.

Hours later, delirious and hot, and with the raw stump swollen and hammering, Long John felt a bottle pressed into his hands. Exhausted as he was, he instantly tried to scream – for every touch was agony – but all that came was a harsh gasp. The rum helped a lot. It took away some of the pain, and what was left was blunted at the edges. Finally, after most of a pint had gone down, it brought unconsciousness.

After that, as far as Long John Silver was concerned, the river of time ran strange and dark: it fled the light, it went deep underground and it went round crooked ways. This was something to do with the rum and the laudanum that Mr Cowdray put in it, and it was something to do with a strong man's pride revolting at the thought of becoming a cripple. But mainly it was the natural consequence of a dreadful injury. At least the stump stayed clean and did not putrefy, otherwise Long John would have died for sure. The ignorant may have laughed at Mr Cowdray's boiling of his instruments, but it drove off the little demons that killed more men than hot lead or cold steel.

For a long and indeterminate time, there was only confusion and pain. Then there was simply confusion, and then there was the first small clearing of the fog, which was an awareness of being out of the stinking hold, in a hammock slung under the fo'c'sle. There were wind-sails rigged to bring fresh air from above decks, and there was the sound of voices. One voice was Selena's, the other was Cowdray's. Long John couldn't move or speak, but he could listen.

'Why not?' she said.

'The amputation is too high.'

'So how can he walk?'

'With a crutch.'

'What?' The voice was angry, 'What? That's no good. No good at all! What sort of a doctor are you? A horse-doctor?'

'God damn you girl! Look here...' And Long John felt them right beside him, laying hands on his bandages. He stirred, trying to let them know he was listening, but the movement was too slight.

'See?' said Cowdray. 'The stump ends not twelve inches from the iliac crest. A peg-leg's no use on that. Perhaps in London or Paris something might be done: a false limb, sculpted, and jointed with springs at the knee and ankle, and secured with a harness. But not out here, beyond Christian civilisation. There are not the tools nor the craftsmen.' Cowdray shrugged. 'He'll have to go on a crutch.'

'Huh!' said Selena. 'Long John's no man for that. He'd rather die!' she sneered. 'You no-account, useless butcher!'

'Hold your tongue, madam!' cried Cowdray, stung to anger. 'He either goes on a crutch or on his belly. Long John Silver is become a one-legged man, and he must make the best of it.'

Chapter 22

30th June 1749
Elizabeth's *longboat*
The South Atlantic

'Ship,' said Hastings, or at least he tried to. On half a pint of water, per day, per man under a scorching tropical sun, it became hard to speak. He reached out a weary hand and pushed at Povey until the other woke. 'Ship,' he mouthed, and pointed. It was so hard to concentrate. It was all he could do to hold the rudder and steer, as the boat plunged onward under a steady blow.

Povey raised his head and blinked dry eyes at the heaving waves.

'Ship!' said Povey. He saw it. He saw topsails and main-sails. It was a ship.

'Corporal, Mr Boatswain,' croaked Hastings, 'rouse the hands!'

But nobody moved. Not properly. Bennet, the acting-corporal, managed to turn his head and at least tried to get up. But that was all. Every man aboard was roasted and feeble, and crumpled in the bottom of the boat, half-conscious and slowly dying. They looked more like the dead of a battlefield than living men.

'Smoke,' said Povey.

When the men still had their strength, Hastings and Povey had set them various tasks, mainly to keep up their spirits. One of these was the construction of a smoke beacon: a wooden bailing bucket filled with sun-dried, unpicked cable mixed with flakes of tar and wood shavings, rigged to be set alight and hoisted up a spar as a signal to any ships they might encounter.

'Here, Povey ... take the tiller,' said Hastings.

'Aye-aye, sir.'

Hastings crawled towards the bow and the smoke beacon. It was slow, hard going, over the barely moving bodies of moribund men. They moaned and cursed, and some clutched at him and had to be shaken off. He'd got halfway before he realised he was wasting his time, and turned back weeping in frustration.

'What is it?' said Povey as Hastings fought his way back and tried to shake Corporal Bennet awake.

'Go way!' said Bennet.

'What is it?' said Povey again.

'Tinder box,' said Hastings. 'Bennet's got it. Dunno where.'

Hastings searched the big limp form without success.

'Where is it? Where is it?' said Hastings.

'Give him a drink!' said Povey. 'Wake him!' With enormous difficulty, Hastings did so. Struggling to the near-empty water butt, lowering the dipper through the bung-hole, filling a cup and contriving to return without spilling it.

But someone saw him do it.

'Here!' said an angry voice. 'Ain't time for water-rations.'

'Wot?' said another.

'Pinchin' the soddin' water, they are!'
'Bastards!'
The dead began to wake. And they woke angry.
'Here!' said Hastings, pouring water into Bennet's mouth.
Bennet's hands came up to the cup and his eyes opened.
'Why's *he* gettin' a bleedin' drink?'
'Bloody lobster!'
'Corporal Bennet,' said Hastings, 'look – a ship! Where's the tinder box? We have to light the beacon!'
'Ship?' cried the living dead. 'Where?'
'There, you idle lubbers!' cried Hastings and pointed to it.
'We're saved! We're saved!'
'Here it is, sir,' said Bennet, hauling his tinder-box out from the depths of his breeches.
'Quick, man!'
Corporal Bennet did his best. He crawled forward – now with ready hands helping him on his way – while those who could were sitting up waving their shirts and raising a thin shout. There wasn't a man aboard capable of standing up on his legs.
'Can't open the bugger,' Bennet sobbed, his weakened fingers fumbling with the lid of the tinder box as he sat.
'Oh Jesus,' cried Povey, 'she hasn't seen us! We'll lose her.'
A groan went up from the longboat as the distant ship ploughed onward with no sign of having spotted them.
'Give me that!' said Hastings, snatching at the

tinder-box. 'I'll do it!'

'No!' said Bennet, determined to complete his task.

'She's passin' us by! She's leavin' us!'

Bennet heaved afresh at the box, which sprung suddenly open, scattering its contents over the bottom of the boat – except for the vital piece of flint, which went over the side with a tiny splash.

'AHHHH!' said Bennet as salvation sank into the depths.

'No!' gasped Hastings. 'Who's got a tinder-box? Who's got a flint? Search, you buggers! Search!'

There was a desperate moaning and muttering and a clumsy fumbling as the men did their utmost to find that which wasn't there.

'Hasn't anybody got one?' said Hastings, 'Not even you bloody marines? Ain't you all supposed to carry spare flints?'

'Oh!' said one of the marines, his dulled mind clearing. He dipped into a pocket. 'Here you are, sir,' he said, and held up a big square musket flint.

'Pass it here!' screamed Hastings, and hand-to-hand the flint sped back to Corporal Bennet, who was busy retrieving steel and tinder and a stump of candle from the bottom of the boat.

Then, hands trembling, Bennet struck steel and flint together, shed sparks on tinder, raised a red glow, blew it into a flame, lit the candle and dropped it into the beacon and ran the beacon up its spar. Soon, white smoke was streaming on the wind and the boat was dry, croaking cheers from stem to stern.

'She's seen us!' cried Povey. 'Look, she's coming about!'

The cheers redoubled and then died. The ship was most definitely coming towards them, but she was flying the banner of Spain.

Chapter 23

25th June 1752
Aboard Walrus
The South Caribbean

It was night. *Walrus* was plunging and twisting in heavy seas. Sharp-bowed as she was, she was a wet ship in a blow and the fo'c'sle was battened down tight.

Jobo had lashed the wounded into their hammocks and Long John swayed and swung with the others. He was boiling hot and delirious. The wound throbbed and burned, and worse than that he was tormented by the knowledge he was now a cripple. He groaned and wept and prayed to the God he'd long since abandoned. He begged for his leg to come back. He cringed and sobbed and implored the maker of the universe to make him whole again, and not turn him into a pitiful one-legged ruin.

And when he couldn't get that, he begged for death. He yelled and swore and called out for an end to it all. He'd have done it himself, there and then, if only he'd had a loaded pistol. So he called out to them all to bring him one. He called to Jobo, and Israel Hands and to Selena. Nobody came, except in his mind. And so he dreamed of Selena. His sanity was hanging by a thread at that moment, but he had just enough wit left, and enough humour too, to cackle with laughter when the desire stirred within him as it always did when he thought of her.

'Well, John Silver,' he said, 'there's still one limb sound out of the three.' And he thought of the first he'd learned of her, even before he'd met her. He thought of a bill posted on a wall in Charleston harbour, South Carolina:

WANTED FOR MURDER

A reward of *fifty guineas* in gold

Will be paid by **Mr Archibald Delacroix**,
for the person, delivered into his hands,
at the Delacroix Plantation, near Camden of

A YOUNG NEGRESS: SELENA

No brand marks,
Sixteen years of age, slim built, five feet three inches tall,
Fine hair, good figure, pleasing countenance, white teeth,
Large eyes, small nose, long limbs,

Formerly the property of **Mr Fitzroy Delacroix**
Whom she has most ***foully*** and ***cruelly*** SLAIN

He slept for a while, dreaming of her, and then woke suddenly. Flint was there. Silver could tell by the cackling of the parrot and the uneasy scratching it made as it shifted its claws on the cloth of Flint's coat. He opened his eyes. He tried to force away the dull nausea and weakness. It didn't do to be weak in Flint's company.

'John!' said Flint, in what passed for tones of anxious inquiry. 'How are you, shipmate? Missing the limb?'

Long John fought to remember where he was and what was happening. He looked around. He was under the fo'c'sle, in a hammock. He peered at Flint's blurred figure with the green shape of the bird bobbing and darting its head and nuzzling at Flint's ear.

'John, my dear fellow,' said Flint, ''Tis your old comrade Joe Flint, come to call.' There was a smile on Flint's face and a hard fright gripped Long John as he realised that he was alone with Flint. The other hammocks were gone, their occupants either recovered or dead.

'How long have I been here?' said Long John.

'Long enough, old friend,' said Flint, his big white teeth gleaming in the darkness. Flint could charm the angels when he wanted.

'Jobo,' called Long John, 'fetch the rum, you lazy sod!'

'He's not here, shipmate,' said Flint, leaning over the helpless man. 'I came down specially, my chicken, just to catch a word with you in private.'

'Jobo! Israel! Geor–' Long John's thin shout, barely more than a whisper, was shut off by Flint's right hand.

'Now isn't this pleasant?' said Flint. 'Just two old comrades together. What a shame it can't last.'

Flint produced a knife with a remarkably long and narrow blade. He shifted so his left hand covered Long John's mouth, clamping like a vice, while the right hand took the blade. Carefully Flint positioned the tip of the stiletto inside one of Long John's nostrils, and there came a fluttering and flapping of wings as Flint's parrot took itself off and found its way out of a hatchway.

'There,' said Flint softly, 'I'll do it as quick as possible, shipmate, for old time's sake. But it has to be done, you see, and it has to be done *right*, so that nobody shall know.' He tensed for the strike: the swift thrust, crunching through bone and into Silver's brain, and then a vigorous corkscrew to mangle and mince. It could be done in a second. Silver would hardly feel it ... would he? And in any case, too much had passed. Too much had changed, and there was no room left for sentiment. Flint tensed again. Sweat broke on his brow. He looked at Silver's yellow-white face and his staring eyes. Flint blinked. It *could* be done and *must* be done. For a third time he tensed to strike...

'What are you doing?' screeched a loud and furious voice.

It jolted Flint like a blow. He was proud of his ability to detect those who tried to creep up on him unexpected, and it was galling to be caught out. Perhaps it was because he was so absorbed in his work. But he moved quick enough and the stiletto flickered out of sight.

'Selena, my dear,' he said, without looking round. Long John heard the quick steps and saw her head and shoulders loom above him beside Flint. He saw Flint's big smile and her fury.

'Israel Hands!' she called. 'Come here this instant!'

More footsteps and Israel Hands appeared. Now there were three of them, blurred and swimming in front of him. It was like a play, a performance in which Long John Silver had no part. They were there: Flint who hated him, Selena who he hoped did not, and Israel Hands who'd been drooling at the mouth for Selena these many months past, but didn't dare touch her, and who now did her bidding like a slave.

Selena ignored Flint. There was no reasoning with that one. She spoke to Israel Hands.

'He must be watched night and day,' she said, pulling Flint's hand off Long John's brow, where Flint had quickly placed it to give an appearance of affection and concern.

'Aye-aye, Miss Selena,' said Hands.

'You fix that, do you hear?' she said. 'You and your mates: watch on, and watch off, by the ship's bell, all shipshape and Bristol fashion – d'you hear?'

Selena had never been to Bristol. She didn't even know it was a place, let alone what its *fashion* might be. But she'd been long enough among sailors to learn their language and to bark it out with authority. Flint snorted with laughter at her doing so, but Israel Hands did not. He knuckled his brow and stamped a foot in the lower deck's most formal salute.

'Aye-aye, Miss Selena,' he said.

'Now, get out of here!'

'Aye-aye, Miss Selena,' said Israel Hands, and vanished.

Selena glared at Flint. Flint was considering this interesting turn of events. This was his ship. His to command. And yet it was not. It was his and Long John's. Each had his following. Just as Billy Bones was Flint's man, so Israel Hands was Long John's, and each with about half the ship's company behind him. Thanks to the recent skirmish, there were less of each now, but numbers were still equally divided. Flint cursed behind his gleaming smile and wondered how long it could go on.

He broke off as shouting and laughter came from the quarterdeck. He frowned, cocked an ear and attended for a while. He judged it was merely some horse-play that the men were indulging in. Nothing to worry about. He turned to Selena.

'Bless you, my dear,' he said. 'I'll leave you to minister unto this poor Christian, for I fear the Almighty may have forgotten the bearings of him where he lies at anchor.' He looked down at Long John, 'Isn't that so, my old chicken?' And then he was gone.

Selena leaned close to Long John and took his hand. The hammock swayed.

'What did he do?' she said. 'Are you hurt?'

'No,' said Long John with great effort, delighted at her interest. A little spark of joy twinkled deep inside him, driving away the dark of pain and weakness that was bearing him down.

'Drink...' he said, and she disappeared and came back with a pannikin of water.

'Here,' she said, and raised his head so he could

drink. Then she laid him back and wiped his brow. The lovely ebony face never smiled. It showed no expression at all. She was a hard creature to read. But her actions spoke, and she stayed for a while, standing guard until Israel Hands came back with Cowdray the surgeon and Jobo the surgeon's mate, who was dripping wet and swaying on his feet.

'Ah, Mr Silver,' said Cowdray, 'I rejoice to see you awake.' He blinked guiltily and added, 'I regret that you were left alone. I ordered this wretch to stay with you.' He looked disparagingly at Jobo. 'But it would seem Captain Flint gave him a bottle and a guinea, and told him to get drunk.'

'Aye,' said Israel Hands, 'but we found the bugger, put a bowline under his arms and heaved him over the side on a line to the yardarm, then all hands hauled him up and down and dunked him till he was sober.' He leered at Jobo. 'You're right enough now, ain't you, shipmate?'

'Aye...' said Jobo uncertainly.

'You'd better be!' snapped Selena, 'You,' she said to Israel Hands, 'stay with him. I'm putting you in charge!'

Cowdray's eyes widened, as Flint's had done, to see a black slave-girl giving orders among men, and Long John tried to laugh. But the effort sickened him and he fainted.

When he recovered, only Israel Hands and Jobo were there. They were bickering and yarning and playing dice for each other's share of the loot. Long John looked at them in fright. He doubted if the pair of them together could keep Flint off, should he choose to come back.

Chapter 24

3rd July 1749
Morning
The Governor's Mansion
Puerto España, Trinidad

George Hastings and David Povey sat in the incredibly cool, elegant room and clutched their drinks. Remembering the long thirsty days, Hastings took a swallow. It was some sort of fruit juice, but like no fruit he'd ever tasted. He emptied the goblet and set it on a table.

Don Felipe Avilia Carreño, Governor of Trinidad, caught his eye and smiled. He spoke slowly, carefully, in Spanish, trying to make himself understood.

Instantly Hastings struggled to his feet, and Povey got up beside him, blinking and frowning.

'I'm sorry, sir,' said Hastings, 'it's no good – we can't speak Spanish.'

'No-no-no!' said Don Felipe and rushed forward to help them back into their seats. Though much recovered, they were still very weak. But at least they were clean – their filthy clothes having been removed and laundered while they slept. Even their uniform coats had been carefully brushed and the brass buttons polished.

Don Felipe turned at the sound of quick footsteps from the corridor outside, and doors swung open to admit a lady followed by two maids.

Once again, Hastings and Povey shot to their feet, this time entirely appropriately, for they needed no Spanish to tell them that they were in the presence of a great lady.

As Doña Alicia Maria O'Donnell de Avilia Carreño entered, doors closed smoothly behind her, maids deployed left and right to stand as statues, and her husband the governor stood forward, bowed and kissed her hand. She was a woman in her forties, statuesque and of regal bearing.

Hastings and Povey stood to the strictest attention of which they were capable, and bowed as Don Felipe presented them. She smiled.

'I came as soon as I could,' she said in excellent English – easy for a girl who'd grown up in Dublin. 'Mr Hastings, Mr Povey – you are heroes! You shall be returned in triumph to England, at the head of your men, and my husband shall send a letter telling of everything that you have achieved.'

For thirty long days, Hastings and Povey had acted like men, and brave men at that. They'd taken command, made decisions, overcome threats and never wavered in doing their duty. They had, in addition, thoroughly absorbed the lower deck's morbid dread of Spain. After all they had endured, the kind words of this lady proved more than they could bear ... for George Hastings was just fourteen years old and David Povey was twelve. They began to tremble and shake.

Doña Alicia looked at the tall but desperately thin Hastings, who'd sprouted, as some boys do, without filling out to a man's strength. And she looked at the childlike Povey. However grand she might be, she was a woman, and she was touched to the heart.

'My brave boys,' she said, stepping forward to embrace them. This broke the last of their reserve and the midshipmen were reduced to tears.

Don Felipe motioned to the maids to leave the room, and quietly went out after them.

Within three months Hastings and Povey were back in London, their promotion assured, Society at their feet. Henceforward, both would be driven by a grim determination to see Joseph Flint pursued, captured and hanged.

Chapter 25

1st July 1752
Aboard Walrus
The Southwest Atlantic

'Diem adimere aegritudinem hominibus!' said Mr Cowdray, as the latest dressing came off Long John's stump. 'D'you know your Horace, Mr Silver?'

'No,' gasped Long John, teeth and fists clenched in anticipation of the pain that came with any handling of his wound. Even now Jobo was hanging on to one of his arms while Israel Hands held the other. Long John had thrown himself clear out of the hammock during previous dressing changes, what with his fighting and screaming.

'In other words,' said Cowdray, '"Time heals all wounds"!' And with that he deftly removed the last of the long-tailed ligaments that hung out of Long John's stump. This wretched remnant of a powerful limb looked like the fat end of a leg of lamb on a butcher's hook, only paler. But there was no trace of inflammation, and granular scar tissue was forming, fresh and healthy, over the raw end, with the bone well covered and invisibly buried within.

'*Venienti occurrite morbo,* as Persius has it,' said Cowdray. 'Which is to say: "Meet the disease in its first stage" – as indeed we have, and so effected a cure.'

Cowdray was blathering on in Latin because he was delighted with this beautiful stump, and proud of his undoubted feat in saving Silver's life despite his appalling injury. As he chattered and applied a fresh dressing, Silver found to his surprise that there was no pain in Cowdray's attentions. This was a first. Silver finally began to believe that he might recover.

When Cowdray was done, he washed his hands in a bowl, rolled down his sleeves and came and smiled at his patient.

'Well, sir!' said he, unconsciously adopting the manners he'd used so long ago to respectable patients in his private practice: merchants, aldermen, even noblemen. 'It is my pleasure to be able to promise you a good recovery, and it is in my mind to have you up and about for the fresh air. What d'you think of that, sir?'

'Aye,' said Israel Hands, 'the lads'd like that.

What say you, Long John?'

Long John hesitated. Even the bravest of men are worn down by constant pain, and he was afraid of being hurt if they moved him. Cowdray recognised this at once.

'Mr Hands,' said he, 'bring another two men so we can hoist him up in his hammock without jolting or disturbing him. And be so good as to have all made ready above.'

Hands frowned. He was not accustomed to taking orders from a sawbones. He looked instinctively to Long John.

'Aye,' said Silver weakly.

So up he went in his hammock, still sickly and dizzy, but with no pain as four men shouldered a spar with the hammock slung beneath it and got him, up on deck with the wonderful agility that sailormen have for shifting awkward loads. And it was worth the effort. Long John's spirits soared. The air was sweet and clean on the quarterdeck after weeks of hot confinement below decks. He could smell the salt breeze and see the fullness of the sails as they drove the ship on. He could see the gulls that hung in her wake.

Best of all, the men cheered as he appeared on deck. They crowded round him, laughing and joking and offering him fruits and grog. Tears came to Long John's eyes and he was perilously close to breaking into sobs at the sincerity of a greeting which was motivated purely by the pleasure of seeing him. Even Flint's followers were cheering. Just for that instant, the whole ship was united in happiness.

Then, as Jobo and Israel Hands made fast the

hammock to a cradle rigged at the taffrail, Selena and Flint joined the crowd. Both were smiling and Long John wondered what might have passed between them. The thought was a dark cloud over the sun – and a solid bank of thunder was coming up astern of it.

'John!' cried Flint. 'Here's yourself come up on deck to see us at last! How are you, shipmate?' Flint noticed Long John's eyes flicking between Selena and himself. He smiled his wolf-head smile and tickled the green plumage of his parrot, 'Selena and I were just discussing my plan to bury our goods on that old island I've told you about.'

Flint paused to enjoy the anger swelling in the face of his helpless enemy. 'D'you remember that old plan of mine, John?' He smiled and smiled. 'Ah yes,' he said, 'I see by the look of you that you do. Doubtless you'll be delighted to learn that Mr Bones and I are taking this ship to the island for that very purpose.'

'God damn you for a bloody rogue!' said Silver, too weak to make an argument, too tired to muster the words, and almost too sick to care.

Flint stared. He saw the effect of his words and almost took a step forward. But he didn't. After all, he'd aimed to wound, and he'd hit the mark. He'd hit it fair and square. Silver groaned at his own weakness and his jaw trembled in self-pity. But then Flint's shot rebounded. There was a surly murmur from the men. Faces scowled and brows furrowed. None of them were entirely sure what was going on, but they could see that it upset the hero of the hour, and they didn't like it.

'Don't you mind, Long John!' said one.

'Long John!' said another. 'He's the boy!'

There was something close to a cheer. Better still, Selena left Flint and came and stood by Silver. She didn't say anything, but she put a hand on his shoulder, just to show that she was now with him facing Flint, rather than the other way around, and that encouraged Silver so wonderfully that it became Flint's turn to scowl.

A week later, Silver's recovery was so far advanced, and his strength so much restored, that Mr Cowdray took a risk and brought forward a moment that in lesser men would have been delayed for months.

Long John was standing upright. He was upright, but he sweated and trembled and the ship heaved beneath him. As she rolled, he, who'd never been seasick since a child, shuddered with nausea. He retched and gasped, though the breeze was steady and the seas calm, and *Walrus* rode the waves like the thoroughbred she was.

All around they yelled and roared and urged him on.

'With a will, John!'

'Come on, shipmate!'

'Handsomely now, Long John!'

'Step out, John!'

'You show 'em, John!'

Long John saw that even Flint was there, and seemed sincere in his encouragement. Certainly Billy Bones and the rest of Flint's faction were intermingled with Long John's men, clapping and stamping and whistling as honest as could be.

Long John held his breath. He found his moment of courage and shook off Mr Cowdray's arm from one side and Jobo's from the other. He braced his back against the weather bulwark by the main shrouds and threw himself forward with the new crutch under his right arm. It was as brave a step as any he'd ever taken ... and thump, scrape, thump, scrape – two staggering steps with the shock jarring up the long shaft to his armpit as the wooden tip struck the deck. Two one-legged steps and two sickening plunges forward, and then he was falling into the arms of the men crowded around the mainmast.

'Hurrah for Long John!' they cried. 'Three cheers for Long John Silver!' They were all around him, shaking his hand and wishing him well. Cowdray took hold of him again and Selena shoved Jobo aside to throw her arm around him too. He felt the warmth and softness of her body, and breathed in the smell of her as she pressed close.

'Give us a hornpipe, John!' cried a voice, and the others roared their agreement.

'I'll race the best of you to the truck of the main t'gallant presently!' said Long John. Or rather, he tried to say it, but the effort was too great and the best he managed was a thin smile and a slurred mumbling.

'Come now, sir!' said Cowdray. 'Enough for today.' He looked among the merry crowd of *Walrus's* crew. 'Where's the carpenter?' he said, and Black Dog stepped forward. 'Well enough,' said Cowdray, looking at Long John's brand-new crutch, shining white with the freshness of its carving. 'But it's a little too long. Take an inch off it and we'll try again tomorrow.' He turned back to Long John. 'Is it padded well enough, Mr Silver?'

'No,' gasped Long John.

'More padding then,' said Cowdray. 'And now, Mr Silver, back to your hammock with you, sir. You have done magnificently to be up and stepping out this early in your recovery, but you must rest now.' So they took him aft again and helped him into his hammock, now rigged with its own shade against the sun, and with a cask for a table, and a chair for those to sit upon who came to keep him company.

Once he was settled, Cowdray and Jobo left and the rest of the crew went to their duties. This was because – aboard *Walrus* – things had always been done man-o'-war fashion, since neither Flint, nor Billy Bones, nor Long John could abide idling. To Long John's delight, Selena stayed and sat by him. She sat close by his head so he could easily speak with her. And he felt better, laid in his hammock. The sick weakness was fading and, having been upright after so long laid on his back, he felt more of a man. He looked at the lovely dark eyes and the swell of her breasts against her shirt, and her backside against her breeches.

Shiver me timbers! he thought. *Haven't one-legged men fathered children before now? Why should I be different? And I've money in the bank besides.*

'Why must you fight with Flint?' she said, breaking his chain of thought.

'What do you mean, girl?' he said. But he knew.

'The other day, when you came up on deck for the first time,' she said, 'you made a fight with Flint. Why did you do that?'

'Make your own damn mind up,' he sighed. 'There's him and there's me. You just choose, my girl, and meanwhile this ship is on course for Flint's blasted island and whatever he plans to do when he gets us there.'

'Why don't you want Flint to put the goods ashore?' She frowned in genuine puzzlement. 'Why are you always twisting the captain's words and making trouble? Always arguing and hollering.'

'I weren't hollering!'

'Maybe so, but you *did* make a fight.'

'Aye, because what's the point of burying the gold when there's banks awaiting and hungry for it? What's wrong with Chancy Neal? He ain't just a receiver that buys stolen pots. He knows names in Charleston, and New York, and even London. And he's honest too. That's my way. A word to Charley and I stows a little here, a little there, and never too much in one place.'

'Yes!' she said. 'And all you've got is paper. Just paper and writings.'

'God pluck and draw me!' said Long John. 'Don't you never mock papers and writings! Papers make laws and pardons and sentences to be hanged by the neck. Papers is power, girl!'

'Says you.'

'Stap me vitals! Lend an ear for the love of Jesus, will you now?'

'Well?'

'Flint says, "Bury the gold so it's out of the ship and we shan't have to fear for it." Ain't that what he says?'

'Yes.'

'And he says, "Then we beat up an down for more, and then we bury that too, and when we've made our pile, we'll have one great divvy-out among ourselves and go our ways." Ain't that what he says?'

'That's what he says.'

'Well, have you ever heard of a gentleman of fortune that don't spend his gelt as fast as he gets it?'

'*You* don't.'

'Damnation, girl. I'm different. I never chose this life.'

'Flint's different too.'

'Not like that, he ain't! He lives for the thrill of the moment. He's got some bloody-handed plan of his own, I stake my 'davy on it, and half the blockhead crew is bewitched by him.' Long John looked the girl in the eye to try to read her mind. 'And you along with 'em, girl!'

'Captain Flint's a gentleman.'

'Shite and corruption!' cried Long John, near the end of his patience. 'Not that again!'

'He's a gentleman!'

'No he ain't!'

'Well, he is to *me,* which is more than *some!*'

Long John dropped his eyes and cursed more horribly still. He remembered Charley Neal's liquor store, and how he'd behaved, and the nonsensical thought ran through his mind that he'd give his other leg to change it.

As for Flint's plan to bury the goods, if he couldn't convince Selena how wrong it was – her that was sharp as a needle and ready to listen – then what chance did he have with a parcel of foremast hands with brains like wooden blocks, and ears flapping to take in whatever Flint told them. He sighed.

'God help every living soul aboard,' he thought, *'for I can't see the way.'*

Chapter 26

15th July 1752
Aboard Walrus
The Southwest Atlantic

Long John smiled and took the pistols from Israel Hands. They were fond favourites of his: a matched pair by Freeman of London, whose name was engraved on the lock plates. Long John held them lovingly to his bosom and polished them with the cuff of his shirt. They were handsomely mounted: the escutcheon, the side-plates, and the fierce oval masks in the heavy butts, were all of hallmarked silver. The barrels were browned, the locks were blued and they were sharp and fast-acting. They were eighteen-bores, taking a twenty-bore ball for easy fit.

'Ah, John,' said Israel Hands, 'now you're a gentleman o' fortune again, I stake my 'davy.' He was genuinely pleased to see Long John up and about at last and now complaining about the nakedness of going unarmed.

'Shiver me timbers!' said Long John. 'How've I gone all these weeks without a pair of barking irons in me belt?' He shook his head.

'Here's powder and shot,' said Israel Hands.

‘The flints are already screwed in place.’

‘Israel,’ said Long John, ‘you’re the finest gunner as ever touched off a piece, I do declare.’ The two men laughed and Long John nipped his crutch firmly against his body with his elbow, and with some difficulty managed to load and prime with powder from a horn, ball from a pouch, and some scraps of old newspaper for wadding.

‘Ahhh,’ said Long John, and sticking one pistol carefully into his belt at half-cock, he levelled the other at the horizon, far away over the bulwark, and squeezed the trigger.

The pistol boomed and jumped in his hand.

‘Avast there,’ cried Billy Bones from his station beside the helmsman. ‘Who the buggery-andamnation’s letting off without leave?’

‘It’s me, Billy-my-chicken,’ cried Long John, and the men laughed. Only Flint called Billy Bones by that name. The colour drained from Billy Bones’s face and his big fists clenched like the roots of an oak tree. He took a step towards Long John, and all present held their breath. But Billy Bones looked at Long John’s haggard face, still bearing the marks of his weakness, and he looked at the way Long John was propped up on one leg and a bit of an old spar; and he remembered everything that Long John had been ... and Billy Bones sneered.

‘Stand easy, me hearties!’ he cried. ‘’Tis only the old cripple, playing with his pops. He’d better mind he don’t blow the good leg off, a-pulling the other barker out of his belt.’

That was a sparking sally of wit by Billy Bones’s standards. The men laughed and Billy Bones turned smiling back to his duties ... and never saw the angel of death that came shrieking down for his soul, and never knew that he would live on for many years more ... *only* thanks to Israel Hands: a man that he'd never liked. For Israel saw the shame and rage in Long John's face and clapped a hand on the butt of the second pistol as Long John tried to draw it.

'Belay!' he hissed. 'Back y'r topsail, John! Not now. For one thing we've signed articles and you'd swing for the bugger...' Israel Hands paused, for he'd another reason for keeping Long John alive. 'And you ain't the only one as don't like Flint's plan for a-burying of the goods. Them as is loyal to you, why, we'll need you when we drop anchor at the island. We need you fighting fit, not ... not...' he blinked and stuttered and fell foul of his own words, and served only to remind Long John of his loss.

'Look at me,' said Silver, 'I was a better man than him before this...' He stared down at where his leg should have been. 'He's felt the toe of my boot, has Mr Billy Bones, and if I had my legs now I'd meet him hand to hand, like a gentleman of fortune, and *according* to articles.'

'Aye, John,' said Israel Hands, happy to think of better times, 'you was the one for that, ever since England's time.' He swallowed hard and delivered the kindly lie that he so much wanted to believe: 'And you'll be yourself again, shipmate.' He gripped the big man's arm and looked up into his face, willing him to go on.

'Aye,' said Silver, wanting in his turn to believe, 'If you say so, shipmate.'

'That I do!' said Israel Hands.

And since it was plain truth that he wasn't the only man aboard that looked to Long John for leadership, for the moment Long John was content to bide his time and to eat hearty and drink deep and gather his strength, which was all to the good when, eight days later, *Walrus* ran into the warnings of such a storm as only the tropics can deliver.

The ship rolled deeply and her sails hung like dirty brown washing. The oozing swell lifted her smoothly up, and softly down. There was no wind and the sun was going down steaming red on a hot and oily sea. There hadn't been a whisper of wind for two days and even leather-faced, seasoned seamen were sickened with the ghastly motion. But now, something was coming. Even Flint's parrot could tell that a storm was in the making, somewhere under the horizon.

'All hands, Mr Bones,' said Flint, 'strike everything aloft. Rig hand-lines and extra lashings on the guns, and batten down hatches.'

'Aye-aye, Cap'n,' said Bones. 'All hands!' he roared. 'All hands!' Billy Bones never had to ask twice, and both watches poured up on deck and set to. The rigging filled with scrambling figures and the topmen raced to pass down every stick that could be struck and secured below, to give the storm the least possible meat to sink its teeth into.

'Ah, John,' said Flint, coming astern to Silver in his accustomed place at the taffrail, 'I assume you'll be going below with the surgeon and the womenfolk? Precious little you can do on deck.' He smiled nastily. 'And we wouldn't want you swept away ... by accident ... would we, now?' The two men stood and looked at each other, standing motionless among a furiously busy crew.

'Aye-aye, Cap'n,' said Silver. He smiled too, but Flint could see the fury held back like water behind a dam. Flint chuckled to himself. He'd told Billy Bones and his other favourites to lose no opportunity of reminding Silver of his mutilated condition, and it was obvious that a good sore had been rubbed into Silver's hide.

'I'll be going below directly, Cap'n,' said Silver. He sniffed the oven-breath air and looked at the sky. 'It so happens that you're right, Joe, for two legs is better than one, when Father Neptune gets angry.' Silver smiled all the harder and took Flint's eye. 'Don't look like we're ever going to find this island o' yourn now, do it, Joe?' he said. 'What with us being becalmed and now this.' He feigned anxiety, as if a sudden thought had struck him. 'Couldn't be as you've *lost* the bugger, could it, Joe? What with peering through your instruments and ruling little lines across your charts?'

'Never fear, John,' said Flint. 'I know what I'm doing, and I know where I'm going.' He leaned forward confidentially. 'You must let me show you how the thing is done. The calculations are simple enough. A child could do it – should he have the aptitude. And it is, of course, the thing of all things that marks out a gentleman from a lower-deck hand.' He grinned and Silver frowned, beaten at his own game. 'Why look,' said Flint, 'here's Mr Bones coming, who hasn't the brains of a bullock munching grass. But even he can plot a course.'

'Bastard!' said Silver.

'Mr Bones,' said Flint, 'help Mr Silver below decks. At the double now!'

Silver took the hint. With Israel Hands and the rest of Long John's men busy about the ship, the last thing he wanted was Billy Bones's *assistance* in making his way down ladders into the darkness of the ship's interior. Without another word, Long John lunged forward, past the helmsman, past Flint, around and between the scurrying hands, and plunged down the nearest hatchway. He'd become agile again. The crutch was slung from a loop of line passed over his shoulder, and he could get along fast by hopping on his one leg. It was faster than walking until he lost balance. But even that was getting better, and the falls were less frequent.

The hatchway ladder was a fearful challenge though, and only the threat of Billy Bones's attentions made him take it at speed. With the crutch dangling, he fell forward and caught the coaming with his two hands, and tried to swing his leg down the ladder. Thump-scrape! His shoe-leather slipped off the rungs and he half fell, half slipped and entirely bumped his way the six feet down to the deck, cracking his head, bruising his knee, and nearly dislocating his shoulder as the crutch jammed into the deck, driving the shock of the impact straight into his armpit.

Rumble-Boom! The hatch ground home over his head, cutting out the light, and a steady hammering told him that the carpenter and his mates were nailing it down tight against the storm. Long John groaned and sat upright. He was battered and bruised, but at least he was alive.

Billy Bones would have killed him, given the chance: pitched head-first down the hatchway, and then Billy-my-chicken's foot on his windpipe till he was nice and quiet. Billy would do it if he could. He'd do it for Flint and he'd do it for himself, for the time he'd felt the weight of Long John's fists.

Long John groaned and beat the deck in shame and frustration. There would have to be a reckoning with Billy Bones, for it wasn't just Bones himself that had to be considered. Where Billy-boy led, others were following, and the very men who'd cheered when Long John first came up on deck were now sniggering behind his back at Billy Bones's mockery of the one-legged cripple. So if there wasn't a reckoning soon, then Long John's own followers would fall behind Billy Bones, leaving Long John entirely at Flint's mercy.

Again and again, Long John cursed the loss of his leg, and he cursed Flint, whose fault it was through his greed and refusal to listen to a word of good advice. But even then, and even in the depths of his despair, Long John grudgingly gave credit – if credit were the word – to an unknown merchant skipper who'd fought like the captain of a ship of the line.

Chapter 27

23rd July 1752
Aboard Walrus
The Southwest Atlantic

With no lights burning below decks, and all hatchways secured, Long John was in total darkness in the narrow space below the quarterdeck hatch. He sat himself beside the ladder and felt around so his hands could tell him what was around him, since his eyes certainly could not. He found one of his pistols, fallen out of his belt, and stuck it back. He decided he'd better crawl than try to walk, for up above there was a howling of wind and the bellowing of Flint and Billy Bones as the storm struck and the ship began to plunge and buck.

The nearest light would be in Flint's cabin, so Long John pulled himself astern as the ship moaned and creaked and chattered to itself. The timbers of a wooden ship are always working to be free of one another, especially in a storm. The joints, lovingly mated and bolted by the shipwrights, will strain and groan. The great oaken knees will wrench against the deckhead and the hull, and the planks of the deck will do their best to gape open and spit out their caulking. To this increasingly loud accompaniment of ship's music, Long John crawled aft. He well knew that this was only the overture, or rather the tuning up of musicians' instruments before the real playing begins.

He found the stern cabin, and shoved open the hatch. Light flooded out: dim light, no more than stars and moon, but it was like sunshine after the blackness outside.

'Who's there?' cried a voice.

'Selena?' said Long John. He'd actually forgotten her. She had the run of Flint's cabin.

'Long John?' she said. 'What are you doing here?'

'Sent below, ma'am, to keep a guard on the pork and beef, and the ship's rats!' He peered around the cabin. Flint's table and chairs were secured to the deck, and everything else was lashed down. There was no movement that Long John could see. 'Where are you, girl?'

'Here,' she said, 'by the window.' Silver looked harder and thought he saw her outline. But even the stars and the moon were going out now, and it was hard to see.

He dragged himself across the dark cabin, towards the row of lights at the stern: lozenge-shaped panes of crude glass, leaded into the wooden frames. Flint had had a padded seat built across the width of the cabin: about ten feet long and three deep. He slept on it sometimes. Now Selena was crouched on the seat, with her back against the side of the hull and her knees drawn up under her chin. Silver hauled himself up beside her, unshipped his crutch, laid it aside, and dusted himself off. Lightning flickered far away and a distant thunderclap sounded. As the storm grew louder, up on deck Billy Bones was bellowing himself hoarse. Selena jumped at the thunder, but she eyed Silver steadily.

'What are you doing here?' she asked again, and for want of anything better to say, Silver told the simple truth.

'Ain't no usc for a one-legged man up topsides.'

'Oh,' she said, and looked away, then jumped as a fizzing bolt of lighting lit the sky, and another thunderclap rumbled, this time much closer. Selena shivered. She had never liked thunder, even ashore, let alone on the heaving ocean. A squall of rain thrashed down upon the ship and the wind began to blow in earnest. Every time *Walrus*'s plunging gave a view of the waves outside, they seamed higher and blacker and angrier. A third thunderclap came simultaneously with the brilliant blue-white flash, and so hideously loud that even Long John twitched in fright, and Selena threw herself at him and clutched her arms tight around him, with eyes screwed shut.

'Aye, my lass,' he said, 'we're in for a blow, and no mistake.' He stroked her hair and patted her back, and searched his memory for words of comfort and tenderness. But he'd lived a hard life and the ludicrous best he could do was borrowing from Joe Flint.

'There, my chicken,' he said. And, straining his powers of imagination to the limit, 'My chick, my little chicky...' And with these attempts at tenderness, there flowered within Long John Silver something that had been waiting to grow ever since that day in Chancy Neal's storeroom.

Meanwhile the wind roared, the seas thundered, the ship's timbers shrieked and crackled and howled, and the entire narrow, dark world of Flint's cabin tossed and bounced like a pannier on a galloping horse. Selena was outright terrified. She clung to Silver like a child to a mother. But let no man or woman think the less of her for doing so; not unless they too have been on board a two hundred ton wooden ship in a tropical hurricane, and managed to bear themselves better than she did – and *that* the first time they've experienced it, besides.

For his part, Long John had near twenty years of seafaring behind him and had seen worse storms in worse ships. He knew that *Walrus* was well found and Flint a masterly seaman. So he wasn't afraid. He wasn't afraid, but he was powerfully confused, because he'd got the very thing clutched to his chest that he'd been hungering after for months. He had an armful of smooth, luscious, youthful flesh. He could feel the plump breasts and the warmth and scent of her body.

It is unshakable truth that none of these foregoing facts were such things as should cause a jolly sailorman to worry. Under normal circumstances, Long John would have known exactly what to do, and delighted in the doing of it. What's more, he knew by happy experience what a splendid trick it was to get a woman frightened of ghosts and hobgoblins in the night, in order to get her braced for a galloping. His heart thumped as he imagined himself hauling the shirt and breeches off her, and rolling her on to her back.

He even got as far as undoing a button or two of her shirt, and getting a hand inside her clothes for a grasp of her bouncers. Jesus Christ, they were juicy! Firm as roundshot and the nipples standing up like marines on parade. He wandered his hand further, sliding down the smooth belly. He shifted the weight of her to spread her legs a little and got his hand right down into the silky-smooth inside of her thigh. The whole of his body prickled, and a ship's bowsprit – hard and fierce – stood up before him. Any doubts he might have had concerning manhood were left drowning in the ship's wake. He searched further...

Selena groaned and her eyes flicked open.

'No,' she gasped. Silver withdrew his hand and sighed.

'Not if you say so, my chick.' And he held her gently in his arms.

'I'm frightened, John,' she said.

'Aye, lass.'

'Are we going to die?'

'No. The old *Walrus*'ll weather this one. Flint'll see her through.'

'He's no good, that Flint.'

'No, lass, he ain't. But nor ain't none o' the rest of us, neither!'

'You are.'

'What?'

'Yes.'

'Well, shiver me timbers!' Silver was genuinely amazed.

'That time, in Savannah...' she said.

'Aye?' said Silver, deeply ashamed.

'You didn't know, did you?'

'No,' he said. 'It ain't no excuse, but I took you for one of Charley's girls.'

'Well, I'm not. I'm not a whore!'

'No, my girl. Not whilst I draw breath...' Long John paused, uneasy with feelings he'd never had before. He struggled to put words to them. His lips worked until the pressures within forced out the strange and unpractised words.

'I love you, my lass.'

Selena smiled and opened her shirt, and took his hand, and placed it over her breast. She turned her face and curled an arm around his neck and kissed him.

'I've never done this before,' she said.

'No?'

'No.'

Silver and Selena were consumed with happiness. Each found the other so very beautiful, even in the dark, even by silky touch alone, relishing the slippery smoothness of cool naked flesh. And what if John Silver was missing a leg? Experiment soon showed that it was wonderful what a one-legged man could achieve when duty called. Selena was amazed and Silver delighted, and between them they managed the task so many times that the forty-eight hours which followed were some of the best in their entire lives, and often in later years when either was troubled or in pain, they would go back in memory to Flint's cabin, on board the good ship *Walrus*, riding out a hurricane in more ways than one.

But eventually, the storm blew itself out, and Flint ordered the hatches broken open. He went down to his cabin to find Long John Silver there with Selena. The noise of freeing the hatch covers had given plenty of warning, but Silver was sat with an arm around Selena, and a hand casually resting on one of his silver-mounted pistols. He stared Flint in the eye, bold as brass.

'Found your island, Cap'n Flint?' he said. Flint's face darkened and the Devil stoked his temper till it rose like the molten rock from a volcano.

Chapter 28

25th July 1752
Aboard Walrus
The Southwest Atlantic

Flint stood at the door of his cabin and saw Silver sitting at ease with an arm around Selena's shoulders, and the girl nestled up against him with every sign of being well content. Emotions washed over Flint like the three tides over a hanged and gibbeted pirate at Execution Dock, Wapping. First there was disbelief that the girl could give herself to a cripple. Then there was fierce, wounding envy that the cripple had obviously done the thing that he was forever incapable of doing. And finally there was poisonous hatred.

Flint snarled, drew a knife, and stepped forward. Silver drew a pistol and levelled it at Flint.

'What?' said Flint. 'Will you murder me? Me with my priming soaked?' He gestured at his own pistols, drenched by the storm, and the two men faced each other, neither moving, eyes locked and limbs shaking with rage. But neither made a move, while Selena, the seeming object of this final outright break between the two men, stared in amazement.

'Come on then!' said Flint.

'Whenever you choose, Cap'n,' said Silver. But still they didn't move. Selena looked at the hard faces and tensed hands. They were a split second from coming to blows, but something was stopping them.

They're afraid, she thought. *Afraid of each other. That's why it's gone on so long*. She'd spotted something nobody else had noticed. But even so, she'd only got part of the truth. Even she never realised that both men would, even now, have healed the breach if only they could, despite the fact that the whole world could see it was past healing. The most painful time of a broken friendship is the time when old friends are making ever more futile and extravagant attempts to compromise, and make allowances, and are steadfastly refusing to face the truth.

Then Billy Bones came thundering down from the quarterdeck and barged into the cabin crying out as he came.

'All secured, Cap'n,' he said. 'Permission to stand down the larboard watch, and issue...' He blinked at the blade and the pistol. He had nowhere near Selena's insight, and simply saw danger to the man he worshipped like a god.

'Uh!' he grunted and instantly stumped forward, unarmed as he was, to stand between Flint and the pistol. 'Gimme the word, Cap'n,' he said, spitting fire and fury at Silver. 'Gimme the word and I'll have the bollocks off the sodding old ruin!'

'Billy-my-chicken,' said Flint, and he barked with laughter. His quick, flickering mind could turn to humour in the instant, and he laughed at Bone's stupidity ... his stupid bravery and his very great usefulness, 'will you split the marrow-bones, of him, my Billy? Will you pop out his eyes with your thumbs?'

'That I will, Cap'n!' said Bones.

'Will you, though?' said Silver. 'Will you, indeed!' And he hopped to his feet, hauling the long crutch under his arm, and shoving Selena out of harm's way. 'Well then, you swab,' he said, 'I challenge you, man to man, and according to articles. I challenge you to face me with the weapons your mother gave you, on fair and level ground and with no man to intervene.'

Billy Bones blinked a while, pondering the legality of this appeal to articles. He searched his memory for what he'd signed, nodded unconsciously as he recalled the article in question ... and a fat, slow grin spread over his heavy face.

'Aye,' he said, 'on fair and level ground, with no man to intervene.' He turned to Flint. 'That's fair and proper, Cap'n. According to articles, and only your permission is awaited. I duly asks for that permission.'

'As do I!' said Silver, and Flint nearly bust himself holding back the hysterical laughter. But it wouldn't do, at this vital moment, to piss into Mr Bones's font. Not when Mr Bones was about to oblige by battering Silver senseless with mighty fists, before kicking in Silver's skull with heavy boots.

And what a fine thing that would be, thought Flint. Once the decks were scrubbed and hosed down, he would make a speech sorrowing over Silver's fall into decrepitude and praising his past triumphs, and so bringing his rival's remaining supporters over to his own side. And then, if anyone thought the worse of Billy Bones for killing a poor old cripple, well, so much the worse for Billy-boy. He could always be replaced.

But first there were formalities to be observed. The crew had to be mustered, the Book of Articles brought forth, the articles read, and the combatants searched for hidden weapons. Finally the hands were warned, on pain of death, that nobody must interfere.

The excitement was immense. Such yelling and shouting and eager jostling, and such innocent delight on all sides at the prospect of so wonderful a fight. So Flint led Silver and Billy Bones to the quarterdeck, where the ship offered its nearest equivalent to *fair and level ground*, and each man took off his hat and coat, and stood to face the other. Bravado drove Billy Bones to haul off his shirt and stand like the pugilist he was, chest matted in black hair and tattooed arms bulging with strength. All of Flint's supporters, and many of Long John's too, roared their approval and admiration at the sight of him, while Long John stood waiting and trembling. He was visibly shaking. His face was white. His lips were black. He looked already dead. He looked a lost man, and Selena gaped in horror and tried to stop the inevitable. She appealed to Flint, and was ignored.

She appealed to Long John, who seemed barely to hear her. She appealed to the crew, who howled and roared and ridiculed.

'So,' said Flint, drawing a pair of fresh-primed pistols, 'I charge all hands to stand back and take no part of this fair and chosen fight, remembering that, if any does interfere, then he shall die by my hand!'

He turned to Billy Bones. 'Are you ready, Mr Bones?'

'Aye!'

'Are you ready, Mr Silver?'

'One thing more–' cried Silver.

'What is it?' said Flint.

'Does Mr Bones agree that I takes no unfair advantage over him?' said Silver. 'Does he agree that I has no weapons other than what he sees. And that *this*–' he gestured at himself, 'as I stand here, is the thing he fights?'

Billy Bones sneered with contempt at the cripple leaning on his crutch. 'Aye,' he said.

'Then go to it!' said Flint, which words were the signal for deafening shouts and cries of delight from the happy onlookers, fiercely shaking their fists and urging on their man to inflict death and mutilation. They filled the shrouds for a better view, they crowded all round in a ring. They jumped and fought to see, and the ship rolled and plunged beneath them. And Billy Bones grinned and stepped forward, waving his fists in little circles to exercise his arms.

'Cripple,' he said, 'I've been waiting for this. I'll stamp your face in!'

And then there was a gasp of amazement.

Long John swung his crutch out from under his shoulder. He balanced neatly on one leg and threw the heavy timber like a javelin. It caught Billy Bones squarely between the eyes. Bones staggered. His knees buckled. His arms drooped. Long John leapt forward and slammed the top of his head straight into Billy Bones's face, with all the weight of his body behind it. Billy Bones's nose crunched like a smashed apple, spraying blood left, right and centre... And down went Billy. Down went Long John too, right on top of him, driving the point of his knee hard into Billy Bones's belly, so the breath wheezed out in a gasp, then heaving him on to his face and wrenching his arm behind his back to twist the shoulder joint till the dazed and semi-conscious Billy Bones woke up again and roared in pain.

'Here we are then, Billy-my-chicken!' cried Long John, and got himself more comfortably seated on Billy's back, and got a better grip of his arm. He might have lost a leg, but he still had plenty of dead weight to hold Billy down, and all the powerful muscles of his arms and shoulders were fighting-fit and ready to put some real pressure to the wrestler's hold he'd applied.

'Bastard!' screamed Billy Bones. 'I'll kill you!'

'So now who's the better man, of us?' hissed Long John, face close to Billy Bone's ear and the sweat dripping off his nose.

'Fuck you!' screamed Billy. 'Fuck your mother! Fuck your father!'

Billy Bones was tough as granite and immune to pain – or so he'd thought. He struggled fiercely to unseat the one-legged man, but Silver hung on. He hung on like a spider round a fly. He hung on and he worked at Billy Bones's shoulder joint until eventually even Billy couldn't stand it any more, and stopped bellowing and started yelping.

'Now then, Billy,' said Silver, when he thought he had Mr Bones's full attention, 'shall I pop this shoulder out of her joint?' He looked up and nodded at the crowd. 'There's Mr Cowdray over there, our surgeon, and he can always put her back in for you ... unless I does a *real* job and tears the flesh and sinews of her, in which case she won't never work again. And *then* who'd be the cripple, Billy-boy? So here's a few more pulls, just to make sure you've got the feel of it. Are you ready, Billy?'

'AAAARGH!' Billy Bones shrieked in agony.

'I asks you once more, Billy-boy: Who's the better man?'

'Ohhhh....' groaned Billy Bones, 'no more...'

'Last time, Billy, or out she comes. Who's the better man?'

'Owww... It's you.'

'Say it loud, Billy-boy. Good and loud.'

'YOU'RE THE BETTER MAN!' cried Billy Bones, and he wept for the humiliation of it.

Long John rolled clear of Billy Bones and stood up, throwing his weight on to his leg and driving himself upright all in one movement. He stood swaying and balancing, hopping occasionally and stretching out his arms for balance. The hands cheered in delight and surged forward, but not before Long John had hopped a few neat steps, and bent at the knee, and stooped, and heaved upright again, retrieving the crutch that had knocked the wind out of Billy Bones. All this he did by himself, and he stood head and shoulders over the men who came forward to acclaim him.

He was Long John Silver again.

Except that he was wasn't quite the old Long John. He was something else. The men didn't clap him on the back as they would have done before. They pressed close and they nodded and saluted. But they didn't dare touch him. There'd been something serpent-like in the one-legged man leaping and hopping; and where the old Long John would have knocked down Billy Bones with his fists, the new Long John had won by cunning and by torture. Long John himself felt the change, but at least he knew by the respect – and fear – in men's eyes that there'd be no more reference to cripples. Not aboard this ship.

Billy Bones certainly felt the change, for he'd always feared Long John before and now feared him twice as bad, and never dared challenge him again. Flint saw it too, and knew there'd be no easy solution to the split in the ranks that left half following himself and half his rival. And Selena saw it and pushed through the men around Silver. She pulled at his arm, and he grinned, and waved the hands away, and they obeyed like sheep, and left him and the girl alone. She was puzzled.

'Why'd you do that?' she said. 'If you'd fight Billy Bones, then why not Flint? Are you afraid of him?'

'Huh!' said Long John. He frowned deeply, and searched within himself for an answer. He might even have managed one, but he was interrupted.

'Sail-ho!' cried the masthead lookout.

'Where away?'

'Two points on the larboard beam!'

'Hands to quarters!' cried Flint.

At the sniff of a prize, all else was forgotten for the moment, and the ship cleared for action at a speed that would not have disgraced a man-o'-war.

It took a speedy, well-found ship like *Walrus* little time to come alongside of the vessel the lookouts had spotted. There'd not been so much as a reef-point torn free during the storm. As Long John had said, Flint was a fine seaman, and now Flint stood by the tiller, hands behind his back, parrot on his shoulder. Billy Bones, still nursing his wounded shoulder was already stamping up and down, bawling at the men, as *Walrus* bore down on a fine little brig that was rolling and wallowing as if no man were aboard of her.

Flint backed his main topsail and ordered a boat's crew to pull across to the brig. He looked at the vessel carefully, and turned to Israel Hands, the gunner, and grinned.

'You can send your cartridges below, Mr Hands,' he said. 'No need to burn powder today.'

Long John also considered the new vessel. Flint was right. There was nobody at the wheel, not a man in the rigging, and the remains of her sails were flapping in streamers where they'd been blown out of their reefs and repeatedly split by the force of the tempest. The brig yawed and staggered, coming into the wind and falling off as the waves and weather played with her. But for all that, she was an uncommon fine little craft and, despite the storm damage, she appeared quite new.

She was about ninety-five foot in the keel, a

hundred and fifty tons burden, and of a most graceful and pleasing form. The hull was painted white, picked out in brown, with actual gold leaf glittering around the frames of her stern windows and the carvings round her broadside of four gun-ports. Her name was *Susan Mary* and a united murmur of appreciation arose from *Walrus*'s men in contemplation of her, for any seafaring man takes pleasure in a beautiful ship.

Under Billy Bones's urging, the men swung out a boat and its crew pulled across to the brig. They went over the side with a customary cheer, and pistols and cutlasses in their belts. But it was more for form than anything else. Everyone could see there would be no resistance. Long John and Selena watched as they thundered across her small decks, whooping and yelling, and then vanished below. The sounds of their busy searching and breaking things open came clearly across the water.

Walrus's men shifted enviously and muttered to one another, feeling left out of the fun. More than that, they feared the natural tendency of small and precious items of loot to find their way into the pockets of the first finders, rather than into the general pile, whatever the articles said on the matter.

Then Black Dog, who was in command of the boarders, appeared at the rail and called across the short space of water.

'Five left living, Cap'n!' he said. 'Six months out of London, and foul winds the whole while...' He paused, and looked at things hidden by *Susan Mary*'s rail from the sight of those aboard *Walrus*.

''Tis the scurvy, Cap'n. The swabs ain't got a tooth in their heads, nor a limb without sores. These aboard is what's left out of twenty-three, and the rest buried at sea or swept away last night.'

'What's her cargo?' cried Flint.

'Plantation goods, Cap'n: herring and slops for the slaves mainly, with bar copper and lead, and some powder and muskets.'

'Well, my chickens,' said Flint, turning to his men with a smile, 'here's a piece of Flint's luck and no mistake. The ship and cargo will fetch a fine price at Savannah, and all without the effort of a fight.' The men grinned and nodded to one another, and squinted at the brig and made their well-practised estimates of what might be their own shares from this excellent piece of business.

'Cap'n Flint,' said Long John, and silence fell as Flint turned to face him and the good humour drained from his face.

'Aye?' said Flint, and his eyes wavered as Silver stared steadily back at him.

'Cap'n,' said Silver, 'all hands knows that there must come a parting, sooner or later, between you and I.'

It seemed as if even the wind and the sea fell silent at these words, for it was the first open saying of a truth that all parties had tried hard not to notice.

'Either that,' said Silver, 'or this happy crew shall split, and messmates shall spill one another's blood.' Flint looked about him, and his parrot hissed and clucked and shifted its claws, sensing the discomfort in its master. As for the crew, they hardly breathed. Even those aboard the brig could hear enough to know that a momentous event was taking place, and they strained their ears and leaned over the rail to catch what it was.

'Perhaps,' said Flint, scowling and ever-suspicious of a trap.

'You *know* it, Joe Flint,' said Silver steadily. 'And I know it. And there ain't no *perhaps* about it.' Flint still said nothing, but looked away.

'So I says this,' said Silver: 'Here's to old times and new luck!' He paused and took a breath and came out with it. 'I'll take that vessel–' he pointed at the brig '–and them as takes the fancy may follow me ... together with our share of the goods.' Flint sneered nastily at this and shook his head emphatically. Silver ignored him and continued.

'And so,' he said, 'we'll sail in company. That way we shall be jolly companions still, without being forced to rub along together, Joe, for we ain't never going to do that again.'

'And who's to set a course for you, John?' said Flint. 'Or have you finally learned the way of it, while below decks these weeks past?'

'Bah!' said Silver, expecting the jibe but still smarting from it. 'No need to worry about that, Joe. Just you give me Billy Bones, there, for you've told us many times it's only you and him as knows how to find your precious island. So lend me Billy-boy until we're done with the island and we come safe into Savannah, and I'll get me my own quadrant-monger after that. I'll hire one, as you would a coachman or a kitchen maid.'

Billy Bones's jaw dropped to his very breast, and he turned to his master, shocked to the marrow, and terrified too. Flint stamped his foot in anger and the parrot squawked and fluttered its wings.

'And is that *all* then, John?' he said. 'A brand-new ship, half the goods, the pick of the crew, and the best man among 'em, apart from myself?' he sneered. 'John, your brains are rotted with the opium the surgeon fed you to stop you blubbering over your wound!'

Silver kept a tight hold on himself, for he could see that Flint had chosen to bargain rather than fight. That was good. That was very good. It was all that mattered. It was now just a matter of settling the details. So Silver argued his case.

He argued fluently and well, just as he always did. Then Flint took his turn, and he argued impressively, just as *he* always did. But the men had to have their say too, and ideas and suggestions were yelled from all sides, and the result was a most excellent compromise; which is to say that it was something both Flint and Silver detested equally.

Chapter 29

25th July 1752
Aboard Walrus
The Southwest Atlantic

A terrible fear gripped Long John when a final agreement was reached on the terms he must bear for getting command of the schooner.

The proposal was put by Blind Pew, of all

people. It wasn't often these days that he had a man's role to play. Mostly he was tolerated as a sort of pensioner, working below decks, getting steadily more peculiar, and somehow managing to do his work as sailmaker entirely by touch.

For a brief time – now passed – he'd cherished hope of getting his eyes back, since they'd begun to feel pain in bright sunshine. He'd thought this proved that they weren't fully dead, and he took to wearing a green shade over his brow, to nurture further recovery. But blind he was and blind he remained, and while the eye shade eased the pain, it gave him a still more sinister and unholy appearance than he'd had already. Mostly men steered clear of him, and the whole crew knew that he was still aboard only out of Long John's pity for the man that was ruined in the same broadside that took off his leg.

But horrid and friendless as he was, Pew had sharp ears, he was fiercely stubborn and intensely argumentative. He loved a debate in a way that few of his fellows did. So having followed the speeches with serious concentration, he'd shouted his way to the front, and when it came to giving a summary of what the hands wanted – to the surprise of all present – none could do it better than Blind Pew. There he stood, thin and grey: a creature from the dark below, brought up into the light, but gifted with a clear voice and even a certain gift of speech – Celtic and poetic.

'So, Silver to take the ship – says I – and Flint to keep the *Walrus*. So, Silver to pick his crew – says I – and Flint to keep the goods. So, Silver to take Mr Bones – says I – and Flint to keep Miss

Selena. So, all shall share the duff – says I – and all shall bear the shite!'

The roars of approval from all hands made the result a foregone conclusion. But Flint meticulously went through the procedures laid down in the ship's articles. He'd grown used to doing things that way, and even he now thought them proper.

'All for brother Pew shall show,' said Flint, and Pew stood tall and proud, nodding and basking in the attention of his mates. He didn't see the forest of hands that went up, favouring his proposal, but he heard the cheer and he grinned. Those around him clapped him on the back and said he was no end of a clever 'un, and they dug him in the ribs and called him a sea-lawyer, and he puffed up with self importance. It was just as well that he couldn't see the look on the face of Long John, who thought this a poor return for kindness.

'Any against Brother Pew's proposal?' said Flint, and a derisory howl greeted the few hands that went up.

'Flint!' cried Silver, filling with anger and ready to fight the whole ship. Flint spun round and laid a hand on his sword, but Selena caught Silver's arm and hissed in his ear.

'Come away, John,' she said, 'now!' And she led him to the stern where they could talk together without being heard.

'John,' she said, 'it don't matter.'

'Stap my heart and soul, but it does!'

'No, it don't. Not a bit.'

'How can I leave you with that bastard?'

'You've got to. Or you'll lose everything.'

'You're my *everything*, girl. Nothing else counts.'
'John, Flint is nothing. He's never touched me.'
'What? Not never?'
'No.'
'But I thought you was his piece. Ain't that why he fetched you aboard?'
'S'pose so,' she said.
'Well, why didn't he touch you? There's not a man aboard as don't want to!'
'*Flint* don't want to.'
'Why not?'
Selena sighed, she laid a hand on his arm and smiled. She knew how it hurt him. It hurt her too.
'Listen, John,' she said, 'he's never so much as laid a hand on me, d'you hear? So you go on that ship, and don't worry about me. Then we'll go to Savannah, after the island, and ... if you're still minded ... then maybe we can get together.' She looked up at him in hope, but with fear too, because even as she dared to speak of the future, a poison worm wriggled in her mind. She knew how white men treated black girls, and she wondered – now that he'd had what he wanted – if he might look elsewhere.
Unfortunately Silver entirely missed the subtle fear. He was turning over the news that Flint hadn't touched her. He was still jealous and, at the same time, questions had sprung into his mind about Flint.
'He could've had you if he'd wanted.'
'S'pose so.'
'An' he didn't?'
'Isn't that what I said?'
'So ... are you saying that Flint's fancy don't

turn that way?'

'Huh! Why don't you ask him.'

'Well, shiver me timbers – Joe Flint's a navigator of the windward passage.'

'John! You get on board o' that ship ... and *no*, he isn't.'

'How'd you know?'

'I know!' She did too. Flint hadn't been quite as careful in his drilling of peep-holes, nor as silent in his lechery, as he'd imagined. Enough gasping and groaning had come through the bulkhead to tell Selena a lot more about him than ever he suspected. But she wisely decided that this was not a good time to let Long John into the secret.

Nonetheless they each had a splinter under the fingernail: she with her fears and he with his jealousy, and there was plenty else for them to argue about over the decision to separate. So they bickered and snapped, nastily and pointlessly, and both grew angry and shouted. Insults were exchanged and tempers lost, and, being so angry, neither could say to the other the three words that would have healed all wounds and given comfort during the weeks to come.

So they parted badly, with Long John going across to his command, taking just under half the men with him. As agreed, one of them was Billy Bones, who had emerged from Flint's cabin after a conversation every bit as fraught as Long John's with Selena.

'I ain't going,' Billy Bones had mumbled, hanging his head and fiddling with his hat. His reaction to Pew's compromise was pitiful to see, and he pleaded to stay with Flint like a child begging to be let into its parents' bed at midnight for fear of the bogeyman.

'Brace up, Billy Bones!' snapped Flint. 'Find some backbone and do your duty! Look at Silver, you fool. He's worst pleased than you are!' It was true, but that only frightened Billy Bones all the more. Flint heaved a sigh and pointed to a chair.

'Billy-boy, just put your enormous backside to anchor and contrive to hold your tongue.'

Billy Bones grumbled and cursed, and plumped down, purple-faced, as he'd been told, while Flint sat facing him on the upholstered bench that ran across the cabin at the stern windows.

'I won't go. Gut and bugger me if I will!' said Billy Bones, but he took care to say it very quietly, almost to himself. Flint heard, nonetheless.

'Billy,' said Flint, starting half out of his seat, with white clear all around the pupils of his eyes, 'not a word ... *not one ... word!*'

Billy Bones gulped in fright, and twisted his hat like a housemaid wringing a dishcloth. There was much that Billy Bones wanted to say. He was terrified of what would happen to him under Silver's command, let alone from Silver's men. Still, he was a damn sight more afraid of Flint, and it was Flint he had to deal with just now.

'So,' said Flint, settling back with a broad smile on his face, 'shipmate ... messmate ... Billy-my-chicken... In this world of pain and sorrow, we many times have to do that which, given free choice, we would not do. And when that happens, a wise man makes the best of things, and he clasps to his bosom such advantages as he has.' Flint paused and contemplated Billy Bones's puzzlement. 'Do you follow the argument, Billy-boy?'

'No,' said Bones, and Flint sighed heavily, like a man who has laboured mightily to see virtue in a particularly stupid bulldog, which is ugly, dirty and foul-smelling but occasionally useful for frightening burglars.

'We must concentrate our minds, Mr Bones,' said Flint, 'on the fact that Silver has you, and I have Selena. That's one-for-one.' Flint saw the puzzlement deepen on Billy Bones's heavy face. Bones, loyal to Flint in all things, had contrived not to notice what most others – and certainly Blind Pew – had noticed concerning Silver's attitude to Selena, and hers towards him. Billy still staunchly believed that Selena was Flint's, and Flint could see the question that he dared not ask.

'You ... need ... no ...worry ... your ... thick ... skull ... about ... that,' said Flint, leaning across and beating time with his knuckles on Billy Bones's brow. Aside from John Silver, any other man who did that would have found his entrails round his neck and his balls hanging from his ears. But Billy Bones took it like a lamb. He knew Flint.

'Aye-aye, Cap'n,' was all he said.

'Good man,' said Flint, and pulled Billy Bones's nose. 'Now then, Billy-boy, can you swim?'

'No, Cap'n,' said Billy Bones, and his face went greasy-white as he cringed before this new terror.

'Hmm...' said Flint thoughtfully. 'But no doubt even *you* would float if buoyed up with sufficient cork.' Billy Bones shifted and frowned at these words. He sailed mortal uneasy upon this tack for he was dreadfully afraid of sharks. Flint grinned at him and laughed. 'Never fear, Billy

Bones,' he said. 'But pay close attention. This is what you must do...'

In due course, Billy Bones's battered old chest with the initial 'B' burned into the lid in poker-work, was hoisted over the side and into a boat, and he and it were rowed across to the brig *Susan Mary*, which Silver promptly re-named *Lion*. Of the remains of her original crew, two died of their scurvy that same day, while two survived and were persuaded to become gentlemen of fortune. One only – the captain himself – refused to be turned from what he perceived as his duty, and so he was put in irons awaiting a suitable landfall for marooning.

He too died few days later, despite all Surgeon Cowdray's efforts in feeding him fresh fruit and greens, and for those few days this honest ship-master thought himself an ill-used and miserable man. But he was merry as a bishop in a bawdy house compared to Billy Bones, whose world was in ruins, and who pondered constantly upon the memory of better days. He groaned in fear of Silver and shuddered at the thought of Flint's orders, for he didn't know which was worse.

Nor did he know the *worst*. As Billy Bones was rowed across to *Lion*, looking back longingly at his beloved master lifting his hat in smiling fare-well, that gentleman was making further plans.

Ah! Billy-my-Billy, thought Flint, *there's long weeks of sailing ahead for you, and all of it on the wide blue ocean. And there's yourself that's never had sole responsibility of navigation, and it always was a wonder, that you could multiply two times two and get the same answer every time.*

Flint smiled as he relished the warmth of his thoughts. *So, Billy-boy, what if you was to lose sight of* Walrus *in the night? What if you wasn't able to keep up? What if you was to get lost entirely, and never find land, and the whole unfortunate crew of you – and dear Mr Silver, too – was to be entered among the hosts of the Lost and Drowned? Why ... in that case there'd be seventy less to share the goods!*

He laughed merrily and called across the water. 'Goodbye, Mr Bones! And good luck!'

'Goodbye, Cap'n,' replied Billy Bones, and came close to weeping in the bitter sorrow of parting.

Chapter 30

25th July 1752
Aboard Lion
The Southwest Atlantic

The brig *Susan Mary*, now to be known as *Lion*, was smaller than *Walrus* and had all the differences below decks in terms of cabins, provision for storage, depth of the hold, et cetera, with which the individual shipwright shows the world that he can do his work better than any other. So there was a considerable bother of cursing and complaining among Captain Silver's men as they moved into their new home. Nothing was quite like what they'd been used to, and each thought the others were depriving him of the cosiest berth and the snuggest corner.

As soon as he got aboard, Israel Hands, who had been Flint's gunner and was now Long John's, elbowed and cuffed his way into a cabin, declared it his own as a senior officer in this commission, posted his mate to guard it, and went to examine the planked wooden cupboard that passed for a magazine aboard this ship. There was just room for him to get inside of it and sit down upon a bench facing a table with rows of pigeonholes above it.

Israel Hands sucked his teeth philosophically. So it had come to this. Israel Hands, who'd once served aboard ships where the magazines held cartridges for twenty-four-pounders, and ninety-pound powder kegs stood shoulder to shoulder in rows, was reduced to this. Ah well, he thought, at least there was a magazine: a proper place set aside for the powder, and lit through a double-glass window by a lantern burning outside. And there was a proper door to it, so that the gunner might keep out lubbers who'd otherwise wander in with lighted pipes in their mouths and blow the ship to splinters.

For that matter, there was plenty of powder aboard too, for the ship's cargo of plantation goods included a dozen thirty-pound powder kegs – far more than the ship herself needed with her pop-gun battery.

He cocked his head and listened to them on the deck above his head, fighting over where they should sling their hammocks. He grinned at the thought of the bruises and broken heads. None of that need trouble Israel Hands now. He was third man in the ship, after only Long John and

Billy Bones. So he grinned and began to examine the flannel cartridges for the four-pounders which were *Lion*'s main battery.

He was thorough in the work, which he did mainly by touch, taking the fat sausages of powder out of their pigeon-holes and running his fingers up and down their seams, feeling for leaks. He didn't trust any other man to do the job. Israel Hands was greedy and violent, and there was a certain depravity within him or he'd never have been where he was today, but he was also a careful and diligent man, or he'd never have been rated as gunner – a job which punished slackness by the loss of the entire ship in one great thundering roar.

He thought over what had happened, particularly the split between Flint and Silver. What an amazing piece of luck it had been that they'd found the brig when they did. Otherwise there would have been one or two aboard *Walrus* whose livers would have been tickled while they slept, for that was the way Israel Hands preferred to do business, what with its being such a safe and quiet way. Given the choice, Israel Hands would have started with Billy Bones, because he kissed Flint's bum-hole every day of the week and twice on Sundays. And now Billy-boy was first mate under Silver! There was a turn of events, and no mistake.

In all, seventy men and three boys came across with Long John into *Lion*. Mostly the men were from the old East India days, when they'd been shipmates under Captain Mason; these included Blind Pew, whom Silver had asked for despite his part in the recent debate, for he was still a better sailmaker than his mates. Every spare sail from

Lion's lockers was being brought up and bent to the masts to replace those shredded by the sea, and more would have to be made.

Among the rest who chose to go with Silver was a small group who'd been with Flint aboard *Elizabeth:* George Merry, Tom Allardyce, and Israel Hands himself. This was a little victory for Long John Silver, since not one of his old East India shipmates had stayed aboard *Walrus* under Flint. Israel Hands paused briefly in his work. Silver was an odd bugger for a pirate, what with his articles and his 'gentlemen of fortune' and his sparing of prisoners and women.

Israel Hands knew more about this than most, for his own father, after whom he was named, had served under Blackbeard forty years ago when it had been butchery on all sides and no quarter asked or given. Israel Hands shrugged his shoulders and reached for another cartridge. Silver might be lily-livered, but his ways meant the crew pulled together. Besides, Israel's father had been lamed for life by Blackbeard firing off a pair of pistols under the table just for fun: exactly the sort of mad game Flint enjoyed. It was one more reason why Israel Hands preferred Silver.

When he'd finished with the cartridges and set aside a few he wasn't happy with, Israel Hands locked the magazine and went on deck to look at his guns. Silver and Billy Bones were getting her under way in *Walrus*'s wake, and men were running in all directions making sail.

Israel Hands went over to the nearest gun and knelt beside it for a close look. He was pleased to see that it was of the same quality as everything else about this sweet little vessel. It was an English-made iron gun, quite new, with a good carriage and fittings, and in all respects shipshape and fit for service. There was shot in the racks and a fresh cartridge ready in the waterproof locker by the gun. A neat wooden tompion kept wet out of the muzzle, and a sheet of lead was lashed over the touch hole, while rammers, crows and a linstock were secured nearby.

'Aye,' muttered Israel Hands, 'pretty enough to look at, but only four-pounders and too few of you.' *Lion* mounted just eight of these guns and the one bright star in Israel Hands's night was the Spanish nine, that by grovelling pleading before Long John, he'd got shipped aboard of *Lion*, along with its carriage and tackles, though these parts were lying in the hold waiting for the carpenter to find time to cut a port into the bow, though the tiny fo'c'sle was already crammed with bowsprit, catheads and other fittings to the point that even Israel Hands admitted to himself there was no room in the bow for a gun of that size.

He admitted it to himself but thought it wise not to mention it to anyone else, for he wasn't going to be separated from his darling for so small a thing as that, especially considering the unpleasant and unavoidable fact that *Lion* was seriously under-gunned in comparison with *Walrus*.

'Mr Hands!' a voice calling his name brought Israel Hands out of his contemplation. It was Silver himself. 'A word, Mr Hands.' Israel Hands stood up and walked slowly towards the quarterdeck, conscious of his dignity as gunner before the common crew.

'At the double, you idle bastard!' roared Silver, his face like thunder. Israel Hands jumped and ran up the ladder and presented himself. From the look on Silver's face, he judged it expedient to salute, navy-fashion, and take off his hat.

Silver and Billy Bones were side by side, and Silver was now dressed in a long blue coat and cocked hat, just like Billy Bones, except that Silver's hat and coat were newer, less faded, and better than Billy Bones's. Since Long John had never had such a coat before, Israel Hands guessed – correctly – that Mr Bones had been required to give up his spare suit of clothes so that Captain Silver might not look less of an officer than his first mate.

Both Silver and Billy Bones were in the foulest of tempers and clearly itching to find a man to discharge their anger upon. Israel Hands vowed that he would not become that man. He stood to rigid attention and answered with the uttermost politeness and subordination.

'Now see here, you lubber,' said Silver, frowning tremendously upon Israel Hands.

'Aye-aye, sir!' said Israel Hands, staring straight in front of his face, arms plumb down by his sides.

'You've been used to festering in your bed all night when it comes to a blow,' said Silver.

'Aye-aye, sir!' said Israel Hands, finding tears to weep, for it was true. A master gunner did not stand watches, nor turn out when 'All hands' was piped. It was a dearly beloved privilege of his rank, and he could guess what was coming next.

'Well, you can belay all that, you lazy sod!' said Silver. 'You shall stand watch-and-watch with me and Mr Bones, here, d'you understand? You're less use than a turd in a teapot, but you're the only bugger we've got, and we must make shift.' Silver and Billy Bones peered intently at Israel Hands. For once they were united in a common cause: that of avoiding twelve-hour watches on deck.

'So,' said Silver, 'are you man enough for the work, Mr Hands? Don't worry about quadrants and dividers–' he turned to Billy Bones '–Mr Bones shall set our course to Flint's island. Either that or we'll follow in Flint's wake. But we must have another man to stand watches.' Pausing only briefly to consider what would happen should he say *no*, Israel Hands forced out his answer.

'Aye-aye, sir!' he said, though his heart was breaking. But it would just have to break. He knew that Billy Bones was furious at being taken away from Flint, while Silver was mad jealous over Flint's black girl, and couldn't bear the thought of Flint ramming and boarding her whenever he pleased. Israel Hands didn't dare anger either of these fearful men, let alone both together.

'Aye-aye, sir,' mocked Silver. 'And you can start by standing watches together with me and Mr Bones until you learn enough of the business not to lose the ship.'

Fortunately Israel Hands didn't lose the ship. And in a week or two he became a passably competent watch-keeping officer: not gifted, but sufficient for the purpose. And Billy Bones didn't lose the ship either, and nor did he lose *Walrus*, though he frequently remarked on how much sail she was carrying, and how she forged ahead of *Lion:*

'You'd think the bugger was trying to leave us

behind!' he said on one occasion, training his glass on the schooner as her topmen set the t'gallants in a strong blow. 'What's Flint doing, carrying that much sail?'

'Aye, Mr Bones,' said Silver, coming up astern of Billy Bones, 'what's he doing indeed?'

'Cap'n!' said Bones, nervously touching his hat and flicking his eyes left and right to check that all present had *seen* him give proper respect. After a few days aboard *Lion*, finding that he woke up in the mornings without a cut throat and walked the decks without being heaved overside, his fears had diminished. But he was still taking care not to give offence.

Silver put his own glass on *Walrus* and thought for an instant that he saw Flint. It looked like Flint – a slight black figure in a big hat – waving at the men, as if to urge them to their duties. But the ocean was heaving and rolling high as the mainsail, and sight of *Walrus* came and went through the glossy green waves, so he couldn't be sure.

'Hmm,' said Silver, 'I think you're right, Mr Bones. He's trying to leave us hull-and-topmasts under!'

'Never!' said Billy Bones instantly, but then he thought hard and bit his lip and dared – very politely – to look Silver in the eye. 'Why would he do that?' he said.

'Mr Bones,' said Silver, 'I leave that to your imagination. But ain't it just a fine thing that our little *Lion*'s so neat and sweet and could sail the arse off *Walrus*?'

It was true. It was a source of pride to all on board, and a wonderful discovery it had been.

Walrus was built for speed and had never met her match – until now. For *Lion* was a thoroughbred from stem to stern. She cut the water like a knife, she was sweet to the helm, she rode the waves like a lady, and she could easily have overhauled *Walrus*, had there been the need. For a second time, John Silver fell in love. If *Walrus* was Flint's darling, then *Lion* was his.

So *Lion* easily kept station astern of *Walrus*, and in due course the two ships found the island, which – to his credit – Billy Bones would have managed all by himself, even without *Walrus* to follow. Flint typically saw no good in any man, and Billy Bones was nowhere near as stupid as Flint thought. Mr Bones, in his slow and methodical way – indeed, with many crossings out and corrections – had managed to multiply two times two and get the answer to *four* every time. And now the two ships were creeping into the southern anchorage, following – at Flint's insistence – a launch taking soundings all the way.

All hands with no immediate duties took to the rigging for a better view of what they were approaching. This was Flint's secret island; the island that had no name; the island that had been the site of so much bloodshed. There'd been much discussion of this on the lower decks of both ships, and many of the hands were already cursing the island as unlucky – as well they might, for some of them had done things there that left them with guilt hanging round their necks like anchor cables.

It was not a happy landfall, not on either ship, and the anchorage seemed to echo the island's ugly reputation. It was entirely land-locked and buried in woods, with great trees right down to the high-water mark. Two little rivers emptied into the bay, though not cleanly, as proper river-mouths, but rather they permeated into oozing swamps. The foliage around that part of the shore was of a poisonous brightness, and a stagnant smell rose up from it: the smell of sodden leaves and rotting wood, where fungus flourished and slimy things crawled.

Nonetheless, *Walrus* and *Lion* dropped anchor, and at the beginning of the morning watch on the day after, a grand council was held, according to articles.

As eight bells sounded, the ships were anchored with their sails hanging limp. It was a hot, still day and the weight of the sun pressed down like a soft pillow laid on old man's face to smother him. The wind was too tired to move and every decent beast or bird crept out of the sun to sleep.

Only the busy mosquitoes were at work. They came up with the steam of the island's marshes and set forth with fever and yellow-jack to kill jolly sailormen, but they couldn't kill Flint's men, nor Long John's neither. These survivors of past epidemics were either naturally immune or too repulsive even for insects to bite.

All hands were gathered aboard *Walrus*, and since this was an exceedingly important occasion, they were turned out in the splendour of their full dress: silken sashes and soiled coats, ruby rings and filthy fingernails, ostrich plumes and sweat-stained hats, glittering ear-rings and knocked-out teeth. And of course, they were heavily armed. At minimum, every man bore a brace or two of pistols and a cutlass, and on top of that there were hatchets, dirks, muskets, knives, and such other arms as the individuals fancied.

Flint, as always, wore the blue coat and bright buttons of an officer, and a hat so laden with gold lace that it was a wonder his head could support it. Unlike his men, he was sparkling clean. His bucket-top boots were shiny and sleek. His shirt was white with fresh-water laundering and his chin was close shaven. Under his arm was a double-barrelled coaching carbine, and gripping daintily on his shoulder, the brilliant green of his parrot, ducking and bobbing her head and occasionally muttering in Flint's ear.

Long John Silver, while not aspiring to the elegance of the Commodore, as Flint now called himself, was his usual, neat self. He too wore a blue officer's coat and, while he must now lean upon a crutch instead of standing square on two feet, his tall figure overshadowed Flint. His free hand – the one not encumbered with the wooden staff – was grasping his belt conveniently close to his pistols. So Silver and Flint looked at one another, and smiled careful, political smiles. Each man was backed by his followers, and each man – at a purely personal level – was almost sure that he could draw and fire and drop his rival before the other could reply... Almost sure, but not quite.

As the two factions crammed aboard *Walrus*, Selena stood apart and aligned with neither. She wore the same clothes she always wore, the outfit she'd settled on, by native wit, as being the most suitable for a single woman among so many men: loose britches to the knee, and a shirt that covered both arms and throat, worn outside the britches both for coolness and to hide the shape of her figure. Nonetheless, when Silver's party came over the side, they ogled her fiercely and whispered to one another, grinning and licking their lips.

At first, Silver couldn't take his eyes off her, looking for some sign, or a look, or a smile. But he got none, and so he forced himself to pay attention to Flint. This was just as well, for Flint looked at nothing other than Long John Silver.

The meeting between the two men was very painful, and all present felt the strain of it. What's more, the peace between the two sides was straining like an anchor cable that's a whisker from snapping under strain. One false word on either side would have been sufficient to start a slaughter. It was an unholy business, totally unlike the moments before normal fighting, when the two sides are strangers. This time, it was old shipmates facing one another.

In some cases there were friendships between the men in either party. In other cases there were scores to settle and injuries to repay. Furthermore, should it come to the extremity of cold steel, then each man had a very good idea who was better in a fight than himself. If it came to it, the thing would be a nasty little civil war. In preparation for it, men felt for their weapons and measured their chances:

Can't fight my old mate Conky Carter…

I'll pistol that bastard Jos Dillon. Thieving sod…

I'll not face Billy Bones. Any o' the others, but not him…

He's a lead-footed swab, that Black Dog. I'll do for him...

For Flint and Silver, upon whom depended the decision to fight or to talk, the strain was heaviest of all. Each man still felt the pain of a shattered friendship, and grief at the loss of so great a comradeship. But more than that, each was afraid of a world without the other. They'd grown so used to depending on one another that they were frightened to be alone, and so they stood ten feet apart and stared into each other's faces, wrapped so deep in their own thoughts that they visibly started when Billy Bones came forward and raised his voice.

'Gentleman of fortune, and jolly companions all!' he cried. 'Silence on the lower deck and let no man strike another, on pain of the yardarm, during this free council of free men.'

Billy Bones had long since swallowed and digested all the lore and custom of those who'd sailed under Mason and England. As far as he was concerned, it was the official way for things to be done. In front of him was a small table, spread with the skull and crossed bones of the black flag. On this was laid – like a Bible on an altar – the Book of Articles under which the company sailed. Billy Bones now respected these things as once he had respected the Union Jack and King George's head on a guinea piece.

'Hats off and give silence for Commodore Flint!' he cried, and there came a rustle of movement as hats were removed.

And then, with the beginning of these formal proceedings, miraculously the tension lifted and everyone let go of their knives and pistols and muskets, and all hands relaxed. Such is the power among men of the images and symbols of authority. Billy Bones was not far wrong after all.

And so the great debate began.

Chapter 31

23rd August 1752
Aboard Walrus
The southern anchorage

'Thank you, Brother Bones,' said Flint formally, and stood forth as the only man present still wearing his hat.

He looked around the dense-packed mass of armed and gaudily clad men, and he spoke with a strong voice that all could hear.

'The purpose of this free council,' he said, 'is to agree finally the plan whereby I propose that our goods be buried safe ashore in this secret place–' He pointed ashore to the green, sweltering island with its line of hills and hidden mysteries. 'This wise step shall enable us to put together, in one stroke, such a fortune for each man as shall make him rich for life!' There was a stir among the men at this. The time was come for debate, and the assembled members screwed up their minds to the process.

In many ways the assembly was far more democratic than the one which sat beside Father

Thames in London, for no man aboard *Walrus* had bought his way in, or was subservient to the will of a political party. And while those aboard *Walrus* had little education – only ferocious prejudices and ignorant opinions – exactly the same applied to the members at Westminster. There were even further similarities: each member had one vote, all motions were decided by simple majority, and decisions were usually arrived at by the previous and secret leverage of promises, threats and bribes: the standard practice of every legislative assembly that has ever sat in the entire history of mankind.

On occasions, however, this time-honoured system breaks down, and the debate over the burying of *Walrus*'s goods was one such. The reason for this was that Flint – who was for the motion – had been denied access to half the members who were aboard *Lion*, while Silver – who was against the motion – had been denied access to the half aboard Walrus. This left only the wildly unpredictable system of members being obliged to listen to the arguments and make up their own minds on the day. But nobody should blame these gentlemen of fortune for turning to so desperate a resort, since the same thing occasionally happens even in the House of Commons.

Flint spoke first and laid out his case.

'Brothers,' he said, 'let's bury what we have, here and now, so we can't lose it by storm or misadventure.' He paused for effect, and looked around at those present. 'And most of all, my chickens, so we don't lose it by spending the whole pile during the first week in port. For isn't that what you always do?'

'Aye!' they said, and grinned and nudged one another and nodded.

'So,' said Flint, 'we bury the goods, then we beat up and down until we have another cargo as good as the present one, and we bury that too, and maybe another besides. And then we return, and lift the whole lot, and divide it up – fair shares for all – and then we go home to England and live like lords for the rest of our lives!'

'Aye!' they roared.

'A carriage and pair for every man!' cried Flint, and others of his men, duly prepared, joined in.

'Ten thousand acres of rolling England!'

'A great house with servants and gold plate!'

'An alderman's daughter for a wife, and a plump tart every Sunday!'

'AYE!' The hands laughed and cheered, and pressed forward to shake Flint's hand: Silver's men and Flint's together. The rivalry between the crews was vanishing like a joint of beef under a dozen carvers.

'Silence on the lower deck!' cried Billy Bones. 'All hands and jolly companions give silence for Captain Silver!'

Brother Bones was at his most officious, like a lord mayor at the opening of a home for orphan paupers. He was grimly determined to be fair to all comers, no matter how undeserving. Give a man public office and he'll bust himself living up to it – at least as far as public display is concerned. So Silver stumped forward, the long crutch thumping on the deck, and his one leg swinging behind. The cheers for Flint were drowned by cheers for his rival, and Billy Bones waved his hands to hush them into silence. This was willingly given and they listened to what Long John Silver had to say.

'Brothers, one and all!' he cried. 'Answer me one question and I'll haul off and not get myself athwart the hawse of this plan, no more.' There was an interested murmuring about this, and a few jeers from the back, where those out of Long John's sight found the courage to oppose him. 'One question, brothers,' repeated Silver. Balancing on his one leg, he beat the deck twice with the stave of his crutch. 'ONE QUESTION!' he cried.

Now there was even more murmuring and jeering, and Flint sneered and tickled his parrot's feathers. This didn't sound like much of a speech.

'Below hatches in this ship,' said Long John, 'leaving aside the bar silver...' Profound silence fell over the company. Long John had struck a spike into the one subject that overwhelmed all others in importance. '...there's such a pile in gold and silver coin as we don't even know how much it is! Such a pile as the hold won't take no more. Such a pile as a few more drops the same would sink the bloody ship!'

He looked around and nodded to himself. *Aye, you lubbers*, he thought, *that's made your ears stand up*. He raised his voice again. 'Seven years I've been a gentleman o' fortune, and others among us longer than that! And *never* has any man of us seen such a pile as sits below these planks!' He slammed the staff of his crutch booming down on the deck. 'Lads, it's gelt that kings'd give their daughters for! It's gelt to build navies! It's gelt to raise armies!'

Flint gulped in alarm as Long John's oratory got into its stride.

'You could buy Savannah with it! You could buy Jamaica with it!' cried Long John. 'You could buy half of bloody England with it!'

Silver nodded grimly; by thunder, he'd got 'em now. Their tongues were hanging down to their boots.

'There's roughly a hundred and forty of us here,' he said, 'leaving aside the extra shares for cap'ns and mates. But even so, the pile's so great that every man shall take enough to live out his life in rum and pickles, and pork and tarts, in his own fine house with his own servants, and his family provided for after he's gone.

'But!' he said, falling into the style that another famous speech-maker had used elsewhere, 'Commodore Flint says you'd spend your share in a week, and Commodore Flint is an honourable man. So, if you'd spend that much in a week, why not twice that, or ten times that?'

Now they were nodding. Such wealth was beyond their understanding, but they'd got the main point. The likes of them would blow their pile no matter how tall it stood.

'So,' said Silver, 'the whole idea o' burying the goods don't make no sense, brothers. You may as well heave it over the side and mark a cross on the sea with ink, in the hope o' coming back to find it.'

'Aye!' they said, and they turned and growled at Flint with the sullen, stupid faces of fools who think they've been duped.

'Avast!' cried Flint. 'Avast there, mateys!'

'Silence for the commodore!' thundered Billy Bones.

'Aye!' cried a few others – those who'd believe shit was gold if Flint told them. 'Let's hear the commodore!'

So Flint got a hearing. And he exerted himself mightily and worked wizardry with words. In all truth, Long John gave the better argument from first to last. But Flint was the better speaker. Flint made them laugh with jokes about one-legged men. Flint made them drool for a triple fortune. And Flint made them afraid of losing their all if they didn't bury it safe in the ground.

But more important than all of that ... and the thing of all, things which won the day, was the doomed, crass willingness of mankind to be seduced by beauty.

For Flint was a splendid creature and Long John was not. Flint stood firm on two legs while Silver went on a crutch. Flint was handsome and gleaming; his clothes were magnificent, his bearing and movements were graceful. Long John Silver was merely big and broad and grim ... and went hopping on a wooden crutch. No man dared fight him, most would choose to follow him, every one of them respected him ... *but nobody wanted to be like him*. And so they were going to believe Flint and spurn Silver. Flint could see it, Silver could see it, even before Flint had finished speaking.

'No man knows of this island but me,' said Flint. 'So nobody can touch the goods that we bury here. And as long as our goods are buried, they're safe from all harm!' So they cheered him and raised him on their shoulders and bore him round the deck in triumph. Flint threw back his head and roared with laughter and his parrot screeched and flapped in alarm.

Long John thumped and staggered through the crowd and found a quiet corner. He threw his hat on the deck in anger, and he cursed and drew out his handkerchief and mopped the sweat from his face. His hands were shaking with anger.

'John,' said a voice at his side. It was Selena, tugging at his arm. She looked up at him in amazement. 'Why'd they believe him?' she said, raising her small voice to be heard over the din. 'It don't make no sense.'

'Neither don't it!' said Silver, and looked away in helpless disgust as the men began to bawl out the words of Flint's song in celebration.

'Fifteen men on the dead man's chest–'

'Why didn't they listen to you?' said Selena.

'Yo-ho-ho, and a bottle of rum–'

''Cos they ain't got the brains of a louse between 'em!'

'Drink and the devil had done for the rest–'

'Why's Flint doing this?'

'Yo-ho-ho, and a bottle of rum...'

'Buggered if I know, lass.'

He sighed and looked at her, and even in that miserable moment he was pierced by her youth and by the sweet loveliness of her face. He raised a hand to stroke her cheek, and summoned a smile. It was as much of a smile as he could manage, and it didn't amount to much. But she put her hand on his and smiled back.

'Won't you ask how I am?' she said. 'Didn't you miss me?'

'Miss you?' he said. 'My little chicky, there weren't never a moment I didn't think of you.' He frowned, and struggled, and dared to ask: 'Did he ... did that sod...?'

'No!' she said. 'I told you, he's never touched me. No man has, but you.'

Silver put an arm around her and managed a real smile. But the roaring mob rolled past at that moment, with Flint shoulder-high grinning down upon him. Seeing the two of them together, he cried:

'Don't worry, John! I kept her warm for you! In fact I kept her *hot*. You just ask the little trollop!' He laughed till the spittle half-choked him, and Silver's face went white with fury and he snatched for his pistols, but Flint was swept away on the instant.

Flint laughed till he ached. He laughed till his head hurt. He laughed so hard that he nearly ruptured himself. It was ... *so ... very ... funny*. Everything Silver had said was true! It was nonsense to bury the goods. It was nonsense for the lower deck to save for a bigger pile. The drunken, whoring, feckless scum would blow the lot in days – even if it stood as high as mountains. There was no point in them burying their treasure. It was nonsense, nonsense, nonsense! At least it was nonsense for everyone except Joe Flint, who had his own plans for the treasure. Plans that did not involve dividing it by so large a figure as one hundred and forty-seven – the precise number of living souls aboard both ships, not counting the six boys and Selena.

At the other side of the roaring vortex of men,

Selena was shouting into Silver's ear, trying to be heard, and him leaning down to listen.

'John! John!' she said, and she reached up and seized his face and made him look at her. If he'd had any sense, he'd have listened to her and believed her, but his whole body was full of anger; anger at his defeat when he knew he was right, and anger and mad jealously at Flint's claim that he'd had his way with her. She shouted louder:

'He didn't touch me!'

'That ain't what he said!'

'Who'd you believe? Him or me? He doesn't want me!'

'Bugger that! What man *wouldn't* want you?'

'He doesn't!'

'Bugger that too! You said he ain't no shirt-lifter!'

'Yes!'

'So? What does he do? Just look at you?'

'Yes!'

'Just that?'

'He looks at me and ... and ... plays with himself.'

'*What?* And you let him?'

Selena blinked. She realised that that was exactly what she did do. Aboard *Walrus*, Flint was god and his power kept her safe from the attentions of dozens of savages whose expressions made it perfectly clear what they would do to her if Flint weren't there. So she didn't dare anger Flint. She didn't dare confront him with his... *Boxing the Jesuit*, that's what they called it; by chance she'd come across some of the ship's boys indulging in this pursuit in a dark corner, and they'd named it and given her the final and complete understanding of Captain Flint's desires where matters of the flesh were concerned.

Those were her thoughts, but all he saw was her failure to meet his eyes.

'So!' he said. 'And you're the one that ain't no whore.'

Selena hung her head. She turned and walked away. The wound Silver had just inflicted was painful beyond bearing. Silver watched her go and all his righteous anger drained away, leaving the growing realisation that he'd just made an appalling mistake. He charged after her, knocking down any man who got in his way.

'Selena!' he cried. 'Selena!' And he poured out words that at first brought laughter from those around, especially from Flint when the spectacle was pointed out to him. But then Flint stopped laughing. He felt the shame of an enemy who'd been such a friend. Soon the whole ship stared silently, for even pirates had their limits. Even they knew what was right and wrong according to their own ways, and they were embarrassed at the sight of Long John Silver hopping along in the wake of a seventeen-year-old black slave-girl who totally ignored him while he begged forgiveness with the tears rolling down his cheeks.

Chapter 32

25th August 1752
In the morning watch (just after dawn)
Aboard Walrus
The southern anchorage

The extent of the treasure was stunning.

For two and a half years they'd fought for it, killed for it, many had died for it – and now it was coming up and out of *Walrus*'s hold and into the daylight. It was a glorious sight: chest after chest, swinging and laden, raised by block and tackle with willing hands hauling to the tune of a shanty.

And now, having got exactly what he wanted, Flint excelled himself in the quality of leadership that he displayed. He was so full of merriment that he didn't need even the smallest flogging to keep him content. He rose in splendour to the occasion, and became – just for once – the officer that he might have been, had Old Nick not tainted his blood with goblin-juice.

So Flint thought the matter through. Flint set aside time. He took a whole day to ponder. And when he was done, even Caesar or Marlborough would have approved his plans – those that he made public at least.

First, since it was necessary, for the present, to keep things sweet among the jolly companions, he invited Silver to join him aboard *Walrus* so that the officers of both ships might confer. As the heat of the island was unbearable except in the morning hours, this took place at dawn, in the open, on *Walrus*'s quarterdeck, where all hands could hear. A table and chairs had been set out for the occasion, and the table was spread with the skull-and-crossbones and the Book of Articles.

Flint even had the boatswain and his mates pipe Silver aboard, man-o'-war style, which was greeted by cheers from all hands, except Silver himself who was plunged into the depths of an enormous sulk.

The great ones took their seats at the table while the lesser hands crowded forward. Flint was immediately joined by Billy Bones – who edged so close to his master that he was almost in his lap – along with Parson Smith and one or two others. Silver had Israel Hands and *Lion*'s boatswain, Sarney Sawyer.

Once Billy Bones had called for silence and healths had been drunk, Flint turned to business.

'We have a heavy task before us, shipmates,' he said, 'for this isn't a thing to be done in an idle moment.'

'Not at all, if we wasn't block-headed!' said Silver.

'Now, John,' said Flint, 'be done! All hands have voted for this.'

'Aye!' said every other voice, and they glared at Silver.

As far as they were concerned he'd lost and was a bad loser. He sighed. He said not one more word. He sank back in his chair, and ignored them all. He did nothing but constantly and uneasily glance round the ship. He was looking for Selena, but Flint had her locked up below. It was fine sport to see Silver tormented, but there were greater matters to consider now and Flint didn't want Silver's temper ignited with unpredictable results.

With nobody to oppose Flint's plans – which were in any case excellent – the business was rapidly concluded and Silver and his men went back to *Lion* to many good-humoured smiles and back-slapping from old friends aboard *Walrus*.

Billy Bones, however, did not go straight back to *Lion*. A word in his ear from Flint – spotted at once by Silver – informed Billy that he needed to search his old cabin for a lucky gold piece that he'd 'lost'. Flint declared that Billy might turn the cabin upside down, if he wished, and return to his new captain – he smiled at Silver – later in the day.

And so to the great works. First a landing party made up equally of *Lions* and *Walruses* was sent ashore under Sarney Sawyer to set up camp. Tents were raised, stores were unloaded, and tackles were rigged – ten-foot lengths of timber with lines in the middle to sling a load by – so that two men, or four if need be, could share the burden of carrying the goods over rough ground to the burial places.

That took most of the first day, which on the island meant working from dawn till noon, then stopping for three hours while the sun did its worst, and then working another three or four hours, depending on how well things were going. Flint had planned for a working day of just seven hours, which was a wise and sensible allowance given the sweltering humidity of the southern anchorage.

On the second day, *Walrus*'s hatches were opened and three teams put to work: one under Billy Bones, who had a dozen men as stevedores to hoist the goods out of the hold; a second under Parson Smith, who had six men and *Walrus's* twenty-five-foot cutter; and a third under Israel Hands, who led a party of four men in *Lion's* fifteen-foot jolly-boat – these being the biggest boats belonging to each ship.

Flint's plan called for the cutter to be loaded – she would take up to forty hundredweight – and then her crew would pull for shore while the jolly-boat was being loaded with her twenty-five hundredweight. He allowed an hour for each boat to be loaded by Billy Bones's men, another hour for Sarney Sawyer's shore party to unload them, and a thirty-minute pull each way between *Walrus* and the shore.

In theory, this would deliver two complete boatloads every three and a half hours. In practice, with the heavy current that swept the anchorage, and the debilitating effect of the climate on men not used to such work, it was found that a mere three boat-loads could be got ashore each morning, and two in the afternoon. So in the end it took four days of heavy work to empty *Walrus*'s hold and get the goods ashore. The final load – greeted with cheers from both ships and the shore party – grounded two hours after dawn on the fourth day, since the mortally tired teams had failed to get it ashore before sundown the previous day.

In celebration, Flint ordered all hands ashore.

The boats were heaving with merry crews, as one hundred and forty-seven men, and six boys were brought ashore, leaving only Selena still locked in Flint's cabin, by Flint's orders.

Laid out in neat rows, just to one side of Sarney Sawyer's camp and under the lines of bending green palms, where they took advantage of a bit of shade, the goods stood finally revealed like a regiment on parade.

There were seventy-one chests of gold coin;

There were one hundred and sixty-five chests of silver coin;

There were four hundred and forty-six bars of silver.

Men gaped and stared. They pushed back their hats. They scratched their chins. They goggled and blinked and wondered. A dull murmuring rose from the mass of men, clinking and glittering in their finery – for they'd come ashore in their best rig for the occasion. Fearful concentration was on most faces as they bent to the inevitable question.

Stood together in their long blue coats, their leaders were at the same game. Even Flint's parrot seemed to be calculating.

'Bugger me!' said Billy Bones. 'What's it all worth, Cap'n?'

'A very great deal, Mr Bones,' said Flint, and turned to Parson Smith. 'Mr Smith, have you made the calculations I asked of you?'

'Ah,' said Smith, 'ahem!' And he studied his sheaf of papers. He'd laboured long and hard over these calculations, and now was his moment of fame. 'Captain,' he said, 'I have made efforts to weigh the cargo...' He pointed to a neat mechanism of spars and ironwork, improvised by the ever-adaptable skills of seamen. Silence fell as the hands realised the subject of which he spoke and gave themselves up to intense concentration.

'We have built a balance, using six-pounder shot as weights, and I have weighed each chest and box with the help of Mr Sawyer's men, whom I commend to you for their efforts.'

'Well done, Mr Sawyer,' said Flint.

'Aye-aye, Cap'n,' said Sawyer.

'Indeed,' said Parson, gravely, 'and here is my tally...' He fumbled with his papers. 'Of gold coin we have a total of ninety-six hundredweights. Of silver coin we have a total of two hundred and twenty hundredweights, and of silver bars we have approximately two hundred and nineteen hundredweights.'

He paused and looked around his audience, swelling with importance.

'As you will appreciate, where the chests and boxes are concerned, those weights are inclusive of the containers themselves, though these will be but a small proportion of the total. You will also appreciate that all weights are approximate, given that our standard of measurement was no more than common roundshot.'

'Aye,' they murmured, still deeply in the dark.

'So give us a sum, Mr Smith,' said Flint. 'A sum in English pounds, however approximate.'

'AYE!' they cried.

Here Parson faltered. He gulped and sweated. He polished his spectacles on a shirt-cuff. He fumbled among his papers.

'The problem is, Captain, the nature of the goods. Considering first the gold coin...'

'Ahhh,' said the audience, eagerly.

'Taking that example,' he said, pointing to one particularly large chest – obviously oriental, with foliate brass hinges and beautiful orange lacquer-work. 'I have opened that, and found it to contain the coinage of half the world. There are Georges and Louis d'ors, doubloons and moidores, and the faces of every king of Europe these past hundred years. Each has a different degree of fineness – which is to say content of gold – and may not be compared simply by weight. Thus each–'

'No doubt,' said Flint, not pleased. 'What about the silver coin? That's Spanish dollars. Give us your tally of them!'

'AYE!'

'Ah! Ah!' said Parson. 'There, too, we come to grief, for the dollar has different values in different places. In England it passes at about five shillings, in Massachusetts at six shillings, in Pennsylvania at seven shillings, and in New York at eight or nine. It depends heavily upon the availability of silver in the place concerned. There is a great crying up of the silver dollar, sir, throughout the colonies.'

A nasty growl came from the hands. Flint frowned. Billy Bones and Flint's parrot – attentive to their master's mood – blinked and shuffled, the one reaching for his cutlass, and the other moaning in anticipation. They didn't quite look at one another and share the moment, but it was damned close.

'Am I to understand, Mr Smith,' said Flint, 'that you cannot make even a *guess?*'

'No, sir,' said Parson. 'But the calculations, sir, they are ... sir, most complex ... sir...' Parson licked his lips, he looked into the depth of his papers. He found no answer there, and he began to tremble.

'Bloody Parson!' cried a voice from the deep of the crowd.

'He's thievin' it, that's what!' said another.

'Soddin' lubber!'

'How much have you stole, you bugger?'

'How much have we got left?'

'Avast!' cried Silver, stirring out of his sulk. 'Belay that!' He stumped forward from where he'd been standing, a little separate from the other blue coats. He pulled off his hat in irritation. He wiped his brow and clapped on the hat again.

'Why, John!' said Flint, with a sarcastic smile. 'Are you joining us, at last?'

'Maybe I am, maybe I ain't,' said Silver and jabbed a finger at Parson Smith. 'But shiver my timbers if I'll stand idle while this bum-sucking lubber pisses in our grog!'

'Go on, Long John!' said Israel Hands.

'Long John!' cried the mob.

'Now see here,' said Silver, 'this is a case for good round figures. First the gold coin...' He looked at Smith. 'You say we've got ninety-six hundredweight of coin?' Smith nodded. 'So,' said Silver, 'bugger your "degrees of fineness" – let's say it was all in English guineas. That ain't precious accurate, but it's good enough. It's all bloody gold at the end of the day.'

'Aye!' said the hands.

'Well,' said Silver, 'a hundred pounds' value, in

English guineas, weighs roughly thirty ounces of weight, and there are roughly eighteen hundred ounces in a hundredweight...' he paused and looked round his audience '...as any gentleman of fortune knows.'

They grinned guiltily, like schoolboys caught out not knowing their lessons.

'So,' said Silver, 'thirty goes sixty times into eighteen hundred, so a hundredweight of guineas is worth sixty times a hundred pounds, which is six thousand pounds. And since we've got near enough a hundred hundredweights of it, that means we've got – in gold coin – close on ... six hundred thousand pounds.'

There was a deep gasp.

'As for the dollars,' said Silver, 'each dollar weighs an ounce, and there's eighteen hundred of them to the hundredweight too. We've got two hundred and twenty hundredweights...' he frowned and closed his eyes an instant '...which makes three hundred and ninety-six thousand ounces. If we takes even the lowest value for dollars – the value in London, which is four to the pound – that's still close on ... one hundred thousand pounds.'

Another gasp and he turned finally to the stacked bars of silver.

'And it's near as damnit the same for them too! About two hundred hundredweights of silver, or ... another hundred thousand pounds.'

Now they were awestruck and helpless before such colossal sums of money, and all of it in precious metal.

'Aye, shipmates,' said Silver, 'I'll leave you to

work out your shares, for I'm done and buggered, and I've said enough. But the grand total must be at least ... *eight hundred thousand pounds*.'

He was right about the arithmetic. He was wrong about saying too little. He hadn't said nearly enough. Not by a long way. The men were brimming with respect for him. They were as grateful as if he, personally, had conjured the money out of the air for them. If he'd seized the moment, he'd have won them back and dumped Flint's burial plan into the bog-house pit where it belonged. But he said nothing. He was still grieving over the loss of Selena and cursing himself for losing the previous debate.

So Flint seized the moment. He'd read the men's mood precisely and suffered a fearful stab of fright. But he bounced back fast and went among the men, laughing and joking, and calling them by name, telling them what wealth they'd enjoy, calling for food and drink, and proclaiming a rest day... And since, as ever, Flint was irresistibly charming whenever he chose to be, they hoisted him shoulder high and carried him round the camp, cheering and waving, with Billy Bones following behind, lost in joy at the triumph of the moment.

Silver gave up completely after that, and proceeded to get heavily drunk when the rum went round. Flint smiled happily and pressed on with the rest of his plan.

'Now, shipmates,' he said, gathering them together, 'here's how we shall continue. First we shall carry the goods off the beach, to an approximation of their three separate resting places: one for the gold, one for the dollars, one for the bar silver. That is a task which shall need all hands, in three crews. Then we shall draw lots for a final crew of just six men, which shall complete the burying in the final, secret places.'

'Aye!' they said, nodding wisely – all except Silver, who was sitting on a barrel all by himself, emptying a mug.

'All hands but the lucky six and myself,' said Flint, 'shall then return to the ships and watch for my signal there –' he pointed to a big spar, raised up as a flag post by Sarney Sawyer's men, with a black flag waiting to be run up to the truck.

'All shall watch for the signal. And until it goes up, none shall interfere with the works ashore. Is that agreed?'

'Aye!'

'And is that sworn upon our articles? Sworn as free companions and gentlemen of fortune?'

'Aye!'

Flint congratulated himself. He smirked and tickled the parrot. He was so proud of himself. He'd won it all. He'd mastered John Silver, and done it with Silver's own jolly companions lore. In the joy of the moment, Flint was moved to add a few more words which were not John Silver's lore but his own. This was entirely unnecessary, and a considerable mistake.

'Thus *Lion* shall guard *Walrus*,' he said, 'and *Walrus* shall guard *Lion*, and either shall fire into the other, should a landing party be seen going over the side.'

'Aye,' they said, and looked at one another, and

were reminded – from that moment on – that they were not one crew of jolly companions, but two crews of rivals.

Chapter 33

5th September 1752
First dog watch (c. 5 p.m. shore time)
Aboard Lion
The southern anchorage

It took six men to put Billy Bones in irons.

Two or three others went down, battered by Billy's fists as the tangle of bodies rolled across the main deck, and Silver clumped about yelling and bellowing while those not engaged in the fight shouted encouragement and blessed their luck that they'd not been chosen for this particular duty.

Finally, when Billy Bone's strength was exhausted and men were hanging on to each of his limbs, Israel Hands hauled off Billy's shoes and put a pair of U-shaped iron hoops over his ankles, then ran a short rod through eyes in the ends of the loops. One end of the bar had a head that wouldn't pass through the eyes, and the other end Mr Hands hammered over so it wouldn't go through either. That left Billy Bones's feet firmly fixed together so he could stand – or hop – but not walk. He was as firmly clapped in irons as any seaman ever had been.

'There you are, Mr Bones,' said Israel Hands, 'all snug and tight.'

'Go fuck your mother,' said Billy. 'I'll do for you yet, you bastard!'

'Not if I do you first,' said Israel Hands, and added mockingly, 'Billy-my-chicken!'

Billy Bones found strength to shake off some of the men and lunged forward in a ferocious attempt to get a stranglehold round Israel Hands's neck.

'Avast!' said Silver. 'Haul off, Mr Hands.'

'Aye-aye, sir!' said Hands, but sneered at Billy Bones sideways when Long John wasn't looking.

'You men,' said Silver to the six holding Billy Bones, 'take him – careful, mind – and get him below to the hold. And you, Mr Hands, come with us and bring your chains and your hammer.'

So they took Billy Bones below, those he'd walloped a thousand times with the rope's end. They took him below with many jolly bumps and cheerful knocks, and they heaved him on to the ballast like a sack of collier's coals. Then they ran a chain between his legs and his irons, and secured him to a timber, and left him sitting on his arse with a lantern to see by. He was a sorry sight: covered in blood and bruises, clothes ripped, hair breaking loose from his pigtail, and one toe poking white and comical from a hole in his stocking. The fall of one who'd been the terror of the lower deck drew jeers and laughter from all sides.

'Belay that, you swabs!' cried Silver. 'Get about your duties!' Silver frowned. The trouble was, lying five days at anchor waiting for Flint to finish with his burying, most of them didn't *have* any duties and the ship was full of idlers. Worse still, the whole crew had seen Silver make a considerable fool of himself and now thought less of him. Silver sighed as painful thoughts filled his mind, and he tried to fix on the business in hand.

'Well then, Mr Bones,' he said when they were alone. 'I'm sorry to see you nailed like this, I take my affy davy on it! You'd not have been brought below like dunnage for stowage if you'd listened to myself instead of Flint. You know you can't trust the bugger, so what's holding you to him? What's he offered you?'

'Ax mine arse!' said Billy Bones, loyal beyond reason to his absent master.

'Is that the way of it, then?' said Silver. 'And there's me thinking we'd sailed a few leagues as shipmates. Can we not make and mend? We're both aground on the same shoal.'

'*Kiss* mine arse!' said Billy Bones.

'Billy,' said Silver, 'I asks you once more – you as knows Flint better than any of us – what's he doing? What's his plan?'

'Don't know,' said Billy Bones. *'An' I won't tell!'*

'Huh!' said Silver. 'You ain't the sharpest, are you, Billy-boy?'

'That's all you know!' said Billy.

'Billy,' said Silver, 'what if I let Israel and some of the others ask you?'

To Silver's amazement, Billy Bones grinned.

'You daresn't,' he said.

'Don't I though? You sure o' that?'

'Aye!'

And that was all Billy Bones would say. Silver got not another word out of him, and made his way slowly up on deck again. He was now very nimble, but climbing would always be hard for a man with one leg. Two bells sounded as he pulled himself through a companionway in the waist. Two bells of the second dog watch – seven p.m. shore time – and it was dark. He glanced ashore and saw a fire burning and heard the faint sound of singing: the lucky six and Captain Flint.

He looked across the anchorage to where *Walrus* lay, visible only by her lights. Selena was somewhere aboard. At the thought of her, the despair sat down upon him. When the grand council ended and *Lion*'s crew went back to their ship, she'd gone with Flint, who'd promptly insisted that Silver should have Billy Bones again ... *in compensation!* Selena he'd not seen since, but Billy Bones had stuck like shit to a blanket ... apart from the half-day he spent aboard *Walrus* looking for his lucky gold piece.

So what did it mean? What had Flint said to Billy? Why should Flint want Billy Bones aboard *Lion?* What was Flint doing ashore, with six men and eight hundred thousand pounds? Silver sighed. He ignored Israel Hands and the others, who were waiting for him to see what he'd learned from Billy Bones, and he went down to the stern cabin and found a bottle of rum.

It was a bad time for Long John Silver. Perhaps the worst time in his life, because he was facing failure – utter failure – at a time when he was still grieving for his lost leg and trying to face life as a cripple. He counted the score in his mind: Item one, he'd found a woman that he loved, and had insulted her and lost her because he couldn't trust her. Item two, losing her was a pain like Surgeon Cowdray's knife. Item three, he'd failed to show the light to Billy Bones. Item four, he'd failed to talk the hands out of Flint's burying of the goods. And item five – if the mutterings and saucy behaviour among the crew was anything to go by – then he'd failed as Cap'n Silver.

He took to the bottle and was well into draining it when, some hours later, a hand tapped at the cabin door.

'Cap'n?' said Israel Hands's voice.

'Go away!' said Silver. But the door opened, and three men entered: Israel Hands, Blind Pew and Sarney Sawyer. Hands and Sawyer had their hats in their hands, and Pew was clutching his eyeshade. They were bobbing and nodding like Flint's parrot. All three touched their brows and stamped the deck in salute, and they stood in a row with their heads bowed. *Lion*'s small stern cabin was too low for men to stand in comfortably, but they'd probably have stood like that had they been in a cathedral. They were nervous.

They were nervous and something else. They were shocked at the spectacle of Long John Silver far gone in drunkenness, stretched unkempt and slovenly in a chair, with his one leg perched on a table and his favourite pair of pistols in front of him. He looked all the worse by comparison with the neat cabin, all white-painted and picked out in gold leaf, and brightly lit by beeswax candles in glazed lamps. The three of them would have been even more shocked had they known what Silver – in his despair – had been thinking of doing with his pistols.

'What's this?' said Silver, peering with red eyes. 'A deputation?'

'Cap'n,' said Israel Hands, 'what did Billy say, beggin' your pardon?'

'Nothing,' said Silver.

'Let *me* ask him, Cap'n,' said Israel Hands, 'with a belaying pin.'

'Aye,' said Blind Pew, 'or a little fire under his toes.'

'No!' said Silver. 'You've signed articles.'

'But we's split,' said Israel Hands. 'An' the articles is broke.'

Silver sighed, hauled himself upright, shoved his pistols out of reach and tried to act the part of a ship's master.

'Mr Hands,' he said, 'bend an ear, for here's the way of it. If this happy company be split – which p'raps it may be – then we needs Billy Bones more than ever, for I reminds you that only he, aboard this ship, could bring us safe home to Savannah. So, even if there was no articles, we can't break his bones nor burn his toes nor anything other than guard him like a mother's child.'

'Oh!' said the three, all together. They'd not thought of that.

'Aye,' said Silver. 'And somebody has explained the matter to Billy, who'd never have worked that out for himself – not for all his 'rithmatic and calculations. Now, who d'you think *that* might have been?'

'Flint,' said Blind Pew.

'Aye,' said Silver. And there was a silence while Silver emptied another glass and the three men stood looking at one another. Then Pew nudged

Israel Hands.

'Cap'n,' said Hands, 'you was right. We are a deppytation.'

'Are you now?'

'Aye, Cap'n.'

Silver knew what was coming. They'd had enough of him. It was the black spot.

'Out with it then, curse you!'

'Cap'n, this crew has been talking...'

'And?'

'Cap'n, you must know...'

Ba-bang! Ba-ba-bang! A volley of shots came from the shore, sounding clearly through the open stern lights.

Chapter 34

5th September 1752
Dusk
The island

Flint was deeply happy. The goods were buried and only he knew where.

Well, the lucky six had an approximate knowledge of the burial sites – he looked at their ugly faces as they sat patiently in the sand, awaiting his orders. They were illiterate clods. Even if he'd given them his notebook with its careful bearings and measurements, they couldn't have used it. Nonetheless, they'd remember trees and rocks and other landmarks, bless their hearts. But that didn't matter. Not at all. Not as far as Joe Flint was concerned, because here on the island he was unchained from any limitations on his ability to deal with these unfortunates.

More precisely – did he but know it – here on the island he'd been joined by his old friend Temptation, who'd returned chuckling and merry, and just bursting with new ideas. Always previously Flint had been constrained by higher powers: King George's law, John Silver's articles, even the stolid conservatism of Billy Bones. But not here! Here he was alone with the lucky six, and boundless opportunity.

He fondled the shifting, muttering parrot that swayed and fidgeted and rubbed itself against his head, and he looked towards *Lion* and *Walrus*, moored out in the smooth waters of the southern anchorage. They were both still visible in the tropical dusk, though a tired red sun was touching the horizon in the west.

Now then, my jolly boys ... thought Flint, studying the ships, *are you awake and lively to your duties, there on board?*

Clang! said *Walrus*, the bell sounding clearly across the water.

'Ah!' said Flint.

Clang! said *Lion* after a pause, for no two ships kept quite the same time.

One bell of the first watch, thought Flint, *time for sunset*, and he turned to those who considered themselves so fortunate to be ashore with him, and he smiled with gleaming teeth as the sun surrendered to the darkness and delivered up the island unto the terrors of the night.

'Build a fire, my hearties,' he cried. 'Build her big, for it's time to feast. Biscuit and pork, sauerkraut and salt herring!'

'And rum, Cap'n?' they said.

'Aye, lads!' said Flint, and playfully pulled the nose of the nearest man. 'Grog for all hands, like the good fellows you are.' They cheered wildly and set to, running about like schoolboys on holiday.

'Aren't they just the roaring boys, though?' he said confidentially to the bird. Two were Silver's men: Rob Taylor, and James Cameron. The rest were his: Franky Skillit, Henry Howard, Peter Evans, and Iain Fraser. Six men: *the lucky six*, as the rest had believed when lots were drawn. Flint positively wriggled with glee at the thought of *that*, and of the downcast, miserable faces of all those whose luck had failed them, keeping them out of the burial party.

The burial party, thought Flint. *God damn and gut me! That's what they called it. Their own precious words!* He marvelled at the eternal truth that no wit is sharper than that of actuality.

So he watched contentedly as they built a huge bonfire, far too big for their needs, and he watched as they skewered chunks of salt pork and fish, and stove in the head of a cask of sauerkraut. He looked around the little camp they'd set out on the beach, all calm and snug and quiet … and inky-black dark without even the moon for company. But the jolly red faces beamed in the firelight and the men jostled one another for the best places to roast their meat, and the rum pannikin went round. Flint laughed, and raised his voice.

'Fifteen men on the dead man's chest!' he sang.

'Yo-ho-ho, and a bottle of rum...' they replied.

'Go it, you bold dogs,' cried Flint, and they took up the song.

Flint took a cut of pork, offered by one of the half-drunk men, bit into it and swallowed and choked himself laughing at the thought that – at the great council – all hands, led by Blind Pew, had solemnly voted that the only man they would trust in the secret burial of the goods was ... Cap'n Flint. He'd not even had to argue the point! Flint chewed the succulent pork and the juices ran down his chin, and his shoulders heaved in silent laughter. He was enjoying himself enormously, and the best was yet to come.

When he'd done with the meat, and wiped the tears from his eyes, Flint sat beside the fire in the sand and took a modest sip from the rum, and became the jolliest companion any of the rest had ever known. He laughed along with them and told them what fine fellows they were, and how they'd drive in their carriages in England, with a tart on either arm, to take their seats in the House of Lords.

'Three cheers for Cap'n Flint!' cried Iain Fraser, and they gave three cheers that set the hills echoing.

'Thank you, lads,' said Flint, and stretched his limbs and stood up by the fireside in the velvet night with the insects twittering loudly and the dull rumble of the breakers ceaselessly pounding the westward rocks and cliffs. 'But there's no cause for cheers,' he said, and smiled indulgently as the fools cheered and cheered again.

'God save the Cap'n!' cried Rob Taylor, who

was a small man and whose curse it was that whenever he drank round for round with his mates, he got drunk first, for there weren't many places in his small body for the drink to go to, other than his head.

'Thank you, Rob,' said Flint, and almost lost control of the mood of solemnity he was now trying to create. The trouble was that the look of spaniel-eyed worship on little Taylor's face was almost beyond bearing. And look at the rest of them! How easy it had been to win their affection with a few days ashore and their bellies full of food and drink.

'Ah-hum!' said Flint, clearing his throat and striking a more serious, pose. 'Lads,' he said, 'on the morrow, with all the digging done, and our spades and picks laid aside, we begin the final task of taking precise bearings.' It was nonsense, of course, for all necessary bearings were already in his notebook. Damn it! He had to cough hard to disguise the unstoppable snigger at their solemn faces.

'So sleep well, like the good fellows you are,' he said, grinding his fingernails into his palms so that the pain would kill the laughter. 'And don't be afeared of anything in the night, for we shall set a guard as before ... even though I doubt there's much to worry about, these days,' and he peered out thoughtfully into the night.

His words set the mood. His manner sent signals to the others, and they too squinted out into the dark, though they knew not what for, since none of them had ever been on the island before.

'I know this place, lads,' said Flint. 'I was here

years ago. It offers a safe anchorage, with good water to fill the butts, and a fine stand of timber for spars and planking, and with goats for fresh meat besides...' he paused and looked into the eyes of each man in turn. 'But every night or so, we'd lose a man...'

Flint had himself well in hand now, and he was playing them like a flute.

'We never did find the cause,' said Flint, 'though we posted guards, and double guards, and doubled them again.' Flint shuddered as if some evil thing had walked past in the dark. 'All we did know, lads, was that it wasn't just men. Not savages even ... but something worse.' He waved a hand towards the dark woods. 'Some said it was hairy apes that hid in the depths of the forest and only came out at night. Others said they'd seen ... things...'

There was dead silence now from his little audience. Meat and drink were laid aside and they gaped at him open-mouthed with terror and wished themselves safe aboard ship, in their own element, with their mates around them, facing dangers they understood, they were brave men; but not here, not against the unknown and the occult. Especially the latter.

'Being as it was a king's ship,' continued Flint, 'we had marines to do the soldiering for us, and they were our guards. One night a whole company of them gave a volley out into the dark, all together at ten paces, when a dark shape was seen creeping towards our camp. But not a hair or a drop of blood did we find in the morning. After that, why, some of the men went looking for silver to cast into bullets.'

'What for?' said Taylor nervously. 'Why'd they do that?'

'Why, Rob,' said Flint, 'I'd have thought you'd have known. ''Tis a proven fact that a silver bullet will kill where a lead bullet will not ... where creatures of the night are concerned ... things that are unholy, if you take my meaning.'

They did take his meaning. They took it into their bones, and their teeth fairly chattered in fright. But Flint merely shrugged his shoulders and sighed. 'That's the long and short of it, lads, so let's be merry again and empty the bowl, and eat hearty. For who knows what the morrow will bring?' He smiled his great smile again, and sat down and helped himself to more food. He ate hearty, just as he'd bid the others to do. He did, but they did not.

'Cap'n,' said Howard.

'Aye?'

'How was it done?'

'How was *what* done, Henry?'

'Them as was killed...'

'Stow it, Henry!' said Fraser. 'No call to talk about that.'

'Aye,' said Taylor and Evans.

'Various ways,' said Flint, shaking his head mournfully. 'But strangulation mainly.'

'And?' said Howard, unable to leave the thing alone.

'Oh, bless you, Henry,' said Flint, with every appearance of kindly concern, 'I'm not sure you'd really want to know. But nasty ways, and silent ways.' He appeared to notice for the first time that none of the others were eating or drinking.

'Why, lads,' said he, 'is none of you hungry? There's work to be done on the morrow. Eat hearty! Drink deep!'

But the merry mood was gone and a dread and fear of the powers of darkness had fallen on the wretched six. Seafaring men have been superstitious since time began, and more susceptible than most to tales of supernatural horrors. After all, they were innocent of education, they lived rough and dangerous lives, they were constantly at risk of death from the anger of the sea, and added to that they really *did* see things beyond the ken of landsmen. So even at the best of times they believed in mermaids and sea-serpents, ghosts and spirits and the lost souls of drowned mariners calling to them out of the bodies of sea gulls. And that was safe at their own mess tables with the grog going round.

Flint saw the terror in their eyes and, yet again, he nearly spoiled it by laughing. But he kept a straight face as they huddled together and drew their weapons and fumbled with them. Howard spilt the priming of his pistols by checking it, and then could barely reload because of his trembling fingers. Evans cut his thumb trying the edge of his knife, and Fraser and Taylor put an arm around each other, seeking comfort, while Skillit chewed his thumb and whimpered like a child.

'Howard'll take the first watch,' said Flint. 'Two turns of the half-hour glass, Henry.' And he pointed towards where their boat lay, out in the darkness fifty yards away and invisible in the deep black gloom. 'You'll find the glass in the boat, Henry, so up-anchor and fetch it, like the good fellow you are!'

Howard swallowed and stared into the dark, imagining what might be out there, waiting to snatch him away with its claws, the instant he set foot outside the firelight.

'At the double now, Henry!' said Flint firmly. 'There's nothing there, lad. Not that I can see ... though you're a younger man than me and may have sharper eyes.'

Howard gave a moan and stared between his knees at the sand, and never moved. Neither did Evans, when he was told, nor Fraser nor Taylor, nor Skillit nor Cameron either, and all the threats and cajoling of their captain could not make them go. They sat in stark terror, biting their lower lips and looking away when spoken to. Flint cursed them thoroughly, then got up himself.

'Why, you cowardly lubbers,' he said. 'Will you make me go myself? Damn you for a set of yellow-bellied codfish!' He shook his head sadly. 'I'd wager a thousand pounds there's nothing out there just now, for it was always in the small hours before dawn that they used to come, whatever they were, so I shouldn't wonder if we aren't safe for *hours* yet.'

So he grumbled and sighed and finally strode off, to a sudden and pathetic chorus:

'Don't go, Cap'n!'

'Please, Cap'n!'

'Don't let them buggers come!'

'Don't leave us alone...'

'Bah!' he said, and ignored them, and vanished into the dark, leaving only the sound of his trudging feet behind him.

Soon even that stopped, and then the night was silent. The six men strained their eyes to see where Flint had gone. They saw nothing. They heard nothing. Seconds stretched into long minutes.

'Where's he gone?' said Taylor.

'He could've been there and back ten times by now,' said Howard.

'P'raps he's lost his way?' said Fraser.

'P'raps something's got hold of ... got him ... got hold … got…'

Evans couldn't bring himself to say it: not fully, not quite, for fear that the saying of it would somehow conjure up the things he feared.

'Shut your trap!' said Skillit. 'There ain't nothing wrong. Cap'n's missed his way, that's all. I'll give a holler.' He drew breath and let go with a mast-head bellow:

'AHOY THERE! FLINT AHOY!'

Silence. Nothing answered. Only the insects and the booming surf. But then...

'What's that?' said Taylor suddenly.

'What?' said Howard.

'There!' said Taylor. He pointed a trembling finger.

'I can't hear nothing,' said Cameron.

'Nor can't I,' said Evans.

'Nor...' began Fraser, then, 'Gawdamighty!' he said. 'I hear it!' He heard it all right, for coming towards them was a heavy, shuffling, dragging sound and harsh, slow breathing as if of some beast. It was faint and some way off, but it was distinct, and every man of them could hear it.

'Who knows a prayer?' said Taylor, who'd had a churchgoing mother.

'Fuck that!' said Howard. 'Pistols, boys!'

There was a feverish trembling and drawing and clicking of firelocks being made ready. But the noise stopped, almost as if the thing had heard them, and for several agonising minutes the six men stretched out their arms, a heavy sea-service pistol in each fist, aiming at the place where they thought the sound had come from. And then there came a low moan from another direction entirely, a ghastly sound like a creature in the extremity of pain. They spun round and aimed afresh. But the sound ceased abruptly ... only to come back from another place.

'Beach and bugger me!' said Taylor. 'There's more than one o' the sods.'

'Back to back, mates,' said Howard, 'so's they shan't take us by the stern.'

'Aye!' said the others.

That was good sense and a comforting opportunity to huddle physically up against one another. They felt better like that and cheered up immensely, until the hideous groaning came again from a third and quite new direction.

'All around us,' said Fraser.

'What are they?' said Evans.

'I don't want to know!' said Howard. 'Just keep the buggers off!'

He was shivering in fright, and when another long-drawn howl came out of the night he jumped and let fly. His two pistols split the night with their flashing and roaring as Howard fired aimlessly. And his mates fired too, in senseless imitation.

Then there was a fearful scrambling for cartridges, and a weeping and snivelling and a gibbering as the wretched creatures fumbled and elbowed each other and spilt powder and dropped bullets in a pitiful rush to reload ... before the things beyond the firelight could fall upon them.

'Ahoy!' came a voice. 'Belay that firing! Who gave the word to fire?'

'Cap'n Flint!' cried Howard.

'It's the cap'n!' cried Fraser.

'Thank God!' cried Taylor.

'Sweet Jesus!' cried Cameron.

'We're saved!' cried Evans.

Flint's familiar figure loomed out of the darkness with a sand-glass in his hand.

'Who gave the word to draw firelocks?' he said sternly. 'D'you not realise you could've shot me as I walked towards you?' But they fawned upon him, these tough, hard, throat-cutting pirates; they clung to Flint's legs like children, they seized his hands, they grovelled like dogs, they all but jumped up into his arms.

'They was here, Cap'n,' they said.

'Shoals o' the buggers.'

'Bearing down upon us, they was.'

'Coming to grapple an' board.'

'By thunder!' said Flint. 'And me not fifty paces off, and I never heard a sound. That ain't natural, lads!'

'Why was you gone so long, Cap'n?'

'What?' said Flint. 'I went straight to the boat and back again!'

'Shite!' said Evans. 'That ain't natural neither, Cap'n, 'cos you was gone for ages.'

''Tain't natural,' they echoed, and Flint plumped himself down beside them and scratched his head.

'Well, shipmates,' he said, 'there's things afoot that no man can fathom, and that's a fact. But we're all true hearts aboard this ship, and jolly companions all, and we shan't be made afraid of that which hasn't the courage to face us man to man.' And he leaned forward and put a hand on Howard's shoulder. 'Isn't that so, Henry?'

'Aye,' said Howard in a tiny voice.

'And you, Peter Evans,' said Flint. 'And you, Rob Taylor, and you, Iain Fraser. I say that if they never came to grips, then they're more afraid of you than you were of them!'

He said it with such conviction, and so boldly, that the men cheered up wonderfully and their fears ran away. In all truth, Joe Flint had the makings of a very fine officer inside of him ... along with all the other ingredients.

'So here's my orders,' said Flint, all brisk and businesslike. 'Howard, you take the first watch, followed by Taylor, then Fraser, then Evans.' He handed over the sand glass. 'And now you, Peter, pile wood on the fire to keep it blazing, while you, Iain, make sure all the pistols are properly primed and loaded, and you Rob – like the sensible man you are – put your head down and go to sleep, which is what I shall do myself.'

With that, Flint laid himself down beside the fire, having first placed his hat as a nest for his parrot. Then, pulling his coat collar up around his ears, he closed his eyes, and gave every appearance of going to asleep.

Greatly comforted, and grinning weakly at one another, his men did as they'd been told. After that, what with the heavy work they'd been doing all day, and what with the quantities of rum they'd been encouraged to drink, within ten minutes only Howard was awake, nodding over his sand glass and shuddering with the need constantly to haul himself out of the seductive pit of slumber. The rest were curled up snoring like happy hogs. And so – it seemed – was Flint.

Howard did his best, he really did. He nodded and started. He stood up and took a turn about the fire. He counted stars and made patterns in the sand between his legs. He gritted his teeth. He even said nursery rhymes in his head, to keep himself awake. But in the end, he slumped over in unwakeable sleep.

'Aaaaaah!' screamed a voice. 'Aaaaaall hands! All hands on deck!'

Howard struggled up towards consciousness, sick and thickheaded from last night's drink. He tried to roll out of his hammock, and found that this could not be done while lying on a bed of soft sand. So he got up on one elbow and looked about him.

The fire was grey ash and black embers. The sun was climbing over the trees and the two ships lay at anchor in the bay. Flint and Fraser were getting up from sleep and Taylor was bawling and howling from some way off, near the edge of the forest. He was staring at a still figure laid face down in the sand.

'All hands!' cried Taylor again. 'It's Peter! They've done for him!' There was a rush towards Evans's body. Flint was first and turned him over. Poor Peter Evans, youngest of all the crew, who'd been abandoned at birth then raised and sent to sea by Coram's foundling hospital. Poor Peter Evans: a kindly soul who'd wished good on all the world – right up to the innocent age of fourteen when he'd knifed his first man.

'Ugh!' said Flint. 'The devils!'

Howard leaned forward for a look at Evans's face over Flint's shoulder. He gasped and a cold fear rolled up his legs like icy water. He'd seen death in a hundred forms, and normally it didn't shock him. But this was different. Peter Evans lay with his eyes bulging out of a swollen face, and a thin length of plaited bark round his neck, biting tight into the flesh and made fast at the back where he'd have been unable to reach.

'Stap my heart!' said Flint in a fury, 'Just like before. This was the way it started last time.' He cursed violently and stared at the jungle as if he'd pierce it with his eyes to find the killers. Then his face turned nasty and he glared at the five remaining men.

'Which of you lubbers had the watch?' he cried. A great shame fell upon Howard and his expression gave him away. 'You, Henry Howard?' said Flint, incredulously, 'I'd have thought better! Under King George it'd be a thousand lashes or the yardarm. But I've need of every man. So your own conscience must be judge and jury.'

Howard was sunk in wretchedness and self-reproach. He tortured himself with guilt and took the entire responsibility upon himself. He groaned and sighed. He wrung his hands and wept and hung his head. In his innocence he thought that nothing could be worse than this. But he was wrong.

Chapter 35

5th September 1752
First watch (c. 10 p.m. shore time)
Aboard Lion
The southern anchorage

'That was pistol-fire, Mr Hands!' said Silver, staring out into the dark. 'A measured volley. All of 'em giving fire together, as if to the word of command.'

'Aye, Cap'n,' said Israel Hands.

'Aye, Cap'n,' said Sarney Sawyer the boatswain, 'Shall I order the boats away, so's we can go ashore to see what's going forward?'

'No!' said Silver. 'You gave oath. All of you did.'

'Oh,' said Sawyer.

'Aye,' said Silver. 'Remember? *Lion* and *Walrus* to guard each other, so none shall interfere with the burying? Whoever puts boats into the water starts a war, and I ain't starting no war in the dark!'

'Cap'n,' said Israel Hands, who'd been thinking, 'them pistol shots... It was at least a dozen rounds. But just the one volley, then no more.' He hesitated, then showed considerable moral fibre by voicing the horror that was in every man's mind. 'D'you think,' he said, 'd'you think ... they was attacked, Cap'n? *Attacked and overwhelmed?'* The thought was appalling, for it might mean the loss – to some unknown third party – of all their precious goods.

'No!' said Silver, and slammed shut the big telescope he'd been peering through. *Lion* was heeled well over, with every last one of her crew up on deck, lining the shoreward rail or up in the rigging, staring at the shore where the burial party's bonfire was still blazing. But there was nothing else to see, nor to hear other than the island's endless, booming surf.

'Why not, Cap'n?' said Israel Hands. 'Beggin' your pardon.'

'Aye!' said the crew and clustered closer.

'Listen to me, lads,' said Silver. He drew breath to speak, for he had much to tell them, and much to persuade them of.

The gunshots had cleared his mind. They'd sent his imagination down fresh tracks. He could finally see what was happening. There had still been some respect for Flint in his mind. Withered and wretched as it was, it was still there – the ghost of their friendship – and it had stopped him taking the final step of reasoning, the one that explained everything. All he had to do now was pass on these thoughts to the men, and hope they'd follow him to the same conclusions.

'Lads, we're in a pickle of shit here, and no mistake,' he said. 'But I'll take my 'davy that the goods is still ashore, exactly where Flint put 'em, and not carried off somewhere by bugger-knows-who!'

'Ah,' they said, and grinned at one another in the darkness. That was better!

'An' I'll tell you for why,' said Silver. 'Silence,

now, on the lower deck! All hands fall silent and listen.'

They fell silent. They listened. Seventy-one men and three boys strained their ears together. But there was nothing to hear. The night was calm. The island was asleep, the sea was asleep. Only a few little noises carried over the still waters: odd sounds from *Walrus* anchored two cable-lengths from *Lion* – a man's voice indistinctly heard, the faint, hollow clunk of some piece of ship's gear. Just that. Nothing else besides the sound of the surf.

'There!' said Silver. 'So even if *Walrus* was bent on breaking oath and starting a fight, how could she have lowered her boats and put ashore a storming party *without us hearing?* Them buggers would've been heard in *Portsmouth*, whooping and hollering as they went over the side!'

'Aye,' said the crew, 'go on, Cap'n!'

'Same goes for an attack by men from inside of the island – even believing there *are* any, which them as what's been there says there *ain't!* I asks you, every man of you ... who knows of a battle without cheering and screaming and the clash of steel?'

'Aye!' said the crew, immensely encouraged. They nudged one another and grinned and nodded their heads. Silver's natural gift for oratory was not only liberating them from an awful fright, it was rebuilding his place as their natural leader.

'No, lads,' he said, shaking his head, 'it weren't no attack. And nor weren't it no fight among them ashore.' He jabbed his thumb towards the still-glowing distant campfire. 'For then we'd have heard them popping off, left and right, one by one, as each man marked his enemy ... not one volley all together!'

'No!' said the crew.

'So,' said Silver, 'I say what I said before: it's some trick of Flint's.' He shook his head. 'I don't know what it *is*...' He looked round, paused for effect. 'But I'll tell you what it's *for!*'

'What?' they said, with round eyes and open mouths.

Here it came. This was the moment. Silver raised his voice.

'Why, lads, can you not see? It's so Flint can keep the goods for himself!'

A deep moan came from the dark mass of men. They'd followed Silver into *Lion* of their own free will, but they'd all been dazzled by Flint. Everyone had been dazzled by Flint. *Silver* had been dazzled by him, for Flint was a dazzling man.

Of the one hundred and forty-seven men who had voted on burying the goods, not a single one had voted against, other than Long John Silver.

The shame of their own stupidity fell heavy upon the crew. That and a self-pitying sense of betrayal and loss. It wasn't only Billy Bones who'd admired Flint. Fortunately, there was now – in reaction – a growing, growling, hatred of the man.

Aye, thought Silver, instantly spotting this, *ain't it just a shame that he's a villain?* And better still, he felt the power that was coming in on the floodtide, full, rich and strong into his own hands.

'Now then, lads,' he said, 'draw closer yet, for there's much to do if we're to come up smelling of roses rather than dog-dung.' He turned to

Israel Hands. 'Mr Gunner,' he said.

'Aye-aye, Cap'n!'

'Where's your Spanish nine? For she's the best gun in the ship.'

'In the hold, Cap'n, wrapped in grease and sacking.'

'With her carriage and all her gear?'

'Laid beside her, Cap'n.'

'So how many men do you need to hoist her up and mount her?'

'Oof,' said Israel Hands, 'she's a nine-foot, twenty-six-hundredweight gun.'

'Never mind her precious pedigree – how many men?'

Israel Hands put his mind to this complex technical matter.

'Best give me two dozen, Cap'n, for with that many we'll do it nice and quiet, as – begging your pardon – I think you'd want it done.'

'That I do, Mr Hands.'

'Let it be two dozen then, Cap'n, and a triple-block on the mainstay to haul her out with, and the carpenter's crew to open up a port for her.' He looked at the ship's four-pounder guns, and the ports that served them. 'For she'll be too high and broad for them little mouseholes.'

'Well and good, Mr Hands,' said Silver, and looked again to the rest of the crew, who'd heard these warlike preparations and were wondering what was coming. Silver knew that his next words must be very well chosen. He paused, and thought, and pointed out into the night.

'Lads,' he said, 'there lies the *Walrus*, and there's few of us that don't have some old shipmates aboard her.'

'Aye,' they said, for it was true.

'But there are times, my bully boys, when a seaman has to face the world as it is, and not as he'd want it to be. Ain't that the truth now?'

'Aye!'

'And truth is, messmates, that Flint has *Walrus* in his grasp. He's got the old ship and all aboard her...' He paused again, for the next step would be the hard one. 'If Flint wants the goods for himself – which I know he does –'

A roar came from the crew.

'Then he'll need a ship and a crew to carry them away, and he'll have told all aboard *Walrus* what a fine thing it would be *not* to share the goods with us, so's to persuade 'em to take his part!'

'Bastards!' they cried.

'Swabs!'

'Thieving sods!'

Aye, thought Silver, *look at you now, you bold bullies. Here's myself and yourselves come safe into port, all jolly companions together ... you as was going to tip me the black spot!*

'Silence now,' he commanded, 'for we must give no alarm to *Walrus*. They can hear us, as we can hear them. Every man that has no duties shall go quietly to his quarters, and make no fuss, nor no noise neither.'

'Aye, Cap'n.'

'One more thing,' said Silver. 'Mr Boatswain!'

'Aye-aye, Cap'n,' said Sarney Sawyer.

'Rig a spring on the cable,' said Silver, 'and bend the spring to the capstan so we can bring the ship's guns to bear on any quarter. All neat and cosy, Mr Sawyer. No noise.'

'Aye-aye, Cap'n.'

'Then get to, my boys,' said Silver, 'with a will now – but all soft and quiet, and no cheering.'

'Cap'n,' said Israel Hands, as the men doubled off to their stations.

'What is it, Mr Gunner?'

'Will we have to fight *Walrus*, Cap'n? Will it come to that?'

'I hope not, Mr Gunner, but best to be ready.'

'Aye-aye, Cap'n.'

Israel Hands put on a stern face, though his heart leapt with joy. For one thing, Silver was calling him *Mr Gunner* again, which Israel Hands loved, and not *Mr Mate*, which meant standing watches. And Israel Hands had other worries – or had done until his beautiful gun was ordered up from the hold. He was sure now that he'd made a mistake in bringing it aboard *Lion* as a bow-chaser, when there was no room in the bow to mount it. That was the sort of mistake that a master gunner was not supposed to make: not in his own special area of expertise. Fortunately, nobody else had noticed, and now it looked as if there was every chance of the gun speaking in anger – from *wherever* in the ship he chose to place it – and all hands cheering their gunner for his wisdom!

Certainly *Lion* had not the slightest chance of defeating *Walrus* without the long Spanish gun: not with *Lion*'s eight four-pounders facing *Walrus*'s fourteen six-pounders. *Walrus* would simply stay out of range of *Lion's* guns, and batter her into a wreck. But she couldn't do that with nine-pounder balls smashing through her timbers.

Israel Hands smiled happily as he went to supervise the bringing-up of his gun. Unlike most others aboard, he hoped with all his heart that it *would* come to action.

Chapter 36

5th September 1752
In the hold
Aboard Lion

Billy Bones was happy. He was happy even in dank, dungeon darkness, with the flesh of his beam ends mortified by the ballast stones. He was happy because he was filled with wonder at Flint's wisdom, and his miraculous ability to foretell the future.

'Now then, Billy-my-chicken,' Flint had said at their most recent parting, when Billy had been 'searching' for his gold piece, giving them opportunity for a private word. 'Billy-boy, did you bring that old box of yours?'

'Aye, Cap'n, according to orders.' Billy Bones smiled a slow smile. 'But I told them buggers – Silver and them – I told 'em I was hoping you'd let me stay on board of *Walrus*, which is why I fetched it with me.'

'And no doubt they laughed – and more fool them,' said Flint. 'Now, here's a present for you. Something of my own creation, which you must cram into your old box, even if it means throwing out your Bible, your prayer book and your certificate of confirmation.'

'What?' said Billy, immune to the subtleties of irony.

'What, *sir,'* said Flint. 'Will you never learn?'

'No, sir... *Yes, sir!'* said Billy, wrestling with the syntax.

'Here,' said Flint, opening a locker and removing a bulky construction of netting and cork. 'You must keep this ready at all times, Mr Bones.'

'What's it for, Cap'n?' said Billy, trembling, for he'd already guessed.

'Rather ask *who* is it for,' said Flint.

'Is it to make me float, Cap'n?' said Billy.

'Well done, Mr Bones! And here are two more presents. Each, as you will see, is quite small and is provided with a linen wrapper, for these items must be secreted about your person, Mr Bones. They must be kept within those sacred corners of yourself into which no sane man would intrude his hand, were you to be searched.'

Billy Bones sweated with the effort of keeping up. Flint sweated with the effort of not laughing in his face.

'Begging your pardon, Cap'n,' said Billy Bones, 'but ... where might that be?'

'In the safe haven of your drawers, Mr Bones, taped with sticking plaster between your most private and intimate parts. I seriously doubt that anyone will want to look there.'

'Oh!' said Billy.

'Oh, *sir*.'

'Oh, sir!'

'Good,' said Flint. 'And now you will appreciate the need for wrappers, since both these objects have nasty sharp corners. Let us look at this one first.' He produced a length of flat, dark steel about the size of a man's finger.

'Why, it's bit of a file, Cap'n,' said Billy Bones.

'Very good, Mr Bones. Indeed it is. And can you guess its purpose?'

'No, Cap'n.'

'It's purpose, Mr Bones, is to release you from your leg irons.'

'Leg irons, Cap'n?' Billy's lower lip trembled.

By now, he'd been tried almost to his limits by Flint's teasing. He did so much want to understand. He did so much want to serve his master. Unfortunately, his master did so much want to torment him.

'Yes, Mr Bones: leg irons. Those that – sooner or later – will be clapped upon you by our friend Mr Silver.'

Billy Bones blinked in relief. This was better. Flint had left the ocean of fantasy and was steering towards the firm shore of fact.

'Silver, the swab! But why, Cap'n?'

'Because, Mr Bones – for reasons which I shall shortly explain – he dares not harm you but dares not leave you free.'

That was days ago, and all of Flint's predictions had come true. Silver had badgered Billy Bones to discover Flint's plans until Bones could stand it no more and had defied Silver on his own quarterdeck before all hands, refusing to go below when ordered. Hence the leg irons. Hence Billy Bones's present accommodation down here with the ship's rats for company.

And they'd searched him, just as Flint had said. They'd searched for weapons and for anything else worth stealing. They'd had the silver buckles off his breeches, the baccy and clasp knife out of his pockets, and his hat and coat were Devil-knows-where. But none of 'em had delved where Flint said they wouldn't. Billy Bones shook his head in religious awe at Flint's abilities. Billy Bones – no less than any other – could see that there was something uncanny about Flint, but Billy Bones worshipped the fact.

So he rummaged down below, took a firm grip, summoned all his courage and hauled. He yelped and shed tears as the sticking plaster came off, uprooting shoals of coarse black hairs.

'Oof!' said Billy Bones, and brought out the two packages, still warm from their recent lodgings. He opened one and took out the file. He felt the rough steel edge with his thumb, and he turned to his leg irons, squinting in the candlelit gloom. His orders were to begin working on them at once, and to leave them seemingly sound, yet ready to be broken open at the chosen moment. At that time, Flint's second little present would come into action.

Chapter 37

6th September 1752
Forenoon watch (c. 8 a.m. shore time)
Aboard Walrus
The southern anchorage

Mr Ewyn Smith, acting-first mate aboard *Walrus*, had a mincing prettiness that at first had made the crew afraid to turn their backs on him when squeezing past in a tight place. They'd warned the ship's boys to steer clear of him too.

But they soon stood easy in that respect. Experience showed that his tastes did not turn to the art of jumping too low at leapfrog, and for a while they accepted him as one of them. After all, they were not a fastidious or particular crew. But then they noticed that Mr Smith was always to the fore when things were shared out, and always to the rear – though bellowing loudly – when boarders went over the side.

Finally, what with him being pompous, and older than them, and a genuine scholar with book-learning, and, worst of all, what with him being suspected of saying his prayers at night – they got the final measure of him and settled on the name *Parson*, which he loathed and they loved, and was therefore a perfect choice.

Unfortunately, that name was now forbidden, since on elevating Mr Smith to his present rank,

Captain Flint had made it blindingly clear that any who uttered the word 'Parson' from hereon would incur his displeasure. Some of those too slow to take heed were now doing their duties with hands bandaged by Mr Cowdray, following severe bouts of Flint's game, and the rest had taken note. But they still called the fat sod 'Parson' when Flint wasn't about.

And this was most appropriate, for Parson happened to be just exactly what he was – or had been – until his appetite for young girls had led him astray. Now he stood by the tiller of a pirate ship in a large black hat and a long blue coat, focusing his glass on the shore and wondering what Flint was up to. Mr Cowdray was beside him, also studying the shore with a glass, and so were some of the hands, in the waist. They were studying the shore and telling their mates what was afoot.

There'd just been a cry of 'All hands!' from the shore, faint but audible. Everyone had heard it, and now Flint and the others seemed to be dragging a body across the sand.

Smith looked around the deck nervously. There was a great deal of muttering and discussion going on.

'What do you think, Mr Smith?' said Cowdray. Smith blinked at the Surgeon, and envied him his light straw hat, loose calico slops and bare legs. He looked cool, while Smith was sweating in his broadcloth and felt.

'Well, sir?' said Cowdray.

'I could not say, sir,' said Smith.

'There was pistol-fire last night,' said Cowdray.

'Do you suppose there is disaffection among the burial party?'

'Hmm,' thought Smith, who knew a great deal more than he was prepared to share with Cowdray. He pondered the offer made him by Flint, and wondered if he'd live to enjoy it. He certainly hoped so. Then a stir and more muttering among the men told him that Selena had come on deck. *How apposite*, thought Smith, and looked at the slim, dark figure in her long enveloping shirt and loose britches.

She'd gained sufficient sense to wear many more clothes now than previously she had. There wasn't the delicious gleam of flesh that there had been. But she was still a most tasty little dish, and the clothes meant all the more pleasure in peeling off the layers before getting your teeth into the meat. And then... Smith had been assured by a considerable authority that she bounced like a rabbit once you'd got the skirts off her. She was only a two-legged animal, after all, and full of red-hot juices. Mr Smith had worked up a considerable lust for Selena.

Maddeningly, as ever she was avoiding his eye. She looked at Cowdray.

'Miss Selena!' said Cowdray. 'Good morning, my dear.'

'Mr Cowdray,' said Selena and smiled briefly.

Clearly she liked the surgeon. Smith didn't like that.

He looked her over again and, as usual, his memory went back to those happy days in Cheshire, when he'd had an excellent living, a fine church and a large and prosperous congregation; a congregation that sent its sons and daughters to him to be prepared for confirmation by His Grace the Bishop of Chester – Mr Smith's cousin, friend and patron.

Happy days indeed! The boys he'd crammed into classes and got rid of as soon as he could. He'd no use for them. But the girls... Ah, the girls! Those he'd given special and personal tuition in his own house.

Mr Smith grew dreamy-eyed at the thought of their fair skins, smooth necks and plump, round thighs. He sighed at the thought of how he'd tickled them to make them laugh, and how they'd come back, day after day, told by their mothers to be good girls for the Parson, and how he'd accustomed them, stage by stage, to him nibbling their ears, pinching their titties, and putting his hand first on an ankle, then on a knee, and then ever upwards, always tickling and laughing, until finally – it usually took a few weeks – it would be a full, bouncing rogering, with him sat in his favourite parlour chair with his britches open, and them with their skirts up and bare legs astride his lap, and their round mouths gasping, 'Oh! Oh! Oh!'

What a tragedy it had to end! But there had been so many swollen bellies and tearful girls telling identical tales that there came a time when his stern denials were no longer believed by their parents. With the bishop's help, and the Church's zeal to avoid scandal, he'd shifted parish several times and carried on as before. But finally, thanks to a farmer named Berwick who'd had a plump young daughter, six big sons, and many friends, the Reverend Mr Smith had been obliged to leave his house by the back door, while the mob came in through the front, and even then he'd taken a charge of shot to the nether regions, of which much remained forever embedded beneath his skin.

'Mr Mate,' said Selena. She stood blinking in the fierce sunshine, and Smith realised she'd been speaking to him, and he'd not been listening. This time she was staring straight at him and saying something. He was pleased at first.

'Look,' she said softly and nodded towards the men, gathering among the packed tackle and gear that crammed the deck. For the moment, they'd lost interest in what was happening ashore, and were lazing in the shade under a sail rigged as an awning. There they were sitting on the guns, chewing tobacco, grinning and muttering, and all of them were looking at her.

'You need to talk to them again,' she said. He looked at the men, and ran a wet, red tongue round his lips – a disgusting habit of his.

'I'm sure these good fellows know their duty,' he said.

'You need to talk to them. Even the boys.' She pointed to the shore. 'Tell them Flint's just over there. He *will* be back soon.'

'Bin gone five days, miss,' said one of the hands, who'd sidled up close enough to hear. He turned to his mates with a grin. 'We heard shooting last night, didn't we, mates? Maybe they done for the cap'n and he ain't never coming back!'

There was a roar of laugher at that. Not that they wanted Flint dead. Oh no. It was just that they wanted a little bit of time, left by themselves, to do something they'd been dreaming about for many long weeks. The pack of them got up and leered at Selena and slowly moved towards the wheel.

'Parrrrr-son!' said a voice, sing-song, soft and mocking.

'Parrrr-son!' said another.

Cowdray took Selena's arm.

'Get below,' he said. *'Now!* And don't show yourself till the captain's back.'

She frowned.

'It's hot down there. It stinks of tar...'

'Good God Almighty, girl ... *get below!*'

Cowdray pulled her towards a hatchway. She took one more look at the men and stopped resisting. He led her down the companionway, towards the stern and Flint's cabin.

'Get in there. Stay in there. Lock the door!' He listened to the growling and arguing now coming from above. He sighed.

'Dear me! Dear me!' he said. 'Give me that–' he pointed to a brass-barrelled blunderbuss hanging in a rack among the armoury of weapons Flint kept in the cabin. She snatched it and held it out. But she hung on to the gun and looked him in the eye.

'Doctor,' she said.

'Yes?'

'Thank you!'

Cowdray sighed. 'Good God, madam, I do but what I can.'

'So where's your fancy words? Your Latin?'

'Madam, there's no time for that!'

'Say some – for luck.'

'Oh... Godalmighty... *Forsan et haec olim*

meminisse iuvabit!'

'What's that?'

'Virgil: "The time will come when this plight shall be sweet to remember."'

'Yes!' she said and kissed his cheek.

This stirred emotions of every kind within Mr Cowdray's breast and loins, for she was very lovely and he was only a man. Still, he'd set himself a role to play – a bold one and a fatherly one – and so he played it. He *was* a surgeon, after all, and the practise of surgery breeds hard decisions and firm resolve.

'Ahem!' he said. 'Poor soul!' And he patted her hand. 'Now, I shall stand here until things are quiet.' He looked nervously towards the rumbling and shouting above. 'Then I shall bring food and water, so you need not emerge till Captain Flint returns. The captain will put all to rights. Meanwhile, shut the door and lock it!'

'Where's the key?' she said.

'Good God, madam,' said Cowdray, 'damned if I know. Search! Search!'

He pulled the door shut and put his back to it. He cuddled the short, heavy firearm and wondered if it were loaded. Then he wondered why he was doing this at all. The men would never listen to him. He was no fighting man. He'd not hold them off for one second, should they come in force. The best he could offer would be a few moments of bravado … perhaps waving the gun at them... It might stop them … though probably not ... and then he'd have to drop it and let them pass, just to save his own life. And in that case a locked door wouldn't stop them either, and God help the black girl.

In fact, everything now depended on Parson Smith, a creature who – in Mr Cowdray's judgement – was a slobbering libertine, and a figure of fun to the foremast hands. Cowdray wondered what in the Devil's name had persuaded Flint to raise such a creature into a position of authority. The bloody parrot would have been a better choice.

Chapter 38

6th September 1752
Late afternoon
The island

'Here it is!' said Flint, and knelt to pick up the shirt, which moved slightly, all by itself. It was rolled into a bundle, tied up by the sleeves. He held it up. It moved again. Something was inside: something alive.

'There's our dinner!' he said cheerfully, and laid it aside in the shade.

Iain Fraser blinked uneasily. He'd noticed Flint wore no shirt. Flint was bare-chested under his coat and had been since he'd gone off alone while the burial party set up their marker. He'd gone off 'to find a site for a bearing'. When he came back, his shirt was gone. Fraser had noticed that, but never mentioned it. Maybe some of the others had noticed it too. But nobody said anything. With Flint it was unwise to mention things that might be unwelcome.

'And now, here we are ... *Farter*,' said Flint. 'Halfway up Spy-glass Hill, and the very spot I marked earlier when I made my reconnaissance.' Flint indicated a rock the size of a house: flat, smooth and sunk in the earth to form a platform about ten feet long by twenty feet wide, and a foot above the ground. 'This will do nicely ... *Farter*.'

'Aye-aye, Cap'n!' said Iain Fraser, so used to his ugly nickname that he answered to none other. At least he did when he was with his mates, who'd almost forgotten why they called him it. But a suspicion itched in his mind that Flint used the nickname more often and with more relish than others did.

'Well then, Farter,' said Flint, 'isn't this just the spot? Don't we have a fine view from here?'

Fraser looked around. The air was fresh and clean. The festering swamps of the southern anchorage and the tropical jungles that surrounded it were nearly four miles away and a thousand feet below. Here was pleasingly open ground: stony underfoot with flowering broom and other shrubs, and with little thickets of nutmeg trees contrasted by a few pines of tremendous size.

Flint breathed the sweet air, he stretched his arms, he tickled the parrot and smiled upon Farter Fraser – the only man of the burial party who would need any special attention. Flint caught Fraser staring steadily at him – and then instantly dropping his gaze. Oh yes! Farter Fraser was by far the most intelligent of them, and would long since have been rated a petty officer but for his hopeless weakness for rum. That and the stink.

'Well,' said Flint, 'go to it with a will, Farter! There's our shipmates down below, working like plantation niggers, and ourselves idling away the hours.'

'Aye-aye, Cap'n!' said Fraser, and he glanced at the four men, little dot-figures in the distance, alongside the spar that they'd raised as a marker. Then, catching the merest hint of a fading in Flint's smile, Fraser swiftly laid down his bundle, opened it and set Flint's compass on the rock, together with his notebook and other tackles. The compass was a heavy, boxed instrument, normally used in *Walrus*'s longboat, and almost the size of those in a ship's binnacle.

'There, Farter,' said Flint, tapping the compass. 'Lesser men than ourselves would build cairns, or blaze marks upon trees and expect to find them on their return. But we shall take bearings from the immovable and the unsinkable!' Flint stamped his heel on the mighty rock and knelt down to take a bearing of the burial site where the gold had been buried.

And then Flint frowned. He laid aside the pencil and notebook that he was using to record the bearing. He stood up. He tipped back his hat. He scratched his head and peered thoughtfully at the burial site so far away and yet in plain sight. And then he shaded his eyes and looked southwards, and miles further, out to the anchorage where *Walrus* and *Lion* lay. There wasn't much that could not be seen from here and Flint managed a mighty sigh.

Out of the corner of his eye he saw that Fraser

had caught the change of mood and was watching intently. Well and good. Let him watch. Flint scowled and bit his lip and took a few paces up and down the rock. He turned as if to speak to Fraser. He blinked and shut his mouth. He paced the rock again. He stopped and stared at the burial party.

'No!' he murmured. 'Not them. Not Henry and James and Franky. Not little Rob!'

'Cap'n?' said Fraser. Drury Lane had lost a mighty actor in Joe Flint, and his audience was too captivated not to respond.

Flint jumped as if pricked.

'Fraser,' he said, 'Iain, lad ... forgive me, shipmate, it's just that...'

'What, Cap'n?' said Fraser, now seriously alarmed, for Flint's face was grey and there were tears in his eyes.

'Iain,' said Flint, 'I'd hoped to spare you this. I'd hoped it would keep until we were back afloat with our comrades around us...' He frowned. 'Those we can trust, that is!'

'Trust, Cap'n?' said Fraser. 'Trust who?'

'It's a plot, Iain!' said Flint, as if sunk in tragedy.

'A plot?'

'Aye, lad! Did you think poor Peter Evans died naturally?'

'No, Cap'n...' said Fraser. He said it very carefully indeed, and avoided Flint's eye, for he'd thought a bit since sunrise and he'd come up with some very plausible explanations for creeping night-time horrors and howls in the dark, not to mention who it might have been that had strangled Peter Evans.

'Ah!' said Flint. 'I always knew you were a sharp' un, Iain, and I am resolved to take you into my confidence, for I'm putting together a new crew – a crew that I can trust … even if it must be a greatly smaller crew.'

'Oh?' said Fraser, instantly appreciating that even so large a sum as eight hundred thousand pounds would be all the more for being shared by less. This beautiful thought cleansed his mind of any suspicion of his noble captain. It cleansed it, purged it, scrubbed it and purified it of any such wicked thoughts.

'Aye, lad,' said Flint and, reaching into his pocket, he came out with a bottle. He pulled out the cork and took a gulp. Fraser smelt rum and licked his lips. The day was improving, minute by minute.

'Here, shipmate!' said Flint. 'Sit alongside of me on this old rock, and take a drop, and I'll tell you the length and breadth of it.'

So Captain Joe Flint and Iain *Farter* Fraser shared a pleasant half-hour, and a full half-bottle – most of it going to Fraser – as Flint explained the burdens of command and the awful iniquities of treacherous shipmates, such that no man could tell whom to trust, nor from which direction a fatal stab might come. The sad conclusion of this tale was that all aboard *Lion* – and most aboard *Walrus* – were back-stabbing, no-seamanly lubbers who were out to steal other men's shares, and so should be denied their own … such that the goods would be shared not between one hundred and forty-seven men but twenty-five!

Farter Fraser beamed happily as he got up to

go and piss, which eventually he had to do. He lurched off on wobbling legs, with the rum warm and cosy in his belly.

'God bless you, Cap'n!' he said. 'And a clap o' the pox on them others!'

'Thank you, lad,' said Flint, pointing. 'And just you go over *that* way, shipmate, and you can bring back that old shirt of mine, and we'll have that rabbit out for our dinner. A bit of fresh meat, shipmate!'

'Aye, shipmate!' said Fraser, greatly daring. He undid his britches, relieved himself, buttoned up, and staggered over to Flint's shirt, which lay squirming in the shade of a broom bush.

'A rabbit?' he said. 'Bugger of a funny shape for a rabbit!'

'Open it, lad,' said Flint. 'You'll see. The rabbits hereabouts ain't like ours in England.'

Fraser fumbled with the shirt. Drunk as he was, he couldn't manage to untie the sleeves. So he picked it up to bring it back to Flint. But he dropped it. He laughed. Flint laughed. The shirt wriggled and gave out a peculiar pattering, scratching sound.

'Whassat?' said Fraser, and Flint's parrot spread its wings and flew away. Flint hardly noticed it go. He was at his sport, as the parrot was well aware.

'It's the rabbit, lad,' said Flint. 'Never mind untying the knots, Iain lad, just out with your knife and cut the damn thing open!'

'But it's your shirt, Cap'n,' said Fraser.

'God bless you, lad, don't mind that,' said Flint. 'We're men who soon shall own half of England! What's a shirt to us?'

'Aye!' said Fraser, shaking his head at his own stupidity for not thinking of that. He fumbled at his belt and pulled out a dirk half the length of his arm. It had a keen edge and a decent point, but in his fuddled state it took a while for Fraser to get it properly into the shirt and rip open a hole.

He peered into the dark recesses of the shirt where it lay writhing on the ground.

'Bugger of a funny rabbit,' he said.

'Just stick a hand in and pull it out,' said Flint, and stood up and moved closer for a better view.

'Aye-aye, Cap'n, God bless you!' said Fraser, still full of wonderful thoughts of riches. After a brief groping, he added, 'Aaaaaaaaagh!'

'Why stap my vitals!' said Flint. 'Do you know, Farter, I think you may be right. I really don't think that is a rabbit after all.'

'Aaaaaaaaagh!'

'Do you know, what I think that is, Farter?'

'Aaaaaaaaagh!'

'I think that may be a snake.'

'Aaaaaaaaagh!'

'A rattlesnake.'

But Iain Fraser paid no attention to Flint. He ran aimlessly in all directions, issuing thunderous farts, while three and a half feet of serpent hung writhing and lashing to his right hand, which was firmly clamped in its jaws, while its blunt tail-tip issued the dry rattling clatter for which its family is named.

'Dear me,' said Flint, as Fraser stormed past on a southern run. 'Could I suggest you retrieve your knife and cut off its head?'

Flint even exerted himself so far as to pick up

Fraser's dirk and to hold it out, butt-first, for Fraser to grab on the return leg. Fraser took the blade, but hadn't the dexterity to achieve very much, left-handed. All he did was anger the snake by scratching its scaly hide with superficial cuts which persuaded it to dig in all the harder.

Eventually, when his breath failed, Fraser sat down, heaving and sobbing, on the big grey rock with the snake still firmly attached to his hand.

'Help!' he pleaded. 'Help, Cap'n.'

'Don't rightly know how, shipmate,' said Flint. 'Though I do believe that they generally let go of their own accord, once they've bitten enough.'

Eventually that's exactly what the snake did do. But by then Fraser was on his back with a fat, blue hand, eyes closed and breath rasping in his throat.

The snake would have made off, but Flint knelt down and played with it, tempting it to strike at one hand, and catching it behind the head with the other as the coils of muscle launched it at glittering speed. The snake was fast, but nowhere near as fast as Joe Flint. It wasn't mad like him, either, and it didn't laugh.

The parrot watched from a branch in a pine tree. It squawked as Flint led the snake, strike by strike, on to the rock, and there stamped on its head and killed it.

Then Flint went over to the recumbent Farter Fraser to make sure of him too. As he wielded the victim's own knife, the parrot squawked and rocked from side to side and shuffled its feet on the branch, and finally it uttered a deep groan. It groaned as clear, and as sad, and as pitiful as any human being.

Chapter 39

6th September 1752
Four bells of the forenoon watch
(c. 10 a.m. shore time)
Aboard Walrus
The southern anchorage

Mr Smith, acting-first mate, had already been sweating, tropical hot in his long blue coat, and now he sweated more.

He cursed in affronted jealousy as Selena followed Cowdray down below, like a lamb. He ground his teeth in rage as the insolent scum of the lower deck dared to sneer and shuffle towards him in mutinous display where he stood at the break of the quarterdeck, by the binnacle and the tiller – the very temple and altar of authority in the ship.

He looked for support and found none. He frowned mightily. There were others aboard – men rated petty officers – who should have stood by him: the quartermasters, the master-at-arms, and especially Mr Allardyce, the boatswain. All these should have done their duty ... but see! They were scowling with all the rest. Scowling and jeering, and now they were brazenly calling him 'Parson' again. They all wanted a go at the black girl, and were damning his eyes if he stood in their way.

It was insufferable! Unsupportable! Outrageous!

It was also throat-slittingly dangerous. But Parson Smith didn't see that. He was so thickly armoured in his own self-esteem that he never stopped to wonder what the crew would do with him once they got their hands on him.

After all, why should he fear this collection of rogues and imbeciles when he was under the personal protection of Captain Flint? He who had been singled out and chosen by the captain and offered great rewards...

'Now see here, Mr Smith,' Flint had said on the voyage down to the island, 'I have sent for you because I know you are a man of learning.' He'd smiled and invited Mr Smith to walk the deck with him, and engaged so openly in conversation that Smith had duly been dazzled.

'You are, in effect, our purser, are you not?'

'Yes, sir,' said Smith.

'Aye-aye, sir!' corrected Flint with a kindly smile.

'Aye-aye, sir!' said Smith.

'Our purser, yet here's myself in need of a navigating officer.'

'Now that you have lost Mr Bones, sir?'

Flint smiled a weary smile. 'Quite so, Mr Smith.'

'Oh?' said Smith, scenting advantage.

'Mr Smith, are you familiar with your Pythagoras?'

'Oh yes, sir!'

'And your Euclid?'

'Oh yes, sir! And Newton's Fluxions besides!'

'I knew it, Mr Smith! I saw the mathematician in you!'

'Oh, sir!'

So Mr Smith got his long coat, and his big hat, and Mr Bones's empty cabin. He was furthermore given the use of Captain Flint's spare quadrant, and was instructed personally by the captain, with the result that, while still some hundreds of miles from Flint's island, Mr Smith – from his own calculations – was well on course for an accurate landfall.

'Well done, Mr Mate!' Flint had said, as Smith showed his latest position on the chart, some few days from the island. 'Now, here's the sun over the yardarm, and the men about to go to their dinners. Will you join me, Mr Mate, for a glass in my cabin?'

'With pleasure, Captain!' said Smith, and puffed up enormously as he sauntered in Flint's wake, with servants taking care of their instruments, and all the crew looking on as he went below to take wine with the captain.

'Your health, sir!' said Flint, seated at his table. 'You have the makings of a damn fine navigator.'

'Yours, Captain!' said Smith, and came near to blushing as Flint beamed at him.

'So you could find this island of mine?' said Flint. 'You could set out from Bristol and find it?'

'Given a good ship and a crew, and charts, sir?' Smith nodded in pompous dignity. 'Yes, sir, I believe that I could.' He was justifiably proud of the fact and it showed.

'Then your future is assured, Mr Smith,' said Flint, showing wolfish teeth.

And indeed Mr Smith's future *was* assured. Like any sensible mariner, Flint wanted a spare navigating officer. Unfortunately, that could not now be Billy Bones, for he was destined for other duties. That had been decided. So, without Billy Bones, what if Flint were to fall ill or otherwise to become incapacitated while *Walrus* was home-bound with a certain cargo under hatches? What then, if there were no man to set a course? What would become of poor Joe Flint?

Hence the time and effort to train up Mr Smith. But once in sight of England, that gentleman's future was assured beyond doubt. Meanwhile there was something else.

'Mr Smith,' said Flint, after a few glasses had gone down, and the acting-first mate's face was glowing nicely, 'Mr Smith – or may I take the liberty of calling you by your baptismal name? Ewyn, is it not? And you must call me Joseph.'

'Oh, sir!' said Smith, enormously flattered, and he licked his lips with so wet a tongue, and peered so bloodshot-misty-eyed through his little round spectacles, that Flint's greatest weakness nearly let him down once more. But not quite, and Flint managed – though only just – to keep a hold on his solemnity.

'Ewyn,' said Flint, 'I seek your advice on a most personal matter...' he paused, '...one so personal that I barely know how to begin.'

'Oh ... *Joseph?*' said Smith, sitting up, and dragging a handkerchief across his sweating face – to clear for action, as it were – for he was an addicted nosy parker, and his greed for other peoples' troubles was unlimited.

'This black girl of mine,' said Flint.

'Yes?' said Smith, and Flint shook his head, and dithered and muttered, and blushed and sighed, and took another glass and sighed again, and dropped his gaze to the polished table top.

'Yes! Yes!' said Smith, and an erection rose between his thighs in sheer anticipation of what might follow.

'The fact is ... Ewyn,' said Flint very softly, 'she has certain *appetites* ... doubtless innocent, and doubtless commonplace among her own folk, but which she wishes me to satisfy ... and ... and...'

'And?' gulped Smith in a half-strangled voice.

'I find that they are more than my strength can achieve,' said Flint. He looked up and saw Smith's goggling eyes and drooling lips, and nearly lost control again. Out of sight beneath the table, he resorted to the technique of peeling back his left thumbnail with his right index finger, which delivered such pain that he was saved from laughter.

'I find, Ewyn,' he said, 'that the variety, the frequency, and the *exoticism* of her desires are more than one man can sustain – at least a white man – and therefore ... Ewyn ... I ask you ... as the only gentleman aboard ... the only man of education...'

'Yes! Yes! Yes! Yes!' said Smith, his mind and member united in their closeness to ejaculation.

'Dear friend!' said Flint, with a grateful smile.

'When? When?' said Smith.

'Ah,' said Flint, 'another glass, Mr Mate?'

'Yes, Joseph!'

Flint gave a small laugh, then smiled like a father. 'Better make it "Captain", dear friend, just for the while.'

'Aye-aye, Captain!'

'Mr Smith,' Flint sighed, 'if only you knew the burdens of command.'

'Captain?'

'And treachery, Mr Smith.'

'Treachery?' Smith's mind was blurred with drink, but this was news.

'We are betrayed by all aboard *Lion*, and most aboard *Walrus!*'

'No!'

'Yes – the burying of the goods is but a ruse to save them!'

'Save them ... *for whom?*' said Smith, who was not quite a fool.

'Thyself and myself, Mr Smith, and those few whom we can trust.'

'Few?'

'Just enough to work this ship back to England – say a dozen hands.'

'Twelve?' said Smith, and his mouth gaped open.

'Yes, Mr Smith. Eight hundred thousand, divided by eighteen.'

'Eighteen?'

'Of course – twelve hands, plus you and I.'

'But does not that make fourteen?'

'No, Mr Smith, for you and I shall have *triple* shares.'

'God love and save us!'

'And of course, you jolly dog,' said Flint, winking broadly, 'once this ship has the goods under hatches, and our business with the traitors is done, and we're safe on course for England ... then I'll give you my cabin and my key, and you can take that piece of black mischief in there, and do what you like to her!'

'Ooh!' said Smith.

'But before that, Mr Smith, there are some

immediate duties for you to perform. You must be my eyes and ears aboard *Walrus*, for I shall have duties ashore. You must hold the ship for me, and beware of John Silver and beware of the crew. So pay close attention to what I shall tell you now...'

Chapter 40

September 1752
Two bells of the forenoon watch
(c. 9 a.m. shore time)
Aboard Lion
The southern anchorage

Israel Hands's Spanish gun was in all respects ready for action. It only needed to be run out and a linstock's match applied to the touch-hole.

'Well done, Mr Gunner!' said Silver. 'And well done Mr Boatswain!'

'Aye-aye, Cap'n!' they said.

'Aye,' said Silver, and nodded in satisfaction as he looked up and down *Lion*'s ninety-by-twenty-foot main deck, which was buzzing and clattering with pointless activity.

Lines were being spliced and un-spliced. Hatch coamings were being levered off with crowbars – to the screeek of nails – and then promptly hammered back again with thundering blows. The carpenter's men were sawing old timbers inch by inch into sawdust, with mighty saws. The topsails were being bent and un-bent and bent again to their yards. A squad of musketeers was drilling by the stern rail, going through the postures of loading – though with empty air – and levelling astern and crying *Bang!* as they pulled their triggers.

There wasn't a busier crew this side of the Bedlam madhouse.

'That's the way, by thunder!' said Silver. 'I defy King Solomon himself to pick the raisins out o' that! Even him what told the wax flowers from the real by the aid of bees!' And he bumped and thumped to the rail, and put his glass to his eye for a look at *Walrus*.

'Them buggers has given up looking, I reckon,' said the boatswain, and nudged Israel Hands cheerfully in the ribs. Hands nodded and nudged him back.

'That they have, Mr Sawyer,' said Silver. 'I don't think there's a soul aboard that even cares. Not now.' He looked at the endless nonsensical labours merrily under way aboard the ship. 'So now, my lads, you can show me over the *real* works, them as *Walrus* don't need to know about.'

Silver's natural excellence in command extended to giving orders then leaving his subordinates to carry them out while he kept out of the way. This he'd learned partly from observing how England and Mason went about their work, but mainly it was his own intuitive good sense in appreciating that no man works better for having his superior beside him. The trick was to pick the right men in the first place, and Silver knew that Sarney Sawyer was as good a boatswain as Israel Hands was a gunner.

And as for Israel's little mistake with the Spanish

gun – the mistake he was keeping so quiet about – why, that could be the saving of the ship ... if it *did* come to fighting, that was. John Silver had been thinking it over very carefully. But first he had to check everything had been done to rights.

'You first, Mr Boatswain!' said Silver.

'Aye-aye, Cap'n!'

Led by Sawyer, John Silver and Israel Hands picked their way across the busy deck, men saluting and making way with utmost goodwill – a most cheery thing indeed for their captain to see when faced with the near certainty of imminent action against a superior ship.

Sawyer took them right into the bow, where two anchor cables ran out through the hawse-holes, the big, three-strand, hemp lines stretching each in its own direction – one to larboard, one to starboard. Each was sixty fathoms long and bent to the ring of an iron anchor fast in the bottom, giving *Lion* a mooring against the powerful tides of the southern anchorage. With a single anchor she'd have swung like a pendulum, scraping her cable on the bottom, and wearing it out worse and worse with every tide.

'See, Cap'n,' said Sawyer, leaning out over a cathead and pointing down at the cables. 'We led a hawser out through the foremost gunport on the larboard beam, and brought the hawser inboard and ran it to the capstan.' He pointed aft to the squat wooden cylinder, 'Then we did the same with a second hawser on the starboard beam, and so – whatever the wind and tide may venture – we can haul on the one or the other of the hawsers, and turn the old ship to face whichever way danger may threaten.'

'Well and good, Mr Boatswain,' said Silver. These were the most basic matters of seamanship, but Sawyer was still new to his rating and needed to know that his captain had an eye on him. 'And has Parson Smith followed your lead, Mr Boatswain? Has he rigged springs?'

'Not him, Cap'n!' said Sawyer, glancing across at *Walrus*. 'From what I seen through my glass, old Parson, he's too busy yelling at the hands. Anyhow, that land-lubber couldn't find his arse with a hand-mirror!'

'Nor couldn't he, neither!' said Silver. 'So, Mr Hands, you've show me how you've mounted your gun. Now tell me why you've mounted her there.' Silver pointed at the second gun-port on the starboard side – the mid-point of the deck – where the Spanish nine stood out from the rest of *Lion*'s battery, like a mastiff among spaniels. Or at least, it would have done if it hadn't been run inboard and covered with a tarpaulin, so it couldn't be seen.

'Aye, Cap'n,' said Israel Hands. 'On the open sea, with Flint in command, he'd manoeuvre to rake us by the bow or the stern – the stern most of all.'

'Aye,' said Silver, for that was the weak point of all ships – the stern, where there were more glass windows than oak timbers. 'So, would you have put the nine-pounder in the stern?'

'No, Cap'n, for even then it would be one gun against seven – my nine pounds of shot against their forty-two. No, begging your pardon, Cap'n, but I'd leave it to yourself to keep him off our stern – ours being the faster ship, and yourself well knowing that, once he's across our stern, we're buggered!'

'Right enough, Mr Hands. So why not put your gun in the bow, which is well-timbered, and would make the smaller target for his guns, and leave it to me to place the old *Lion* bow-on to the foe, where you can play your gun upon him?'

Israel Hands blinked, and sighed, and thought, and bit his lip.

'No, Cap'n... Can't be done. For there ain't no room in the bow, and that's the Gospel truth.'

'No, Mr Hands, there ain't,' said Silver. 'And we'll say no more of it! So why've you mounted her on the beam?'

Israel Hands cheered up enormously.

'First off, Cap'n, we ain't on the open sea. Flint ain't in command, and there ain't no manoeuvring to be done by nobody – not even *him* – here in the anchorage. So it might come to distant fire with guns elevated, or it might come to boats and boarders. In either case, I'd want our four-pounders able to bear – with grape and cannister – as much as I'd want the long gun sending shot into the enemy's hull.'

'Aye!' said a chorus of voices, for others were listening now. Duties or no duties, free companions were not King's navy seamen and each was an individual who took a keen interest in matters which could mean life or death to himself.

'Well and good, Mr Hands,' said Silver. 'And have you had your pick of the shot?'

'Aye, Cap'n,' said Israel Hands. 'See there–' He pointed to a chest brought up from the hold, and laid alongside the Spanish gun. 'Them Dons is a sight better iron-founders than they's given the credit for. I've gone through that shot locker and I ain't had to heave out more than one in five of 'em. Round as a baby's bum and smooth as a milkmaid's tit!' He looked at *Walrus*, less than two cable-lengths off. 'What I say is this: let it come to long bowls, and ourselves at anchor with the deck steady, and myself with a good crew, and I'll put shot into that bugger where she lays right now, and they can stick their six-pounders up their arses!'

'HUZZAH!' cried the crew, and surged forward to slap Israel Hands on the back.

Silver waited till they were quiet.

'Well done indeed, Mr Hands. And well done, Mr Sawyer...' Silver paused, looked round his crew, and spoke.

'But there's one more thing, lads,' he said. 'Is there any man here now as doubts that we was made fools of by Flint?'

'NO!'

'So what about them over there?' said Silver, pointing to *Walrus*. 'They ain't all swabs and lubbers. Don't you think some o' them won't have wondered? Flint's been ashore best part of four days now. Four days on a duty that should've taken two! And them aboard *Walrus* will have heard the same firing we heard, and the screaming in the night, and all they've got for a cap'n is Parson Smith!'

There was a roar of laughter.

'Cap'n,' said Israel Hands, 'what course are you steering? We can batter spars off 'em. We can sink 'em! We don't need to worry about 'em.'

Silver shook his head.

'Listen, lads,' he said, 'once we was jolly companions, one and all. Once we fought side by side and was messmates–'

'Long John!' said Israel Hands, guessing what was coming, 'Don't–'

'So there's one more thing to do before it comes to fighting, and that's to give 'em one more chance!' cried Silver. 'We signed articles! We *all* signed, every man of us, and there ain't been no vote to dissolve them articles!'

The crew fell silent.

'John! John!' said Israel Hands.

'So I'm taking a boat,' said Silver, 'and I'm going across. And just before we all blind one another's eyes and blow one another's bollocks off... Why! I'm giving 'em that one more chance to be jolly companions again!'

'It's the black girl, ain't it, John?' said Israel Hands, hanging on to Long John's arm, and looking up into his face. He dropped his voice so no other should hear. 'You're soft on her, ain't you? You don't want her hurt in a fight.'

'Bugger that!' said Silver. 'That's done and ended. It's *articles* I'm worried about, for if we ain't true to them, then what are we? We're just a set of thieving pirates!'

Chapter 41

6th September 1752
Four bells of the forenoon watch
(c. 10 a.m. shore time)
Aboard Walrus
The southern anchorage

Parson Smith – landsman, lubber and budding navigator – was now within seconds of a nasty death, and it was a wonderful thing to see how ignorant he was of the fact.

'Garn, you bugger,' said the crew as they closed in on him, a sea of cruel faces and eager hands fingering knives.

'Out the way, Parson!'

'Give us the black tart!'

'Fair shares for all!'

'Flint's gone! It's our turn!'

'You can have a bit yourself, when we're done!' said a wit, and there was a nasty laugh.

Smith stamped his foot in anger. He lifted his head in defiance. He advanced to the quarter-deck rail. He gripped it with both hands and took up a noble pose – the pose of an innocent man shamefully abused.

This was exactly how he'd behaved in England whenever he'd been denounced, and it was a fine act that had served him well – until he wore it out. It had worked so well because he had such a wonderful capacity to believe his own lies. Thus he could denounce an innocent sixteen-year-old girl as a shameless trollop, and he could do it with flawless sincerity ... even while recalling her outrage at the first time he got a hand up her skirt and squeezed her buttocks.

Parson Smith could do this because he was gifted with no ordinary hypocrisy. He was possessed of first-rate, copper-bottomed hypocrisy with line-of-battleship timbers, and a hand-picked volunteer crew.

He had something else, besides. He had a tremendous voice.

'HOLD, YOU MUTINOUS DOGS!' he cried.

He shook the topmasts and shivered the rigging ... and the men stopped. They were used to the Billy Bones school of discipline: big voices and hard fists. They too had their illusions, and thought the one must be inseparable from the other.

'AVAST!' roared Smith, seeing the effect of his words ... and nearly ruined it. It was the right word, but from the wrong man. They laughed at him. It was a sailor's word, and they could never see him as anything other than a landsman.

'Bloody lubber!'

'Farmer!'

'Parson!'

'Parrrrrrrr-son!'

So they laughed. Which saved him.

They put their knives away and simply jeered. The killing mood was gone for the moment, and they listened as he took the opportunity to deafen their ears with thunderous words.

And so he preached them a sermon. He preached the Gospel According to Joe Flint. He preached the Word of Flint, the Will of Flint, the Commandments given by Flint, the Worship due to Flint... And the Terrible Vengeance of Flint upon the Sure and Certain Day of His Return ... *when sinners shall be judged!*

Old and familiar ground for Parson Smith, but terrifying to Flint's crew, for once they'd started to listen, they found there was not one word of it that wasn't directly relevant to them, and not one word that wasn't true. Eventually – when Smith got on the matter of judgement – he had them trembling and hanging their heads.

It was, without doubt, the most powerful sermon that Smith ever preached. And this was not surprising, for even the most faithful of rural churchgoers had never actually *seen* God, nor did they expect to meet Him in church on Sunday, whereas Flint's chickens knew their master from severe personal experience, and knew for a fact that he might appear at any moment – incarnate, smiling, and brimming with spite.

They shuddered, and the Catholics among them crossed themselves.

So finally Acting First Mate Smith was able to send the crew to their duties, which meant little enough, but in their sombre mood it moved them away from the quarterdeck and dispersed them out of their threatening mob, and back to sitting in the shade with their mates, harmlessly chewing tobacco.

By George, thought Smith, *that's put the rascals in their place!* and he puffed up even more than he had when Flint had favoured him with promotion. He strutted to and fro, and made a great business of taking his glass and scanning the horizon, and looking over *Lion*, where all sorts of noisy activity was under way – but none of it threatening and no sign of them putting a shore party into their boats, so that was all well and good.

Then, in his majesty and triumph, a very naughty thought crossed his mind. He stopped in his tracks. He pondered on the vengeance of Flint – the vengeance of which he'd just spoken so eloquently – and he pondered on what might happen should certain agreements be pre-empted. But Flint had not yet returned ... *might* not return at all ... and the naughty thought swelled and grew.

He turned and went down a hatchway and into the gloom, and was soon outside the door to Flint's cabin, where Mr Cowdray was standing guard with a blunderbuss, and an agonised expression on his face.

'Thank God!' said Cowdray. 'Me damn bladder's bursting. Can't stand here another second. Here – take this. She'll probably be safe now, but you never know.' And he thrust the blunderbuss into Smith's hands and darted off, thinking of the pewter chamber pot in his own cabin. 'Well done, Parson!' he said. 'Heard every word of it.' And he was gone.

And Parson Smith was alone in the dark narrow space in front of Flint's cabin. He reached out and tried the door. It was locked.

'Who's there?' she said from inside, and Parson licked his lips.

'It is I, my dear,' he said.

'Go away!' she said.

He smiled and produced a key: Flint's spare key to the cabin. Flint had given it to him as a token of things to come. He put it into the lock. He turned the key, and he was in, and locking the door behind him.

'Ah!' he said. It was even hotter down here than up on deck. She was wearing just a shirt. It was open at the neck and left her legs exposed from the knees down. Every hair on Smith's body prickled with delicious excitement.

'Dear me, dear me!' he said, and took off his hat and coat.

'What do you want?' she said.

The look on his face gave the answer. There followed a brief series of manoeuvres – he trying to get at her, and she keeping the big table between them.

Smith laughed. 'Too hot for such games!' he said, and pulled out a chair and sat on it. He peered at her. 'Do you know your catechism, my dear?' he asked, and slapped his leg at the joke. That was how he'd always begun! He wiped his eyes with the sleeve of his shirt, and licked his lips. He stood up again. He darted one way and she jumped to avoid him. He darted the other way: she jumped again.

He sniggered: a dirty, wet snort at the back of his nose. He wasn't trying to catch her; not yet. He was happy with things as they were. He was in the shadows while she was in front of the stern windows, wearing one of Flint's fine, lawn shirts – such that he could see every curve of her naked body as well as if the shirt had been transparent.

So he was quite happy for the moment, just licking his lips at the sight of her breasts bouncing as she moved.

He laughed. He sat down again. He cleared his throat. He became serious and turned to business.

'And now, my dear, I must tell you that Captain Flint and I have discussed your future.'

'What?' she said. 'First I've heard of it!'

'Doubtless,' he said with the invincible self-assurance of a man who knows what is best for others. 'But you will be pleased to know that your time of dissatisfaction is at an end! Your vital needs shall no longer go unmet.' He licked his lips again, very slowly. 'You shall not be denied those services so indispensable to a woman of your race.'

'Just what the Hell do you think you are talking about?'

He told her, and received – thrown as hard as her arm could deliver – a savage shower of every object on her side of the cabin that was not fixed, clamped or nailed down.

'Bitch! Slut! Trull!' he cried, springing out of his chair and racing round the table, roaring threats of horse-whipping, and she was running and running ... and tripping over a tumbled chair ... and down she went and down he leapt, grabbing and reaching ... and caught the hem of her shirt, and enjoyed a second's wonderful viewing of the luscious flesh beneath the linen, before one of the gleaming limbs pounded, hard and heel-down, into the middle of his face, leaving him blinded with pain and dizzy with shock.

'Damn you, you nigger slut!'

'Damn you too!'

Smith hauled himself up, and wiped his nose on the tail of his shirt, which had come out of his britches and was dangling round his knees. He was hot and tired, and out of breath. For the moment, lust was driven from the field, leaving only hypocrisy standing fast. Parson cleared his throat loudly and drew himself up once more into *innocence abused*.

'So much for my attempts as a Christian,' he said, 'to minister unto the needs of others.'

'What a heap o' shit! I'll tell Flint when he gets back. Know what he'll do to you?'

That gave Smith a fright.

'Oh,' he said, 'I really cannot imagine any reason why the captain should be involved in this small disturbance.'

'Can't you, though?'

'Err ... no.'

She sneered. He frowned. He looked down, locked in fearful dilemma. He'd known in the first place that it was madness to lay a hand on her before Flint gave the word, but he couldn't keep away. He couldn't keep his hands off anything female – girl, woman or child – once she was in his power. He moaned to himself.

'Parson?' cried a voice outside.

A fist beat the door.

'Parson? A boat's pulling over from *Lion*. Silver's coming!'

Chapter 42

6th September 1752
Seven bells of the forenoon watch
(c. 11.30 a.m. shore time)
Aboard Walrus
The southern anchorage

If Silver had been standing level with Parson Smith, he would have won. But he was sitting on the thwart of a miserable jollyboat with *Walrus*'s crew looking down on him, while Parson strutted the quarterdeck and boomed and roared in majesty.

As Billy Bones had done before, Parson marvelled at Flint's prescience. Flint had warned him that Silver might try to turn *Walrus*'s people, and Flint had ordered that *under no circumstances* was Silver to be allowed aboard *Walrus*.

'If you do that, Mr Smith,' he'd said, 'then you are lost. In the eyes of the crew he is the greater man. He stands head and shoulders above you all, both figuratively and in reality.'

So when Silver came across from *Lion* with six men pulling and himself at the tiller, and called for a parlay, Smith sternly refused, and wouldn't let him come aboard. He protested that this would break the promise that all hands had made not to interfere with the burial of the goods.

'No, sir!' cried Smith. 'We've taken an oath, sir!'

'Which ain't nothing to do with me coming aboard *Walrus*.'

'It is, sir, for what else would you speak of?'

'That bugger Flint! That's what!'

'There!' cried Parson. 'Condemned from his own lips!'

'Bladderwash!' cried Silver. He gave up with Parson Smith, and turned to the men, 'Who knows me?' he said. 'Come on, shipmates – who knows me? Who knows me, and who knows Flint?'

There was a stirring among the men packed along *Walrus*'s rail. There wasn't one man of them that didn't know Long John Silver. They knew him and they knew all that he stood for. He stood for jolly companions, fair shares for all and none left out, and no comrade ever abandoned – not even Blind Pew. Others might speak of these things, but Long John Silver believed in them and lived by them. Oh yes indeed! They knew Silver and they knew Flint, and Parson Smith blinked in fright.

'Don't listen to him!' he cried.

'Bollocks!' cried someone.

'Shut your trap, Parson!'

'Go on, Long John!'

'Go on, Cap'n!'

Captain! They were calling him captain! Parson Smith trembled.

'When did I ever tell you lies?' said Silver. 'When did I ever twist or turn? Let any man of you stand forth who's ever heard me called a liar!'

'Not you, Long John!'

'Never!'

'NEVER!'

He nearly did it. Even sitting in the boat. Even

under the disadvantage that Flint had contrived. He nearly had them, and a few more words would have had them out of Flint's grasp. But success – or near success – betrayed him. Greatly encouraged, Silver attempted to stand in the boat. He attempted to stand, to make the better figure of himself … and the boat swayed, and one-legged he stumbled and crashed headlong into his own oarsmen.

The fickle audience laughed. They laughed and Parson darted forward and picked up a shot from the rack beside a gun. He hurled it over the side towards Silver's boat.

'See him off!' he cried. ''Ware boarders!'

The shot missed, and Parson heaved another. One or two of the men copied him in vicious glee, being the sort whose pleasure it was to kick a man when he's down. The shot plopped and walloped into the water, none hitting the boat, but splashing the crew and making them look foolish. There was more laughter.

'Wait! Wait!' cried Silver, white-faced with anger. 'You stupid, shit-head lubbers! Listen to me!'

But the moment was gone. Israel Hands, at the stroke oar, called for the men to pull clear. He didn't want shot through the bottom of the boat. And then, as the boat gathered way and the current slewed her back past *Walrus*'s stern, where the big windows were wide open, a voice cried out.

'Long John! Long John! Get me out of here!' She was leaning out as far as she could, waving a handkerchief.

'Selena!' said Silver. 'Mr Hands, get this boat under the stern there!'

'Can't be done, Cap'n!' said Hands. 'They'll sink us!'

He was right. Parson Smith was foaming and roaring and spouting the Word of Flint. With none to oppose him, he was back on his safe ground of terror and retribution, and *Walrus*'s taffrail was black with figures waving shot in their fists and howling abuse: the self-same men who, seconds ago, had nearly been Silver's to command.

'Then get us as close as you can, without coming into range.'

'Aye-aye, Cap'n. Give way, you buggers! Back larboard pull starboard!'

The oarsmen heaved mightily and the jolly-boat spun in her own length.

'Together now – *heave!*' cried Silver, and steered the boat as close as he dared while the shot dropped heavily into the sea an oar's length away.

'Can you swim, girl?' cried Silver.

'Yes!'

'Then swim! Jump and swim to me!'

'No!' cried Parson Smith. 'Listen, lads – he's stealing the black girl!'

There was an angry howl from the men.

'Give me a match!' cried Parson, and hauled the tarpaulin cover off one of the two brass swivel guns mounted on the taffrail. 'And you there–' he pointed at one of the men, 'Stand to the other gun!'

Instantly, a pair of two-pounder swivels, was levelled at Silver and his boat. The range was twenty-five yards, and each gun was crammed with half-ounce pistol balls. Parson swelled in triumph as a smouldering match was pressed into his hands. 'Haul off, Silver,' he cried, 'or I'll blow you to Hell!'

'John!' cried Selena. 'Help me!'

'Can't be done, lass!' said Silver bitterly. 'Back off, Israel.'

Silver waved. Selena waved. The jolly-boat pulled clear, and turned for *Lion*. Silver looked back until he could no longer see the small figure at *Walrus's* stern. He turned and faced the crew, pulling together to speed the boat back to *Lion*.

'Well, lads,' he said, 'it's hot lead and cold steel from now on.'

Chapter 43

7th September 1752
Late afternoon
Spy-glass Hill
The island

Franky Skillit crept very quietly. He crept crab-wise, in the manner of the practised knife-fighter, his left hand feeling the way, and his knife low and easy in his right hand, with the arm tensed for a thrust.

Franky liked a knife, because it was nice and quiet. So he'd taken off his baldric with the big silver buckle and the cutlass. He'd taken off his belt with the pistols; he'd taken off his calico waist-coat with the pockets for cartridges and flints. He'd even taken off his prized leather boots that he kept so nice and clean, and he'd taken off the red silk handkerchief that was normally tied around his scalp. That wasn't for the noise, but 'cos its colour caught men's eyes and drew attention.

Now, all Franky wore to cover his nakedness was a pair of loose cotton slops tied at the waist. He went forth barefoot, bare-armed and bald, for there wasn't a hair on his head, which he shaved for the coolness. He left behind a neat little pile of clothes and gear, at the place Flint had set them to guard.

Where are you, Jimmie, my boy? he thought. *Just show yourself to your old mate Franky and take what's coming.*

With utmost softness, not making a sound, Franky Skillit crept down from the summit of Spy-glass Hill. So intent was he upon his mission that he was immune to the beauties of the spectacular view, the sweet freshness of the air, and the grandeur of the noble trees. Franky was concentrating on the bushes where James Cameron had gone for a shit.

'Ugh!' came Cameron's voice in a constipated grunt.

There you are! thought Franky Skillit. *Heave away, my jolly boy. Heave away with a will.*

He quickened pace. He darted out from the bush that was screening him. He sped across open ground. He did it with utmost skill. He was a fine woodsman for a sailor. A Huron or a poacher would've heard him coming, but not Jimmie Cameron – not with drawers down and bowels open.

'Uh-ugh!' said Cameron, and 'Aaaaaah!' as finally his efforts were rewarded.

Yugh! Thought Skillit, getting wind of it. For he was now very close. Close enough to jump, and stab from behind, and be done... But not just yet. Cameron wasn't placed right for the knife. Cameron was crouched down low, scrubbing his beam end with a handful of grass that he'd brought along for bum-fodder.

'Ah!' said Cameron, smiling, and he stood and hitched up his drawers.

'Right!' said Skillit, and made his leap. It was almost perfect, spoiled only by Cameron's attempting to turn – as every man does – for a proud glance at what he'd brought forth. This movement threw Cameron's right side to the fore, and out of the way of Skillit's knife *just* as it swung round looking for entry.

Thump! The knife scraped on spine, digging through muscle, and almost missed the pulsing rivers of blood that flowed through the kidney – the plump favoured target of the back-stabber, the assassin and the sneak.

'Bastard!' said Cameron, and turned furiously on Skillit as the two jammed together in the impetus of the attack. They fell to the ground, and gouged and throttled and butted and rolled – getting a good smear of hot droppings as they wallowed through Cameron's pyramid – and burst through the broom bushes, and out into the open, and on to the dust and the stones.

There, Jimmie Cameron strove might and main to get his left hand into his right boot, where his own knife lived, while squeezing Skillit's windpipe with his right hand.

Skillit, for his part, wriggled and struggled and

kicked and tried above all to break free. Cameron was stronger, so Skillit knew he'd lost his chance and must escape or die.

'Uch! Uch!' choked Skillit, and burst his neck out of Cameron's grip, which was weakening. Skillit thrust his head forward and bit off the end of Cameron's nose. Cameron screamed, foul breath stinking in Skillit's face. Skillit spat out the end of nose and drove his knee into Cameron's crutch ... *and Cameron let go!* Skillit rolled and rolled and rolled ... and was free.

He got to his feet, chest gasping and heaving and every limb a-tremble.

'Bugger you, you bastard!' said Skillit, and staggered back as Cameron got himself first on to his hands and knees, and then, with much effort, heaved himself upright.

'Look what you done!' said Cameron, feeling the knife handle that stuck out of his back. Tears sprang to Cameron's eyes, mingling with the snot and blood of his nose. 'Look what you done, you sod-you-are!'

'Serves you right, you thieving lubber!' said Skillit. 'You and all the rest of Silver's crew.'

'Look!' said Cameron, displaying a blood-dripping hand, fresh from feeling the knife. 'I'm bleeding, you sod! You done that!'

'Good job an' all!' said Skillit.

Cameron slumped back on to his knees. He lurched forward, nearly falling on his face, but propping himself up with his two hands. He raised his head and glared at Skillit.

'Sod!' he said.

Skillit laughed and grew bold as he saw

Cameron's strength. was dying.

'That's you done for, you swab,' said Skillit. 'An' I thought I'd missed, an' all!' He darted forward and kicked Cameron across the face with his bare foot. 'That's for you, you no-seaman!' He stepped forward and stood close to Cameron. 'Not so bold now, are you?'

Cameron lurched as if reaching for Skillit's foot. Skillit laughed and danced out of the way. Cameron groped his hand forward again. Skillit laughed louder. Cameron groped again ... and...

'Bugger me tight!' cried Skillit as he realised that Cameron wasn't reaching for his foot. He was reaching for a pistol, half hidden in the dust and stones.

'Here's for you, shipmate!' said Cameron, and cocked the lock and raised a wobbling hand and tried to bring the weapon to bear on target.

Skillit skipped back, arms outstretched for balance, and he darted from side to side. He sneered at his half-dead opponent.

'Go on then,' he cried. 'You couldn't hit the fucking mainsail, not if you was wrapped in it!'

'Oh!' said Cameron, and lowered his arm. 'I'm bad, shipmate.'

'You'll be even badder soon, Jimmie boy!'

'Help me, mate. I think I'm going.'

'Serve you right, too!'

'Come here, Franky, old messmate, for the light's a-goin'.'

Franky did come here, lured in close by Jimmie Cameron's little act. It was an act, because Cameron wasn't quite gone.

His pistol jerked up quick-sharp and fired three

feet from Skillit's belly.

'Ha!' said Cameron. 'Now who's feeling bad?'

Skillit staggered back under the impact of the ball. His ears were ringing, his slops were smouldering, and there was a scorched black hole below his navel. He got a finger right inside of it when he felt for it, and he howled in anguish, and fell over backwards, and sat himself up again, and howled some more, and wept and moaned and called on the mother who'd sold him to a Pudding Lane brush-maker fifteen years ago when he was five, and spent the money on gin.

Cameron sneered and flung the empty pistol away. He looked for its mate with the thought of finishing the job. He saw it, but it was no good. He couldn't drag himself that far. He looked at Skillit, sitting twenty feet off, nursing his wound.

'That's you done for, you sod!' he said. 'That'll see *you* off!'

'And you too, you sod!' said Skillit.

'Bastard!' said Cameron.

'And you're another!' said Skillit.

There they sat for some time, weeping and whimpering, and getting slowly weaker. Soon, their anger faded and self-pity grew.

'Couldn't I just take a swig right now!' said Cameron.

'Me an' all,' said Skillit.

'There's a canteen o' water up top o' the hill,' said Cameron.

'Can't walk,' said Skillit.

'Me neither,' said Cameron.

That was all their conversation for a while. Then, as the sun was sinking and night approaching,

Cameron spoke again.

'Here, Franky – why'd you do that, anyhow?'

'What?'

'Stick a fucking knife in me!'

'Cap'n told me to.'

'Why?'

''Cos you're Silver's man.'

'So what?'

''Cos you'll thieve the goods and leave us *Walruses* marooned!'

'Bollocks! We're loyal-hearts-and-true, aboard *Lion*.'

'Says who?'

'Says I! And so says all aboard of us. And Long John too!'

'Oh,' said Skillit, severely puzzled. 'But the Cap'n said...'

'Sod the cap'n! I *told* you thems was screams we heard yesterday.'

'It wasn't!'

'It *was*. When we was a-raising the spar... It was Fraser!'

'Wasn't!'

'It was! It was that bugger Flint, a-doing for him!'

'Was it?'

'Who else could it sodding be? It wasn't any of us, was it?'

'P'raps it was them ... *creatures*...'

'Horse-shit! D'you know what Fraser said to me?'

'No?'

'He said them noises was Flint playing games in the dark.'

Both men fell silent again. They were thinking over all that they'd heard about Flint – none of which was very nice. They were doing this with rudderless, fog-bound minds, while weak and wounded, and laid out helpless in the open, and in agony … and with darkness approaching when daytime certainties about the non-existence of *creatures* would not be so certain any more.

'Franky?' said Cameron.

'What?'

'What was we s'posed to be guarding up here?'

'Dunno. Flint said guard the hill. That's all.'

'What if he comes back?'

'Oh, bugger me! What if he wants the goods for himself?'

'Oh, shag me ragged!'

'Come on, shipmate, up anchor! He'll do for the pair of us if we don't.'

Thus Cameron and Skillit began their descent of Spy-glass Hill. They scraped and dragged and crawled. They set their teeth against the pain. They helped one another like jolly companions, each encouraging his shipmate when the other seemed likely to fail. They even did what they could for their wounds: Skillit hauling the knife out of Cameron's back, and Cameron using it to cut one leg off Skillit's slops to make a bandage for the bullet hole.

Sadly, the removal of the knife only made Cameron's wound bleed all the faster, and Skillit's bandage was promptly dragged off by his slithering over the ground.

Nonetheless, since it was downhill all the way and along a goat track, they made steady progress, covering nearly a hundred yards, until finally, just before it got properly dark, they heard – faintly in the distance – a cheerful voice singing, and the steady beat of a man's footsteps coming up the track towards them.

'Fifteen men on the dead man's chest!

'Yo-ho-ho, and a bottle of rum!'

It was amazing how this put life into Cameron and Skillit. There was no more lizard-like dragging themselves over the ground. Not for them! Somehow – heroically – they struggled up on to their legs. Then, leaning heavily on one another, and clutching their wounds, they stepped out at double their previous pace, even though it was now *uphill* all the way.

They got a remarkably long way before the cheerful singer caught them.

Chapter 44

7th September 1752
Night
Spy-glass Hill
The island

Flint was puzzled. The parrot wouldn't come back. It fluttered in the darkness like an owl, except that owls didn't cackle and groan.

Flint was used to the parrot flying off on certain occasions. He was far too sharp not to have noticed that. He'd put it down to the little peculiarities that all creatures have, parrots as well as men. But this was different. Usually the bird would settle in the rigging, or here on the island it would find the branch of a tree. He peered into the warm, smooth darkness and looked up at the enormous pines. Crickets chirped, the surf rolled, the stars glittered ... *and there came the bird again* ... a screeching fury like those in the Greek legends.

'Ah!' said Flint, as a claw scratched his face, dangerously close to his eyes, almost as if the bird were attacking him, almost as if it disapproved.

It came back again and again. It came out of the dark, howling and squawking. And all he'd been doing was settling Skillit and Cameron. Just a bit of fun, tickling them up with an inch of the cutlass point to make them run: just a jab here, and a stab there. And then a bit of sobbing and pleading from the pair of them, and one of them calling for his mother – Flint couldn't remember which – while the other fell to screaming and raving and damning Flint's eyes. And then Cameron managed to pop off all by himself, while Flint laughingly explained to Skillit that he'd taken such a liking to that gentleman's ears that they must come off for keepsakes before their owner was sent upon his way.

That was the source of the problem. Once Skillit and Cameron were quiet, the parrot had come back to Flint's shoulder. It was then that he'd attempted – in all innocence and meaning no harm – to feed it one of the ears. And that, unaccountably, seemed to have turned the bird's mind.

Screeching manically, it came again, and this time caught Flint an outright blow on the brow.

It was attacking and no mistake. Flint was unnerved. He could have drawn steel and cut the bird out of the air. He could have used his pistols. But the bird was his companion and he wanted it back. He didn't want it dead.

Another strike, and that was it. Flint ran. He held his hands over his head and sped down the goat track to the forest with its undergrowth and intertwined branches where the bird could take no advantage of him.

And there he found darkness: utter, smothering darkness. So dark that nothing could be seen and nothing could be done. Not even the stars shone here. Not here in the foetid, stinking mould of rotting plants and wriggling insects: centipedes, millipedes, slugs and spiders, every one far bigger than a decent man would have wished, and proceeding in company with whatever *else* there might be that slithered through the night-time jungle. It was neither a cosy nor an inviting place. For once, Joe Flint had found a billet as slimy as the entrails of his own mind.

But billet it was. Flint was here for the night. He couldn't go forward through the invisible jungle, and he couldn't go back – not in the dark with an airborne demon trying to take his eyes out. So, with utmost reluctance, Flint sat down, his back to a tree, put his cutlass and pistols across his lap, and resigned himself to sleep. He told himself that he was bound to be safe, for the island had no leopards or panthers – not so far as he knew – and he had no fear of snakes, not in the daytime at least.

Just as he was falling asleep, he heard a

fluttering high up above his head. He recognised this as the parrot, settling in for the night. His last thought was that at least he had a friend nearby.

Chapter 45

8th September 1752
One bell of the afternoon watch
(c. 12.30 p.m. shore time)
Aboard Walrus
The southern anchorage

Parson Smith kept his mind off rape for nearly a day and a half.

He managed this because he had become a very considerable seaman and officer – at least in his own eyes. For one thing, after his triumph over Silver, the hands were treating him with a reasonable approximation of respect, rather than merely stifling their contempt through fear of Flint. For another, he truly enjoyed the pleasures of mathematics, and was full of self-satisfaction with his constant polishing of his calculations of latitude and longitude.

So, Mr Smith strutted around thinking himself a man of action and a gentleman of fortune, and he fantasised that, on his return to civilisation, with the enormous wealth that would be his – why – he might well continue in some honest and profitable seafaring venture, a venture such as would make him the master and owner of a huge

East Indiaman: a man recognised as a prince of commerce, a nabob and a millionaire!

It was by that very route that he fell – inevitably – into sin. For the East Indies conjured up visions of sybaritic pleasures and harems full of perfumed women ... and so, in the end, he couldn't keep his grubby little mind off the succulent flesh locked in Flint's cabin, where that bastard Cowdray – who was probably after her for himself – was taking her food so she need never come out.

Now, even fear of Flint was suppressed by his lust. So he waited until the hands were paralysed by the noon heat. He waited till all but the lookouts were in the shade, dozing ... and then he crept below.

He took off his shoes for silence. He took off his hat and coat as well. Then, in an ecstasy of anticipation, he glided to the door of Flint's big cabin. He made no sound. He turned the key ... slowly ... slowly ... slowly ... *clunk!* He pushed the door with utmost gentleness. He slid inside ... he locked the door ... he looked around. Oh! A moment of doubt – where was she? All he could see was the furnishings – the big table and the chairs. He took a step forward and caught sight of her at last, and the load inside his britches strained to spilling point.

She was asleep, *naked!* She was stark-shining-luscious-delectable-beautiful naked, stretched out in the boiling heat on the padded seat that ran under the windows. The table and chairs had been in the way, that was all. Parson ground his teeth. He struggled tremendously. He exerted Herculean efforts. He was throbbing with lust and agonising to contain himself. He tried and tried and tried ... but...

'Agh!' groaned Parson in wasted ecstasy.

'Get out! Get out of here!' she said, up and awake at the sound. Her legs swung forward she ducked down for something Parson couldn't see.

'Bah!' said Parson, and slumped into a chair, wiping the slobber off his lips with his shirt. When he looked up a very nasty surprise was waiting for him. He was staring down the barrels of two heavy pistols. The sight so gripped him that, for the moment, he didn't even look at the naked figure behind them.

'Oh!' he thought, and blinked at the realisation of his own stupidity. Flint's cabin was hung with arms. It was festooned and decorated with them. He should have thought of that. He sat for a while, wondering what to do next. She backed against a bulkhead, arms outstretched, shaking with the weight of the pistols.

'Get out of here,' she said, 'or I'll shoot you dead!' Parson sneered and shook his head.

'No,' he said, 'I don't think you will, my dear. Because, if you do that, you'll bring the crew down here on the instant. And who will defend you then?' He laughed.

The first shock had worn off, and Parson had taken a closer look at the pistols. One of them wasn't cocked at all. The, steel was thrown forward and the powder-pan open. The other looked as if it was on half-cock, though it was in the shadows and hard to see. He smiled. Stupid moll! She obviously knew nothing of firearms. He was safe. All he had to do was sit quietly till his own armament reloaded, and then he'd do her on his lap – just for old times' sake – and after that in as many different ways as he fancied. He was a man of powerful appetites, and could usually manage three or four courses at a sitting. His confidence came back. He smirked.

'You must ask yourself, my dear,' he said, 'would you not prefer my own gentle attentions to those of seventy violent men? I really would recommend that you make no noise at all, let alone fire off a pair of pistols!'

But this caused quite the wrong result.

'Bastard' she said, and hauled on the triggers with all her might. As Parson had noticed, one couldn't possibly fire, and didn't. But the other – which *was* fully cocked, snapped in a shower of sparks that shocked Smith's bladder into passing a brief spurt of water into his drawers. What a mess was now accumulating down below aboard the good ship Parson!

'Bitch!' he cried, and threw himself across the broad table to grab the pistols and pull them from her hands. But she hung on, and she had a better grip on the butts than he did on the ends of the barrels, and his arms were fully extended and his feet off the ground and, after a brief tug-o'-war, she wrenched the weapons free and flung one at Parson's head.

'Ow!' he cried and retreated, clutching a bloodied brow and wincing in anticipation of the arrival of the second pistol. He crouched behind a chair, and spat venom. 'I'll skin the arse off you, madam! I'll flog you to within an inch of your life!' By God he would too, and what pleasure it would be to do it. *There* was a novel thought! One that opened up fresh horizons, and he looked around the cabin for something to serve as a whip. But she wasn't listening. She was standing in her silky nakedness, with her tits quivering and the second pistol up-ended, trying to load it with a cartridge snatched out of a locker.

Parson looked, and giggled. She hadn't the least idea how to go about it. She was missing out the ball! It was tied up in its own little recess at one end of the paper cylinder, and she didn't even know it was there! She just threw it aside with the empty cartridge paper.

Well, thought Parson, *the pistol won't do a lot of harm without that!*

He stood up and dusted himself off as Selena fumbled with the rammer, then dropped that too, and grabbed another cartridge, and bit that open and showered gritty black powder down the barrel and all over the wood and steel of the pistol. Another cartridge followed the first two. She was like a cook, dusting flour over a pie.

Parson was right. Selena had no idea how to load a gun. And why should she? Plantation slaves weren't trained in the use of arms, and the only time she'd ever seen a pistol fired had been in Charley Neal's liquor store when Flint shot Atty Bolger. Neither had she any interest in guns, so she'd never asked how to load one. Whenever *Walrus* had gone in to action, she'd been sent below, and had never even *seen* a gun loaded.

She just knew it was something to do with gunpowder and steel and flint, and she did the best she could.

'Selena, my dear,' said Parson, creeping towards her, 'I was so disappointed in you when you called on Silver to save you, for he is a ruined man.'

'He's ten times the man you'll ever be!'

'And even if you had jumped, the current would have swept you away.'

'Shut your mouth!'

Selena looked at him. She was done loading. She thrust the pistol into Parson's face.

'I'll shoot!' she said.

'You won't. You didn't load the ball. You didn't prime the pan.'

'I'll kill you!'

Parson smiled grimly. Making ready for action, he took off his spectacles; the white showed round his eyes as he turned nasty.

'Now listen to me, my saucy doxy. You will not kill anybody. You will behave yourself, and you will be quiet too, unless you want more than me to deal with. And then, my girl,' he licked his pretty lips, 'you will take a damn good thrashing and a damn good shafting.'

She pulled the trigger. Nothing happened.

'You didn't cock it,' sneered Parson. 'You have to pull this back–' he reached out and touched the flint. She hauled it back with a fat click.

'And you have to pull this back too,' said Parson, tapping the steel. In terror, Selena snapped down the steel.

'Fire at will!' said Parson, and touched his nose to the muzzle.

Click! The flint showered sparks as it scraped the steel. But the pistol didn't fire.

'I told you,' said Parson, and in bravado he took

the muzzle of the pistol and popped it into his mouth, while reaching out a podgy hand for a good fondle of Selena's left breast. Ahhh! The feel of it pumped fire, and up stood Parson's best friend like a soldier at attention.

Click! Selena tried again. Click! Click! Click! Again and again, hauling back the mechanism and pulling the trigger.

Parson sniggered. He gripped the muzzle with his teeth and smiled happily. He reached out the other hand and got a grip on the vacant breast. It was just like old times, those times so long ago and so fondly remembered.

Click! Click! Click! And silence.

A firelock needs a good pinch of powder in the pan to feel the sparks from the steel, and so to explode, sending a flash through the touch-hole and into the barrel to explode the main charge and drive the ball thundering on its way. In her ignorance, Selena hadn't put in that pinch of powder, nor loaded the ball.

But she *had* poured most of three cartridge-loads of powder into the bottom of the barrel, where it accumulated in a pile, of which just a very few grains – what with Parson Smith's shoulders heaving with laughter and shaking the barrel – just a few adventurous grains decided to make their way *out* through the touch-hole, and into the pan, where they lay waiting for the next time that Selena pulled the trigger.

'Click!' said the lock.

'Scrape!' said the flint.

'Fizz!' said the sparks.

'Whoof!' said the grains.

And...

'BOOM!' said the powder in the barrel. There was plenty of it, and there wasn't the least need for a ball.

Parson's face tore wide open, jagged and bloodied and raw. His tongue and cheeks spattered in fragments round the cabin, while white-hot flame blasted down his throat, bursting lungs and windpipe, stomach and gullet, pallet and eardrums. Smoke poured from his nose and ears and from the hideous, blackened cavity that had been his mouth. Roast flesh sizzled and crackled and split.

But he didn't fall. He staggered and swayed and lived. He raised hooked fingers to the monstrosity that was his face. His eyes stared. His ruined lungs drew agonising breath, and spat out a hissing stream of blood and mucus in the attempt to force a scream from the incinerated apparatus that had once delivered Smith's voice. And then he was crashing on to his back, kicking and twitching and frothing and bubbling. He'd only stood a few seconds, but it was a miracle he'd stood at all.

Selena's stomach heaved up its contents at the sight of him. She retched and groaned and crawled into a corner as Smith drummed the deck with his heels and elbows. He was a long time dying: a long, hard time. He made enough noise that someone came to see what was happening.

'Parson?' said a voice. 'That you? What you doing? Was that a shot?' The door rattled and shook. 'Selena?' said the voice, 'You got Parson in there?'

'Get a crowbar,' said another voice. 'She's done

for him, or he's done for her. Get this bloody hatchway open!'

As the door shivered and splintered, Selena did what she wished she'd done when Long John called her to his boat. She jumped from the stern windows and swam.

Chapter 46

8th September 1752
Mid afternoon
Haulbowline Head
The island

'*Fox's Book of Martyrs*,' said Flint. 'It was the constant companion of my youth.' He sighed and shook his head. 'Given to me by my father on my thirteenth birthday – which birthday, by Mosaic Law, made me a man, and which book, my father said, was "the bastion of our Protestant religion against the Anti-Christ Bishop of Rome"!' He turned to his audience. 'Those were his very words, lads. What do you think of that?'

'Mm,' they said.

'He was a man of powerful views,' said Flint, which was true. The Reverend Mordecai Flint, Presbyter-General of the Revelationary Evangelist Church, had held opinions that were rooted like mountains. Flint smiled. 'And yet, he was hated by all who knew him. Hated ... but feared!'

Flint dug into the rich, black soil of memory,

and turned up a thing that smelt bad, even to him. He paused. He gathered himself. He spoke.

'Do you know, lads, *he* ... my father ... he had a particular disgust for the physical act of procreation. D'you know that? And he never ceased to punish me for my own conception.' Flint raised a warning hand. 'Not that he beat me! No. He never touched me. Not once, not ever. Indeed, he never touched anyone. But he had the most wonderful ability to inspire guilt.'

'Mm.'

'And so I took refuge in that beloved old book. It was the London edition of 1701, in two folio volumes with hundreds of wood-cut illustrations, most lavishly and beautifully worked. What do you think of that?'

'Mm.'

'We had two other books in the house: the Bible, of course, and *Pilgrim's Progress.*' He frowned. 'But I could never take to them. It was always *Fox's* for me, and many's the happy hour I spent in study of it.' He chuckled confidentially. 'Well, lads,' he admitted, 'if the truth be known, it wasn't so much the text I studied, for I mainly looked at the pictures.'

'Mm.'

Flint shook his head.

'You wouldn't believe the things I saw, and the lessons I learned. You wouldn't believe the ingenious cruelties inflicted by one man upon another in the name of faith, and the agonies suffered by the blessed martyrs. And you wouldn't believe the artistic skill – and the precision of detail – with which those horrors were depicted: the rack and strappado, the stake and the thumbscrew; decapitation, immuration, ex-sanguination, and the winding-out of the gut...' He mused a while, savouring the memory. 'Have you ever seen that, lads? The winding-out of the gut ... with a windlass?'

But his audience said nothing. They'd said little enough before, had Rob Taylor and Henry Howard, because each had a ball of cloth jammed into his mouth, secured in place by a strip of the same cloth knotted firmly at the back of the head. And now they said even less because they were tied hand and foot, sat together propped up against a tree looking at the iron windlass that Flint had brought ashore with him, and which they'd all supposed was to be used for the burial of the goods. But though they'd laboured to carry the thing round the island, it had not been used – until now.

'*Fox's Book* says there's over five fathoms of guts inside a man,' said Flint. 'I've often wondered if that really is the case.'

Silence.

Flint got up from the rock on which he'd been sitting and took a turn around the little camp: the camp where Rob and Henry had – with a little encouragement – got so profoundly drunk that morning, and fallen so very deeply asleep in the midday sun.

'Here we are, then, at Haulbowline Head,' said Flint. 'Named and mapped by myself, these three years since.' He waved a hand, as if to introduce it to them. 'And d'you know, lads, I can't even remember why I gave it that name!' He laughed and looked around. It was a fine place, bracing and fresh. The view over the sea was magnificent. Like Spy-glass Hill, Haulbowline Head had a small number of big trees – not enough to constitute a forest, not enough to obscure the view, but tall and old and gnarled, for these weren't pines but something more tropical.

Flint marvelled at the variety of the island, for here was another little world within itself, as different as could be from the jungles of the southern anchorage, or the Alpine heights of Spy-glass Hill. The surf thundered even louder here than anywhere else, for the sea was ever beating at the foot of the massive cliffs, with tumbled rocks and seething white water at the base. A strong wind blew inward off the South Atlantic, driving into the wet cliffs and broken waters, and swirling up with steaming wetness that kept Haulbowline Head forever damp.

It was a fine and noble place. It was also the most dangerous place on the island, for the cliffs fell sheer as a right-angle, such that no man who went over them need ever have the least fear of being hurt. The drop was three hundred feet, straight down on to jagged rocks, and certain, instant death.

The drop was only about twenty yards away from where Taylor and Howard sat by their tree.

'Now, where's that bird of mine?' said Flint to himself, and he looked up into the branches of that very tree. 'Ah! There you are.' The bird squawked as he looked at it. It swayed and bobbed its head. It was peering steadily back at him, meeting his eye with an insolence that he'd never have tolerated from a man.

'You rascal!' muttered Flint, knowing that he wanted it back. In fact, he wanted it back very much indeed. It was like the first time he'd fallen out with John Silver. Flint frowned. These were strange and alien thoughts for him.

'Pah!' he thought. But he couldn't take his eyes off the bird. When first he'd confiscated it – stolen it – from some lower deck ape, he'd taken it for the swagger and colour of the creature, and the fine figure that he cut going about with it, and also for the fun of its uncanny gift for words – especially oaths and curses. But later he'd learned how intelligent it was, for it was *very* intelligent, and used its store of words in proper context.

'Oh dear! Oh dear!' it would say if Flint dropped something.

'Bugger off!' it would say when it disliked someone.

'Salve!' it would say to Cowdray, who always greeted it in Latin.

'Bump! Bump!' it would say on sight of John Silver and his crutch.

'And I don't even know the sex of you!' said Flint. 'Don't know if you're he or she.' All he knew was that he missed his constant companion. It was the only living thing that stood by him, night and day, and showed him affection... Or it had been.

'Why?' he asked himself, completely failing to make the connections that any other man would have spotted instantly. He'd even had the bird back, briefly, when he got himself out of the jungle that morning, on the way to his rendezvous with Taylor and Howard. The parrot had been waiting. It had been circling above. It had been looking for him.

'Here, my pretty!' he'd said, and for a moment it had fluttered down and alighted on his shoulder, and nuzzled his face in the old way, and a surge of happiness had filled Flint's breast. But then he'd tried to pet it ... and off it had flown, screeching and howling. Flint couldn't understand it. He'd got rid of Skillet's ears, so it couldn't be them. Perhaps some of the smell of them was hanging about him?

'Ah well!' he said. 'And so to business.' He took off his hat and coat. He drew the pistols from his belt and pockets. He laid his cutlass aside and picked up a small bag of tools he'd brought for the occasion, and rolled up the sleeves of his shirt, smirking at the rips and cuts inflicted in it by Farter Fraser.

'Now then, Mr Taylor and Mr Howard,' he said, 'who shall be first?' The two men wriggled and moaned. They did their utmost to hide, or to get out of Flint's way, and above all, *not* to be first.

The parrot screeched and flapped its wings.

'Taylor!' said Flint, and darted forward, grabbing the smaller man by the belt and dragging him towards the iron windlass.

'Mmmmmm-mmmm!' said Taylor, and the parrot spread its wings and took flight.

Flint sat on Taylor's legs and punched him heavily in the face, throwing his head and shoulders back to the ground. Stunned for the moment, Taylor lay still: helpless and doomed. But Howard did his best to wriggle away. He strove might and main. He contorted like a clumsy caterpillar, trying to put ground between himself and terror. Flint smiled at the sight of him, and turned back to Taylor.

'D'you go much to the theatre, Mr Taylor?' he said. 'For we learn from that wonderful drama *The Duchess of Malfi* that "strangling is a quiet death", which indeed it is, and by that means I could have seen off the six of you while you slept, and none the wiser!' He shook his head in contempt. 'But any fool could've done that.'

Flint opened his bag.

'Now then,' he said, and drew out one of Mr Cowdray's surgical knives, and cut Taylor's shirt from top to bottom. He further produced a pair of carpenter's pincers, a large needle, and some strong linen thread.

'The trick is ... to find a loose end,' said Flint. 'Or so I believe.'

Taylor stirred.

'Mmmmmmmm!'

'We'll start here,' said Flint, and carefully slit Taylor's belly.

'MMMMMMMM!'

The parrot dived like a kestrel. It dived silently and gave no warning. Claws first, it struck Flint on the top of the head. Then it took hold, and bit. It bit to the bone.

Flint screamed and raised his hands in defence, only for the bird to savage the flesh of his fingers.

'AAAAAAAAAH!' Flint leapt to his feet and struck desperate blows at the manic fury that was digging raw meat out of him. Finally, his greater strength prevailed. He tore the bird free and flung it to the ground and tried to stamp the life out of it. But the bird was off and flying free, only to turn in the air and come down again in attack.

Flint ran to where his arms were stacked. He drew his cutlass and slashed, taking feathers from a wing as the bird dodged. Then down came the bird again, and clawed for his eyes. Flint screamed and swung the blade again, and cut more feathers as the bird flew clear.

Bang! Flint fired and dropped his first belt-pistol. Bang! He fired the second, dropping that. Then the two smaller pistols. All missed, but the bird took the warning and settled in the tree again, furiously stamping and swaying and flapping and turning its head, all the while groaning and sighing and moaning.

'Look what you've done!' screamed Flint, staring mad-eyed at the bird. *'Look what you've done to me!'* The red blood streamed down his face, and a great flap of scalp hung gaping open, raw and ugly and sore. He cried out in pain and in protest at the atrocious cruelty of the universe. For in all his career Joseph Flint had never taken a wound. He'd seen blood and fire and mutilation. He had – with relish and a light heart – inflicted dreadful wounds on others, but he'd never, ever, been wounded... *And it hurt!*

'You filthy swine!' he said, and, casting around for someone to punish, he fell upon Taylor and Howard, spattering blood and spittle and spite. Considering what he'd had in mind for them, they were lucky that all he did – in his rage – was haul them, one by one, to the edge of the cliff and heave them over.

Chapter 47

8th September 1752
Mid afternoon
The southern anchorage

Selena swam like an otter: sleek and gleaming and easy. All the children on the Delacroix Plantation could swim. They learned to swim as toddling babies in the local creek, where they would dive and leap and shriek and splash. It was a happy place. Even the mistress and her daughter used to come down to the creek, just for the pleasure of seeing the tiny, beautiful bodies, laughing and shining in their little time of innocence. That's how Selena had met Miss Eugenie. She'd taught Miss Eugenie how to swim.

Feet-first and naked, Selena dived into the waters beneath *Walrus*'s stern. Wet, booming silence filled her ears as the sights and sounds of the air-breathing world were shut out. She was up again with a few kicks, and her head broke surface. She gasped and struck out, to get away from the ship, to get anywhere. Just away and clear.

There was shouting. She wondered if they'd point their cannons at her, as they had at Long John. She wondered if they'd launch a boat. Taking a deep breath, Selena dived, and swam and swam and came up, gasping, and turned and saw them calling to her from the windows and from the stern rail. They were angry. Gaping mouths and waving fists ... and some pistols spouting balls of white smoke. She was already a good way from the ship and the gunshots seemed small and weak. She never even thought to be afraid of where they'd strike, her mind still full of the pistol in Parson Smith's mouth. She shuddered, took another breath, then dived and swam again: kicking and kicking to get away.

This time when she came up, the ship was far off. She trod water and looked for somewhere to go. She turned, round and round, and the little waves bobbed and nodded round her head. The taste of salt was on her lips and all the universe was a flat, glossy-green, liquid surface just level with her chin.

Where should she go? Where *could* she go? Not ashore. Flint was there. And *never* back to *Walrus*. Once again she was running from a dead white man. She didn't think the pirates would be any more understanding than Fitzroy Delacroix's sons, and this time she had personally and deliberately killed someone. That left *Lion*. The choice was not a hard one. Selena struck out, intending to swim wide around *Walrus*, which was blocking her line of sight towards *Lion*, and then to head straight for Long John and his ship. It was only a few hundred yards and she'd been used to swimming all day. It would be easy.

But she immediately discovered why she'd got so far so fast from *Walrus*. There was a powerful current sweeping round the anchorage, and it was carrying her away faster than she could swim. She tried, briefly, to beat it, but sensibly gave up. That was a sure way to exhaustion and drowning. So she rolled on to her back and floated gently, with minimal movements of hands and feet, and concentrated on keeping her head above water.

It was warm and peaceful. The sun was hot, the water was calm, and there was no sound. It was a gentle delivery from the threats she'd lived under for so long. It was so relaxing that Selena fell into sleep – or something like it – and she thought of John Silver and Joe Flint. She dozed and dreamed and floated. It went on, and on, and on. There was no feeling of time.

Then her heels grated against sand. She started, and pushed down with her hands. She'd come ashore. She sat up. She was in water just inches deep, and suddenly she was heavy and clumsy: not a weightless water-sprite.

'Ah!' she wiped her eyes, and awkwardly stood up and looked around. The two ships were over a mile away, out in the bay. The beach – sizzling hot underfoot – curved like a new moon, stretching for miles, with dense palms bending down to meet it. The sand was much churned up here, and there were many footprints and trails where heavy objects had been dragged. This must be the site of the camp they'd built when they were unloading their treasure. She supposed that even in their boats, the current must have made it easier to come here than anywhere else.

She took a breath, and ran across the beach as quickly as she could – the sand was too hot for bare feet. She tripped and skipped, trying to make the briefest contact, and then she was in the cool shade. She sat down and sighed. She had no food, no water, no tools, no arms, no clothes. She looked into the jungle and wondered what animals might live there. That was not a pleasant thought, and fear came back. A different kind of fear, but fear nonetheless.

Selena hadn't the least idea what to do next. So she did nothing, and a long day passed, followed by a long, cold night. But no beast with teeth or claws came out of the forest and the sun rose at last. Selena was now getting hungry and was very thirsty. She'd heard the pirates say that there were streams on the island, and if there were streams they must run into the sea somewhere, so she started out along the beach to find one.

She found no water but found something else. She found it just before it found her. A little away from where the camp had been, there was a pole set up in the sand, and firmed into place with rocks. It was what they called a *spar*, and it had lines fastened to it for a flag. She was walking under the palms, next to the jungle, because the sand there was a little firmer than out on the beach, and so she heard the crashing of something moving through the trees, a little in front of her.

She darted behind a tree and looked out as a man emerged from the forest and staggered out on to the beach. He plodded heavily through the sand towards the flag pole. There, he hauled on a line and up went the flag – a big, black pirate flag with a white skull and crossed bones. Then he drew a pair of pistols and fired them off, and waved towards *Walrus*. It was Flint. Selena wept in despair.

But very visibly hanging across Flint's shoulder

by a strap was a canteen. Selena had taken no drink for nearly eighteen hours. She'd licked drops of moisture from the leaves around her, but that wasn't enough in a tropical climate. Thirst, cruel and unreasoning, drove her to stand out from the trees and walk across the sand – which at this time in the morning was not yet hot.

'Flint!' she cried. 'Here!' and walked towards him. He spun round, and even at fifty yards she was shocked at the sight of him. His head was bound up in a bloodstained handkerchief and his face was black with dried blood. He was swaying on his feet and his eyes were glaring and staring.

'Selena!' he said, then contorted with rage and pulled another pair of pistols and fired them towards her. She cringed, but he wasn't aiming at her. He staggered forward, cursing and blaspheming hideously at his parrot – which was fluttering overhead. He dropped to his knees and fumbled for powder and shot to reload.

She went up to him and laid a hand on his shoulder. He ignored her. He carried on with his pistols and let her pull the canteen from his shoulder and take a long drink.

'What happened?' she said.

'Damned bird!' he said. 'It's gone mad!'

'Why?'

'Don't know.'

BOOOM! A gun sounded from *Walrus*. Flint looked up.

'Ah!' he said. 'They're launching a boat.' He looked at her and noticed her nakedness for the first time. 'Better take this,' he said, and gave her his coat, then turned to gaze at *Walrus* and the boat pulling for the shore. But he said nothing else. He divided his attention between the on-coming boat and the green bird circling over the trees.

Then the boat grounded, twenty yards off on the shallow shore. Sand crunched under the bow, six men shipped oars with a rumble and rattle, and Tom Allardyce leapt out and splashed towards Flint and Selena. He stared at Flint in horror.

'Where's the lucky six?' he said. 'What's happened? What's wrong?' Then a more immediate thought occurred to him: 'Cap'n,' he said, pointing angrily at Selena, 'that moll's done for Mr Smith. Blew his fuckin' face off, she did!'

'Huh!' said Flint, who was worried with matters far greater than the life or death of the miserable Smith, with his all-too-obvious flaws. He looked at Selena. 'Do I take it that he couldn't keep his filthy hands off you?'

'Yes,' she said.

'Then serve the lubber right!' Flint looked impatiently at Allardyce, and waved a hand as if to brush away a fly. 'Pah!' he said. 'I'll hear no more of Parson bloody Smith, and you may give the word to all hands in that regard. Now! Pull for the ship and Devil take him that don't break his back!'

That was shrieked at them in fury. The men bit their lips and avoided his eye. Flint had never screamed at them before. He'd always been smooth as silk and slick as grease. He'd never visibly lost his temper. His voice had been soft as a mother's kiss, even when smashing fingers with a belaying pin. They didn't understand this. It was frightening. So they pulled like red-hot buggery and were back aboard in no time, even with the current in their faces.

There, Selena was shut up down below again, in the cabin smeared with Smith's blood. She found herself some clothes and sat with her head in her hands, and made the best of it. At least she was safe with Flint aboard. And it was no good swimming back to the island. She would have to be patient and hope for better days.

Up on deck, Mr Cowdray was summoned with his instruments, and he washed and dressed Flint's wounds on the quarterdeck, blathering Latin and claiming that soap and sunshine cured all, and wielding a razor to clear the skin for sewing.

'There, sir!' said Cowdray, after a busy half-hour, for he was proud of his work, and felt that no man could have done a better job of putting Flint's scalp back into place. He finished with a neat bandage and a word of warning.

'There will be some scarring, sir, at the brow, near the hairline. But mostly there will be little to be seen once the hair grows back.'

Flint nodded. He'd borne the surgery manfully, since his mind had been far away while Cowdray was cutting and stitching. He'd been pulling himself back from the edge. He'd been very close last night, and even closer this morning, for there are worse depths than those which swallowed Taylor and Howard: depths which are ever-waiting for a man with a mind like Flint's. But now he was back. He was back and safe, and the edge was far away, so he thought.

'Will you take a pull of rum, Captain?' said Cowdray. 'It's usual at such a time.' And Cowdray's assistant, Jobo, held out a bottle.

'No thank you, Doctor,' said Flint. 'I need a clear head, and a word with the hands.' He looked Cowdray seriously in the eye. 'For we have been betrayed, Doctor.'

'Betrayed?'

'Betrayed by John Silver – that unconscionable scoundrel – who put ashore a landing party, in secret and at dead of night – and murdered all my dear comrades, leaving me the sole survivor.'

'No!'

'Yes! And therefore I must take this ship into action against his, if we are to have any chance of reclaiming our buried goods, the which he is resolved to steal and keep for himself and his men – for they are as bad as he!'

'In breach of his oath and his articles?'

'I heard him say it, sir! When I was forced to hide in the woods, and he did not know I was near!' Flint bowed his head in sorrow. 'I know we did not part as friends, yet still I had thought more than that of John Silver.'

'Good God Almighty!' said Cowdray, horrified. He raised his voice, 'Gather round, you men. Come closer! The captain has fearful news!'

Chapter 48

9th September 1752
The forenoon watch (c. 10 a.m. shore time)
Aboard Lion
The southern anchorage

A nine-pound shot was only half an inch wider than a six: about four inches as compared with three and a half. But the greater weight of shot, and the heavier powder charge behind it, gave the nine-pounder gun its famously long reach, and a far greater capacity to smash timbers and beams. The six-pounder was a good enough gun for grape and canister, or for chain-shot to dismast, but the nine-pounder was a proper ship-breaker.

'Can I fire, Cap'n?' pleaded Israel Hands, 'before them buggers comes into range of us?' He crouched down and took two more sights over the barrel of his beloved Spanish gun: one sighting through the top notches to train the gun, and a second, for range, through the side notches.

Range was the hard one. Training was easy: just a matter of pointing of the gun at the target, by sighting through the top-centre notch on the breech-ring, and the top-centre notch in the muzzle-ring.

But range had to be judged – which meant *guessed* – and then the side notch on the muzzle-ring had to be lined up with one of a series of side notches at the breech, giving from one degree to five degrees of elevation. As Israel Hands had never yet fired the gun, he was ranging by guesswork and the hope that the two and a half degrees he'd chosen would reach *Walrus*, which he guessed was about four hundred yards away.

'Can I fire, Cap'n?' said Israel Hands again, and blew on the match-cord in his linstock to make the end glow nice and red.

'No,' said Silver, 'not yet. All they've done is make sail.'

'But that's against–'

'Silence on the gun-deck!' bawled Silver, and stumped about behind Israel Hands and his gun-crew. Silver was in anguish. It was torture. His was the final decision. Should he fire on *Walrus* or not? Should he take the final step that would set jolly companions to murdering each other?

Israel and the rest looked at Silver and waited. The ship was at general quarters. Guns were run out and loaded. Decks were sanded and the ship's boys crouched ready to run cartridges from the magazine. The larboard spring was bent to the capstan, and hands stood at the bars to swing *Lion*'s battery to bear on any quarter. She was as prepared as ever she could be.

Silver looked at *Walrus*. He'd been studying her through a glass since just after dawn when Flint's signal had gone up. He'd seen Allardyce take a boat ashore and come back with Flint: just Flint and none of the burial party. Just Flint, and Selena in Flint's blue coat, the sight of which set Silver's mind wrenching and churning and doubting all over again, wondering what in

Heaven and Hell was going on.

And then *Walrus* had upped anchor and made sail! And all without a word sent over to *Lion*. Silver had immediately made ready to fight, knowing that, with springs on his cables, he couldn't be out-manoeuvred, and equally that there was no way out of the anchorage for *Walrus* other than past *Lion*, for on *Walrus*'s side it ran to shoals and sandbanks.

He'd not set sail either. With the navigable waters of the anchorage over half a mile wide, it was possible that Flint would pass well clear of *Lion* and avoid a fight, heading for the open sea, but Silver couldn't see him doing that. That would mean leaving the island free and open for Silver to go ashore and search for the goods. And Joe Flint would poke his own eyes out before he'd do that.

'What's he doing?' said Silver, and put his glass on *Walrus* again. There was the breath of a south-westerly wind in the anchorage where the steady westerlies swirled around, and Flint – having recovered his anchors and cables – was creeping towards *Lion* under topsails and jib.

'*Please* let me knock a spar off him, Cap'n,' said the gunner, wringing his hands. 'Please, Cap'n...'

'Aye!' said the gun-crew.

'Aye!' said all hands.

'What's he doing?' said Silver. 'Look! He's going about...'

Walrus was turning. She wasn't bow-on any more. She was turning her broadside towards *Lion*.

'DOWN!' cried Silver, and dropped to the deck as white gouts of powder smoke burst out of

Walrus's side, followed a heartbeat later by the thunder and flash of her guns.

Voom! Voom! Two shots from *Walrus* sped high over *Lion*, harmless and aimless, and the rest went totally unmarked.

'BOOOOOM!' said the Spanish nine at last, as Israel Hands concluded that no further orders were required, and dipped his linstock.

Silver struggled to his feet in the swirling smoke as the nine-pounder crew leapt to their work, sponging, ramming, and running out: five men each side, and a second gun captain, ready with a powder horn to prime the touch-hole. It was blessed relief for John Silver, and he felt it. No more doubts and agony. Just a straight fight.

'Left! Left! Left!' cried Israel Hands with his left arm extended, and ten men hauled on tackles and heaved with handspikes to train the gun.

'Right!' cried Israel Hands, throwing out the other arm – it was always *left* and *right* to avoid confusion with the ship's *larboard* and *starboard*. Then it was 'Left-left!' and finally 'Well!' as the smoke-shrouded silhouette of *Walrus* lined up with the gun. The elevation he kept at two and a half degrees, and fired again.

Boom! The gun bounded back and sent another shot on its way, to the cheers of all aboard *Lion*. With ten men for a gun-crew, Israel Hands got off yet another round before *Walrus* replied with a broadside.

'Block-headed buggers!' yelled Israel Hands into Silver's ear, and pointed at *Walrus*. 'They're out of bloody range! They couldn't hit St Paul's bloody Cathedral from there.' He smiled like the sunshine. 'But I bloody well can!' And he turned to his gun-crew again. 'Go on, my fine boys!' he cried. 'With a will now, lads!'

'Heave... Heave... Heave!' they chanted, pulling together to run out the gun.

BOOOOM!

Silver got himself out of the way and into the stern, for a better sight of *Walrus,* clear of the Spanish nine's smoke. *Lion*'s people were leaping and yelling and waving cutlasses. They were like the crowd at a cock-fight, all merry and bright and cheering their gunner and his men.

BOOOOOM! At the very instant Silver put the glass to his eye and focused, a nine-pounder shot tore into *Walrus,* showering wooden splinters across the deck and bowling men over. It looked like Israel had got the range. Then *Walrus* fired again, and missed with every round, and Israel Hands fired twice more, sending shot crashing into *Walrus's* hull. Silver could see the damage Israel was doing. Men were being killed, and at least one gun had been knocked over and blown clear out of its carriage.

What's up with you, Joe? he thought. *You ain't moving. You're just making a target of yourself. And why are you firing so slow?* He looked again and, just for an instant – though he wasn't sure – he thought he saw Flint aiming a musket upwards, and shooting at something, and others beside him doing the same. Then the smoke of *Walrus*'s guns covered them up.

'Shiver me timbers!' said Silver. 'We'll wreck and sink him if he don't move sharper than that. And him not laying a finger on us.' He shook his head in disbelief. 'What are you doing, Joe?'

It was too easy. Silver couldn't believe it. Something was wrong. Flint wouldn't just give up. Nor would he give an enemy the chance to shoot him to pieces and not hit back. Silver was still wondering when he smelt smoke. Not powder smoke. Wood smoke.

He turned. In the middle of *Lion*'s quarterdeck was a small raised skylight that lit the ward-room just forrard of the stern cabin. The glazed windows were open, and smoke was pouring out, glowing red with the reflection of flames beneath. It was the worst of all a seaman's fears: the ship was on fire.

Chapter 49

9th September 1752
The morning watch (c. 10 a.m. shore time)
Aboard Walrus
The southern anchorage

'Commence firing!' said Flint, and hugged himself in delight as *Walrus*'s seven gun captains touched off a harmless broadside, and the guns roared and the smoke billowed and the ship crawled forward, and round-shot flew God knew where.

Voom! Something flashed between *Walrus's* masts with a ponderous, heavy note, but Flint ignored it. He'd made his plans. He was full, fat and happy with them. He had no concerns at all.

'And again, my bully boys!' cried Flint. 'Give 'em another!' He was himself again: Captain Flint, sparkling clean in fresh linen, bedecked with arms, and the neat bandaging hidden almost entirely by his hat. He was so pleased with himself that the headache of his wounds was blown away on the four winds.

He ran his glass over *Lion* and picked out Silver, just visible through a cloud of smoke. It seemed *Lion* had returned fire – Silver was clustered together with some of his men, in the waist.

Ah, John, my fine fellow! he thought, *there's you with guns run out and matches burning, and springs on your cables, and ready in all respects for action – not knowing that the real danger is creeping up behind you!* Flint smiled. *And all I have to do is persuade you to open fire, and then keep out of the way of your shot. All else has been arranged.*

He smiled in complete satisfaction ... which departed with hideous speed as a gun fired aboard *Lion* and a shot struck *Walrus* with a rending crash, and two men died instantly and another three were ripped open and thrown down, bleeding savagely. Flint put his glass on the smoke and felt the first, dismaying fright. *Lion* was supposed to be out of range. *Walrus*'s six-pounders were close to useless at this range and *Lion*'s little pop-guns should be utterly outclassed.

There was a flash as *Lion*'s gun fired again. That was no four-pounder! It was something very much bigger. And where had that new gun-port come from?

'No!' said Flint, in the horror of realisation. It was that poxy Spanish gun, the one Israel Hands had taken out of the treasure ship. Flint realised with profound shame that he'd forgotten it. The pit opened and beckoned as guilt and self-loathing fell upon him, for this was his own fault, his very own fault and could not be unloaded on to any other person.

CRASH-CLANG! Ten feet away, a six-pounder vaulted backwards out of its mounting, spraying iron fragments in all directions and throwing more men dead and wounded on to the deck.

'Cap'n!' said Allardyce, running up to Flint and yelling over the din of gunfire. 'They're hitting us, Cap'n. Permission to make sail and get out of range?'

Flint turned to look at Allardyce, on the point of saying *yes*. But a flash of green caught his eye. It was the bird. It had flown out to the ship. It was nestling in the maintop. Flint shook with anger. There was the cause of all his ills!

'Small shot!' cried Flint. He stamped and roared and shouted with such passion that, beneath his bandages, stitches parted and fresh blood began to flow. 'Fetch me some small shot and a fowling piece!' He leapt on to a gun-carriage and grabbed the mizzen shrouds. 'There!' he screamed, pointing at the parrot. 'There's the swab!'

'What is it?' said Allardyce nervously to one of his mates.

'It's the Cap'n's parrot,' said the other. 'Look, it's come back!' But there came another rending crash and the two men ducked in fright with their hands over their heads as another nine-pounder ball ripped into *Walrus*.

'Cap'n, sir!' cried Allardyce, 'we got to get her

under way!'

'Damn your eyes and bones, you mutinous bugger!' said Flint. 'I said *fetch me some small shot and a fowling piece!*'

The men looked at one another in fright.

'Well? Well?' cried Flint.

'Don't rightly know that we've got any, Cap'n,' said Allardyce. 'Not small shot. And we surely ain't got no fowling piece on board.'

Flint's hands were around his throat in an instant, throttling and spattering blood from his fresh-opened wound.

'Then get me a bloody musket, and cut up a ball with a knife. Cut it into many pieces and load it well, or I'll cut the liver and lights out of you!' He turned on the rest of them who'd left their guns and their duties and were gazing in horror at their captain. 'And all hands, out with your barking irons and shoot me that bloody bird!'

He set an example by dragging a musket out of a rack by the mainmast and blazing away at the unfortunate parrot, which abandoned the maintop and fluttered to the foretopmast.

His deeply puzzled men fired a reluctant volley at the creature who had been Flint's pride and joy. They all hated it, but none had dared lay a hand on it. Not in Flint's sight, anyway. And now, since none dared oppose him, men were loading and firing at it as if nothing else was happening, while Flint sat on the deck, making parrot-shot out of musket balls, in company with Allardyce and one or two others who were more afraid of Flint than they were of death.

And *CRASH!* – another round from Israel

Hands, who'd got the range nicely and was hitting *Walrus* at a comfortable, steady rate of about one shot every two minutes. They could have fired much faster, but Hands had a firm deck under his feet, and a good crew, and a target that was sitting still and not hitting back.

It was just a matter of time before *Walrus* was knocked into splinters.

Chapter 50

9th September 1752
The morning watch (c. 10 a.m. shore time)
Aboard Lion
The southern anchorage

The boom and rumble of a gun reached Billy Bones, where he sat in his chains. The sound came down through two decks, loud and clear and unmistakable, and it set the very ballast stones a-tremble.

'Ah!' said Billy Bones, throwing off the leg-irons that he'd long since filed through and had left in place only for appearances, to keep Silver's men happy when they came down to feed him and to empty his slop-bucket. He frowned, for they'd done *that* none too often. It was usually the nippers they sent down to do it and the little bleeders delighted in spilling the stew on Billy Bones's legs – God an' all his little angels help 'em if Billy ever got his hands on 'em!

He stood up and stretched. He'd been fourteen days down here. He was cramped and stiff. He'd been sat on his behind the whole time, unable – in his irons – even to take a step, and afraid to take them off to exercise for fear of losing them in the gloom and blowing the gaff. Now he wriggled his toes for the pins and needles, and he rubbed his arms and worked his shoulder joints. He grumbled and mumbled a bit, but he was a stoic beast. He was no more capable of self-pity than a cart-horse or an ox.

'Now then!' he said, as he took a good grip of the iron bar that had held the shackle-loops to his ankles. It was about eighteen inches long and three-quarters of an inch thick. He felt the weight of it. Not really big enough, should it come to fighting, but it would have to do. Then he felt in his pockets for the tools that Flint had given him. The file had done its job, and now it was time for the other.

BOOM! Billy Bones looked up at the deckhead as a gun went off above. Oh yes! *Lion* and *Walrus* were at it hammer and tongs – not that he hadn't guessed it already, what with Silver bellowing, and the crew clearing the decks and hoisting out the boats. Billy Bones grudgingly approved of that. It was man-o'-war practice, was hoisting out the boats: getting them out of the way of shot, and ready for use in case of need, especially in shoal waters like this, where a captain might need to haul his ship out of danger by putting out a kedge anchor.

He took a step forward, wincing at the stones under his stockinged feet, and he paused and looked at the big ship's lantern that had been his sun and moon the past fortnight. He was tempted to take it, but he had much to do and couldn't do it heavy laden. He looked about and made plans.

They'd put him next to the well that fed the ship's pumps – the well and the shot locker. There was a little area of naked ballast down here, but the rest of the hold was taken up with water-butts and other heavy stores. It was crammed and dark. He pursed his lips and thought heavily ... and started forward.

Round the well he went, and up on to the water-butts and aft, where a half-deck began, packed with more stores, then up a ladder, now in darkness beyond the feeble light of the lantern. He stopped for an instant to get his bearings. There should only be a thin bulkhead, now, between him and the wardroom.

BOOM! The gun fired again, and Billy Bones heard *Lion*'s men cheering and the unmistakable sound of Silver's crutch thumping the deck.

'I'll show you, John Silver,' he thought, 'won't I just!' And he felt in the darkness for the hatchway that he knew was there... There it was. He ran his fingers round the coaming and tried to get the iron bar into the small gap. It was too big to fit. But never fear: out with the file, a bit of scraping and cutting, and he'd opened up a gap for his lever. A moment later he'd forced open the hatch. It wasn't properly locked, just fastened with a wooden catch on the other side.

Light stabbed his eyes. After almost a week in the gloom, the brilliant tropical sun was blinding and painful – even when it had to make its way down through a skylight and into the shadowy wardroom. Billy waited, blinking and rubbing his eyes. Everything was bright and loud, and a companionway led straight up to the quarter-deck, just to his left, letting in more light. The crew were yelling and cheering, and Israel Hands was calling out as he trained a gun...

'Right! Right! Right!'

Billy Bones hesitated a moment. *Lion*'s crew were all around him. They were only a few feet away...

BOOOOM! The gun fired and the men cheered.

Billy bent to his task. This wasn't really a wardroom. Not like the real thing on board a warship. They just called it that as a sort of joke. It was a narrow space, lit from above, with cabins on either side for the ship's officers: little boxes four feet wide and just over seven feet long.

Quickly, Billy pulled all the doors open. He dragged out everything from the cabins – especially papers and small timbers – and scattered them on the deck. Then he found a knife and ripped open all the straw mattresses he could find and shoved some of them in a pile and dragged others into the stern cabin, aft of the wardroom, and heaved the cabin furniture on them, and opened the stern lights.

From his own cabin he dragged his old sea-chest, and hauled it back through the hatchway and into the hold. Then he opened it, pulling out the papers that Flint had given him, and a gallon bottle of olive oil. That went all over the pile of rubbish in the middle of the wardroom and stern cabin, and slopped towards the hold.

Then Billy Bones got himself back into the hold with his box, and looked out through the rectangle of light before producing Flint's final gift. It was – or had been – a gentleman's pocket pistol, one of the tiny, box-lock kind with a screw-off barrel that enables it to be loaded at the breech. With the barrel removed and the wooden butt cut away, there was very little left of it: just a few inches of steel mechanism.

In that condition, and loaded only with powder and wadding, it was useless as a pistol ... but excellent as a fire-lighter.

Billy Bones cocked the lock and held the thing close to the trail of papers that led aft from the hold. As Flint had ordered, he had a nice, dry pile of torn and crumpled papers for his target, and the oily papers were stacked behind that.

'The oily ones won't take the spark, Billy-boy!' Flint had said. 'So the dry ones must be first, and the oily ones must feed from them.'

Billy marvelled at Flint's wisdom. Was there *nothing* he didn't know? He thought of that last conversation with Flint aboard *Walrus*, when – not that he knew it – Flint had been so astonishingly honest with him. All others had received lies tailored to their tastes. But Billy Bones had received the truth.

'I'll not share it, Billy,' he'd said. 'Not a penny, not a grain of dust!' He hadn't even said, '*We'll* not share it.' He took Billy Bones so much for granted that he didn't make the small effort of pretending to include Billy Bones in his plans, not even when talking to Billy face to face. He'd laughed and pulled Billy's nose and allowed him plain sight of the Great Truth: the goods were not to be shared at all. Not among one hundred and forty-seven, nor among seventy-four, nor twenty-five, nor even two. The goods were all for Joe Flint.

'The only part I have not yet fully arranged is how I shall proceed on sighting England,' he'd said.

'England, Cap'n?' Billy had said, as ever wallowing in Flint's wake, and trying to keep up.

'Aye, Mr Bones, England! For we shall need a ship to carry the goods home, and the ship will need a crew – even the reduced crew that will have survived the perils of the seas so far as the sight of Plymouth, God help their precious souls! But nonetheless there must be some hands to haul on lines, and they will expect their shares. Even *I* wonder what shall be done with *them!*' Flint had laughed merrily. 'But something shall be done, trust me, Mr Bones!'

And Billy Bones did trust Flint. In his mind there was no future without Flint. There was only service to Flint. In so far as he'd ever even thought about a future when Flint owned a palatial mansion and rolling acres, Billy Bones only assumed, vaguely, that he would be provided for as chief and favourite retainer.

But these were abstract matters, and Billy Bones was a practical man. He squeezed the trigger. The lock sparked, flame spurted, and the fire was under way. He waited to make sure that it was really taking hold and then backed away, dragging his sea chest, and leaving the hatchway open for the draught.

He looked back at the red flames and felt the

heat on his face. The wardroom's little cabins were made of thin, pine boards and the doors were painted canvas stretched over frames. There was no better place to start a fire, and he knew it. It was then he felt his moment of doubt... Billy Bones was a seaman from the crown of his greasy head to the dirt of his blackened toenails, and he had just done a thing for which a seaman's God would damn him to a seaman's Hell, and even Jesus bloody Christ would never forgive him.

Despite being armoured in his loyalty to Flint, the guilt arose. No man knew better than Billy Bones how terrible a monster is fire afloat. Landsmen in their ignorance wonder how a ship can burn in the midst of endless water, but not seamen. They know the truth. A ship was made of seasoned timbers, pitch and tar and canvas and rope – all of which burn like the Devil, especially in the tropics.

But he'd done it now, and that was that. *Lion* was doomed, and now it was time to save Billy Bones. He pulled the collection of cork and netting out of his box. He closed the box and said farewell – a sad wrench, for it contained his all and everything. Then he went forrard in the hold. He fumbled and groped in the dark. He made his way through narrow corners and dark ways, and broke through one or two closed hatches, and kept himself as quiet as could be when he went by the magazine, where a man was working, and one of the ship's boys was running down every couple of minutes for a powder charge.

Billy recognised the little bastard as one of the shit-sloppers, and had to hold back. This was no time to draw attention on himself. He looked aft, and thought he could see a red glow, though there were bulkheads in the way. He sniffed for smoke ... none just yet.

Then the nipper was gone, scrambling up a ladder with his cartridge box, and Billy pressed on and got himself as close to the bow as he could, and just beneath the main deck, where he could be out and on to the fo'c'sle and over the side in a trice ... when the moment came.

'You must wait your moment, Billy-boy,' Flint had said. 'Let the fire be in the stern and yourself in the bow, and then it shall be a clear run for you, over the rail, once all eyes are elsewhere.'

As usual, Flint was right.

'Ship's a-fire!' roared Silver. 'Ship's a-fire! *Allllll* hands! *Allllll* hands!'

Billy Bones heard him. Everyone heard him. There was a rumble of feet. Even Israel Hands and his crew abandoned their gun. Every soul in the ship leapt to face the deadliest danger of all.

Up and out into the daylight, climbed Billy Bones, and with no man paying him the slightest attention, he waddled forward on his stiff, awkward legs, encumbered in his cork floats. He stopped at the rail and looked at the backs of *Lion*'s people fighting the blaze, and Silver's tall figure in command, and the nine-pounder gun that had been making all the noise, and the smoke-clouded, distant *Walrus* and the sweep of the southern anchorage, and the blue skies and the hot sun. Finally ... finally ... he forced himself to gaze upon the hideously wet and terrifying expanse of the deep salty element upon which he'd floated all his life, but always in a ship or a boat. He'd never attempted to swim, nor wished to swim, nor could even bear the thought of swimming. He gazed upon it in dread, for he, who was a sailor, was terrified of water.

At the stern, Silver and his men were fighting heart, soul, mind and strength with pumps and hoses and buckets. Nobody looked forrard as Billy Bones crouched hidden in the fo'c'sle, trembling like a virgin on her wedding night.

If courage and loyalty are virtues – which they are – then Billy Bones showed virtue that day: valiant courage in the conquest of fear, and selfless loyalty to his cause. He showed such courage that some might forgive him for spending it in the service of so cruel and worthless a cause.

Billy Bones stood up, he held his nose and – with a sob – he jumped.

Chapter 51

9th September 1752
The forenoon watch (c. 10 a.m. shore time)
The southern anchorage

Selena came up on deck and looked around. *Walrus* seemed ruined. Dead bodies lay ripped and gutted, wounded men screamed and groaned, and Flint – armed with a bloodied cutlass – was busy killing two more who were busy trying to get away from him.

She'd left the stern cabin through fear, having stayed there only through fear. The door was smashed and couldn't be locked, but she'd been afraid of the crew, even with Flint aboard. She hadn't the strength to swim for the shore again, and she'd huddled in a corner when *Walrus*'s guns had fired. The sound of that had been bad, but not as bad as the sound of the cannon ball that had come in through one side of the cabin and out at the other, ploughing a furrow across the deck on its way. That was too much. She just ran.

'Black spot?' cried Flint. 'I'll give you black spot!' And he caught one of his victims a slice across the back of the neck and ran the other through the chest.

Walrus's main deck was a jumble of shattered wreckage. The ship had been heavily pounded, half the guns were dismounted and the men were surly and muttering. For the moment, discipline was broken, and Flint – having just despatched two of his men – was in the centre of a ring of the rest. Some twenty men stood loosely around him, armed with axes and pikes and cutlasses. They weren't exactly threatening him, not quite, and they were wary of him – desperately wary – and kept out of his way. They knew Flint and they feared him, and they were trying to find their courage. They were shifting and moving all the time, none willing to be in the front rank, each seeking protection behind some heap of wreckage, or clambering on it for the advantage of height.

As men do – when they lack the courage to fight – they went to law instead.

'You can't do that, Cap'n!' cried Allardyce,

pointing at the two dead men, 'It ain't according to articles!'

'No!' said the rest.

'And you're bugg'rin' mad, you are!'

'Aye!'

'Shooting at bugg'rin' parrots!'

'Aye!'

'And we ain't bugg'rin' having it! We's gennelmen o' fortune, we are!'

'Aye!'

'And you must take the black spot and you may not harm him as brings it.'

'No!'

''Cos it ain't according to articles!' roared Allardyce.

'Rubbish!' cried Flint, with the blood of his wounded scalp streaming down his face. 'There's no mention of any black spots in the Book of Articles!' That was true. Flint knew it for a fact. Allardyce was thrown into doubt, because he couldn't read and was nervous of Flint, who could.

'Well ... well ... then ... it's according to *tradition,*' said Allardyce, who was one of those who'd been a King's Navy seaman. 'It's ... it's ... according to the *immemorial traditions of the service!*'

'Service?' shrieked Flint, incredulously. *'Service?* You blasted nincompoop!' His temper snapped. He charged. Allardyce had the sense to run, but three others attempted to fight. It was a very brief combat. One found his right hand off at the wrist. One found himself bleeding to death from a slashed throat. One found nothing at all, being cut down, stone dead, on the instant.

Which marked the end of the mutiny. Those whom Flint had killed or wounded had been the boldest, the ones who'd actually dared to face him in arms. Now there was only groaning and bleeding from the survivors, and muttering from those who were whole. Nobody looked Flint in the eye, and nobody mentioned black spots again. They sat around in groups and did nothing. Flint wiped the sweat and blood from his eyes, caught sight of Selena, and gave a mad, mocking bow.

'Look!' she said, and pointed. They'd all been so busy with fighting one another they'd not seen the fire that was blazing aboard *Lion*. The stern was leaping with red flames.

'Ahhhh!' said Flint, and seized advantage in the instant. 'There, my lads!' he cried. 'See what your captain has contrived. Those swabs aboard *Lion* are roasted pork. Our ship's saved, and it's double shares of the goods for every man jack of us!'

They cheered him for that. They cheered and they jumped to his orders when he called on them to clear the decks and make all shipshape.

'Selena, my dear,' said Flint, in a manner that was quite like old times, 'you may not have noticed – not being truly a seafarer – so I shall tell you: while we are somewhat knocked about in the hull, we are entirely sound in our masts and sails!' he looked in satisfaction at *Walrus*'s pristine rigging. 'Israel Hands always did prefer roundshot below to chain-shot aloft, and today that will be the ruin of him!'

So Selena watched as Flint achieved the impossible. He turned the half-ruined *Walrus* back into a fighting ship. Wreckage was cut free and heaved over the side, with the dead and the dying. Small arms were reloaded, and able seamen promoted to fill ratings made vacant by death. Dismounted guns were hauled from the larboard ports, and others brought over from the starboard side, to assemble a complete seven-gun battery, and the guns were loaded...

'With cannister, my dear,' said Flint. 'Which means a flannel bag filled with a good, round hundred of musket balls.' He smiled. 'Which is the best possible thing for men struggling in the water, having left their burning ship.'

'Long John,' said Israel Hands, 'there's a dozen thirty-pound powder kegs down in the hold, just forrard of the magazine. We've got to abandon ship!'

'No!' said Silver. 'We've lost her and no mistake, but I'm thinking of us ashore with nothing to eat but our boots and belts. So I want them stores!' He pointed to the men heaving *Lion*'s stores out of the hold and into the skiff. The jollyboat was already pulling for the shore with a full cargo.

'Go to it, lads!' cried Silver. 'Jolly companions one and all! Heave together, boys!'

'Aye!' they cried, in their sweat and struggle, as Long John Silver did what the gods had made him for. He led his men in the face of danger and inspired them to do their best. He stumped about, cheering them on, slapping backs and calling them by name, and even managing a laugh as *Lion* burned beneath him and the decks grew fearfully hot. No King's officer, bred by years of training, could have done it better.

He had a team at the pump with a hose rigged and spouting into the open cavity where flames roared out of the stern. Beside them was a bucket-brigade of a dozen men, heaving sea-water onto the flames. At the same time, all hands that could share the task were trying to get *Lion's* stores of food and drink, and tools and arms, out of the ship and into the boats.

'Long John,' said Israel Hands, 'the fire's at the magazine. I've been down and cleared it, but them powder kegs is just forrard and they're already hot to the touch. We've got to leave, the ship, John!'

'No, dammit! We're over seventy hands aboard of this ship, and the ship's lost and ourselves marooned, and I want pickles and pork and biscuit for all hands, and rum too, if we're to be stuck on that bloody island.'

'But the powder, Long John, it won't wait!' Israel Hands was frightened. Nobody knew the strength of gunpowder better than a master gunner. If a dozen kegs went up in a ship with seventy men, there wouldn't be enough wood for kindling nor enough meat for seagulls.

Long John looked around. There was nothing more that could be done on deck. The hands were working well ... and none had remembered the cargo of powder in the hold. Best not to tell them about that. All men have their limits.

'Mr Gunner,' said Silver, 'you were right to remind me that that-there powder is a danger to the ship.' He clapped Israel Hands on the shoulder. 'So let's you and I get it out of her!' That wasn't at all what Israel Hands had been hoping to hear, but he didn't dare show cowardice in front of Long John.

'Aye-aye, Cap'n,' said Israel Hands miserably, raising a knuckle to his brow.

'And bring your hammer and chisel, Mr Gunner,' said Silver. 'It's time we let Mr Bones out. Can't let the bugger burn!' He turned to the men and raised his voice, 'Keep at it lads!' he cried. 'Mr Hands and I have some instruments to recover.' He looked around, 'And you, Tom Merry, and you, Black Dog, come along o' me, for I'll need your help.'

And down they went, down into the hot smoking dark – except that the hold wasn't dark any more. It was full of red light. It had never been so bright, not since the ship-builders had planked over the deck above, and shut out the sun. Silver led the way, with Israel Hands behind, and Tom Merry and Black Dog at the rear. Silver led one-legged, for his crutch was no use in narrow spaces and on ladders, and he'd left it up on deck.

'Billy-boy?' cried Silver, when they came to Billy Bones's little corner. But he found only a length of chain. He looked around.

'Where's he gone?' said Israel Hands.

'Bah!' said Silver. 'Who knows. At least he ain't chained up here, a-waitin' for the flames.'

He pressed on to the magazine – a small compartment sealed off from the rest of the ship. Its pine planks were dark and smouldering and giving up their resin in bubbling beads. It was very hot down here. Silver could smell his hair singing, and the smoke stabbed his eyes.

'God help us!' said Israel Hands.

'Where's the powder, Mr Gunner?' said Silver.

'There, Cap'n.'

'Ah!'

Silver lurched forward, bracing his hip against the side of the magazine and reaching for the first powder keg, where it lay stacked on top of a line of water-butts.

'Back off, Mr Gunner,' said Silver. 'Get yourself to the companionway and hand this up to Mr Merry!'

Silver couldn't walk with the thirty-pound keg, not with one leg, so he rolled it towards Israel Hands. It was very hot to the touch, especially the copper bands that encircled it.

'Oof!' said Israel Hands, and heaved the keg up towards Tom Merry.

'Here,' said Merry, 'this ain't no instruments!'

Israel Hands's reply was so violently profane, so ferociously obscene, and bellowed in so menacing a voice, that George Merry – though not the sharpest man aboard – instantly understood that further discussion was inappropriate, no matter what he might be handed. He took the keg without a word, and passed it to Black Dog, who gave it to the team loading the skiff.

The second keg came out as quick as the first, but the rest came slower and slower, as Silver's arms tired and the heat and smoke grew unbearable. Israel Hands was shielded by the magazine, and George Merry was halfway up a ladder, but Silver was directly in line with the flames. By the tenth keg, the heat was singeing the cloth of his coat, and the magazine planks were smoking, getting ready to burst into flame.

'Leave it, Long John!' said Israel Hands. 'If there's one loose grain on them kegs, they'll blow!'

'No,' gasped Silver, 'Job's nearly done,' and he rolled number ten and reached for number eleven. This was far back and almost out of reach.

'For Christ's sake, John,' said Israel Hands, 'leave the bugger!'

'No!'

Silver went back for the last keg. Only he, of all aboard, could have reached it. For any smaller man it was out of reach, back against the ship's hull, and even he had to stretch. A hiss of steam rose as sweat dropped off his chin and on to the copper bands of the cask. He flinched as a tribe of rats scampered past, across the water butts. The fur was burnt off their backs and their tails were blistered.

'John! Give it up!' said Israel Hands.

'Cap'n?' said George Merry. '*Walrus* is making sail!'

'Uh!' said Silver. The heat was burning his exposed skin, the nearby flames were roaring in his ears, and his coat and stockings were smouldering. The final keg was nearly too hot to touch. He turned, and stooped to roll it to Israel Hands ... and dropped it ... and fell flat as he reached for it. Then he grabbed it once more and embraced it and crawled forward with it.

'*Walrus* is bearing down on us, Cap'n,' said George Merry.

'Here!' said Silver. 'This is a hot 'un. Heave it

straight over the side.'

'Ouch!' said Israel Hands at the feel of the keg.

'George Merry? You hear that?' he said.

'Straight over the side!' said Merry. 'Aye-aye, sir.'

'Ahhhh!' cried Silver, as smoke poured from his coat. Any material other than wool would have burned. But wool saved him.

'Get him out!' cried Israel Hands, 'George Merry, lend a hand!'

Silver was exhausted. His limbs ached. He was crawling and unable to stand. Israel Hands and George Merry cleared the last keg, and heaved Silver up and away, and got him back on deck and threw off his coat, and poured a bucket of water on him to cool him down.

'Thank you, lads,' said Silver, and gasped and spluttered. 'Another one,' he said, 'right over me head,' and 'Aaaah!' as the water cascaded over his shoulders. They gave him his crutch and stood him up, and he saw the awe-struck respect in their eyes. But the ship was well and truly lost. More than a third of *Lion*, from the taffrail to the mizzenmast, was blazing.

'*Allllll* hands!' cried Silver, and they turned to face him. The pump fell idle, the bucket-chain stopped, the unloading of stores came to an end. The busy teamwork ceased and the flames thundered unchecked.

'Lads,' said Silver, 'the game's up. But well done every man of you, for I'm proud of you!' They grinned and called back to him, but he raised a hand for silence. 'In a trice we'll be over the side, but first – as jolly companions one and all – I calls upon you to give three cheers for the old ship. Three cheers for *Lion*,' he cried. 'Hip-hip ...'

Lion had been Silver's first command, and he'd have loved her anyway, even if she hadn't been so beautiful. So he'd spoken from the heart when he called for three cheers, not knowing that he was following the lead of many captains before him, and many after, in honouring his ship as he lost her. Likewise, there was hard practical sense in lifting men's spirits at such a time. Any decent captain hopes to keep his men together as a crew, and not as a broken mob.

'Now, lads,' said Silver, 'steady as can be ... them as *can* swim, shall go over the side, and them as *can't* shall man the boats, and shall do it like British tars: old 'uns last, and young 'uns first. And now...' he paused and forced himself to speak the dreadful words: '*Abandon ship!*'

Even then he wasn't done. He went among them with a cheerful word for all as they set to work heaving over the side anything that would float: gratings, hatch covers, spare masts, and all the rolled-up hammocks that could be found. Then, just twenty of the seventy-one aboard went over the rail and swam, or clung to whatever they could grasp, and struck out for the shore with the current behind them.

With over fifty-one men and three boys still aboard, it took two trips of the jolly-boat and three of the skiff to get everyone ashore, with Silver the last man over the side, and the fire now raging forrard of the mainmast.

As the skiff pulled away from *Lion*, Silver sat in the stern sheets and glanced at *Walrus*. She'd proved to be no threat at all. The wind had failed her. She had no steerage way and her sails hung like washing on a line. She was harmless, just a cable's length off, and gently wallowing in the water. He put his glass to his eye and looked her over, from stem to stern ... and nearly leapt out of the boat at the sight of Selena struggling in Flint's arms.

Chapter 52

9th September 1752
In the forenoon watch (c. 11.30 a.m. shore time)
The southern anchorage

Flint studied *Lion* through his glass. She was well ablaze but bustling with activity. They'd got a pump rigged and buckets dipping over the side on lines, and they seemed to be discharging cargo into their boats. He didn't like that. Not at all.

Walrus was idle as a floating log. She couldn't move. The charges of canister he'd hoped to spray into Silver's men were sleeping in the iron cradle of their guns. What a pity. What a damned, bloody, infernal shame!

It got worse. *Lion*'s crew went over the side and into the boats. Steadily and efficiently Silver got his whole crew ashore, right under Flint's nose and just out of cannon shot.

'So what are you going to do, *Captain?*' said Selena, standing beside him on the quarterdeck.

'Looks to me like Long John's got the better of you.'

'What?' he snapped. 'How in the Devil's name do you calculate that?'

'He's given your ship a beating. He's killed half your men, and he's got the island and the treasure.' She sneered, 'And I thought you were the clever one.' She was baiting him out of hatred, and the desire to hit back after being the victim for so long. More important, *Walrus* was much nearer the shore than she'd been when at anchor, and Selena was feeling ready for a swim again. She was feeling bold because she could hop over the rail in an instant and it was Long John ashore now, not Flint. The only problem was the ship's guns and their hundreds of musket balls.

Flint's eyes went round and white. The parrot or Billy Bones would have seen the danger signs. But they weren't there. She'd hit the mark. She'd hit it right in the centre.

When the sun rose that morning, there'd been a full crew aboard *Walrus*. There'd been seventy-three men. Now there were just thirty-one able-bodied men aboard, the rest were either enjoying Mr Cowdray's attentions or were dead. Flint had killed at least four of them himself, which he now rather regretted because he was left with nowhere near enough men to fight Silver's seventy-one for possession of the island.

'Bitch!' he said, and raised a hand to strike. But she jumped back, and turned and leapt up on one of the guns, and would have been over the side ... if Flint hadn't caught her. She struggled fiercely and he – of necessity – held her close and dragged her away from the ship's side.

The struggle had a strange effect on him. An unexpected effect, since it was the first time he'd had close physical contact with a woman since certain highly unsatisfactory experiments with Portsmouth whores in his early youth.

'Well,' he said, clutching her to him, his lips half an inch from hers, 'I think we'll keep you nice and tight, my girl. I think we'll get the carpenter to mend my door and pop you back inside.' He smiled, and risked a tiny kiss. Earlier thoughts of strangulation and throat-slitting, which had then seemed so appealing, were now replaced by other desires entirely.

The skiff grounded. The crew leapt out and hauled her up on to the beach. Long John got out, struggling as ever with the soft sand, and his crutch digging itself into holes.

'Look, Cap'n,' said Israel Hands, 'I think she may be burning herself out.' Silver looked back at *Lion.* He stared at her for a while, judging the progress of the flames. Everything aft of the mainmast was gone, but it looked as if the fire was not advancing any further forrard, and might even be dying out.

'Aye,' he said, 'There's a bit of the bow that might survive. But we shan't sail the seas in *that.*' He looked at Israel Hands and the others. 'What did we save? How much did we get ashore?'

'Plenty of pork and biscuit, Cap'n,' said Israel Hands. 'And rum too, and most of the ship's small arms and shot.' He grinned. 'And a great deal of powder!' There was a roar of laughter at that. 'And much more besides: all the charts and suchlike, and a couple o' compasses.'

Israel Hands turned and glanced towards the woods and hills. 'And we got this old island too!' he said. 'I been here before, Cap'n, along of Flint, and – why – there's water and there's fruits and other things to eat, and there's goats too. There's even a blockhouse somewhere.'

'Ahoy!' cried a voice. 'Look what we got!' It was the boatswain, Sarney Sawyer, leading a group of men coming towards them from the jolly-boat. Sawyer was carrying something and the others were prodding a man forward with their cutlasses. It was Billy Bones, festooned with cork floats and clearly in mortal terror.

'We found the swab in the water, Cap'n,' said Sawyer. 'He says he went over the side when the ship burnt. But the bugger's got out of his irons somehow. And where did he get the cork, an' all?'

There was an ugly roar from Silver's men and calls for a rope and a good tree with a strong branch.

'Silence!' said Silver, and struggled towards Billy Bones, who wouldn't meet his eye. 'What's this, Billy?' said Silver, grabbing hold of the cork and netting. But Billy Bones said nothing. 'This weren't made in an instant, were it Billy-boy?' said Silver. 'It looks like a thing of purpose. Something prepared in advance of need.' He frowned and put his head on one side. 'And how did you get out of them irons, Billy? *And how did the bloody ship take fire?*'

It took every ounce of Silver's strength, leadership and powers of persuasion to save Billy

Bones's life. Without that, Billy would have been lucky if he'd got it quick rather than slow. And the only reason Silver bothered was the old, old reason.

'He's the only blasted quadrant-monger of our whole blasted crew!' said Silver. 'We're on this island for ever if we ain't got *him*.'

So Billy Bones lived. And so did another member of Flint's crew.

'It's the parrot, Cap'n. It must've flown ashore. Been shot about something wicked.' Sarney Sawyer held out the bedraggled bird, bleeding from a number of small wounds, and missing feathers from its wings. He put a hand round the bird's neck. 'Shall I pull it, Cap'n? 'T'ain't no bloody use, and it was Flint's own bird, damn him!'

'No!' said Silver. 'I've just pardoned a far worse bugger than this poor bird, which is only a creature, and which ain't to be held to account for what Flint did.' He took off his hat and put the bird in it, just as Flint had done when it needed a nest. 'There, my pretty,' he said. 'We'll find you some fruit and seeds to eat, and a little drink of water.'

Silver smiled. He'd always admired the parrot and he'd always been the only man other than Flint who could touch it without losing fingers.

'No, Cap'n Flint,' he said to the parrot, 'we shan't pull your neck – not you, my pretty bird!'

Later that evening, just as a wind got up in the anchorage, Flint himself came ashore – or rather, not quite ashore. He came in *Walrus*'s cutter, with a swivel mounted in the bow, and oars double-banked for speed and the crew ready to pull clear on the first sign of any danger. He came waving a flag. He came for a parlay and stopped just out of musket shot: far enough to be safe, and close enough for a shouted conversation.

'What is it, Joe?' cried Silver, with his men around him, armed and ready. 'What have you got to say to me?'

'Not much, John,' said Flint, and smiled. 'And is that Billy Bones there, standing among you. Why, Mr Bones, have you changed sides?' Billy Bones broke free of the men holding his arms and ran forward. He ran till he was up to his waist in water, and dared go no further.

'Let him go,' said Silver. 'He ain't going to swim and Flint ain't going to fetch him!'

And Flint didn't, despite Billy's desperate plea that he was Flint's man for ever and only following Flint's orders.

'So what is it, Joe Flint?' said Silver.

'It's a promise,' said Flint. 'One to keep you warm at nights.'

'Which is?'

'Which is this... Looks like you've got the island, and I've got the ship.'

'Aye!'

'Oh! And I've got your black girl, too, who stays with me of her own free will, having entirely lost patience with a one-legged cripple that cannot meet a woman's needs.' Flint laughed. 'Do you understand me, John?'

'Bastard!' said Silver.

'No,' said Israel Hands quietly and laid a hand on Silver's arm. 'It's hoss-feathers, Cap'n. All hands knows the moll were yourn when you was on board of *Walrus*. And that day when we pulled across to speak to Parson, she'd have jumped in and swum to you on the instant but for them bloody swivels!' He looked at Flint, standing laughing in the bows of the cutter. 'And as for that bugger ... who's ever seen *him* poke a woman?'

'Hmm,' said Silver, and thought of what Selena had said about Flint. He raised his voice, good and loud, for all to hear.

'Won't do, Joe!' he cried, shaking his head calmly, 'That girl knows a man when she sees one – and you ain't no man. Do *you* understand *me*, Joe?'

For an instant Silver thought of telling everything. It would win a roaring laugh: the tale of Flint's fiddling while peeping through holes in bulkheads! It would stab Flint to the heart. It might even lose him his crew and his ship. But if Flint were pushed too far, he'd want his vengeance and might take it out on Selena. Silver couldn't risk that. Not for all the treasure in the island.

Silver was right. He'd judged the matter nicely. Flint blinked. He sat down, and shut up. The riposte had been devastating. He knew exactly what Silver was talking about, and the bounce went out of him and the fright shot up his spine: fright and hideous embarrassment. In his vanity, he'd never dreamed anyone knew. Not Selena, not anyone, and certainly not Silver. He'd always been so careful.

'Pull for the ship!' he said. 'Pull with all your might!'

'Leaving so soon, Joe?' cried Silver, and his men laughed and jeered.

But Flint recovered fast. Just before the boat pulled too far out for his voice to carry, he stood up, and called back in a final farewell message.
'I'll be back, John, with a full crew to skin the hides off every man of you, sparing none, and that over a red-hot, roasting fire!'

Chapter 53

12th September 1752
The forenoon watch
Aboard Walrus
The South Atlantic

Selena knew now that Flint was mad. But mad in his own special way.
Just as he'd promised, the door to his cabin was mended and herself locked in. But once the ship was properly under way, and the island out of sight, he'd let her out and welcomed her back on deck, and given her every kindly consideration, just like the first time she'd been brought aboard, and he called her 'My dear' and 'Madam' and 'My Nubian princess'.
She could see he wasn't the same man though, for he would fly into tempers as he'd never done before, and was highly dangerous when he did so – dangerous to the men, that is, not to her. She thought that perhaps this was because of the headaches he was suffering from the wound in his head, and which Mr Cowdray had had to

close up again where Flint had popped the stitches. And perhaps he missed the parrot, although he never spoke of it.

Fortunately the crew were even more afraid of him now than they'd been before, since he was unpredictable, and old certainties had had to be thrown over the side. And this was just perfect as far as Selena was concerned. Indeed, she hoped that they sizzled and fried in fear of Flint, because it meant that they behaved themselves better towards her. There were no more hungry leers from the men, nor dirty words from the boys. It was all 'Yes, Miss Selena' and 'No, Miss Selena' and she could go where she liked on the ship and never worry.

Nor was Flint peeping through his holes in the cabin walls. Those, mysteriously, seemed to have been closed up – she'd long since found out where they all were. On the other hand, he'd taken to kissing her hand, and putting an arm round her waist whenever she stood beside him. This seemed to please him, and she suspected that it was a new alternative to his old games.

Beyond that, she had to face the fact that she was parted from John Silver, with no prospect of seeing him again. And that was bad. She could only wait, and watch for opportunity.

To encourage opportunity, she made a point of getting Flint to explain to her exactly how a pistol was loaded and fired, which he did with much amusement until – with daily practice – she learned the business so well that she could load without looking and could hit whatever she pointed at.

Chapter 54

12th September 1752
Morning
Spy-glass Hill

Silver was getting about more easily. The carpenter had fixed a disc of wood round the bottom of his crutch so the staff stuck out an inch for use on firm ground, while the disc stopped it digging too far into sand, or the soft, boggy ground of the jungle or marshes. Now he was taking stock of the island, and was up on its highest point, for a good view. But the view wasn't good. Not at present. And neither was the air as fresh as usual, not with the hot sun and the present company.

'Who'd this be then?' said Silver, looking down at the bloated, maggot-wriggling corpse lying stretched out under a nutmeg tree. 'Jimmie Cameron, wouldn't you say?'

'Aye, Cap'n,' said Israel Hands. 'And Franky Skillet's over there, with his arse as bald as his head and a pistol ball in his belly. It must be him, 'cos he's the only one of the lucky six as shaved his noggin.'

The parrot squawked and rubbed its head against Silver's.

'Ah, my pretty,' said Silver, and tickled its feathers, 'you've seen a deal of wickedness in your time, ain't you now? And I don't doubt you could tell how these poor sailormen came to die.' The parrot bobbed its head, and gently nipped Silver's ear. It had taken to him at once. Its wounds hadn't been serious. It had been tired mainly: tired in body and in spirit, that was all. In a couple of days it was flying again, and had hopped on to Silver's shoulder as if it were the natural thing to do. Silver was the one who'd been feeding it, after all.

'That makes four of 'em, Cap'n,' said Israel Hands, 'what with Peter Evans on the beach, and Iain Fraser over there–' he pointed towards Flint's great rock. 'D'you think it was Flint what done for 'em?'

'Well it weren't their mothers!'

'And what about Rob Taylor and Henry Howard?'

'He'll have done for them too, somewhere... Ugh! It stinks up here. Come on, Mr Gunner, let's go below.' He set off, and then stopped as a thought came to him.

'Israel, old shipmate,' he said, 'don't you wonder what'd have happened if you and Blind Pew and Sarney Sawyer had tipped me the black spot that night aboard *Lion?* Maybe you'd have made your peace with Flint and had a ship under your feet this very minute.'

'No, Cap'n,' said Israel Hands. *'No!'* He said it vehemently, as if he'd been accused of a foul deed. 'We wasn't coming with no black spot! Not us, Cap'n! We was coming to say we was all with you. We'd talked it over, and we'd decided we should've voted with you on the burying of the goods. Flint gave the game away on the island when he said

Walrus and *Lion* was each to fire into the other, should either try to go ashore. *The bugger was setting us against one another!* You was right all along, and we was come to say we was sorry.'

'What?'

'Aye, Cap'n! There weren't a man aboard then, nor ain't there a man on this island now, as wouldn't follow wheresoever you lead, and I take my affy davy on it!'

John Silver had to take a hard grip on his emotions to avoid giving way like a woman. He closed his eyes and clenched his teeth.

He sighed, and rubbed his eyes, and smiled at Israel Hands. There was much to do in this vile place, for never doubt that Flint would be back, and back with plenty of men, just as soon as he could contrive. And there was still the awful fear for Selena, and the thought that he might not see her again. But Long John Silver could face up to that, as long as he had a good crew behind him.

He turned and led the way down the goat track. He was quick and nimble on stony ground like this, and he was head and shoulders taller than any other man. He wore his scorched blue coat with the big brass buttons, and under his hat was a red silk handkerchief bound round his head as a sweatband. There were two pistols in his belt and a cutlass at his sides and the green parrot was perched firmly on his shoulder.

'Come on, Mr Hands,' he said, 'there's work to do!'

Afterword

WRITING *FLINT AND SILVER*

I wrote *Flint and Silver* to resolve the questions that Robert Louis Stevenson left unanswered in *Treasure Island*, one of the best-loved classics of English literature, but one which delivers a story plucked out of history like a carriage from the middle of a train. Questions are begged from end to end of the book: How did Long John lose his leg? Where did he get the parrot? Who was the black woman that he married? Who was the hideous Captain Flint? And above all, the question of questions that surpasses all other others: Why did the pirates bury their treasure?

This is a puzzle that bellowed and roared for explanation because the concept of buried treasure has so deeply penetrated our mythology that almost nobody sees a question there at all, despite the fact that there is a profound contradiction in the idea of pirates burying their treasure.

Burial means safe storage. It means planning for the future. But pirates had no future. They did not look forward to retirement in Eastbourne with a service flat, BUPA and a plasma TV. They lived fast and died young with the navies of at least three countries trying to catch them and hang them. So when they got hold of some money they blew it on sex, alcohol and gluttony, and then went out and got some more money, and so on and so on, until the hangman got hold of them.

Faced with these questions, and knowing that Robert Louis Stevenson was not going to answer them, I decided to do so on his behalf by writing a series of books about what happened before *Treasure Island*, and hoping that, if I did it well enough, he might forgive me should we meet in some other place.

To increase my chances of forgiveness, I read and re-read *Treasure Island*. I went through it page by page, taking notes and producing a cross-referenced file of information with which my book should be in harmony. If *Flint and Silver* is to be a 'prequel' it should contain nothing irreconcilable with *Treasure Island*. This does not mean that I never departed from – or even contradicted – some of Stevenson's detail, but that I did my best never to do so in ignorance, or without good reason. For instance, *Treasure Island* is a children's book, because Stevenson wrote it for his thirteen-year-old stepson Lloyd Osbourne, who wanted no women in the story: a perfectly reasonable sentiment for a thirteen-year-old, but I am older than that and I write no books without women and the delights and sorrows that go with them; so my work is not for children.

Conversely, I was absolutely true to Stevenson in correcting a false impression, universally held, of Long John Silver himself. Almost everyone knows Robert Newton's incomparable representation:

'Ah-harr, Jim lad!'

of Long John. But who knows that this boozy, greasy, squinting creature is nothing like the Long John that Stevenson created? The real Long John was, in Stevenson's words:

...very tall and strong, with a face as big as a ham. Plain and pale but intelligent and smiling ... clean and pleasant-tempered.

Of all the actors who have played Silver, the closest, in my opinion, was Charlton Heston, and even he was too old at the time. If you want to picture Long John, think of a young Charlton Heston, swinging a broadsword as he did in *El Cid*.

I kept Silver's speech and character as close as possible to Stevenson, though stressing Silver's belief that he was a 'gentleman of fortune' and not a pirate. But I plead guilty to making him younger than Stevenson did. He imagined Silver as middle-aged, while I've re-incarnated him in the prime of manhood. Likewise I've romanced Silver's lady, Selena, very considerably. Stevenson refers to her as an 'old negress' and she never makes an appearance in his book, whereas my Selena is young and delectable, for she is the heroine, and must be lovely, as an irrefutable requirement of good story-telling.

Flint, the other major character, was long dead in *Treasure Island* and Stevenson gives no clue to his appearance, though his many references to Flint point to a monster in the shadows. 'He was the bloodthirstiest buccaneer that ever sailed,' says Squire Trelawney. 'Blackbeard was a child to

Flint. The Spaniards were so prodigiously afraid of him, that, I tell you, sir, I was sometimes proud he was an Englishman.' Here was the opportunity to create something special, and I have tried. He could not be a simple brute but someone with glittering talents as well as psychotic menace. Hence Joe Flint with his holy-sadist father, his lightning reactions, his amoral cunning, his beautiful clothes, his gleaming, smile ... and his little problem with women. Flint, of course is the answer to the great question 'why was the treasure buried?' It was buried for Flint, to be exhumed by Flint, for Flint's exclusive use, and perhaps with Billy Bones allowed to carry the weight of it.

Poor, loyal Billy Bones. He is a brute: a thumping, bruising brute, just as Stevenson described him, though younger and bigger. But the notebook and quadrant in his chest in *Treasure Island* showed that he was a literate, numerate brute and capable of plotting a course. So I made him a master's mate. He was no mere 'hand before the mast' and he was much wronged by his idol and master. Left to himself in the Royal Navy, Billy Bones would have been a perfectly decent ship's officer, no worse than many others with thick boots and heavy fists.

Further characters likewise spring from Stevenson. I have described the flogging of Ben Gunn which began his descent into insanity. Blind Pew, who terrified me as a child, I made into 'Mad Pew': sinister and peculiar even before he lost his sight. Israel Hands in *Treasure Island* was the drunken thug who chased Jim Hawkins up the mast with a knife. But Stevenson also said that

Hands was Flint's gunner, and a gunner was a senior officer, responsible for guns, carriages, shot and powder. He kept written records of these expensive stores, and he held the keys to the magazine, where a single act of carelessness could destroy the entire ship. Apologies to Stevenson, but this is inconsistent, and my Israel Hands is a sober and thoughtful man. He is Silver's chief ally, and a considerable expert in the use of the nine-pounder gun.

My favourite character is Cap'n Flint, the parrot. I had almost finished writing the book when, by chance, I met a parrot at an antiques fair in Staffordshire. It was a huge bird, sitting on the shoulder of a lady – one of the traders – nuzzling her ear and preening her hair, taking a strand in its beak and gently running down the strand towards its end. Later I read of Dr Irene Pepperberg whose research suggests that parrots have an intelligence equal to that of the higher primates, with the bonus that they can speak. Thus I learned that the fantasised intelligence I had given to Cap'n Flint was perfectly reasonable. Parrots really are that clever. And they can crack Brazil nuts in their beaks, or bite off Black Dog's fingers.

Other characters such as Captain Springer, Midshipman Hastings and Midshipman Povey are entirely mine and are as true to the period as I can make them. Thus midshipmen were sometimes very young. Nelson famously went to sea at twelve and his contemporary, William Dillon, states in his memoirs that he went to sea aboard HMS *Saturn* in 1790 aged nine and a half years.

Research is vital to historical novels but it should

never show, because nobody wants a history lesson while reading for pleasure. Nonetheless, here are a few points that might be of interest:

CARIBBEAN PIRACY: THE REALITY

Piracy in the West Indies flourished in the seventeenth and early eighteenth centuries, when it was practised under every shade of legality from official, state-licenced 'privateering', through bribery of the authorities, to outright criminality. Among this varied company there were indeed some who considered themselves 'gentlemen of fortune' and sailed under articles. Long John would have been pleased to know that a set of articles – those of Bartholomew Roberts – is on the internet today for all to see.

Likewise there really was a pirate by the name of England, namesake of my England who tried to teach Long John the art of navigation. But the real England died in 1720, and in historic fact the various royal navies, especially the British, French and Spanish, had stamped out much of West Indian piracy by the middle of the eighteenth century. In earlier times piracy had flourished because the governments who paid for navies baulked at enforcing their laws on a raw frontier half a world away. Suppressing piracy meant sending out many ships for long periods, and politicians doubtless wept and groaned at the cost of this until the pain of piracy grew unbearable, which it did in the early years of the eighteenth century when such fabulous wealth was generated in the region, especially from sugar, that no government would share it with pirates.

But Stevenson set *Treasure Island* in the second half of the eighteenth century, as can be calculated from the only date in the book: 20th July *1754*, written by Billy Bones on the treasure map. My guess is that the map was at least five years old when Jim Hawkins found it, placing the action of *Treasure Island* in the 1760s. Probably Stevenson did this because his story was about the consequences of *past* piracy: buried treasure, long since lost.

A final word on the real captain England and those whom he exemplifies: he was regarded as a *gentle* pirate because he used torture only when necessary, other means of persuasion having failed. Most of the rest were not so kind, and all those persons who like horror – real horror – should study contemporary accounts of these pirates.

And so to the treasure itself...

WHAT WAS THE VALUE OF THE TREASURE IN MODERN MONEY?

Long John's estimate was that the treasure was worth about £800,000 in the mighty golden pounds of 1752, representing a truly enormous sum in the miserable paper pounds of the twenty-first century. It was worth all the more in the eighteenth century because then so much was bought on credit via written promises to pay; a system even worse than plastic cards in the slippery ease with which it led into debt and inability to pay. Thus ready gold or silver was warmly welcomed.

Turning to actual figures, Research Paper 99/20 of the House of Commons Library February 1999 calculates that prices rose by a factor of 118 between 1750 and 1998, which seems seriously too low a figure, reflecting the fact that politicians now, as in the eighteenth century, should never be trusted with money. But even that dubious figure would turn Silver's estimate into £94.4 million.

Substituting honesty for statistics, an able seaman RN was paid 24 shillings (£1.20) per month in the 1750s, while his modern equivalent, a trained rating, is paid £15,500 to £26,000 per year, say £20,000 on average, or roughly £1,666 a month – approximately 1,400 times inflation.

Similarly, a dockyard clerk, a middle-ranking, white-collar professional, earned £30–40 per year in the late eighteenth century, while an equivalent, middle-grade, modern administrator might reasonably expect something like £30,000–40,000.

Factors such as tax and the relative cost of manufactured goods versus services have turned dizzy cartwheels over the past two hundred and fifty years, but we will not go far wrong in adding three noughts and assuming that, in modern money, the treasure was worth something like £800,000,000.

Which brings us up to date so far as the value goes. But how do we reckon the date?

JULIAN AND GREGORIAN CALENDAR

On Friday, 15th October 1582, enlightened

Catholic Europe adopted the new Gregorian calendar proposed by the Calabrian astronomer Aloysius Lilius, and decreed by His Holiness Pope Gregory XIII, after whom it is named.

This calendar corrected faults in the previous Julian calendar, which had caused natural events like the equinoxes (twice-yearly occasions when the day and night are of equal duration) to 'drift backwards' through successive Julian years, occurring later and later as each year passed.

The change to the Gregorian Calendar required that Thursday, 4th October 1582 be followed by the newly reckoned Friday, 15th October.

Protestant Europe, including England and its overseas possessions, fiercely resisted anything Catholic – including the Gregorian Calendar – until the stupidity of this policy became too gross to be ignored.

Finally, grudgingly, one hundred and seventy years late, and with riots by the ignorant, howling:

'Give us back our eleven days!'

the British adopted the Gregorian Calendar, with the result that Wednesday, 2nd September 1752 was followed by Thursday, 14th September.

Events described in this book – particularly the burying of the treasure – take place both before and after the switchover date. To avoid confusion, all dates are given in the Julian, or old-style reckoning.

The publishers hope that this book has given you enjoyable reading. Large Print Books are especially designed to be as easy to see and hold as possible. If you wish a complete list of our books please ask at your local library or write directly to:

Magna Large Print Books
Magna House, Long Preston,
Skipton, North Yorkshire.
BD23 4ND

This Large Print Book for the partially sighted, who cannot read normal print, is published under the auspices of

THE ULVERSCROFT FOUNDATION

THE ULVERSCROFT FOUNDATION

... we hope that you have enjoyed this Large Print Book. Please think for a moment about those people who have worse eyesight problems than you ... and are unable to even read or enjoy Large Print, without great difficulty.

You can help them by sending a donation, large or small to:

The Ulverscroft Foundation,
1, The Green, Bradgate Road,
Anstey, Leicestershire, LE7 7FU,
England.
or request a copy of our brochure for more details.

The Foundation will use all your help to assist those people who are handicapped by various sight problems and need special attention.

Thank you very much for your help.